JUST LIKE MOTHER

JUST LIKE MOTHER

ANNE HELTZEL

NIGHTFIRE

A TOM DOHERTY ASSOCIATES BOOK

NEW YORK

JUST LIKE MOTHER

A Nightfire Book
Published by Tom Doherty Associates
120 Broadway
New York, NY 10271

www.tornightfire.com

Nightfire™ is a trademark of Macmillan Publishing Group, LLC.

Library of Congress Cataloging-in-Publication Data

Names: Heltzel, Anne, author.
Title: Just like mother / Anne Heltzel.
Description: First Edition. | New York : Nightfire, 2022. |
"A Tom Doherty Associates Book." |
Identifiers: LCCN 2022000329 (print) | LCCN 2022000330 (ebook) |
ISBN 9781250787514 (hardcover) | ISBN 9781250787538 (ebook)
Subjects: LCGFT: Novels.
Classification: LCC PS3608.E4676 J87 2022 (print) |
LCC PS3608.E4676 (ebook) | DDC 813/.6—dc23
LC record available at https://lccn.loc.gov/2022000329
LC ebook record available at https://lccn.loc.gov/2022000330

Our books may be purchased in bulk for promotional, educational, or business use. Please contact your local bookseller or the Macmillan Corporate and Premium Sales Department at 1-800-221-7945, extension 5442, or by email at MacmillanSpecialMarkets@macmillan.com.

First Edition: 2022

Printed in the United States of America

0 9 8 7 6 5 4 3 2 1

FOR ELISABETH

JUST LIKE MOTHER

PROLOGUE

M other with the lazy eye spoons soup into our bowls. "Eat up," she says. She smiles, and the eye rolls outward, landing on the crow on the windowsill before it rolls back in. My cousin and I lift our spoons to our mouths and swallow. The other girls—Susie and Beth and Frances and Gloria—are still too little for meals with us. They nurse of the Mothers' milk in the bedrooms. I dip a crust of bread into my soup until it softens enough to chew. Mother doesn't like it when Andrea and I don't finish our lunch.

There is a *thud, thud, thud* from the room next door and wild grunts like pigs at the trough. Our spoons pause midair and our heads, nearly identical, pivot at the neck. Three sets of eyes fix on the locked door. Mother rises from the table to stand behind us, placing one hand on top of each of our heads. "Finish," she says. She begins to hum, and the words take shape in my head.

A sailor went to sea sea sea
To see what she could see see see.
But all that she could see see see
Was the bottom of the deep blue sea sea sea.

By the time we are done, the sounds have turned to whimpers. We push back from the wooden table and carry our bowls to the sink. Andrea takes mine and washes it, while I linger at her elbow and Mother observes with her good eye. My cousin is taller than I am. They say it doesn't matter what we are, we're all family regardless, but she and I may as well be twins.

Boy has crept in unnoticed. He is just walking and always underfoot. I slip him the heel of the bread that's been abandoned on the counter. He latches on greedily. I keep an eye on him while he eats; as long as he's out of the way and quiet, he'll be okay.

The locked door comes unlocked, opens. We freeze. The water is still running. Mother with the red hair and chipped tooth comes out of the room. Her face is red. Her freckles stand out against the cast of her skin. Her hair is straggly and damp and she smells like sweat.

"Good morning," she says, her voice even. She locks the door from the outside with a key. The whine continues behind her.

"Good morning, Mother," we reply in tandem, while Mother with the lazy eye observes. Mother exits the room, her musk trailing her, and Mother scrubs the kitchen table until I'm sure she'll bore a hole straight through. None of them seem to notice Boy; it's as if he's invisible.

"Let's go weed the garden," I whisper to Andrea. Mother always says "No idle hands." When we weed the garden, we can talk and sing and make up stories. Andrea looks at Mother.

"May we weed the garden, Mother?" she asks. Mother nods without looking up. Andrea is the favorite. Mother can never say no to her. Boy looks panicked when we move toward the door, so at the last minute I sling him over my hip and take him with me. Andrea rolls her eyes.

"You're too soft with him," she says, her voice crisp.

"Just keeping him out of the way." My heart twitches when Boy buries his face in my neck and wraps his chubby arms around my shoulders.

In the yard the sun is hot against my back, but the chill in the air makes me wrap my sweater tighter around my frame. The garden is far enough from the house that we won't be heard. It is our project: a patch of order amid acres of wild brush and water and woods. Mother with the blond hair to her waist—one of the two who looks most like us, the one who sometimes slips us sweets or gives us hugs—is removing sun-dried sheets from the line on the other side of the yard. Just beyond her is the swimming hole where Andrea and I pretend to be minnows on the hottest days, and beyond that are the trees. We don't know how far they stretch, with their bright green leaves that look like jewels against the blue sky. We have never seen the other side of the woods.

I settle Boy in the grass next to me and hand him a worm-eaten apple to play with. He amuses himself while I crouch low.

"What do you think is in there?" I keep my voice soft, and tug not hard enough at a weed, which breaks above the root. "A puppy?"

"In the locked room? A new baby, maybe," Andrea says, shrugging. She's dragging her finger through the dirt, draw-ing patterns instead of weeding. "A girl, hopefully." She shoots Boy a look of disdain. She hates when I coddle him.

"No," I shake my head hard. "Not behind a locked door. I think for sure a puppy. It must be a surprise they don't want us to see yet." My birthday is approaching. I have wanted an animal to love as long as I can remember.

Andrea looks at me, her eyes wide. "You think so?" She must be remembering the time we found a dog and tried to keep it in our room in secret, but the owner came to get it, and afterward we stood in separate corners of the kitchen for two hours. It had a chip in it, Mother told us later. The owner could track it. We could have gotten into big, big trouble if people came here and saw things they didn't want to see. We've wanted a dog forever.

"Maybe," I tell her. I'm already exhausted from the heat and crouching in the dirt. Andrea's feet are flat on the ground, her bum resting on her heels, while the weight of my body balances on the balls of my feet, my torso angled forward and heels hovering inches from the soil. I am awkward and unwieldy where Andrea is graceful and composed.

"Let's look," Andrea suggests.

"Mother would never let us."

Andrea pushes a strand of hair from her cheek, and her eyes sparkle green with mischief. "I know where they keep the key," she confides, then bites her bottom lip as she tugs halfheartedly at a stubborn root. My pulse accelerates, causing my fingers to turn cold. We never disobey. But I think of the puppy. Alone in the room. Scared. Making those noises.

"Maybe tonight," I concede. I am equal parts afraid and alive with the urgency of need. We both know it could be tonight or some other night, that we are not the ones who will choose when. It'll be chosen for us, when things line up just so, during the narrow glimmers of our days when all eyes are elsewhere. And Andrea will not be satisfied until her curiosity is sated. The promise is, we do everything together. Never alone, never apart, no matter what.

Mother at the wash line has bundled all the sheets into her wicker basket and begins making her way back toward the house, her ankles red and raw where unruly brush scrapes them above her sandals. Even so, she is elegant like Andrea. Now we are alone outside, and the sun is high in the late afternoon sky. The trees shift gently in the light breeze. Their shade looks cool, inviting.

Andrea sees me staring into the woods and juts her chin in that direction. Her mouth is quirked, the remnants of mischief seeking a place to land. I glance back toward the house. There is no movement from behind the curtains. It is late afternoon, the time when they take their naps. I stand, dusting filthy palms against my thick wool sweater. I nod. She leaps up and throws her arms around me.

"Shh." I clap a palm over her mouth, stifling her squeal. But I laugh, too; there is nothing better than making Andrea smile. First, I take Boy back to the house. I drop him in the kitchen and leave a pinch of sugar in his palm so he won't cry. And then we are off toward the trees, hand in hand.

As we pass the swimming hole and approach the division between the backyard and the woods, I stop. Our palms separate, and I feel a physical ache at their parting. The sun is setting earlier than ever now, since winter is near. "Maybe we shouldn't go," I suggest, stopping to catch my breath.

The house looks small from where we stand, and I'm starting to feel afraid. But Andrea has already crossed the border and disappeared into the thicket, fearless as always. I hear her laughter and the sound of branches crunching beneath her feet. I can barely make out the flash of her red ribbon against her blond hair as the distance between us increases. I glance at the house, at the empty kitchen illuminated in the waning light through its narrow window. Then I look back into the trees, where the invisible string between me and Andrea is pulling taut, until surely it will snap. Before I can think about it anymore, I'm running after her, eager to relieve the awful anxiety of separation. The woods at night are terrifying, but the thought of Andrea leaving me behind is worse.

I'm sweating and thorn-bitten when I find her. She's sitting on an upended log in a clearing, drawing in the dirt at her feet with a stick. She doesn't look at me as I ease down next to her on the fallen tree.

Until she does.

She turns to me slowly, her neck moving stiffy—unnaturally—as if on a wire. Her expression is blank, her eyes empty. I can't make out their green in the fading light.

"Andrea?"

"I am not Andrea," she says, and the voice that always brings me comfort is gone. It has been replaced by something low and gravelly, the sound of sandpaper on a wooden door.

"Stop." I giggle nervously to show her I'm not mad. "Come on, Andrea. Let's go back in the yard."

"I'm *not Andrea*," she says, her voice still guttural. She seizes my forearm. "I am Bloody Mary."

"Ow!" I exclaim, trying to pry her fingers from my arm. With every struggle, her nails dig deeper. "Stop! You're hurting me. Andrea, stop. Please."

She removes her hand from my arm and slaps me across the face.

It's so sudden that I don't fully register what's happened until it's over.

"I am Bloody Mary," she repeats. "Say it."

I stand and back away. I won't say it. "You're Andrea," I tell her, more firmly now, certain I can talk sense into her. "You're my cousin who loves me. You're playing a mean game."

"I am Bloody Mary," she snarls, reaching for me, pulling out a clump of my hair, scratching my face with her hands until I'm running, breathless, and thrashing through the woods in what I hope is the direction of the house.

After what feels like hours of twisting among the trees in waning light—but is probably only minutes—I break the border and find myself in the calf-high wild of our yard. By now my heart is threatening to crack through my ribs. I cross the grass; it's crisp and deadened from the summer sun. I stumble—nearly falling once—until finally I hurl myself up the back steps to the kitchen, banging on the door.

"What is it?" Mother with the lazy eye looms large against the light of the kitchen. She doesn't let me in right away, and I wonder suddenly if I've made a mistake. "Where's Andrea?"

Mother with the long blond hair walks into the room and stands with her arms folded, waiting for my reply. I touch a pain on my head, and my hand comes back red. Boy isn't anywhere, and I'm glad for it. I don't want him to be scared.

"In the woods," I tell them, my cheeks wet. "She said she was Bloody Mary."

Mother with the blond hair glares at Mother with the lazy eye. "I told you not to speak of such things around the girls. They're still too young. They don't know what they're hearing."

"They need to learn."

Mother with the blond hair grabs my shoulders. Shakes me. Her eyes skitter past my bloody temple. "What's happened to Andrea? You left her in the woods? Where? What were you thinking, you willful girl?"

Without waiting for my reply, she runs into the backyard, screaming Andrea's name over and over. When Andrea emerges—almost as if she was right there, lying in wait for this moment—Mother grabs her, crying. She holds her tight. Together at the edge of the lawn in the dusk, with their honey-colored hair blending together, they look like one being.

Before Mother can bring Andrea back in, Mother with the lazy eye grabs me by my collar and hauls me toward the closet. "You'll stay in here until you repent. One hour."

"No," I protest. "It's dark."

"Well, now you'll know how Andrea felt when you abandoned her to the woods. Lucky she didn't go missing out there in the dark. 'If you're born to be hanged, you'll never be drowned,' you know. That child was born under a good sign." She pushes me roughly to the ground and stares at me with her good eye, the other lolling.

"What did Mother mean?" My voice is small. Mother doesn't like questions. "About not speaking of certain things?"

There's a heavy silence, as if the air around us has condensed.

"You will know someday. Oh, you will." I shift backward

on the closet floor, frightened, as she points down at me with
a trembling finger. "You were born under a bad sign. Rotten
through and through. A bad apple, that's what I always say.
Boy-loving and difficult. Not one of *us*. No loyalty. She's a
bad, rotten fruit, that Maeve. She'll be a Bloody Mary one
day, mark my words. She'll abandon us all."

She's still muttering when she locks the door with a key.

Abandon. I abandoned Andrea. I broke my promise.

The space is too small for me to stretch my legs. Long,
threadbare coats hang over my face, tickling my cheeks. Each
one smells faintly of the Mothers. Amber and tobacco and
sweat and something earthier. My shivers have given way to
a warmth so oppressive I can't breathe. I draw thick, ragged
breaths until I am light-headed.

I wrap my arms around my knees and lean against the wall.

> *A sailor went to sea sea sea*
> *To see what she could see see see.*

I murmur it to myself. It is our song. If we're singing it,
nothing can hurt us. That's what Andrea says. But will it work
when we are apart? I imagine the words wrapping themselves
around me like an impenetrable cloak. I squeeze my eyes shut.
It feels as if the walls of the closet are drawing closer.

> *But all that she could see see see*
> *Was the bottom of the deep blue sea sea sea.*

I sing myself to sleep. When I wake up, the space feels
tighter than ever. It's as if the closet is shrinking, until I'm
certain I'm not in a closet at all but a small coffin built exactly
for me. I don't realize I'm whimpering until I hear Andrea's
voice. It brings me back to myself.

"Maeve." She's whispering from right outside the door. I

feel a dampness in my tights and realize I've peed myself. I'm seven—too old to pee myself. "Listen to me, Maeve," Andrea says. "I'm right here." She knocks three times on the door. "I won't leave you."

"Why did you do it?" I say, sniffling. Even as I ask, I find my anger ebbing.

"I'm sorry," she tells me. I hear her hand shift against the wood of the door. "It was only a dumb game. I'm so sorry. I didn't know how scary it would be."

"What dumb game? How did you even know it?" I ask. For as long as I remember, we know the same things. We share the same thoughts. There are no secrets. Now Andrea is silent. "I thought you'd left me," I explain, starting to hiccup. "I thought you'd become her."

"I'm just me," Andrea replies. "I can't open the door, Mae. Mother has the key. But I'm going to sit here with you."

"Okay," I say. "Please don't go."

"I will never, ever leave you," my cousin tells me. "I am here always, no matter what. I won't leave you like you left me."

Like you left me.

"I wasn't going to say this, Maeve. But it wasn't just a game. I was testing you. I wanted to see how much it would take for you to betray me."

"I'm sorry," I whisper quietly, tears streaming down my cheeks.

Andrea slips a finger under the door and wiggles it around until I find it with my own.

"Who is Bloody Mary?" I ask. In her silence, I forget to breathe.

"Something bad," she says finally. "It's what the Mothers call a very bad woman. Forget it. That isn't the point."

"I'm sorry," I say again.

"Now I know," she says. "There are holes in our promise." Her voice sounds sad.

"No! I will never, ever leave you," I whisper back to her, honoring our pact. "I am always here, no matter what."

"But you did, Maeve. You did leave. At the slightest scare. When we promise to stay together no matter what, it needs to mean as much to you as it means to me."

Distantly, I begin to recognize faint sounds of unrest from the other side of the closet wall. The locked room.

"Never again," I swear, distracted. I bend my fingertip as far as it will go around hers. I mean it. I failed this test, but never again.

The sounds beyond the wall turn to strained grunts, then heavy thuds. The closet wall shudders slightly, and I move closer to the door.

"Okay," she agrees. "We'll start from scratch. People make mistakes." At her words, I am awash with relief and gratitude.

"A sailor went to sea sea sea." She starts the old, familiar rhyme. The thing behind the wall grows louder and more furious. There's a clanging sound that threatens to override Andrea's voice. I raise my own, trying to drown out the sounds in the room. But the louder I get, the louder it gets, as if our song is stirring the thing's unrest. It isn't a puppy, I know now. Or if it is, it's large and feral.

I curl against the door as the thing grows louder, its noises joining with our own rising voices to create a strange melody. We match its pitch. Its exertions match ours in turn. Then there's a terrific thud, the clanging of metal, the sound of something breaking, and more thuds against the closet wall so powerful I worry it'll splinter inward, crushing me dead. I huddle against the door, willing it to open, and clutch Andrea's finger more tightly in my own. The banging grows louder, the closet's flimsy wooden beams bending against the weight of the thing I'm now certain is a monster, not a dog at all. I hear the Mothers' voices, the patter of their feet as they move toward the locked room. I try not to cry out as the creature's efforts threaten to break down the wall and swallow me whole. Andrea's voice, louder now, grounds me.

I repeat the words—*all that she could see see see*—even as I hear the Mothers enter the room, hear the beast grow wild. Even as I lose control of my bowels and a dank, putrid odor fills the air and makes me gag through my words. Even as I hear sounds of chaos through the thin slats and the tremble apparent in Andrea's chanting. Our voices blend together until I can no longer tell hers from mine. Until it feels, again, like our promise is true.

1

It had been years since I'd searched for my cousin. In the early days, I entered fringe-style message boards with a feverish enthusiasm, hoping to find lost girls but more often than not finding derelicts who hoped I *was* a lost girl, who asked things like whether I was tight or loose long before I knew how those words might apply to my anatomy. Sometimes I'd ask to be dropped at the mall, where I'd comb the shops I thought she'd like, lingering for hours over scents at Bath & Body Works, debating whether she'd like peach or raspberry, before stalking the aisles of Hot Topic.

It plagued me constantly, then, that I didn't know what she'd become. I imagined all sorts of variations on Andrea: Goth Andrea with pink and green hair and fishnets and a deep love for Joy Division; Andrea who snuck out to kiss older boys on the middle school jungle gym after dark; Andrea who mastered a fouetté and went on to perform at the Palais Garnier. It drove me mad, not knowing. More so than not having her in my life, maybe. It was the lack of connection to who she was, the absence of noise where I'd once been able to read her thoughts almost as easily as my own.

Patty and Tom—my adoptive parents—might have known what I was up to or might not have. Patty had a strict rule: No dwelling in the past. What's done is done. Put one foot in front of the other. Et cetera. To her, that meant no talking about anything that happened before I came into their home. She was desperately afraid I'd be perceived as abnormal, and in the way she fretted, I knew I must be. But Tom was the one who most often drove me to those solo outings, and sometimes the look he gave me when he dropped me off was so nakedly pitying and sweet that I'd have to jump quickly out of the car with hardly a good-bye in order not to cry.

When Facebook finally went wide, I scanned endless pages of anonymous profiles. Every time I saw a girl who looked like me, I clicked, leading to a string of dead ends. Same with Google. My late teens and early twenties were spent skipping parties to stay in and search "Andrea Indiana" and "Andrea Mother Collective" and "cult bust 1990s kid survivors" and a million other iterations of the same damn things. My college roommates would stumble in at five a.m., lipstick smeared, eyes glazed, limbs weak and trembling from dancing, and I'd still be sitting there at my desk. Searching obsessively.

My whole life revolved around Andrea, and Andrea wasn't even there.

One day I spit in a cup and mailed it in to one of those DNA websites. When that didn't yield results, it occurred to me to ask the social worker who had been on my case. It seemed so obvious a solution that when I thought of it, I laughed aloud. After that didn't turn up any results, I gave up. Andrea had disappeared altogether, lost to the foster care system. With no last name or birth certificate, she may as well have ceased to exist the night I tossed a metaphorical grenade into the center of our childhoods.

It wasn't what I'd intended, of course. As an adult, I have realized that the biggest mistakes usually aren't intentional so much as idiotic and tragically avoidable. One little error. A misguided tweet, a rogue email, a forgetful, harried disposition and your reputation is ruined, you've lost your job, you've left your child in the back of the car on a hot day.

It was the start of summer, a Saturday. I had my window open and a soft breeze was filtering through the screen. The piece of tape I'd used to patch it had come dislodged and was flapping around. A mosquito had found its way in and drunk heavily from my left shoulder before I noticed and squashed it, spreading a fine streak of blood across my palm. I'd been editing a manuscript and fighting off drowsiness with Skittles and Diet Coke. I intermittently scrolled through Twitter, following a viral debate over whether Taylor Swift, at thirty, ought to consider having babies before her looks faded and all her eggs turned to dust.

Working well into the weekend evenings, when everyone else was presumably out living their full, rich lives, had become typical for me aside from an occasional happy hour invitation from my supervisor, Elena. Ryan—the guy I'd been hooking up with—worked weekends at a bar, and most other people I knew disappeared at five p.m. Friday, receding into the glow of their relationships and family lives just as I receded into the glow of my computer screen. On the plus side, weekend hibernation saved me money—or rather, prevented me from sinking further into debt. The negative side, of course, was that it made me acutely aware of having nowhere to go.

I'd once been one of the kids Ryan catered to at the bar. I knew the game too well—was intimately familiar with the thin border between adolescence and adulthood. It was how I'd met him myself—drinking to casual oblivion as I began to cross that very threshold. Mine was a neighborhood for youths, artists, and leftovers. As one of the thirtysomethings who still lived there, I fell into the "leftover" category, though it could have been worse. It could have been a neighborhood populated by pregnant women, nannies, and strollers. I'd graduated from a vibrant, hopeful twentysomething with an alluringly blank future to what I was now—an adult with little to show for it other than a job and a cramped, dingy studio apartment.

The radiator in said apartment was inconsistent, and when it worked it was so hot to the touch it had actually given me a scar once. The second-floor light outside my unit turned off and on at a whim, and more often than not I had to fumble my way home in the dark. The refrigerator worked—kind of—except for the condensation that gathered up top, never falling, like hundreds of small stalactites. I slept on a mattress a former roommate had handed down when she moved in with her boyfriend; all other décor consisted mostly of street finds. The only thing I ever splurged on—my one concession to vanity—was the set of hair extensions I replaced each month to cover the alopecia I'd had since I was a kid.

Even the large canvas that graced the wall above the patio set I'd repurposed as a dining table had been confiscated from a garbage bin outside an artist's loft during Open Studios. It was a painting of an empty boat, drifting away from its intended occupant, a woman trapped on an island. It was unsigned, and clearly someone hadn't thought it was very good, but I liked its mood: it had a relentless, lonely sort of beauty to it. I was glad to have saved it. I was proud of all my motley treasures. It was squalor of a kind, but I was comfortable in it. It was my own very small footprint in an oversaturated, overpriced city. Moreover, it was the only proof of progress I could point to.

I toggled fluidly between news headlines, email, and edits on nights like these, when time seemed infinite, so when I saw an email announcing "New DNA Relatives," it didn't really register. I absently clicked the See New Relatives button under a message that informed me one new relative had joined in the last thirty-one days.

Every now and then over the years, I'd clicked that same button to find a sixth-plus cousin or to be reminded of the gene mutation that allowed me to smell asparagus in my pee. After more than ten years on the site, I did not expect my one new relative to be Andrea. *My* Andrea.

Andrea Rothko, the site listed. *1st Cousin. 13.8% DNA shared.*

My heart accelerated. *Cousin.* There it was, confirmed in

stark serif font. I clicked on the site's notifications tab. I had one new message, four days old.

She was cordial, even casual.

Maeve! Is it really you? It's Andrea. Andrea Rothko, now. I can't believe this thing worked. I've tried to find you forever . . . why don't you have your last name listed? Look, I know this probably feels as shocking to you as it does to me, but text me when you get this, okay? Here's my number.

My fingers went cold and my head swam. I'd imagined this very moment for so long. For more than two decades, I'd fantasized about our reunion. Now she was here. Like it was nothing at all. Like an entire lifetime hadn't separated us. I had a sudden, visceral urge to slam my computer shut. To stuff headphones in my ears and drown out whatever *this* was, this seemingly benign interaction that was actually as life-altering as it got. For a second, I was angry. She'd foisted herself on me, knowing there was no way of going back.

I switched over to Instagram and searched her name. Andrea Rothko. She wasn't even private. I clicked on her profile and felt my heart begin to accelerate as I flipped through her photos. There she was in a wedding dress, with a ruddy-complected man who gazed down at her adoringly. There they were together, posing in an apple orchard, laughing as he hoisted her high, she straining toward a top branch.

The normalcy of it cut me to my core.

I forced myself to take a breath. To pick up my phone, program in her number. It wasn't even eight p.m. yet; I could text her right then. Casual, confident, just like she'd messaged me.

Or I could ignore it. Go back to my easy, predictable routine of before. I stared at her message on my laptop. I felt hot. I ran a palm across my forehead; it was slick with sweat. I was about to shut my laptop and pretend the whole thing hadn't happened when a green dot appeared next to her name in the messaging tab of the DNA site.

She was online.

Which meant she'd see that I'd opened her message.

I quickly X-ed out of the site and slammed my laptop closed.

"Fuck, fuck, fuck," I whispered. I stood from my desk and paced the room in circles. If I didn't text her soon, it would be weird. She'd know how badly I was affected. Or I could pull myself together and send her the same kind of breezy text she'd sent me. *Yes.*

I picked my phone back up, casting around for appropriate words. I could do this. This was practically my forte: putting on "normal" for Patty as a kid, continuing it throughout college and on into my professional life that way, imposter syndrome lurking long after I'd succeeded in passing. The irony was, I'd managed to convince everyone except myself. Andrea didn't need to know that, though.

Andrea! I just got your message. It's me. If our DNA percentage wasn't proof enough, I can assure you I'm the right Maeve. 😊

I pressed Send and waited her out, my fingers trembling just above the keys. Why had I included a smiley face? *Idiot.* I reached for my wineglass, eager for something to do with my hands—I didn't trust myself not to start typing every single thought firing through my brain.

I took a long sip as the three dots appeared, then stopped, then appeared again. My palms dampened and my breathing had become audibly labored.

I'm so glad I found you, she wrote.

I kind of can't believe it. Where do you live? She hadn't listed her location on the site.

New York, she replied. *Upstate. Just moved here from the West Coast.*

Mere hours from where I sat.

Happy birthday, she typed, after a long pause.

I froze, frowning, my fingers hovering over the keyboard. I

was about to be thirty-three the following month. June 16 was the birthday my adoptive parents had assigned me, to commemorate the day I came to live with them. It was the date on all my official documentation. So it took me a second to understand the significance of her words. My eyes flickered to the calendar date on my phone. It was May 7: the twenty-fifth anniversary of the raid on the Mother Collective. I'd celebrated my eighth birthday that same day. How had I forgotten?

I'd love to see you, she wrote. *It's been so long, and*—She stopped. I imagined her casting about for words the same way I was. Everything had a subtext. *We could celebrate your birthday? I've*—Her typing trailed off again. There was a long pause as the ellipses started, stopped, started again. So she wasn't sure-footed. Something about the realization calmed me.

—*missed my cousin.*

Cousin. A word we'd never really been allowed to use. We'd whispered it anyway, in secret, behind closed doors and in the dark of night. We'd huddled under the covers in a shared bed and whispered it: "Cousin, I love you. Cousin, sleep tight." It had implied ownership, security, a sense of belonging to someone else when we didn't know who to belong to. It blew my mind that our relationship was finally confirmed.

I wanted to say yes; I really did. Yet I found myself hesitating. I clicked through her photos again. I scrutinized the images of her with all those smiling groups of people, their arms casually draped around one another. I studied her face for any evidence of artifice or hints of lingering trauma. But she looked happy and well-adjusted. *Normal.*

It would have been largely my fault if her life had turned out otherwise. My fingertips rested gently on the keyboard. Seeing Andrea again would link my present to my past in a way Tom and Patty never would have wanted.

I'd like that, I typed. Because what else could I say? To

reject someone whose life I'd already upended once would be unimaginably cruel.

She was heading to the city the following Tuesday for some meetings, so we agreed to get together that morning for breakfast. After we said our good-byes, I took a long breath and reopened my laptop. It still felt surreal. Now that I had Andrea's last name—Rothko—I was hungry for more. According to her LinkedIn, she was CEO of a start-up that had been making the news for its groundbreaking contributions to the lifestyle market and billions of dollars in recent funding. So Andrea wasn't just a cog in the tech machine; she was crucial to its operations. She'd actually been in the news a lot, though mostly in science journals.

I could hardly blame myself for not knowing the esoteric underpinnings of Silicon Valley. These were the kinds of things you didn't really pay attention to when you resided on the East Coast with your nose buried in novels. Wealth, tech—they were as distant and theoretical as the luxury buildings in Dubai I'd read about, so tall they punctured the sky.

"NewLife Dazzles with Its Cutting-Edge AI Technology," one front-page headline in a major national newspaper read.

"Female CEO of NewLife 'Marries' Groundbreaking Vigeneros™ Tech with Humanity for Better Family Planning," read another.

I clicked away, eager to absorb everything about Andrea and the details of her world.

I typed "NewLife CEO" in the search bar. The only photo of Andrea that popped up in Images was her LinkedIn shot. I switched back to the news tab.

Andrea was mentioned in articles featuring NewLife, but she was mostly absent from Google Images. Instead, photos of a colleague, Emily, flooded the results page. Emily seemed to be some sort of tech goddess, worshipped by the top tier of Silicon Valley.

Andrea's professional life was, admittedly, intriguing. Even in my childish imaginings I had mostly assumed she'd struggled too. It hadn't occurred to me that she'd be wealthy, accomplished, renowned, and *loved*. My cousin had made a real life for herself. What did I have to offer, after all these years? If my life was a lazy river, Andrea's was the Autobahn. I couldn't help but feel that all those years I was looking for her, she'd been jetting in the other direction.

2

As a nondriver subject to the whims of a limited bus schedule, I couldn't easily travel upstate to where Andrea lived, so she had offered to drive the two hours to New York. We planned to meet in a café in the West Village so we could catch up "for real." I'd had to take the day off for the occasion—a possibility Andrea hadn't seemed to have considered, and one I wasn't comfortable broaching.

When I got there she was already seated, but she rose quickly and threw her arms around me the second I walked in. Then she pushed me back, gripping my forearms and staring at me hard. "My god," she said. "I still can't believe it's really you. Have you been in New York all this time? How could we have been so close without ever knowing it? What am I talking about? *I* haven't been in New York all this time. I only just moved out here from the Bay Area a year ago." She shook her head and a strand of perfectly highlighted hair tumbled charmingly over one porcelain cheek—healthy, strong hair, unlike my own unreliable strands.

Andrea looked good. Amazing, really. Like a better, more polished, fitter version of me. She was wearing a pair of loose-fitting high-waisted jeans with ankle boots and a white silk button-down, which was carefully tucked into the jeans. Her glowing skin appeared poreless, and I spent a second wondering which expensive laser treatments had produced such perfection. A delicate gold chain encircled her right wrist. And there was the diamond on her left hand: the kind of solitaire that was on the large end of the tasteful spectrum. The sum effect was that of casual luxury.

"Wow." I drew back, separating from her grasp, and indicated her ring. "That's beautiful. So you're married, then." I knew this already from my sleuthing, obviously; she'd had that wedding photo on her Instagram feed. Still, I was experiencing a nasty mixture of envy, possessiveness, and—bizarrely—FOMO. Andrea blushed and glanced down at her hand as if she was surprised by it too.

"I am," she asked, forcing a smile. "And it is. Thank you. Funny how everything looks from the outside, don't you think?"

I tilted my head. It was a strange admission for the first thirty seconds of our reunion.

"Things aren't good?" I pulled out my chair and slid into it. "Are you . . . is everything okay?" I suddenly wanted to know her entire story all at once. The juicy stuff, not the curated content I'd found online. If it were possible to reclaim all twenty-five years through immediate osmosis, I would have. My stomach twisted. I clasped my fingers in my lap to still their trembling.

"I'm fine," she said, sliding into the booth across from me. "Or I am now, anyway. It's been a difficult year. Rob—my husband—well, he's been a saint. Seriously. The silver lining, I guess, is that I found you." She stopped, took one look at my confusion, and shook her head as if to clear it. "Let me back up," she said. "But first, coffee."

Andrea motioned to the waiter for some water and he brought over a pitcher, filling each of our glasses.

"Coffee, when you get a minute." She flashed him a dazzling smile. Andrea oozed the kind of authority that had eluded me my entire life. There were years when I held my breath every time I spoke to a stranger, half expecting to be met with scorn for breaking a random social convention I'd never learned. Half wondering if I'd even gotten my phrasing right. If I was honest, it was part of the reason I'd become an editor: the meticulous attention to detail made me feel more controlled. And it gave me a reason to study people. Most people thought editing was about fixing grammatical errors, but that was the work of copy editors and proofreaders. In its way, being an editor was a blend of sociology and psychology: the study of characters and the worlds they moved in. What motivated them. What drove them. What their individual microcosms looked like. What it meant to understand and empathize to an immersive extent. And above all else, how best to craft an authentic-seeming narrative.

I was fascinated by people's stories. Over the years, I'd become adept at telling convincing stories of my own—namely, the overarching narrative that I was just like everyone else. Despite my knack for blending in, I often caught myself apologizing for basic requests. I was that person who waited to contact her landlord until the cockroach problem was out of control and who preferred to go home empty-handed rather than ask the salesperson for a different shoe size. Andrea, on the other hand—while clearly emotional—exuded self-possession where it counted. This was a woman who never had to wonder how to be. It seemed that for her, moving through life was instinctual.

Our waiter placed two cups of coffee in front of us.

"Cream, please," she told him, offering another warm smile.

I hadn't told her I drank coffee. But coffee with cream was exactly what I'd been craving.

"I just . . . assumed," she said, motioning toward my mug. "We were always so alike, you and me. But if you want something else . . ." She trailed off, her eyes questioning.

"No, no. This is perfect." I added cream to my mug and took a long sip to prove it.

She relaxed into the booth.

"Maeve, I can't tell you how happy I am to see you," she said. "I thought—I wondered—Well, none of it matters now."

I exhaled loudly. I hadn't even realized I'd been holding my breath. My napkin, which I'd been clutching in my lap, was shredded.

"You wondered whether I was alive or dead," I clarified. "What had happened to me, whether I'd turned out fine. Whether I ever thought of you over the years."

She nodded, her eyes brimming. "It was the same for you, then."

"Yes, exactly," I told her. "It was like losing a part of me. I'm just so glad to see you're okay. Or—*are* you okay?"

"I am." Andrea dabbed at the corners of her eyes with her napkin. "God." She laughed. "I really hadn't planned to start like this. I'm a little vulnerable, I guess. Oh, hell. I may as well just be candid. I lost my daughter five years ago."

"Oh god, Andrea—" Taken aback, I was the first to look away.

"No, no. Don't say anything," she said. "I've made peace with it . . . mostly. We didn't find out about Olivia's condition until after we took her home from the hospital. She lived for three months at home, and then she was back at UCSF Benioff and fully reliant on machines. In the end, we made the decision to let her go. It's been . . . well, she was so little when we lost her. Some might say we were lucky. It was probably easier than losing a child we'd had more of a chance to get to know. But I don't know. It was no easier than the night I lost you," she confessed, meeting my eyes again. "I just wanted a *family*, you know? Which is why finding you feels like a gift from the universe. I still can't believe it."

"I can't either." It was weird how simultaneously awkward and normal it felt to be sitting across from her. "I've got to say, I've spent most of my life wondering if you even *wanted* to find me. Finding each other on a DNA website is just so fated. And obvious."

"What can I say; I'm a tech girl. Thank goodness you took one of those DNA tests."

"Yeah, but like a thousand years ago. I didn't even know I had email notifications enabled."

"Are we ready to order?" The waiter interrupted us. He was young and very handsome, early twenties, with slicked-back hair and the sort of angular chin people paid good money for. Likely an actor or model. His smile was from another world, where cousins brunched casually without a lifetime of baggage to unpack.

"I'll have the fruit bowl," Andrea said. "And a spinach omelet with turkey bacon on the side. And a tomato juice with a wedge of lemon. Thank you."

"I'll take two poached eggs," I told him. "Thanks."

"Oh, Maeve. You should have more than that."

"I'm not really a breakfast eater," I explained. "Sometimes it's hard for me to force food down before noon."

"I get it." Andrea fidgeted with her bracelet, her forehead crinkled in thought. "I was that way, too, for a while. Then, when I was trying to get pregnant, I started eating a lot of fiber and protein at breakfast. I guess it kind of stuck." She shrugged, losing herself to memories. Then she met my eyes again.

"I'm sorry," she said. "I didn't mean to launch into that whole sad story so soon. But I guess . . . Honestly, it's probably good that you know. It's so wrapped up in who I am now that it would have felt strange to hide it."

"I appreciate you sharing it with me," I told her, meaning it. "I'm so sorry you went through that."

"Thank you." She smiled tightly. "Do you have kids?"

"No," I said. "I'm single. No kids. No significant other. Just me."

"Oh." There was an awkward silence. Then, "Well, you're a high-powered career woman, by the look of it. I checked you out online," she admitted. "What do you edit?"

"Fiction," I said, embarrassed by her idea of me. "The occasional nonfiction. But mostly I love escapism."

She laughed. "Of course! You had the most active imagination when we were kids. And a penchant for overanalyzing. Yeah, I could see you being great at that gig."

I found myself smiling back. "I guess I needed an outlet for that imagination. You remember how you were always teasing me about it? I'd have these ridiculously detailed dreams and force you to listen . . ."

"But then I'd interrupt you to tell you *my* dream, which usually I was just making up on the spot because I was jealous you could remember yours."

"Wow. I never knew that." I paused, touched that she'd admitted something so personal. "You had a great imagination, too." We both laughed then, longer and harder than the conversation warranted. It was as if someone had hit the release valve on everything I'd been bottling up.

"You have no idea how incredible it is to see you," Andrea said quietly, as the waiter set down her tomato juice and refreshed our coffees. Andrea added more cream to her coffee from a small pewter pitcher.

"I do know," I said. "I feel the same way." Being with Andrea again felt like getting back an essential piece of me, that part of me that had died when I was eight and she was eleven. I knew all along how much I'd missed her; I simply hadn't realized how much of *me* had been missing as well.

"I just wanted to say . . ." I started, hesitating momentarily. "About that night—"

Andrea sucked in a breath. "Actually, I don't want to talk about those days. If it's okay with you. The only thing that matters anymore from back then is that the two of us were together. And now we can be together again."

"Okay." I nodded, confused. It was hard for me to think about those days too, let alone discuss them aloud. But how could we *not* talk about it? Our history was the entire basis for our relationship. It struck me that we actually didn't have much in common other than our past, that I knew of, and I fumbled for something to ask. Then a smile crossed her face and she reached across the table to squeeze my hand.

"Tell me everything. What's been going on all these years? Besides your badass career, I mean."

I laughed awkwardly. It had been so long since anyone had even asked. I was painfully aware that I had nothing to say.

"You first. What do you do professionally?" I bluffed. "And who's this guy you married?"

"Oh, I can't wait for you to meet him," Andrea gushed. Part of me lifted at that—the acknowledgment that there would be opportunity to meet him, that this wasn't it for us. As she talked about Rob, the way they'd met, and the house they'd just recently purchased upstate after a year of renting, I couldn't help but lose myself in the fantasy—becoming friends with both of them, spending holidays at their home. Being part of a real family.

"And so that was when he proposed!" she finished. "Can you believe it? It was the biggest surprise of my life."

I nodded, then shook my head, realizing I'd spaced out. "No!" I exclaimed. "Wow. That's so great."

"What?" She looked at me closely. "What is it?"

"Nothing," I said. "I'm just really glad you found someone you love."

Andrea set her fork down—she was long finished with her omelet and had been tracing absent patterns on her plate. "And you? You must at least be *seeing* someone. Who's the lucky guy? Or person," she amended.

"No one special," I said. "I'm as unattached as it gets." I wasn't about to get into my relationship with Ryan. The ongoing casual sex that represented the sum total of my love life seemed at best immature and at worst a little tainted. Andrea nodded, her face full of questions.

"I was really lucky, though," I said, bringing the subject

back around to the things I really wanted to know. "A great family adopted me almost immediately after the raid." Andrea's eyes flickered to her plate. I pressed on. "Tom passed away when I was in college and Patty's in a nursing home—they were an older couple—but we got really close for a while. Did anyone take you in? I was hoping—"

"Maeve." Andrea cut me off, glancing around. A short, embarrassed laugh escaped her. "I told you. I really don't like to dwell on those times."

"Oh." I shifted uncomfortably in my chair. "I guess I'm just wondering if—"

"You want to know?" She leaned forward, lowering her voice. "It was bad. Really bad, okay? I know you were just a kid, and I am glad you were adopted, but nobody wanted me. I was in and out of foster homes. Four, five, I lost count after a while." She raised her eyes to meet mine. "I didn't want you to know because I didn't want you to feel responsible for what happened to me. But it wasn't pretty. When I was eighteen, I was out of there."

"I'm sorry," I whispered. "You seem so *together*. So amazing. I just assumed . . . I'm so sorry."

"I did fine—I just had to do it on my own for a while. I got a full ride to community college. Did really well. I guess by then I'd learned I could only really rely on myself. I got into a good grad school, got my MSW and my MBA. I used my business background to create my own company—I started as a life coach. That's around when I met Rob at that conference I mentioned. He was one of the presenters. He was doing a talk on getting into tech." She stopped, her face flushed. "I built this life for myself," she continued. "And I forgave you a long time ago. But I don't talk about the past anymore. And I'd appreciate it if you don't ask me about it. Please. Can you do that for me?"

"Okay." But I was disappointed. I'd never been permitted to talk about the past in front of Patty and Tom. Here was the one person who'd been there. Who would understand. I had thought she could validate my experiences or offer a perspective that might bring me closure. Maybe it was selfish.

When Andrea addressed me again, her voice was gentle. "Maeve. You were the best part of childhood for me," she said. "When Olivia died, it took me a while to put what happened with her behind me. And when I came out on the other side after a lot of work and spiritual growth, I just wanted family. Rob—my husband—is my family," she said simply. "But I wanted my flesh and blood."

I nodded, meeting her gaze. I felt homesick every day for a family that had never existed in any tangible way in the first place. I knew instinctively that despite what she seemed to have now—a doting husband, financial security—Andrea felt the same way.

"I'm here for you," I found myself saying. "Flesh and blood. I'm so glad you found me."

Andrea smiled and squeezed my hand tighter. "Now that we're together again, I'm not letting you go."

* * *

The server ended his shift, and Andrea settled up without me noticing. After the initial discomfort of dancing around our pasts, our conversation picked up. I thought this must be what it was to have a life, to feel alive. At some point Andrea motioned for a cocktail menu.

Soon Andrea was tipsy enough to repeat herself. I wondered about the meetings she'd mentioned having, but I was enjoying myself too much to question it. It was only one in the afternoon, so we'd graduated from coffee to very respectable mimosas, and the mood had lightened. "Rob's in tech," Andrea was explaining again. "He's a developer. A total genius. But I'm the alpha of the two of us." She laughed.

"Oh?" I smiled, enjoying this. "Somehow that doesn't surprise me at all." Andrea had always been the one in charge.

"Rob's completely dedicated to me," she went on, waving away my comment. "He's amazing. He's the only man I've met who just . . . allows me to spread my wings."

"That's fantastic. I'm so glad to hear it." I meant it. As much as I had this fantasy of the two of us coming back together into the inseparable unit we'd been as kids, I was happy she'd found a partner.

"So do you have a picture of the hot fling guy?" she asked. "Does he have a name?"

"Oh god." After a single mimosa and fielding a lot of Andrea's prying questions, I'd admitted to my casual affair with Ryan. Rather than being disapproving, Andrea had been delighted. She'd asked me a million questions, right down to the specifics of our sex life. I was too overwhelmed by it all to play defense; and anyway, it felt like what family probably did. Now I reached for my iPhone, flipping through my photos until I landed on one of the two of us grinning into the camera against the backdrop of his Brooklyn bar. "His name's Ryan," I told her.

"He's *cute*," she said admiringly, waggling her eyebrows. "I'll have to live voyeuristically through you, I guess." Before I could ask her what that meant, she switched the subject. "Oh man. If I could go back to my single days . . . I love my husband, but you're only young and in Europe once."

She explained that she'd lived all over, even Paris for a year, where she'd had an affair with a French woman nearly fifteen years her senior. It was from Adele that she learned the ins and outs of investing and was inspired to go to business school when that relationship went up in flames. "Very hot flames," she clarified. After business school she began to build her life coaching business, and it took off around when she met Rob. She didn't even have to work if she didn't want to. But as it turned out, she did want to. Then she got pregnant with Olivia and switched gears to coaching in the lifestyle space: more specifically, family planning. After Olivia's death, she added grief management and recovery from loss. She began holding workshops and retreats. She and Rob developed an offshoot product that was starting to pick up. Andrea and Rob had been together for eight years. They were determined to build a family of their own, one way or another.

"But *we're* family. Right?" She looked eager as she searched my eyes, then reached out to squeeze my hand.

"God, you've lived such a full life," I exclaimed, buzzing from the drinks. "I can't believe you even thought of me after all those adventures."

"Oh, Maeve," Andrea exclaimed, cupping my face in her palms. "There's no one more important to me than you. No one at all. There's something special about people who have known each other their whole lives. We can all reinvent ourselves. But who we were as kids never really leaves us. You do know how much I love you, right?" I nodded, even though I'd never have believed it if she weren't in front of me, staring directly into my eyes. They were the words I'd wanted to hear for so long, and never in a million years thought I'd hear again.

"I love you, too," I told her. Getting to say it felt like a gift.

Andrea beamed. Suddenly I wanted to make her even happier, to hold on to that fleeting feeling.

"Hey . . . You know, my birthday's next month," I said. "My legal birthday," I clarified, when she looked confused. "The one my foster family gave me. My friend—well, technically she's

my supervisor . . . kind of a mentor, but we've gotten close.
Elena is her name. She organized this drinks thing for me. We
all do it for each other," I explained. "It's sort of obligatory
by now." I paused, realizing it would mean giving Andrea a
glimpse of my life—possibly ruining any image she had of
me as ultra successful and beloved. I was sure if Elena hadn't
planned it, not one of my colleagues would have remembered
my birthday. There was a long silence, and I laughed awkwardly. "You know what? Forget it." I trailed off. Letting her
into my life would mean she'd see me, really see me. Maybe
she wouldn't like what she saw. Maybe she would regret having reached out.

"Maeve," she said, interrupting my train of thought. "I'd
love to come to your birthday party."

"It's not a party," I said quickly. "Just a low-key drinks
thing at a bar by my office. I'm talking, like, dollar shots. An
expedient happy hour before everyone gets on with their regular evening plans." But a smile lit up her face.

"I'd really like to be there. You're the only person left in the
world who's known me forever. And I can't wait to meet your
friend Elena."

"My supervisor," I corrected her. Then I caught myself. "A
friend too, I guess." I met her gaze; Andrea's face was flushed,
her smile childlike and pleased. It made her look vulnerable.
I smiled back at her. "All right," I said. "Okay. Let's do it. I'd
love for you to be there."

Later that day—back home in my Brooklyn studio—
everything seemed more muted without Andrea. I was charged,
electric; something had changed within me. It was as if I'd
finally discovered a sense of purpose.

Thanks again for the amazing day, I texted her. *I'm so glad to
have you back in my life.*

She replied with a simple *xx.*

JUST LIKE MOTHER   33

Two letters: a future that a week ago hadn't existed. A family I never thought I'd have. I knew without a doubt I could never go back to the way things were. It seemed like the world had finally granted me a kindness.

3

A month passed—a month of tentative texting with my cousin that had caused time to simultaneously speed up and slow down—and then it was my birthday. The bar where we'd gathered smelled dank and yeasty, and five of my colleagues were occupying various points on the inebriation spectrum. A tray of room-temperature cheese cubes I'd bought myself sat untouched on the bar counter.

Andrea had texted me last minute to see if she could bring her "crew." Rob, her husband, was just as doting and attentive as she'd said, yet funny and charming and smart too—a perfect man; the kind of man I'd have dreamed up for myself if I could. Then she introduced me to her best friend and colleague, Emily Lee of NewLife fame: a strikingly beautiful woman with delicate features and dark hair that fell in easy waves over her shoulders. When I extended my hand to introduce myself, she enveloped me in a hug instead.

"Happy Birthday, Queen. We're going to be great friends; I can feel it." Then, when I offered her a drink: "Oh, I wish. I'm pregnant—just a few months along. Do you have kids? Don't worry; there's time yet. Better to wait for a guy with great genes. They're few and far between." An eye roll, then a playful wink. And with a glance at Rob, a nudge of the elbow. "Sweet, isn't he? Andrea could have done worse. But men are only good for one thing, am I right?" She didn't bother to clarify what the thing was. Sex? Getting people pregnant? Emily was all winks and nudges, from what I could tell.

At one point, Elena rose from where she'd been sitting on a cracked-top stool, its stuffing spilling out from beneath green laminate. She pulled me aside and wrapped me in a hug before handing me a small, brightly wrapped gift. "Open it later," she said. "And *shh*—don't let the others know you're my work wife."

"Oh, Elena. You didn't need to get me something."

"I wanted to. I may have hired you, but we're friends, aren't we? Anyway, that's how I think of you."

"Yes," I agreed. "Friends. I'm so lucky to have you. Where's Lesley?"

"She's home with the kids. We couldn't get a sitter. She sends her love, though." Elena gave me a nudge. "Aren't you going to introduce me to your friends?" She nodded toward Andrea and Emily, who were standing a few feet away.

"Of course," I said. "That one's my cousin." Soon the group was chatting animatedly in the corner—Andrea causing Elena to laugh, then look intrigued, then whisper as if they'd known one another for years.

My cousin in my world, the thread to my past worming its way into my present.

There was shot after acrid shot and the flash of cameras and a tray of cupcakes that someone ran out to grab at Whole Foods—horrible cupcakes, dry as bone, which we wolfed down anyway, after I blew out a tiny lit match and made a wish.

I was thirty-three. I was drunk enough to forget none of these people were my friends, that we were all gathered here not to celebrate the birthday of a loved one but out of obligation and a mutual appreciation for binge drinking on a weeknight. I was overwhelmed by gratitude and the urgent need to pee.

"A twelve-house auction," my colleague Thomas was shouting into another colleague's ear.

"What?" Emory gaped. "That book wasn't even good!"

"I know. And I heard she didn't write it herself." Thomas leaned closer, confiding. "Good luck speaking to your process on tour, honey." He laughed, rested a hand on Emory's fore-arm. I rolled my eyes and stepped between them.

"I'm going to the bathroom," I announced.

Thomas was an entitled prick in his late twenties who'd grown up in New York and gone to Horace Mann and Prince-ton, where he'd been a member of the Triangle Club—facts I shouldn't have known, except for his frequent and unneces-sary mentions of his pedigree. He'd been trying to fuck Em-ory ever since she started three months ago, and I had made it my personal mission to divert his course. Emory was twenty-three and beautiful, with smooth, dark skin, high cheekbones, and thick, shoulder-length braids. She was an editorial assis-tant, very smart and brand new to publishing. She deserved to stay innocent at least until she had a salary high enough to pay for out-of-network therapy. "You have to go too, right?" I said to her. She looked confused. Then her face cleared and she gave me a knowing look.

"I've got this," she said, patting me on the shoulder. "You don't need to watch out for me." I nodded. I'd wrongly as-sumed that just because she was young, she was easily ma-nipulated.

"Happy fortieth, Maeve," Thomas called out spitefully, as I made my way to the bathroom. I was next in line for the single-occupancy, all-gender "WC," according to the sign on the door. By then my head was swimming.

"I've got to go so bad." Andrea's voice materialized behind me. "How long have they been in there?"

"I don't know." I shrugged. "A while."

She reached around me and knocked hard on the door.

"Andrea, stop! They're going to think it was me," I told her, just as the door opened and a peeved-looking woman with a platinum pixie cut stepped out. She glared at me hard, and Andrea burst into giggles.

"Come on," she said, taking my hand. "I can't wait another second. And besides, we're family."

I allowed myself to be whisked into the tiny room in a cloud of perfume. She promptly pulled her tights down and sat on the naked toilet seat. I raised my eyebrows.

"What?" She stared. "*What?* Ohh. Are you one of those people who puts down a layer of toilet paper?"

"Maybe," I said, facing the mirror. I turned on the sink and washed my hands, avoiding her eyes. She was beautiful, even perched ridiculously over a filthy ceramic seat. I could hardly stand the intimacy of it—as if we'd done this a hundred times before.

When she was done, Andrea washed her hands and motioned for me to use the toilet. "I'm just going to freshen up super quick." I watched as she spread a layer of red onto her bottom lip. She turned and giggled slightly, lipstick held aloft, as I lined the seat with wads of toilet paper.

"I've got a present for you," she said, when she finished applying her lipstick. I was still on the toilet. She handed me an envelope, and in it was a postcard. On the front was a house, enormous and majestic and rambling and slightly Gothic looking. On the back was a message: *For thirty-three, what's yours is mine, what's mine is yours.*

"What is this place?" I asked, confused. I balanced the card on the toilet paper dispenser as I wiped, then pulled up my jeans and headed for the sink. Andrea was smiling at me, a mischievous expression on her face.

"It's our house," she exclaimed. "Rob's and mine. I told you, we bought a home in the Hudson Valley in April. It's historically preserved, and I found those postcards at the local library."

"Wow," I said, shaking off my hands and holding them in front of the dryer. "It's beautiful."

"We've been renovating it," she said, "at least within the constraints we're allowed. It's a bitch renovating a house that's preserved. It's been a crazy four months, let me tell you, but most of the guest rooms are done." I tried to focus; things were getting a little blurry. *Most?* How many guest rooms were there? "And so you'll come? This weekend?" she asked.

"What? As in, tomorrow?"

"Yes, tomorrow! I know it's a little spontaneous, but why not? I meant what I said in the message." She took my hands in hers, and repeated it: "What's yours is mine; what's mine is yours. I'd love to throw you a real party. A relaxing, fun weekend. Just us. Oh, and maybe Emily and Micah. That's her husband. And Rob, obviously. You'll come? We've got this big, beautiful house and no one in it. Come on, let me spoil you a little bit."

I hesitated. I was touched . . . and nervous. A weekend was a long time to spend together. On the other hand, I'd been dreading being alone over the weekend, so soon after my birthday. For once, I could celebrate with family. *My* family. A warm glow flooded me.

"Oh," she said, noticing my hesitation. "You already have plans."

"No, no," I said. I didn't—I never had weekend plans. "I just . . ."

She frowned, her forehead wrinkling.

"I'll come," I told her. "I requested the day off anyway, for my birthday."

She squealed and jumped up and down until someone banged on the door with their fist, just as she had, and yelled at us to hurry the hell up, and we slipped back out. Then Andrea reached back for my hand and led me into thirty-three.

A few hours later, back home in my studio and restless, I picked up my phone and texted Ryan.

Hey baby, I wrote—the kind of greeting I utilized only

when I was feeling especially needy. *Come over? We need to celebrate.*

I remembered the wrapped box from Elena, shoved at the bottom of my purse. While I waited for Ryan's response, I pulled it out and tugged off the wrapping. It was beautiful wrapping: thick lavender stock, hand-stamped with intricate gold patterns. She'd topped it off with a black ribbon and a tiny paper flower inserted at the knot. Elena always put such care into presentation; it was why she was good at evaluating book covers. Anything with her eye on it was always gorgeous and fresh, with some unexpected detail that set it apart.

I opened the small blue box inside the wrapping and gasped. It was a business card holder—sterling silver and engraved with my name. It was gorgeous. I was admiring it when my phone dinged. I set Elena's gift carefully aside and retrieved my phone.

Gotta close tonight ☹, he wrote. An ellipsis appeared on the screen beneath his first message. He started typing, stopped, started again.

Won't be out till 4, but I can bring u breakfast in the morning? What are we celebrating?

I stared at the screen, a knot forming in my stomach. *What are we celebrating?* I'd told him once in passing when my birthday was, but I couldn't have expected him to remember. Boyfriends remembered that type of thing; fuck buddies didn't. It was strange to have spent a year getting to know someone—a year of being as physically intimate as two people can be—and still feel so alone. I clicked off the text screen without responding, then lay on my side and pulled my knees into my chest, drifting off to sleep fully clothed and with the light on. I was ready to feel loved, I thought, as I drifted off. I was ready to let someone in.

*   *   *

I had only just managed to shake off my birthday hangover
the next day when I found myself wedged in the back of Emily
and Micah's Range Rover between Truman, their black lab,
and Henry, their three-year-old, on our way to Andrea and
Rob's home in the Catskill Mountains. I'd been relieved when
Emily reached out to offer—*Hey lady, can we give you a lift?*—
with the upbeat, confident affect I'd started to recognize as
her trademark. I hadn't been looking forward to enduring
the itchy cushions of a Trailways bus. A rental car wasn't an
option—I've been afraid of driving my whole life. It was one
reason besides publishing that I was bound to New York, one
of the few cities I could navigate easily without a car.

That said, I hadn't envisioned myself adjacent to a toddler
in a car seat for several hours. Being close to Henry—who
was an absolute cherubic vision—made me break into a cold,
anxious sweat while simultaneously feeling a disparate tug of
affection. Half of me wanted to wrap him in my lap and snug-
gle him right then, and the other half thought the Trailways
bus looked a lot more appealing.

The trunk was stacked with luggage and provisions: wine
and groceries from specialty shops in the city. There was a
tense air to the journey, a weird vibe between Emily and Micah. It was augmented by Henry's attentions to his mother,
from whom he apparently hated to be separated. Emily had
told me quietly, while stowing my bag in the back, that they
hadn't yet explained her new pregnancy to Henry, and as
such, I shouldn't mention it in front of him. She wasn't showing much either—just a cute little bump easily disguised under a loose-fitting button-down. Still, it was as if Henry could
sniff it.

"When I was pregnant with Henry, I could hardly keep
anything down," Emily was explaining, as we merged onto
the George Washington Bridge. "I was a walking vessel for
regurgitation."

"Babe," Micah said absently. "I'm a little carsick. Could you manage the rest of the trip, if I pull over somewhere?"

"Micah. Really? I mention morning sickness and suddenly you have nausea by association? You're fine. Car sickness is approximately one-tenth as bad as first trimester morning sickness." She met my gaze in the rearview mirror and rolled her eyes conspiratorially, as if to say *Men are such pussies*.

Micah clenched his jaw. I had to admit, Emily was clever. It wasn't as if he could argue with her over whether her stats were accurate.

"Anyway. This time has been smooth sailing so far." She smiled brightly.

"You look incredible," I offered, figuring if she could indirectly mention her pregnancy, I could too.

"Doesn't she?" Micah agreed, his face more relaxed than it had been a moment ago. "I got to marry the smartest and most beautiful woman in the world. Life is good."

It was true that Emily pulled off pregnancy better than anyone I'd seen. She oozed vitality. Her skin glowed. Her hair was thick and shiny, and tumbled in waves past her shoulders. Her lips and cheeks were perfectly flushed. She was even prettier in person than she'd looked online.

"It suits me, I know," she said, keeping her allusions vague for Henry's sake. "But I really appreciate you saying so, Maeve."

Okay, then.

She glanced back at me, giving me an appraising look. "It'll suit you too; I can tell." I laughed, shaking off my annoyance. Her default assumption was apparently that I wanted children—that every woman did.

"You laugh, but I know these things. It's why I'm good at my job. I'm very intuitive."

Micah cleared his throat and switched the radio station. Emily switched it back. To my surprise, Micah shot her an indulgent grin.

"What Emmie wants, Emmie gets."

I'm good at my job. I thought back to the headlines I'd read, back when I'd looked up Andrea online. There'd been at least one about Emily—I knew she worked with Andrea, but what did she do, exactly? I pulled out my phone and typed "Emily Lee" into the search. Immediately, a dozen images popped up. There she was, looking confident and self-possessed. It was evident in the upward tilt of her chin, the direct focus of her eyes, a mouth lifted in a smile that conveyed a hint of a challenge.

I clicked back on "All." The first headline was from *Forbes*. In 2018, Emily had been named a Top Thirty Under Thirty for "shaking up Silicon Valley with radical feminism." Huh. Impressive. And Emily was the same age I was. I clicked the back arrow and scrolled to a link on a lifestyle blog. "Meet the Woman Who Has It All." There was Emily again, holding a newborn in one hand and a kitchen scale in the other. Rather than seeming antiquated, the mischievous tilt of her mouth made the photo convey irony and empowerment. I scrolled through the article: "In a study wherein random participants viewed Ms. Lee interacting with two NewLife AI infants and her own child, forty-seven percent of the focus group incorrectly identified one of the NewLife models as the human baby." Emily was quoted as saying,

As a Korean American woman married to a Black man, I am often asked if our child—who inherited my husband's complexion—is adopted. I suspect this test was distorted somewhat due to racial bias; none of the three children "look" like me.

Neither my husband nor I had any trouble bonding with our child. Evolutionary studies say we bond more quickly with children who resemble us. Vigeneros babies are customizable, of course. But they're designed to appeal to families—

both grieving the death of a child or planning for a child—on a completely different psychological level. Most of our prototypes are biologically female, to inspire a protective instinct where it might otherwise be lacking.

What if a couple grew attached to their female prototype and wound up having a son? And why was it assumed that female babies needed more protection than their male counterparts? I typed in the question and flicked to an article in *The Atlantic,* quickly scanning the page. It linked to an interview with Emily. Others were asking the same questions I was. Emily explained:

Once the maternal or paternal protective instinct is activated, the child's gender becomes almost irrelevant. Think of it as a switch: Once it's on, it's on. This is especially intriguing when it comes to shielding an expecting parent from postpartum depression or facilitating paternal bonding.

Female infants activate the protective instinct more quickly than males due to their relative physical vulnerability. It's somewhat counterintuitive, since studies also show that females live longer lives and are more physically and emotionally hardy than males over the course of a lifetime. Still, we have found that tapping into these primal instincts via our AI models allows for closer bonding with one's human offspring—biological or not, and regardless of gender.

It was fascinating. I opened my mouth to ask Emily about it, when Henry, who had been relatively quiet up to then, broke in. I jumped, rattled. I'd almost stopped noticing his presence.

"Fing-ah," he said, peering at me from his car seat. "Fing-ah." I tensed. His voice was shrill and grating.

I clicked off my phone and shoved it back in my jacket pocket. Henry continued to stare, his eyes frantic. "Finger."

At least, I thought that's what he was saying. I felt my blood pressure beginning to rise.

"Emily," I called over the din of nineties alt-rock. "Henry wants something."

"Hmm?" Emily looked at Henry, her brow furrowed. "What is it, sweet pea?" Henry's eyes immediately welled, the space between his eyebrows wrinkling in distress. "Hang on. Daddy will get you a snack."

"Finger," Henry demanded. The back of my neck prickled. Desperate, I offered him my extended index finger. Maybe there was some sort of routine where he liked to clutch a hand, which he was now being denied because I was seated next to him, rather than his mother.

Henry broke out in a true wail then, a fake, deafening sound that reminded me of the moirologists I'd read about in a course on ancient Egypt my freshman year. It was obvious to me that it was attention seeking, yet Emily shot Micah a look, a fleeting expression of irritation crossing her features.

"Can you handle this, or do you need me to jump in?" she asked him pointedly.

"I've got it." Micah twisted in his seat, keeping one hand on the wheel as he fumbled for an oversize tote from the back, near where I was sitting. I picked it up and handed it to him. He thanked me, then looked up, studying me in the mirror.

"You know, you look a lot like Andrea," he said. I forced a smile, my attention on Henry's sobs, which weren't getting any better.

"That's a compliment. He thinks Andrea is hot," Emily remarked. The comment was matter-of-fact, devoid of jealousy. The previous night, Emily had fawned over Andrea, wrapping her arms around her shoulders and nuzzling her neck as they swayed to the bar music. *This* version of Emily was cooler, more detached. As if the one she was in love with—who made her flutter—was Andrea, not her husband.

"Micah, please turn the music down," she said absently, while she fiddled with her phone. "Or, actually, why don't you put something on that Henry would like." Micah fumbled with the sound system, tote lying untouched on his lap, until a Disney sing-along piped through the car's speakers. "It's hardly the death metal I listened to in college," he joked, meeting my eyes again. "But I guess it'll do."

Truman sat quietly beside me, apparently used to all the activity; but then, I knew Truman had been fed a tranquilizer in a marshmallow before the trip began. I found myself wishing I had some of that marshmallow, as Henry's cries increased in pitch and urgency. My own Klonopin stash was in my suitcase in the back.

Micah deftly navigated a lane change and signaled to exit I-278 onto 87. Once on 87, he reached in the bag and pulled out a bag of cheese puffs, handing them back to Henry, who snatched them without requiring interference. He stuffed cheese puffs in his mouth, but still he wailed, sodden flakes spattering his car seat and my leg. I shifted in my seat, brushing off my jeans and fighting the urge to scream. Emily flipped through a magazine, unfazed. Finally—*finally*—she shot Micah a beseeching look.

"Well, what do you want me to do while I'm driving?" he asked. He fumbled through the tote again, retrieving a pacifier attached to a stuffed dinosaur. I reached for it, Henry's cries filling my head and making my heart pound frantically. *Make. It. Stop.*

"Micah's got it," Emily said quickly. Then she turned back and smiled, mollifying. "Sorry. I know you're trying to be helpful, but you should relax. You're our guest. Micah has it covered. Don't you, babe?"

"Relax," I repeated. Yeah, no. That wasn't happening.

Micah nodded. "Absolutely. On it." When he transferred the tote off his lap to the floor of the backseat, I didn't bother helping. But when Micah broke into the lyrics from *Frozen*—a little desperately, I thought—and Henry's sobs still continued, I wanted to scream along with Henry. The kid just would not be placated. I looked at Henry, who returned my gaze. I narrowed my eyes, willing him to shut up. His eyes spilled over with tears, despite him having everything he could ever want: a sippy cup filled with juice, his choice of entertainment, a plastic baggie of cheese-flavored puffs.

"I know you're faking," I told him in a low voice. His eyes widened, but his features calmed, and he trained his eyes on me. A strange, measured chill replaced my frantic nerves. "I have magical powers and can always tell when a cry is real," I continued, my voice muffled by the din of the music in the front. "Did you know Auntie Maeve is a wizard?" Henry abruptly stopped whining, his jaw slack and his small, dry lips ringed with mucus and cheese powder. "That's right. And when kids are bad, I can cast an evil spell."

He sniffled, then reached out with an orange hand to touch my arm, as if testing my powers. I jerked it away, the spot he'd touched tingling.

"What did you do?" Emily asked, staring at me intently in the rearview mirror. For a panicked moment I tensed, certain she'd heard me. "Wow, you're really amazing with him," she said then, the corners of her mouth turned up in a wry grin. "I don't know how you did that, but if you hadn't been here, that was a Category 10 waiting to happen. Micah, maybe you should take a page from Maeve's book."

"Oh. It was nothing," I assured her, fighting to keep my voice neutral. "Henry and I are just buds. Right, kiddo?" I tickled his knee and Henry smiled warily.

Emily clapped, loving it. "Seriously, Maeve. You're a natural." I offered her a stiff smile and pulled out my novel, reading until I felt sleepy enough to wad up my lightweight jean jacket into a pillow against the window and rest my head there, hopeful that sleep would come soon.

* ' * *

I awoke to the sound of a loud gasp from Emily and a "Holy shit!" from Micah.

"Micah! Language," Emily reminded, but I could tell her heart wasn't in it. The car rolled slowly up a long dirt road. We were surrounded on both sides with trees, as if a forest had swallowed us up. My ears popped, and I blinked a few times to clear the sleepy haze from my contacts, then squinted through the front windshield into the narrow gap between Emily and Micah.

I sucked in a breath. "That can't be it," I told them, certain there was some mistake.

"It has to be," Emily said, her voice hushed. "I'm so glad we finally get to see it. Andrea's been particular about needing it 'set up' before visitors could come."

"This is a one-way road to Mansionville," Micah said, sounding a mixture of bitter and envious. "Why didn't they tell us their new house was an estate?" A pocketknife had materialized in his right hand, and he began absently fiddling with it.

"And say what? 'Hi, the house we bought, it isn't a house so much as a crumbling old mansion'? Seriously, Micah."

The house was even more impressive than it had appeared on the postcard I'd left in the bathroom that night. It was a Gothic stone fortress with multiple balconies, stained glass windows adorning the uppermost level, and trees on all sides. We pulled closer, finally arriving at a stop in front of the behemoth structure. I pulled out my phone and took a quick shot through the window, then sent it to Ryan.

Check out my 5-star digs for the weekend, I typed. *Try not to drool.*

Ohh . . . send photos of your bedroom, he responded immediately. *Ideally of you in your bedroom. Ideally unclothed. That'll
get me drooling.* A second later, the phone buzzed again. *On
second thought, need a bedmate?*

I smiled and sent a wink emoji, then clicked off the screen.
I needed to see more of this place. I had to crane my neck
from my vantage point to make out its third story. The tow-
ers converged in a sort of pyramid shape, a fourth-story attic
looming above them, adopting the role of an imperious sen-
tinel. It was massive and austere, almost like a British manor
buried deep in the woods.

"You good?" asked Emily, as she hopped out of the car,
leaving her window cracked. "Andrea and Rob. Always full of
surprises, right? NewLife must be having an even better year
than we thought."

"Sure," I replied. But didn't she know how the company
was doing? She was obviously right there at its helm. I reached
for my own door handle and cast a glance at the slumbering
Truman.

"Let him be," Emily instructed through the open window.
"He's just sleeping off the tranquilizers. If you keep the door
open, he'll hop out when he wakes up."

I did as she said, cracking the door for the dog and sliding
out of the car to the gravel driveway below.

"God. What *is* that?" I asked no one in particular, as a shrill,
squalling sound—not unlike an animal being tortured—
pierced the quiet country air.

Just then Andrea pushed her way out of her house, her
left arm gripping a perfectly oblong bundle, her glossy blond
waves draped over one shoulder. Micah was right. We did look
alike, but I was predictable and average, where everything
about her was unpredictable—a study in one of the paintings
Ryan had hanging in his apartment: a precise kind of chaos,

every erratic line planned for effect. Even her rumpled linen shirtdress and pallid skin, devoid of any makeup, looked purposeful.

Now Andrea dashed down the stairs and threw her petite frame around Emily as Emily passed Henry to Micah. Andrea hugged Emily tightly, the bundle shoved to the side, *knocked aside* really, and twisted behind her, nearly. I felt a swell of bile building in my throat. Why was Andrea carrying an infant? Emily's words played back in my head: *Andrea and Rob. Always full of surprises.*

"You made it," Andrea murmured, burying the side of her face in Emily's neck as she peeked out at me with a warm smile. She gave Micah and Henry warm hellos, then presented us with the bundle—which had finally ceased its crying. Its face, turned outward, was fixed in a stiff expression of agony. It wasn't an infant at all. I recoiled at the sight of the doll in her hands. It was even more lifelike in person than it had appeared online. It was fake . . . and terrifying. Why was Andrea carting it around?

I expected Emily to look as weirded out as I felt. Instead, her expression was pleased—delighted, even. "Take Henry inside," she said to Micah.

"Come on bud, help me carry the luggage in," Micah told Henry, clapping him on the shoulder, as though nothing were amiss. Henry obediently accepted his Thomas the Tank Engine backpack and allowed himself to be scooped up and hauled indoors by his father.

"Meet Olivia," Andrea instructed us, jiggling the doll against her hip. The bundle bounced with an unnatural weightlessness in her arms. "Oh, come on," Andrea said, noticing my discomfort. "She's beautiful. She looks just like her."

She tilted the doll in my direction, inviting me to inspect its features. While I had never seen the real Olivia, the doll *did* bear a startling resemblance to Andrea, with its wide green eyes, shock of blond hair, and perfect, rosebud-shaped lips. I turned away, bringing a hand to my mouth.

"You should hold her," Emily suggested, turning to me with shining eyes. "Then me! She looks incredible. I can't believe she's finally ready." I shot them both a worried look. *Ready?*

"Do it," Emily insisted. She plucked the doll from Andrea's arms and placed it in mine before I could refuse. "There. Hold her closer. See, Maeve?" She looked up at me, eyes bright. "Doesn't she make you feel good?"

I looked down at its face. Something about holding the doll—its solid heft pressed against my thin frame—*was* comforting. It felt sturdy and permanent. It reminded me of holding Boy when he was small, cuddling him close, feeling the heavy weight of his down-covered head against my arm.

"What is this, Andrea?" I asked softly.

"It's that product I was telling you about," Andrea started. "The one we developed. I figured it would be easier to show you in person."

"It's for preparing for motherhood," Emily jumped in. "Everyone needs a license to drive a car, but no one needs a license to be a parent. Which is ridiculous, because it's so much more intense and serious, and with higher stakes—don't you agree? I've never met a new mom who wasn't terrified. It would be so easy to make a mistake, yet there's no manual on how to be a mother. So that's exactly what we're offering—training for motherhood. And a guide for grieving, too." I arranged my face into something I hoped appeared surprised and intrigued. Emily was enjoying giving me the entire pitch. It was practiced, but her enthusiasm for what she was selling was sincere.

"Andrea thought of it after Olivia died," she went on. "How helpful it would be for grieving families to have custom dolls to help them ease some of that awful despair. That empty space you feel in your arms when your baby is no longer with you. But the dolls didn't exist. So we started it ourselves. We used Henry as a model for the soft launch. Then we made some improvements, and Olivia is the new version. I'm *so* excited." She actually clapped.

"You sound like a walking ad." Andrea laughed, amused. "You explain it so well." She turned to me. "We ship the product this fall and . . . I have to say, our preorders have been tremendous. We're lucky. It's part of why we felt comfortable buying this house. The investments were strong from the beginning. But . . ." She paused, reaching for the Olivia doll. She pulled it away from me, patting its back where it rested on her ribcage. I watched as the gears in its face rearranged into something peaceful, its eyes lowering gently as if to imply the doll was fighting a losing battle against sleep.

"It's not just a product," Emily said. "It's a cause we really believe in—it goes hand in hand with the life coaching arm of the business. Our focus has always been family planning, but we're actually developing a whole extension of the program around these dolls, for expecting families and grieving families. We call it NewLife."

"I've heard of NewLife," I admitted. "But I didn't know your life coaching was part of the business, Andrea. I guess I assumed they were separate things."

"Nope. One and the same. We have a top psychoanalyst on board acting as a consultant, as well as some leading educators. I can't say who. NDAs and all."

"Expecting and grieving. Start to finish," I remarked, before I could stop myself.

"It's just beginnings, Maeve," Emily corrected. "And the Olivia doll is helping Andrea and Rob ease into their new stage of life. It's part of the process."

"It's true that I'm beta testing our product to help cope

with my own grief," Andrea said. "Kind of a perk of the business. I'm hoping you'll even participate, if you like."

"The technology is really incredible," I admitted, staring. The doll was uncannily lifelike. I gazed at it, awestruck. "What do you need me to do?"

"Just that, while you're here, you treat Olivia as you would any other baby when I'm engaging with her," Andrea said.

"Like playing house?" I laughed, incredulous.

"Maeve, we've been working toward this for a long time. All of us have. Please don't diminish our efforts." Emily frowned. "It's extraordinary. This will change so many women's lives for the better. It's our chance to make a real difference."

Andrea clasped my hand in hers. "Mae," she said, calling me by the name she'd used when we were kids. "I think it might help me. I know it's a little strange, but can you try? It's all I ask."

I looked into my cousin's eyes, which were so earnest, so full of emotion. I was here to forge a new path for us, after all. If this was how I could make up for upending her life so many years ago—well, there were worse, stranger things.

"Okay," I told her, squeezing back. Grateful for her hand in mine again, back where it was meant to be. "I'll do whatever you need."

Her face broke into a smile. "We're so glad to have you, Maeve. Now let's put your things down, shall we? And Emily, you too."

"Let me hold her first." Emily reached for the doll.

"Of course!" Andrea replied, smiling up at her. "Say hi to Auntie Emmie, sweetie," she told the doll, as she passed it over to Emily. Then she shot me a wry wink. *Thank you,* she mouthed silently, shooting me a grateful smile.

"Hi, Olivia," Emily said. Olivia blinked twice. Her nose had the perfect, upturned slope of her mother's. No, I corrected myself. Not "her mother"—she was just a doll. But then, there was something so real about her it made me hurt. How many photos and videos of Olivia had the designers had to study in order to get her just right?

"She's beautiful," I told them, and was immediately glad I did. Andrea appeared pleased.

"Well," Andrea said wryly, "babies certainly are expensive enough to make! Best to get it right." Truman barked from within the car, then came bounding out of the backseat to where we stood, spittle flying from his jowls as he ran. Andrea backed away from the previously docile dog. Truman was suddenly not only wide awake but also jittery, the ridge of fur on his back standing skyward.

"I'm so sorry," I said, even though the dog wasn't mine. "Quiet, Truman." I reached for his collar, whistling softly, but he growled viciously, baring his teeth, and I loosened my grip. As Andrea grabbed Olivia from Emily, cradling the doll protectively to her chest, Truman lunged forward. In turn, Andrea took a step back toward the base of the broad stone staircase that led up to the porch. The edge of her heel connected awkwardly with the lowest step, not quite landing.

It happened almost as if in slow motion: she lost her balance and tumbled over, landing on her tailbone on the steps before Emily or I could react. Olivia flew from her arms and the doll soared through the air against the backdrop of the gray sandstone exterior. I gasped and reached for Olivia, missing her by inches.

The baby's head hit the ground first.

Then Truman was on Olivia, sinking his teeth into the soft, fleshy folds of her face.

There was a shriek of despair so guttural and wild, I thought it was coming from Truman at first. But Truman was otherwise occupied, puncturing those gorgeous green eyes with his animal teeth, muzzle sinking into the guts of her.

"Truman! Back!" Emily shouted, and the dog whimpered, releasing his hold and slinking away behind the tires of the SUV.

Andrea stared at the doll, its face mutilated and in pieces beside her. Then I realized: the animal shriek was coming from me.

4

Maeve," Andrea said, seeming frightened. "It's okay. It's only a doll."

"I'm sorry," I said. "I don't mean . . ." I took a great, gasping breath. "It looked so real," I finished helplessly.

Emily placed an arm around my shoulders, drawing me to her side. "I knew we should have left the dog in the city. But Henry is so attached. Andrea, I'll leave him with a dog sitter next time."

"It's okay, really," Andrea replied. "We have more models upstairs. But this was a good learning experience. I'm actually glad it happened. I should build accidents like this into the curriculum. Or maybe think about reapproaching our engineering team about what materials we're using. Clearly, we don't want dogs thinking these are chew toys," she said with a nervous laugh. "Come on, let's go inside. I'll show you both around and let you get settled."

The house felt smaller on the inside than it appeared from the outside. Or at least that's how I felt as I unpacked my things in the small tower room on the second floor—the only room with twin beds, as far as I could tell. To be fair, much of the house was closed off, not yet furnished. And anyway, the window in my little room offered an extraordinary view of the mountains, the endless and rolling expanse of trees, which made me feel immediately more at peace.

"Champagne problems," Andrea had explained, as she ushered us upstairs, towing my roller bag herself. "Turns out, when you buy a lot of house, you have to buy a lot of furniture."

"That sounds like the fun part," Emily had commented. "Trolling antique shops, picking out vintage armoires . . ."

Being there—surrounded by people who were coupled and monied—I felt a strange regression pulling me backward, an insecurity I hadn't felt in years, one I associated with my youth and thought I'd mostly left behind me. Maybe it was the way Micah and Emily had demurred at my offer of pitching in for gas on the way up, as though they were the parents and I was the child. Maybe it was the sheer enormousness of this house and the unfathomable level of Andrea and Rob's wealth— money I knew all too well I'd never have access to. Maybe, god damn it, it was the *room,* the one I'd been instructed to settle into. Clearly meant for a child. *Children,* actually—twin bed, times two. How odd, I thought, that this was how Andrea had chosen to furnish one of the few initial guest rooms. It struck me that it wasn't all that different from the room she and I had shared as girls. I shivered at the thought. There were even similar yellow bedspreads with white coverlets, the only difference being that these were fresh and new.

And how tiny it all felt for such a massive structure. Almost as if I'd been placed in a box inside a box. I willfully exorcised my train of thought and reached for my toiletry bag, eager to freshen up and desperate to pee after the long ride. I stepped into the hall and was confronted with a maze of doors, a disorienting prospect. They seemed to stretch endlessly, entrances upon entrances—a bit like a book I'd read in my teens about a funhouse with endless mirrors and no exits. Were the stairs to the ground floor not directly in front of my room, I'd have doubted my ability to find my way to dinner.

I reached for a doorknob at random, but when I opened it, it revealed a set of spiral stairs moving upward and covered in dust. A wing of the house they hadn't gotten to. I tried not to think of all the spiders that must populate places like this before people moved in. I tried another door and found a closet, stuffed to the brim with blankets and towels. I made a mental note for later. The mountains could get cold at night, even at the height of summer.

The third door was cracked open. I assumed it might be Emily's, and knocked lightly, thinking she or Micah would point me in the direction of a bathroom. When I received no answer, I pushed open the door and peeked around its edge. I startled, momentarily short of breath, because in that tiny room rested a crib, white and well worn, one side adorned with a flourish of green paint that read "Olivia."

I moved toward the crib, which appeared to have been dusted recently. The thought of Andrea lovingly wiping the crevices of the space that used to hold her daughter made my blood run cold. There was a blanket folded over the edge of the crib, slightly pilled from use and embroidered with Olivia's name, and a worn spot at the front of the crib where the original wood showed through. I placed my fingers over the spot and imagined Andrea resting her hand there as she watched the baby sleep. I moved toward the blanket then, inching closer as if summoned. It was soft. Cashmere, maybe, or silk and cotton. I imagined the celebrations they must have had when Olivia had been born.

A photo hung on the wall by the crib. In it, Andrea posed on a rocking chair. Holding the infant Olivia, she beamed up at the camera. My eyes darted to the rocking chair in the corner of the room where I stood, then back to the framed photograph. The room in the photo held the same crib as this one. Also pictured was a changing table, just like the one set up against the wall that was shared with the hallway—out of sight until I'd entered the room. On it rested a baby monitor. The whole setup was identical to the room in the photo. They'd *restaged the room,* I realized. It was exactly as Olivia's room had been before her death. All at once, I felt light-headed. My poor cousin, made insane by her grief.

A low, crackling noise startled me from my reverie, and I drew in a breath, taking an involuntary step backward. The noises sounded again, something like static, and I moved my eyes to the baby monitor, for the first time noticing that it flashed green for On.

An icy hand clasped the back of my neck. I shrieked, yanking away from it so quickly, I caused myself to stumble and fall against the nursery floor. "Maeve!" Andrea's face registered concern. "I'm so sorry. I didn't mean to frighten you." She offered me a hand. I allowed her to pull me to a shaky, kneeling position, then I stood, using the wall as my support.

I took a breath, steadying myself. Unsure of my footing. "I just don't understand all this," I told her, gesturing around me. "In New York, you seemed . . . fine. You seemed like things were going well for you again. After Olivia, I mean."

"What are you talking about, Mae?"

"This," I said cautiously, gesturing at the nursery. "Is it part of your grieving process? Something to do with New-Life? Will the doll sleep in here?"

"No, silly," Andrea replied with a small smile. "This bedroom is for Henry. We figured Emily and Micah shouldn't have to pack all that stuff when we had it all right here from the move. Our movers brought over everything we had in storage. We could never quite get rid of this stuff. The crib folds out into a trundle bed."

"I'm sorry," I stammered. "I thought—"

"You thought . . . Oh, you thought I was keeping Olivia's room? Like a shrine or something?" Andrea smiled and raised an eyebrow. "Oh, Maeve." She laughed, pulling me into a hug and planting a light kiss on my temple. "You must have thought I was looney tunes."

I felt my cheeks reddening, but then I laughed too. "I'm so embarrassed," I admitted. Then we were both laughing. "I'm truly sorry," I told her. "You've been so kind, welcoming me into your home like this—into your life—"

"Listen, it hasn't been all that easy," she said, interrupting me. "But I'm doing the best I can." She paused, her expression clouding. "A lot of days I'm fine. But then there's the smallest reminder and . . . I don't know how to explain this to someone who hasn't been through it," she said. "I'll never be over it. Not really."

I moved toward her, reaching awkwardly for her hand and clasping it in mine. Andrea's eyes had begun to well.

"I'm sorry," I told her. "I was startled. I'm so, so sorry you went through it."

"It was pure hell. It's still pure hell. The kind you can only feel if you've held a baby in your arms, loved her, felt that love transform you . . . then lost it all. I carried Olivia for nine months and then cared for her for three. I've never loved anything the way I loved her. Except . . ." She paused, as if wrestling with her words. "Except for you. You're the only person who's ever come close to that kind of love, for me." She met my eyes again, hers bright, and my heart ached for her. Andrea shook her head once, blinking, then drew a breath. "You can't know—" she started, then breathed in again, long and slow, eyes raised to the ceiling. "Can I be completely honest with you?"

I nodded. We had to talk honestly, if our new relationship had any hope of succeeding.

"Every year since we've been apart, I think of the day I lost you: your birthday . . . the one you had before, I mean. And after Olivia died, the sum total of my losses became unbearable."

"But—"

"No." Andrea cut me off, her tone firm, deliberate. "Just listen. Right after her death, I was in a fog. Your birthday was a few weeks later. I still thought of you, but I was too consumed by my own sadness to try finding you again. And I was afraid. I thought, how could I bear it if I searched for you one more time and failed? At the time, I couldn't withstand the possibility of that pain.

"Several years passed and I began to feel stronger. I thought, why would I willingly go through the loss of my cousin, year after year, when there's still a chance I could have you in my life? I couldn't get Olivia back, but maybe I could be close again to someone else who shares my blood. Then you appeared, like magic, without me even having to try very hard. I hoped this trip would be a chance for us to rebuild. And just have fun together and celebrate your birthday. I still do."

"I want that too," I said, my voice small, as my eyes flickered to the framed photo on the wall.

"Then please accept me as I am, as I choose to grieve," Andrea told me, squeezing my hand hard. "I need to be honest about it. All of it. And you need to give me your trust, or this won't work. I saw how you were at your birthday party. You aren't that close to any of those people, are you?"

Her words stung. My eyes welled, more from the embarrassment of her seeing through me than from the truth of her words. I pulled my hand from hers. "No," I said, shaking my head. "Other than Elena, they're just colleagues. It's how I've always liked it. Elena's the only one I've opened up to."

"Well. Trust takes vulnerability," Andrea pointed out. "And bravery. You're a strong person, Maeve. You have the capacity to let people in."

"I want to trust you," I said, my throat tightening. "I just— for so long, after everything—" I faltered, mindful of our pact not to speak about the past. "I've been alone, for the most part. I'm not used to this."

"No one knows more than I do how scary it is to love someone when you might lose them," Andrea agreed. I burned with embarrassment again—at my self-centeredness, her magnanimity. "For what it's worth, I *love* who you are," Andrea told me. "You have nothing to prove. I've always loved you. You're family. Come on, Maeve. This is your birthday celebration! Let's have a good time."

I hesitated, then something shifted inside me and I reached for her spontaneously. She folded into my embrace. She was right. If I was going to have any kind of life, I needed to let people in. Most importantly, her.

"I wouldn't have brought you here if it didn't make me happy," Andrea said. "Same thing with NewLife. What Emily said was true . . . The company is more to me than just a cash cow. It's the way I give back."

I nodded. It made sense, wanting to take our tragic history and turn it on its head by helping to create happy families. It was, in some benign sense, a form of revenge, of taking back control. I wished I'd found a healthy way to handle our shared past.

"I have a great feeling about this weekend," Andrea continued. "Now let's go eat. I figured we'd grill salmon, throw some vegetables on . . . I pulled a great South African blend from the cellar. You'll love it." She pulled her shirt down where it had ridden up. It was then that I noticed there were small blotches on her chest, symmetrical wet ovals, as if fluid had leaked through her bra. I froze.

"Oh, don't worry about that," Andrea said, following my gaze. "A little snot and tears never stained a shirt of mine."

Snot and tears. *Mine.* Not breast milk. I nearly laughed aloud at the absurdity of what I'd thought.

You've always had a vivid imagination, Maeve.

5

The wine was red and flowed endlessly into our glasses. I drank mine like water, and every time I looked down, my glass was full again. That was okay with me. I asked Rob how the business was doing, and Micah immediately brightened. Now Micah was leaning toward me, his hands clasped, dark eyes glittering, while Emily looked on proudly.

"It's not just grief management," he was saying. "Or even family planning. It doesn't stop there. It's a lifestyle. A value system."

"I hadn't realized you were involved," I admitted. I was getting a little tired of the preachy thing he and Emily seemed to share, but I felt bad. I knew Emily and Andrea had met through work; Andrea had told me Emily was one of New-Life's very first hires. I hadn't bothered to ask Micah about his own life.

"Oh yeah. Emily got me into it," he said. "I was at a tech start-up before. God. Bunch of Silicon Valley assholes, all they care about is the bottom line. That, and doing coke." He laughed, leaning back in his chair with his arms folded over his chest. "Then I met this perfect woman right here"—he turned to Emily and chucked her under the chin playfully—"and she brought me out of the dark and into the light."

"Oh—did you know Rob, then? You were in tech out there, too, right?"

"We didn't know each other until Emily and Andrea brought us together," Rob broke in. "I'm more of a backend developer. All the things they say about techies are true. We're not the most social."

"I find that hard to believe." I meant it. Rob was charismatic and handsome. How reclusive and awkward could he really be?

"It wasn't quite so simple as us becoming friends and hooking up the men," Emily said, rewarding Micah with a smile, then turning to me. "Andrea was our life coach—Micah's and mine—before we all went into business together. She coached us when we were preparing for Henry's arrival," she explained. "Then she brought Rob on board when demand grew higher, and I officially joined the company when she expanded to events and merch. I'd been a publicist beforehand, so it was a perfect fit. Eventually Micah came over on the tech side. He heard me talking about how much I loved it and finally said . . ." Here, she paused. "Sweetie, what was it?" Emily laughed, looking fondly at Micah. It was the happiest I'd seen them all day.

"If I have to hear my wife evangelizing all day, I have two choices: convert or divorce," Micah said. Everyone at the table laughed.

"Basically, 'If you can't beat 'em, join 'em,'" Andrea clarified.

"You are way too modest," Rob told her, giving her a peck on the cheek. "NewLife is a fantastic company to work for. Perfect five stars on Glassdoor," he informed me. "And that's all due to you, babe."

"So how does it work?" I asked. "How is the company structured?"

"Rob and Micah handle tech," Andrea explained, "which includes the website and development of the AI and app. Emily and I handle the really important stuff." She winked. "Strategy, client base, that sort of thing. Emily's the face of the company, really. It wouldn't exist without her."

"Oh, please." Emily brushed off the compliment. "I'm just glad I got to go into business with someone who would become my best friend." Was she giving me a pointed look, or was I imagining it? "It makes work way more fun. And when Andrea came to us all with the idea for the dolls, well . . ." Emily settled back in her seat and dabbed a bit at her lips with a cloth napkin. "It was an opportunity we couldn't pass up. That's when NewLife became less a job and more a vocation, really. We didn't feel like we were making a choice. We felt like we were answering a calling. And seeing how it's all turned into something real with the Olivia doll is incredible. We wanted to dedicate our lives to something with more meaning, you know?"

"It's true," Micah agreed. "You spend your life working, for what? I realized when I met Andrea, after all she did for us with Henry, that I wanted to work for a cause I believed in. I wanted to give back."

I finished my glass of wine, having lost count of how many I'd had. "It's so incredible that you did all this, Andrea. Especially given our history." I realized my error the second the words spilled from my mouth. And when I looked up to see Andrea's stricken expression, I cleared my throat and hurried to change the subject. "So, uh, you all became friends after that?"

"We did," Micah said, staring at me intently. "Hey—why haven't you guys talked in twenty-five years?"

I met Andrea's eyes, uncertain. "Well, I—"

"We fell out of touch when we were kids," Andrea interrupted. "Our moms weren't close, Maeve's family moved . . . the usual. Then we found each other on one of those DNA websites! We struck it back up, and here we are." I searched her eyes, wondering about this glossed-over version of events. She gave me a wink, quick and subtle enough that no one else noticed.

"Huh." Micah examined me. "And you just hit it off, just

like that. BFFs after all these years." He reached into his pocket absently and retrieved the pocketknife I'd noticed him playing with earlier. "That's really nice, actually," he added, with a faint smile.

"Yep," I said, softened by his comment. I returned his smile. "Just like that."

An hour later, most of us were completely sloshed and Emily had moved on from one of her two favorite conversations (NewLife) to another: motherhood. I suspected Micah had hardly been exaggerating about the "convert or bust" thing.

"What else is there really? Besides motherhood?" Emily was asking rhetorically. "Like, what is the point of *anything* else?" she went on, motioning theatrically with her water glass.

Micah raised his eyebrows. "Oh, I don't know. Love for your husband?" he suggested with irony.

"Of course." She laughed, grabbing his wrist to still his hand. "If it weren't for you, we wouldn't have our perfect Henry. But no one else wants to hear about that, sweetie." She patted his leg, and he appeared mollified.

"But I mean, just look at all these people who are so driven by money or dead-end careers they forget what's really important. And miss out on all that joy," she added, addressing the entire table like she was giving a TED Talk she'd performed several times already. "Then regret it when it's too late." She shuddered. "God. What a sad life."

Andrea shot me a sympathetic look, which did not go unnoticed by Emily.

"Oh, Maeve, I didn't mean—"

"It's okay," I told her, waving a hand.

"You've got loads of time," she told me, smiling generously. "A woman from my book club got pregnant at forty-two."

I'm not waiting for anything, I wanted to say. *There's no ticking clock.* But I bit my tongue.

"I wouldn't say *loads* of time," Micah contributed. "What?" he asked, raising both hands in the air. *Don't shoot the messenger.* "It's just a fact that ninety percent of your eggs are gone by age thirty. You still look great, though," he assured me. "You won't have any trouble finding a partner. Unless you have some skeletons in your closet you haven't mentioned." He laughed like it was the most hilarious thing in the world. I tasted something sour in the back of my throat.

"Actually," I said quietly, "I don't want to have children." *Why won't this conversation end?*

There was a silence, and I wished I had waited to say something without Emily and Micah there. I understood their passion for the company—for helping people build families—but it seemed to come with a dose of judgment I was having trouble swallowing.

"Oh," Andrea said faintly.

"Look," I continued. "I realize I am saying this to exactly the wrong crowd. I know motherhood is your business," I told them. "And I have a ton of respect for that. I think the company sounds incredible, really." I gave Andrea a small smile. "I've just never thought motherhood was for me." I hoped Andrea would understand and stand up for me again, but Emily plowed on.

"I've never met a woman who regretted having kids," Emily insisted.

"I have," I replied, more sharply than I intended. "A lot of women who give babies up for adoption do. Maybe they don't regret their decision to bring a kid into the world, but some might regret needing to make that decision at all. And other women . . . women I've met who weren't sure it was worth it, giving up their careers and lives for this whole other path they chose to follow because everyone said they should, not because they truly wanted it. Those women love their kids, sure. Still, they sometimes find themselves mourning another life they can never reclaim. And what about the women who have kids because it's 'just what you do,' then realize they aren't cut out for it?"

"Well, it sort of *is* just what you do," Emily replied. "Right? It's the greatest power we've been given as women. It's what we were *made* to do."

"Like I said, skeletons," Micah broke in, shaking his head. "This is probably why you don't have a partner."

"I—"

"Whether you're religious or not," Emily barreled on, "you can't deny the science of pregnancy and childbirth is semi-miraculous and incredibly empowering. It's one thing if a woman can't physically have children. Obviously those situations are tragic. But to deny your body its natural right when you're able to have them sounds . . . confused, at best."

"Who wants dessert!" Andrea interjected, moving to clear the table. Rob, who'd been mostly quiet through all of dinner, shot her a look. It was all I could do to bite my tongue, and I did, for her sake.

"It's a choice, Emily," Andrea said sternly, as she brushed past her. "Everyone has a different path." Emily looked like she'd been slapped.

"Will you excuse me for a minute?" I said, fighting to compose myself. "I have to use the bathroom."

I pressed my palms against the table and hoisted myself to my feet, swaying a little from the wine as I made my way out of the dining room. I passed through the kitchen and found the hall bathroom, breathing a sigh of relief as I settled onto the seat and began to pee. I rested my elbows on my knees as I let out a steady stream of urine. In this new light, I could look at the situation more calmly. Micah and Emily were laying it on thick, and Micah was being a bit of an ass, but we were more than a little tipsy. And they meant well; Emily had just drunk the Kool-Aid, big-time. I washed my hands and made my way back to the dining room.

"Hey, Andrea, something's up with your toilet. Wouldn't flush."

"Rob will have to fix that," Andrea said absently. Rob nodded next to her.

"First thing tomorrow," he agreed.

The ritual of dessert seemed amplified in the silence that followed: forks clicking, the unpleasant smacking of lips, the grinding of teeth, the sickening swallows. There was something unseemly about the sounds of our enjoyment. We all scraped the last morsels of pie from our plates and leaned back in our chairs. I racked my mind for something to break the silence.

"Can we *please* have a house tour? A full one, I mean. Pretty please?" I asked.

"I've got a better idea," Emily told us, wiggling her eyebrows up and down. "Let's see the secret passageways! Andrea told me about them when she bought the place. I *love* spooky old houses." I hadn't seen this playful, giddy side of Emily. So far, it was a refreshing change.

"We guys will take a pass and get these dishes done," Rob said, standing up and beginning to clear the table. Micah followed suit, pushing back from the table and beginning to grab dishware and utensils. Then he followed Rob into the kitchen with his precarious stack.

"Secret passageways? Could we just keep to the nonsecret ones?"

"Maeve's a little claustrophobic," Andrea responded. "And they *are* pretty creepy." My heart quickened—she'd remember my childhood claustrophobia.

"I'll come see," I told them. "But I'm not going in them. Why are there secret passageways, anyway?"

"Our realtor told us this home can be traced to Freemasonry, and that members of the brotherhood liked to seal secrets within the walls," Andrea explained, as we headed for the back staircase—one of two, the one farthest from my room—and began to ascend. "I think she's full of shit about the secrets. The house apparently does have Masonic roots, though. The passages are insanely elaborate. They wrap all around the exterior of the second floor. It's one of the construction elements we aren't legally allowed to touch."

"No way." Emily wrapped her arms around her chest. "Think of the history that's in these walls."

"Huh," I said. "I knew the house seemed kind of small inside—Not *small*," I clarified, when Andrea shot me a faux insulted look. "Smaller than it looked on the outside. That must be why."

"Pauper," Emily said with a laugh. Andrea was the furthest thing from it. That's why we could laugh and make privileged jokes about it. I, however, essentially *was*, with my barely livable salary and a cool twenty thousand in credit card debt. I brushed off the thought—and the resentment that came with it—and followed them down the second-story hallway, watching Andrea run her fingers over the moldings. I had to remember that no one *deserved* anything. Feeling entitled wouldn't help my cause.

"Didn't Freemasons hate women?" I asked then, remembering some bit of history long suppressed.

"Hate? Seems extreme." Andrea shrugged. "I don't think women were allowed in the organization, though. Can you imagine?" She tilted her head back, toward the ceiling. "Well, here we are!" she shouted into the walls of the house. "I *own* you now."

"Don't make them mad," Emily said, in all seriousness. "We cannot be one hundred percent sure their ghosts aren't haunting this place."

"Just showing them who's boss. Here," Andrea said, having

apparently reached what she was looking for. She dug her fingers under the base of the wainscoting and tugged. A door popped out of the wall, sending a puff of dust in its wake.

"Holy crap," Emily said, coughing a little and waving one hand in front of her face to clear the air. "This is wild." She shined her cell phone flashlight into the passage, which looked to be wide enough to fit two people side by side. "Let's go in!" she said.

"I'm not going in," I repeated.

"Maeve. Come on! It's fun," Emily urged.

"It's cool." Andrea shrugged. "Stay here, Mae. We're just going to have a quick peek. We'll call for you if we need help slaying any ghosts."

They slipped through the doorway to the passage, cell phones held aloft to illuminate their path. I listened to their laughter as they made their way through what I assumed was a mess of cobwebs, and possibly worse. Their voices began to fade.

I typed out a quick text on my own phone to Ryan.

This place is crazy, I wrote. *Too much to type . . .*

2 more days and you can tell me in person, he replied, followed by a string of emojis: the smiley with the tongue sticking out, the peach, and the eggplant. I rolled my eyes.

I was just beginning to type a message back when I heard a shriek from within the passageway, then a silence. I pointed my phone toward the dark expanse, but it only illuminated the few feet in front of me. There was a sharp turn, tracking with the corners of the building.

"You guys?" I called into the passageway. "Everything okay?"

Another silence, then Andrea's voice.

"No," she said. "Not really. Emily fell."

"I'll get Micah," I called back.

"Jesus, Maeve, get in here and help me!" Emily yelled back. "My ankle really hurts! We don't need Micah. We need you."

"Shh," Andrea was saying, soothing her. "I think it's only a twist. You'll be fine. Maeve, hurry up and help us. We have to help her walk out of here."

I really, really didn't want to go in that passageway.

I took a tentative step into the dark.

"Hurry, Maeve," Andrea urged, her voice pinballing against the narrow walls, sounding louder than it had from the hall. "You can do it. You're stronger than you think."

I nodded, despite the fact that she couldn't see me—despite the fact that I couldn't tell how far away they were. The echo was everywhere, surrounding me, even as the walls threatened to close in. My breath was coming shorter as I took several baby steps. I forced myself forward. It was all in my head. The space was fine. It wasn't closing in; it was plenty big enough. I could breathe. I was a capable adult.

I let out a sharp yelp when my phone flashlight illuminated a thick spider the size of a silver dollar hunkered against the wall. "Ugghh," I muttered, ducking past it. *At least something can get me moving in here,* I thought. Claustrophobia was the lesser of two evils in this scenario. I stumbled again, feeling disoriented and woozy. If I didn't pull myself together, there'd be two women down.

"How far are you guys?" I said into the void. They'd gone silent.

I put a hand to my forehead. I suddenly felt drunker than I had before. The ground tilted toward the ceiling, and a tingling sensation started in my fingers and worked up my arms, like thousands of tiny, relentless daggers. When the stabbing stopped, I felt numb, confused. Worse, my vision was obscured with flashing lights, the type I get sometimes at the start of a migraine. I fought hard to stay upright. I was covered in sweat.

"We're not far." Andrea's voice sounded distant, but I could hear Emily's faint moaning. I took three more steps. Then I shone my flashlight up. And screamed.

There was a nest. A whole nest of them. Wriggling, creeping spiders that seemed to ooze from a central point above my head, as if they were being birthed right then. I stared upward, paralyzed by fear.

And then I heard the door to the hallway slam shut.

I ran. I stumbled. Fell to my knees. Heard through my fear Andrea's voice, dimly. I felt around on the ground, seeking purchase, and jerked my hand back when it touched something sticky. I felt my breath coming in short gasps. I realized suddenly that my phone wasn't anywhere; the light had gone out when I fell. I was alone in the dark, fumbling.

A sailor went to sea sea sea
To see what she could see see see.

I pressed my hands over my ears and sank down against the corridor wall.

No, no. I was imagining it. The words flowed around me, as clearly as if someone were singing it next to me. As clearly as if they were coming from my own mouth. Thuds echoed through the wall at my back, and I sank further into delirium.

But all that she could see see see

"Stop," I whispered. "Andrea, stop. It isn't funny."

Was the bottom of the deep blue sea sea sea.

The words kept coming. And the walls pulled closer, until I couldn't breathe.

Then, blackness.

6

It rained the following morning, torrents of it slashing against the living room windows and pattering atop the tin roof. It was the kind of day best spent indoors under the folds of a blanket or behind the pages of a novel, and that was exactly where I wanted to be, after my anxiety attack and subsequent embarrassment the previous night.

"I am *so* sorry," Andrea said again, when Emily left for the kitchen in search of sparkling water. I noticed she was tacitly avoiding mention of the *way* my fear had manifested—the nursery rhyme that had guided them to me. I'd imagined it was Andrea singing to me, but she'd told me later that it had been me all along. They'd found me singing and muttering, curled in a ball on the ground. "We never should have done that while tipsy. Hell, I never should have brought you up there under any circumstances. Can you forgive me, Mae?"

"It's okay." I set aside the manuscript I was reviewing and pulled the faux fur throw up to my chin, nestling deeper into the sofa cushions. "I'm so embarrassed. Your friends must think I'm a lunatic."

"Absolutely not." Andrea's tone was firm. "You crawled into a nest of spiders in some creepy old passages and lost your light source. That would have scared the bejesus out of anyone, claustrophobia or no."

"Do you think we'll be able to find my phone up there?" It was somewhere in the passages. Possibly aglow with lewd texts from Ryan, possibly home to a nest of spiders. Possibly dead.

"We'll make one of the guys do it," Andrea assured me,

cradling her new Olivia doll and taking notes in her computer. *One hour per day,* she'd explained. *Our consulting psychologist says that's all the time it takes to alleviate symptoms of grief. Kind of like what light therapy does for depression.*

"Make one of the guys do *what?*" Rob asked, entering the room, with Emily trailing behind him, slightly favoring her right foot.

"Rob," I said, grateful for the distraction. It was still a little disconcerting to watch Andrea with her therapy doll, crooning and rocking it like a real child. "Could you do me a huge favor?" Emily sank to the sofa, where she propped her ankle on a stack of pillows before reaching for her laptop.

"Depends on what it is." Rob winked at me.

"Could you go into the hidden passageway and find my phone? I dropped it last night, when . . . well. When I lost my shit." I laughed weakly, a strained sort of bray that fell flat.

"Sure," he agreed. "No problem. I'll go take a look in a minute." He approached Andrea, giving her a kiss on the forehead. "How's my little bean?" he asked her of Olivia.

"Terrific," Andrea told him. "See? Falling asleep already." It was true that the doll's lifelike eyes had begun to close. Andrea caught me staring and smiled. I smiled back at her, eager to be perceived as supportive.

"Let me hold her." Emily reached for the doll when Rob left the room, bound for the passageways. Her expression was inscrutable. "I should probably reacquaint myself with caring for an infant," she explained, as Andrea handed her the doll. "Besides, Henry could stand to get used to the idea of having a sibling around."

"How far along are you?" I asked. "And how's your ankle feeling?"

"Five months," she said. "And the ankle feels mostly fine. Thank you for asking, Maeve."

"You're *five months?*" I'd had no idea. She'd favored oversize shirts and sweaters the few times I'd seen her, but she had a small frame and I'd assumed it was a style choice. She was hardly visible at all.

Emily laughed. "I'm only showing a little," she confirmed, tightening her pullover against her torso to demonstrate.

"It's coming so soon," I remarked. I'd pegged Emily for the type to gush endlessly about a new baby—her due date, its sex, everything she'd bought for the nursery.

The timer on Andrea's phone dinged. "The hour's up," she told us. "We can put Olivia away now."

"Why don't I take her upstairs?" Emily asked. "I'm going to lie down for a nap anyway, I think."

"Really?" Andrea looked surprised. "That's not like you. Are you feeling okay?"

"Fine," Emily snapped. Then she looked contrite. "Sorry. I'm . . . still shaken up from my fall, I guess. What if I'd fallen harder and the baby had been hurt? Or I'd had to take time off work?"

"Well, thank god it was a twisted ankle," Andrea said. "No use catastrophizing."

"I know." Emily worried her bottom lip with her teeth, biting off her deep red lipstick. "So, can I have Olivia?" She reached for the doll.

"Sure. And later today, why don't we special order you one of your own? Then we can test both ends of the spectrum, expecting and—" Here, Andrea grimaced slightly. "Recovering."

Emily limped awkwardly to the door, cradling the doll in her arms.

"How long have you known she was pregnant?" I asked my cousin, after Emily had gone.

"Since she was a few weeks along," Andrea replied. "The fact that she's talking about it openly now is a good thing. She's been anxious about the pregnancy, and the first few months were rough. She's the face of NewLife, you know. Incredibly capable. Leads all our retreats and workshops and puts a lot of pressure on herself to be perfect and run the show. With Henry, she enjoyed being pregnant and embraced every aspect of it—the nursery decorating, that sort of thing. It was frankly hard to keep up with her. It's been different this go-around. She's usually such a ball of energy, never fazed by a challenge. I don't know. She doesn't seem quite herself."

"Did she not want another child?" I asked carefully.

"Oh, of course she did," Andrea said, surprised by the question. Mistaking my silence for skepticism, she continued, "You heard her talking last night. She sees motherhood as a vocation. Probably even more than I do."

Just then, Rob walked in, wielding my phone triumphantly, with Micah trailing him. "Got it," Rob said, handing it to me. "You can thank me later."

"Oh. Amazing," I told him. "Thanks so much." I clicked the power button, but my phone was dead.

"You should try one of those sweet external battery cases like I have," Micah suggested. "My smart case holds charge for like a day and a half, I swear."

"Well, it's not often I plan on losing my phone in a hidden corridor, so I think I'm set. I'm going to charge up and enjoy my reunion with my device for a few."

"A few" turned into a few *hours* of catching up with Ryan—who had sent no fewer than seven texts while my phone was lost—and continuing my edit in the bedroom. There was always work to be done on the weekends. Meetings and calls and emails consumed the weekdays, and so reading and editing were relegated to stolen hours. Sometimes it felt like a perverse luxury to spread out into the empty space of a weekend like that—at the very least, it provided me with purpose. And just now, in an unfamiliar setting, my familiar routine served as a buffer against the most socializing I'd done in years.

Around six, we left for dinner at the local pizza spot. "Henry loves pizza," Andrea explained, once we were all settled around a broad, round table toward the center of the room. "But we have to be home before his bedtime." Henry was the focal point of dinner for Emily and Andrea.

"Sweetheart, cut his slice for him," Emily commanded Micah several times, before finally doing it herself. Andrea was watchful, drawing my own eyes to Emily's hands, which visibly trembled against the cutlery. For his part, Rob helped mop Henry's spill when he tipped over his chocolate milk.

"Party foul," he said. "No worries, kid." He dabbed sauce off Henry's cheeks and held him while Emily focused on her own food. Rob would have made a good, dedicated father to Olivia. I hoped they would have another baby someday. It was clear how much joy it would bring them.

"Maeve, stay put," Andrea said, when we returned to the house. "Keep an eye on Henry for a minute, will you? We have a surprise for you." She and Emily disappeared into the kitchen, trailed by Micah and Rob. I sank into a sofa in the small sitting area just off the foyer. Henry toddled over with his Hot Wheels cars and began making *vroom, vroom* noises. He handed me one of the toys.

"Want to play crash?" he said hopefully, then continued to make car noises, vibrating his lips so forcefully that flecks of spittle landed on my hands.

"Crash?" My hands went cold.

Henry nodded, then powered his car into the one he'd handed me, hitting my fingers with so much force it stung, and I dropped my car with a shriek.

"God damn it," I shouted. "Why would you do that, Henry?" I wrung my right hand against my left, pressing out the sting. It hadn't hurt so much as shocked me, but I was still trembling.

Henry stared, his eyes wide. Then they crinkled in the corners and his lips pulled down. I took a breath. I was the adult. He was just a child. He hadn't meant anything by it.

Crash. Twisted metal. Broken glass. Blood all around me.

"It's okay," I told him, offering a ginger pat on the shoulder. "Please don't cry. I was just a little startled." I'd made efforts to keep my distance from Henry, and it was as if my reticence had compelled him to try harder. He'd twice climbed into my lap at dinner, making Emily raise her eyebrows and grin, as if to insinuate that my inherent maternal prowess had tempted him over. But I'd toggled between the desire to wrap my arms around him and the overwhelming urge to scoot him off me as soon as possible. And the thought of being left alone with his tears caused a sharp ripple of panic to work its way from my gut to my chest. Luckily his shifting mood didn't evolve into a full-blown tantrum, because a second later, Emily, Micah, Rob, and Andrea burst into the room, carrying an enormous chocolate cake ablaze with candles.

"Happy birthday to you . . ." Rob started, and the others joined in, Emily filming it with her iPhone.

My throat tightened, and I blinked furiously against the surge of emotion. Andrea placed the cake on the coffee table in front of me. "Happy 33, Maeve!" read the white frosted scrawl.

"Make a wish!" Emily exclaimed, beaming. For all her tiredness earlier, now Emily was hyperalert, almost manic. Maybe this was the "usual" Emily, the one no one could keep up with. I hovered over the flames, which danced vigorously, casting shadows across the tiny, dimly lit room. I drew in a deep breath and made my wish—the same wish I'd been making most of my life, for the only thing I'd ever really wanted but had never seemed able to create: a place to belong, and people to belong to.

I exhaled hard. Not a single flame of thirty-three remained.

* * *

Later that night, when everyone else had gone to bed, Andrea and I sat wide awake on the living room floor, talking. "Floor party!" she cheered, pouring us generous glasses of wine— sparkling, in honor of my birthday. "Doesn't something about a picnic on the floor make you feel like we're kids again?"

I nodded, and impulsively curled up onto my side on the rug, Prosecco abandoned. I rested my head in her lap, the way I'd done when we were little, and she absently ran her finger-tips through my hair. I felt drunk on the intimacy of it, and be-hind my overwhelming sense of happiness lay a tiny, niggling worry that I wouldn't get to experience it again, or at least not soon enough. I wanted this time with my cousin to be my daily reality, not merely an escape from my bleak, everyday life.

"What are you thinking about?" Andrea asked, giving my scalp a light scratch. She leaned against the base of the sofa and lifted my head in her palms just briefly, in order to un-cross her legs.

"Just that tomorrow came way too soon," I told her. "I'm not ready to head back to the city yet."

"I hope that means you had a good time," Andrea said. "I'm rooting for us, you know. It isn't every day you get a second chance."

I sat back up, curling my legs underneath me. "I had an amazing time," I confessed. "And I feel the exact same way. It's fate. It's honestly hard to believe we were ever apart." I swallowed, feeling myself getting emotional. "Really, Andrea. This is the best birthday I've ever had. The cake was such a sweet gesture."

"Well, but with the weather . . . you were probably a little bored." She picked at her fingernails, sneaking glances at me. She looked vulnerable—it was the first time since we'd reconnected that I'd seen her looking truly defenseless.

"I wasn't," I insisted. "I was so happy just being here. Catching up with you." My cheeks flamed. I wasn't used to speaking so candidly about how I was feeling. "And enjoying your gorgeous house," I added, redirecting. "I am *not* eager to sleep in my studio tomorrow night."

"You need more than a studio at your age," Andrea mentioned, looking concerned. "No offense. Your job must pay you pennies for the amount of work you do. I'm sorry. That probably sounds so rude. I only want you to be comfortable."

"Believe me. I know it." I shrugged. "I enjoy my work. It's interesting and challenging. But I *am* tired of barely scraping by," I admitted.

"What if I told you I could possibly fix that?" Andrea asked.

I laughed outright. "How? You're going to have a word with my supervisor? Offer me a job at a rival publishing house?" Her expression was serious. "Oh god. Andrea, are you offering me a job at NewLife? That's incredibly generous, but—"

"No, no." She waved her hand dismissively. "Not NewLife. It's just . . . I didn't tell you everything about Olivia's death."

I nodded, unsure of what she was getting at, or what it had to do with me.

"Well . . ." Andrea paused, then gnawed again at her bottom lip. "It's really hard for me to talk about, but it's important that I share this with you."

I reached for her hand. "What is it? Tell me."

"I can't have another baby," Andrea explained, choking up a little. "The chances of what happened with Olivia happening again are too high. The doctors told me I can't try again without risking my own life. It's ironic, isn't it? I've built my career around motherhood, and I can't be a mother." She paused here, blotting her eyes with a tissue.

"Oh, Andrea," I said, drawing her close. "I wish there were something I could do."

"Well, actually," she said carefully, "there is." There was a long silence, and I had the sense that there was something crucial I hadn't yet grasped.

"I know you don't want to have a baby of your own, Mae, and I respect that," Andrea went on. "But what if you gave one of your eggs to us? To me and Rob?"

I was stunned. I opened my mouth to interject, but she plowed over me.

"It would help us tremendously, and it would allow us to have a baby with our DNA, and you and I look so much alike. It's kind of perfect. The way you just appeared in my life out of nowhere—*poof*—made me think there was a reason for it. We would pay you handsomely. Think about it: I get to have a child and you get financial security. I'm not asking you to be a surrogate," she clarified. "We could hire someone else to be the surrogate."

The weight of what she was asking had begun to sink in. I pulled back, scooting a few inches away from her without thinking about it. When I didn't respond immediately, she rushed to continue. "You could live your life however you want. Take the money and quit your job, keep working . . . anything."

"Andrea." My voice was flat, flatter than I'd intended. What she was asking wasn't possible. I knew it in my heart, but it still broke me to disappoint her. "I can't do that. I'm so sorry."

She recoiled as if she'd been slapped. "You didn't even let me finish. We'd pay you half a million dollars for one extraction," she said, as if I hadn't given her my answer. "You could have your own apartment, a nice one, no more crashing in studios or in some bartender's bed." I winced at this, as a wave of nausea rolled through me.

"Andrea, I wish I could," I told her. I did, so fervently. "But I just can't put myself through that."

"Please, Maeve," she whispered, her eyes welling. "It could be so easy. For all of us. All of our problems solved."

"Can't you get another donor?" I asked desperately, already knowing her answer.

Andrea's eyes brimmed. "We want our child to look like Olivia," she told me. "Like us. Our blood."

I hesitated. I wanted to say yes. More than anything, I wanted to please my cousin. But I couldn't reproduce, not even by extension, not even for her.

"I'm sorry," I told her again. I couldn't look at her. "I've known my entire life I don't want to bring children into the world. Egg retrieval is no small thing; it's hard. I know someone at work who froze hers. And even with you as the mother, it would be too hard for me to be around it. To watch you raise it. Besides," I pointed out, "I may well have whatever you have, that caused Olivia's death."

"It isn't genetic," Andrea said coldly. "I already told you that. Don't you think you owe me?" she pleaded. "Even a little?"

"What?" I straightened. I always knew she blamed me for that night—for leaving her. How could she not? This was merely the first time she'd said it.

"Because of you, I never had a family. I was in foster care for years. Bad foster care, sometimes. One man beat me." Andrea's laugh was choked with tears. "All I want is your eggs. Even one, for god's sake. Whatever one retrieval can yield. It's so simple, Maeve. You aren't even using yours; it doesn't matter to you. You aren't—"

"Andrea," I interrupted, my voice gentle, yet firm as I could manage. "I am so, so sorry. I would give you anything else you asked me for. I swear. Not this." Anything at all except this.

"What if you didn't have to see the child?" Andrea's voice was desperate. "You can give me your eggs and I'll pay you and disappear. I would pay a million dollars, Mae. All your problems would be solved. You just give us whatever you get from one round, we vanish from your life. Done. You'd never have to see us again."

"Done?" I whispered. "That's it? You take my eggs and our relationship is over?"

"Of course I don't want it that way," she protested. "What I want is that we raise the baby together." She was crying now, tears streaming down her face. "But if that's not what you want, we can make it easier for you, make sure you don't have to be around the child. That's all I mean. I mean we'd do what makes you comfortable."

"I can't believe you have a million dollars to give away," I said, more to myself than to her. I stared into the distance for a moment. Pressure was building in my chest, and my own eyes were wet. I could hardly see straight. "What I'm hearing is that my fertility is transactional to you," I told her, choking out the words.

I stood, my resolve returned. I'd spent my adulthood working through my past, setting boundaries, establishing normalcy. What Andrea was suggesting would damage me. I knew it with gut-level certainty, the kind that can't be explained. Andrea knew enough about me to understand why this would be my choice. Having to justify it was deeply painful. And the realization that she could cast me aside so easily in exchange made my stomach turn.

"You've always been selfish," she said, staring up at me with cold eyes. "But refusing outright? Not even taking the time to consider the offer? This is beyond."

"You just admitted you're willing to discard me as long as

you get what you want," I hissed back, fury coating my words. "I said no. Please respect that. There are some things you can't throw money at."

I stood and left the room. I went straight to bed, my hands shaking as I turned the lock to my door with definitive purpose. How quickly our evening had morphed from something magical into something sickly and laden with old tensions. I hadn't even known we had so much animosity simmering between us. It had been laid bare, and there was no going back. I resolved to get up early and take an Uber to the bus station, where I would board the first bus back to the city.

It took hours to fall asleep. I felt sick, feverish with the intensity of the fight. I had had everything, briefly, and then I'd lost it. Maybe she was right. Maybe I *was* selfish. But this was one thing I couldn't bend on, not ever.

As I slowly drifted off, I realized it had been more than two decades since my heart had last been broken, on another fateful birthday. Until now, I hadn't thought there was anything left to break.

7

Happy birthday to you . . ." Mother with the long blond hair and upturned nose, the one who looks like us, places a cake in front of me. She is beaming. She kisses me on the forehead. Andrea claps, but I can see Mother with the lazy eye frown. She discourages displays of affection. She thinks it promotes favoritism. Andrea is the oldest, but the Mothers want us to think they love all six of us daughters the same, even if it's not true.

Boy nuzzles my leg. He wraps his arms around my calf and presses his cheek to my knee. He's tiny still, newly walking. I wrap my ankle around the wooden leg of the chair in which I sit, nudging it away from him. It wouldn't do for him to be seen loving me, for me to be seen letting him. He isn't even supposed to be here. Boy was supposed to be a girl. I can't help but love him anyway, or something that feels like love. An urgent compulsion to protect him, no matter how much I ought not to care.

"Eight," Andrea says in a whisper, her face flushed with happiness. "My little cousin, growing up."

I bend to blow out my candles, making the wish of a traitor. My wish about Boy flashes through my mind before I can stop myself, and once it's done, it's done. There is nothing I can do to take it back. I seize up, wait for something to go wrong. For Mother Superior to lash out. For my heart to stop beating. None of it happens. Andrea laughs, then kisses my cheek. Soon, she tells me, she will let me know all the secrets she's begun to learn about becoming a woman. And then—when I am a woman too, and there are no more secrets between us—we will be best friends again.

Andrea has known what it is to be a woman for nearly two months now. When she turns thirteen in a couple more years, she will receive the ritual and become a Mother. It is the greatest privilege, the only way to know love, says Mother with the red hair. It is the fundamental reason for life.

Andrea doesn't know she isn't the only one with secrets.

I have a secret too. A secret about the locked room. A secret so horrible I half wonder if I dreamed it.

The cousins huddle around me, eager for a slice. Boy watches as Susie, Beth, Frances, and Gloria eat cake, crumbling it in their fists and shoving it into their tiny mouths with abandon. He looks at the ground, eager for a crumb to fall. When no one is looking, I slip him a wedge. Just a few bites. He gobbles it down gratefully, his face rapturous with pleasure. Sweet Boy.

He reaches his sticky fists up for more. Everyone else is distracted now, Boy forgotten. Mother with the red hair is scraping dishes at the sink and the cousins are playing a game in the corner. Andrea is busily gathering my gifts: a knitted sweater, pristine other than a pulled thread at the cuff; a pair of shoes a size too big, lightly scuffed on the soles.

"Shh." I place my finger against my lips, willing Boy to be quiet. But he's fallen under the spell of the sugar. He throws himself to the floor, squirming, writhing and red-faced, the way he was when he came out of Mother's womb.

"Boy!" I try to quiet him. I give him my finger to suck on, but he swats it away. He lets out a bellow, as though he's been holding it in all his life. The activity in the kitchen stops. Mother carefully places a dish towel on the counter, then straightens, turning slowly to the source of the shrieking. Mother pushes her chair from the table and stands, her eye rolling wildly. Mother comes in from the next room, her mouth set in a hard line. Mother looks worried, twining her blond hair in both fists. She nibbles her bottom lip and avoids my eyes.

Mother moves to stand next to Boy, peering over him while he's thrashing on the floor.

Mother stands over Boy.

Mother stands over Boy.

Mother surrounds him.

It is then that I spot the telltale streak of blue frosting—smeared by his tears—that's been transferred from his fists to his cheeks. My heart stops beating. I know what happens when boys disobey. Mother says boys will never become important or powerful. But they have other purposes when they grow older. They make themselves useful in small ways, despite their inadequacies. Despite Boy's limitations, I feel tender toward him in a way I know I should not.

Boy sees Mother surrounding him. He reaches his chubby baby arms out, hopeful. His sobs begin to quiet. He hiccups and keens for their love.

Mother stares down at him.

Mother's neck jolts up as if on a marionette string. She looks at me.

Mother's eyelids flutter as they do when she is very angry. She places one palm atop the knife we used to cut the cake.

Mother is vacant, looking beyond it all, as if to ignore what comes next.

Before I can think, I act. I reach down for Boy. I lift him, cradling him to me. I right myself, gathering his energy into me, until it propels us both from the house, through the yard, weeds twisting at my ankles and rocks nipping the soles of my feet. Andrea's cries follow me all the way down the hill. My cousin's feet pound the ground behind me, but I'm flying with more than just my own energy. Something bigger, more powerful, is carrying me. I wonder if it is the same thing that might strike me down.

O n Monday, Elena called me into her office. I had a serious emotional hangover from the weekend. Dark circles graced the skin beneath my eyes, and I was exhausted
from turning my fight with Andrea over in my head for hours
on end. It was a relief to be at work, where there was some
semblance of routine. Where I could forget the void that had
opened in my heart.

I grabbed a pen and my favorite notebook, a pink-and-gold
number with the phrase "Choose Your Own Adventure" foil-
stamped on its cover. I kept it as a reminder that I'd very much
chosen my own adventure in terms of my career, never bowing out of my competitive and low-paying field even when
things got tough. I was proud of how far I'd come.

"What's up?" I asked, closing her office door behind me.
"God, I had a rough weekend." I settled into the chair across
from her desk and ran a hand through my hair. "I went upstate to see my cousin—you know, the one you met at my
birthday drinks. You wouldn't believe the conversation we
had." Normally she'd have piped in right away to ask me what
happened, her eyes alight with curiosity, but today Elena was
uncharacteristically silent. I examined her closely; her shoulders were tensed and her own eyes were red-rimmed.

"Oh god. I'm sorry. I've been babbling about me. Is everything okay? Elena. What is it?"

"Maeve," Elena said carefully, "there's no easy way to say
this." Her voice faltered. "You're being let go."

"What?" My mind went blessedly blank. "Is this a joke? I
don't understand."

Elena took a long breath, then looked me in the eye. Her own were glistening. "I want you to know this wasn't my choice. I fought for you. But Edward . . ." She trailed off. Edward, our editor in chief, and I had had a strained relationship ever since I'd turned down his advances two years prior, at an after-party for a prestigious literary award. Elena, of course, knew none of this. No one did.

"What did Edward say?" I snapped.

"Quokka isn't bringing in enough revenue, compared to the other imprints. We need to make staffing cuts in order to justify the kinds of big-ticket celebrity investments we envision for it. Those six-figure commercial acquisitions are what set Quokka apart from the other imprints here, you know that."

I sucked in a breath. "So you're keeping Quokka? I brought more to it than any other editor in terms of sales last year. I was the first editor hired to launch it. How can he cut me like this?"

"He feels we're too top-heavy," Elena explained. She looked down at her hands, which were folded on her desk. "Obviously I wasn't planning for this, or I wouldn't have gotten you . . ." She trailed off.

"The business card holder," I finished bitterly. "I guess I won't be needing that now. Who's staying?"

"Mallory, Anthony, and Faye," she said.

I went cold. "Mallory is at my same level," I pointed out, fighting to keep my voice even. "And she didn't achieve a fraction of what I did these past three years. She spends her days curating Pinterest boards." Then I paused, taking it all in. "I'm the only one leaving," I said as I realized the truth.

"It isn't fair," Elena agreed. "Believe me, I fought for you. I value you so much. You know that. You're not just an employee to me; you're my friend. But he needed to get rid of one top-level editor. And he thinks Mallory's recent acquisition—

that TikTok star, whatever his name is . . ." She waved it off. "He thinks that program has legs."

"Can't I take a reduction in salary instead?" I knew the answer without having to hear it. And there was no way I could have lived on a reduced salary anyway.

"No." Elena shook her head. "There are legal reasons we can't do that. HR will walk you through it all."

I felt my phone buzzing in my pocket. Likely Ryan with some sexy and inappropriate plan involving my various anatomy later that evening. I silenced it without looking, and refocused. The mention of HR seemed so impersonal. I was reeling; my fingers were trembling in my lap. It was all I could do to not cry.

"He's going to make her editorial director." I choked out the words. I knew it, suddenly, with the same certainty I knew the real reason he'd let me go, which wasn't smart of him, not really—I could always reveal what he'd done at that party. But he knew I wouldn't, if I ever wanted another job in the industry. Besides, what he'd done was gray, murky. He hadn't crossed the line in any way I could explicitly define. Without me around, he could forget about it altogether *and* he had the budget to promote Mallory. Was he trying to groom her? Gain her loyalty and dependence so he could do to her what he'd done to me?

"You could have fought harder for me," I said to Elena.

"Please don't make this more difficult." Her voice was strangled. "You can take the day to pack your things and transfer any documents you may still need," she went on. "And we're offering three months' severance." I nodded, numb. Three months' severance was generous, by publishing standards. And technically it was kind of her to let me access my computer at all after a layoff. They were letting me go gently, but the pay wasn't going to get me far. I felt panic bubbling deep within me. I had no savings and a steep hill, if not a mountain, of credit card debt. When my severance ran out, I'd be ruined. I didn't have any options.

"Believe me, I will recommend you to every publisher I know," Elena continued. "You'd be an asset to any team, Maeve. Edward is making an egregious mistake. I told him as much. And if I ever leave here, which I very well might, if things keep heading in this direction, I'll hire you in an instant. Not that you'll need it. You'll be snatched up immediately. I'm sure of it. You *will* come out on top."

She went silent. It was clear I was supposed to excuse myself. To do anything other than sit there, frozen. I couldn't muster the willpower. She reached across the broad wooden desk and clasped both of my hands in hers. "I'd like to remain friends," she said.

Was this what friendship was? Maybe I'd never known friendship. Suddenly I felt lonely there with her, lonelier than I ever had alone.

"Bye, Elena," I said, rising to my feet. "Thank you for everything."

When I returned to my desk, I fumbled in my bag and retrieved my bottle of Klonopin, glancing around to make sure no one was paying attention. I popped one milligram dry to quiet my jangling nerves, then pulled out my phone and saw that Andrea—not Ryan—was the source of the buzzing. She'd sent three messages. My pulse quickened. It was as if she was a drug I'd been craving.

I clicked on her name with a trembling finger.

Mae, I'm sorry, read the first message. The apology was followed by a long paragraph explaining how terrible she felt and how much I meant to her. *Our relationship is my top priority. I would do anything to preserve it,* she finished. The following two texts simply read *Can we talk?* and *?*.

My heart lifted. It was strange to feel so devastated and so elated at the same time. All I wanted, in that moment, was to call my cousin and tell her everything. My gratitude over having her to call in a moment like this stole my breath. *That* was how she'd changed me. She'd given me something that, if taken away, would leave me emptier than I'd been before she'd swooped into my life.

*　*　*

It was 1:30 a.m. that same day—the next morning, technically—and Ryan was reclining against my headboard, spreading his legs wide like he owned the place, letting his body occupy the bulk of my bed as he casually rolled a spliff.

"So, what, they fired you for no reason?" he asked, leaning over to kiss me on my temple as though he knew his words might sting and he wanted to soften the blow.

"I don't know, Ry," I told him. I didn't feel like explaining it to him—how, after million-dollar net gains yearly and three *New York Times* bestsellers in the last season alone, I could be so unceremoniously fired.

I was curled to the right of him, occupying a comparatively small amount of space despite it being my bed, my room, my rules. I leaned into him, biting his shoulder lightly, and he reached over to pull me close, giving my hair a gentle tug, which made me self-conscious, even though he knew all about my extensions.

"Andrea is sending a car for me on Friday," I told him. I'd talked to Ryan from behind my closed office door right after my firing, then taken a minute to reply to Andrea's texts. She'd then called to explain herself. I wound up apologizing, too, before telling her about my firing. She'd immediately begun planning, offering me the world.

"She said I can stay with them upstate," I explained. "Save on rent, make my severance last longer. But honestly, I'm a little afraid of being up there semipermanently, after what happened last weekend. I hope Andrea doesn't push the issue.

I want to rebuild slowly. I definitely want to go up there this weekend—the quicker we can get past this fight and back to normal, the better . . ." I trailed off. I'd been rambling. "You think I should do it. Give her my eggs."

"I mean, it's a million dollars, Maeve. I'd give my left nut for that kind of money."

"I'm sure." Ryan knew nothing of my past. He couldn't understand the significance. "It isn't something I feel comfortable doing. I know you think it's crazy, but I'm not changing my mind on this one. The money isn't worth it to me."

Ryan looked doubtful. He nodded anyway, accepting my position. "So get back out there, make nice with your cousin for the weekend, have a good time, clear your head, then come back to the city," he said, drawing me in to his chest. "Can you freelance for a while?"

"I probably can. Maybe even through Elena. So you've been paying attention after all," I teased.

He took a long drag of the weed, giving me ferocious side-eye. "You think just because you're slumming it with me, I'm not a gentleman?" he asked. I laughed. Ryan was the only one who possibly could have made me laugh like that after being fired. He grew up in a rough part of L.A. and always teased me for slumming it, and I always said *How can I slum it with a sommelier?*, and we went back and forth like that even though neither of us was concerned with pedigree. Then he leaned over to tickle me, making me laugh even harder.

"Oh god," I said. "Seriously. Stop." I didn't mean it; I was enjoying the relief this moment of lightness provided.

I knew I'd sleep two or three hours, as I usually did on the nights Ryan swung by. It mattered less, now that I didn't have a job to preserve, though I did have a doctor's appointment the next day. I knew I'd wake up late, as I always did, pull on a "future dress," as Ryan called them—half of my wardrobe had no adornments or zippers—slip my feet into a pair of black heels, carefully conceal the shadows under my eyes, and kiss Ryan good-bye. I was never sure what he did in my bed once I was gone. I didn't particularly want to ask.

I had met Ryan in the most unflattering of circumstances. He was bartending and I was at his bar, blind drunk. I'd been eyeing him for weeks, and that time I'd decided to tell him I wanted to fuck him. Or so the story went, according to Ryan. All I knew was, it was that easy. He walked me home—which was when, according to him, I threw myself at him—and I woke up the next morning, fully clothed, on top of my bed, with a text from a strange number saying *I'll call you,* and he did.

By the night of my firing, Ryan and I had been fucking for nearly a year. *Fucking*—such a boring word. But what we were doing was fundamentally boring. And sweet, despite its gently sadomasochistic undertones. Ryan liked to call me "Fifty Shades of Maeve." He thought it was hilarious as well as complimentary, which said something about the ways Ryan and I differed and the ways we were the same.

The truth of it was, Ryan made me feel sexier and more adored than I'd felt in years. And I needed it. I felt adored when he fucked me from behind, clutching my extensions in a fist and tugging my head backwards. I felt sexy when he flipped me over and placed a hand on my collarbone, near enough to my throat to excite me but far enough to offer me ease. Everything was like that with him: just near enough, but not too close. Which was why, when Ryan ground out his spliff in the jewelry dish on my nightstand, I let him, knowing what would come next. Ryan had an appetite for things and people. I happened to be one of those people, for now.

I was lying on my back, relatively disinterested, which excited him more. He bent over me, hovering his naked torso inches from my frame. He ran a finger lightly down my sternum, making trails over my loose-fitting cotton tank top, then lower. I felt my body responding, but I held myself motionless. Ryan liked this game. He liked to see how long it would take to excite me, and I in turn liked the way every response I gave, however minor, made him harden. Sometimes my tells were practiced, sometimes involuntary.

He pressed his hand between my thighs. It was a gentle pressure, and I moved my hips against him, allowing my mouth to part. I was sore from the first time. Sore, raw, and turned on by the weight of his hand in the place that was most sensitive.

I shifted backward, my breath quickening. Every nerve in my body was on fire. The aching pain of want was indistinguishable from the pain of his palm against me. He slipped a finger beneath the elastic lining of my underwear and teased my outer edges until I lifted toward him. He knew what I liked. When his finger entered me, I felt my eyes roll back in my head and I succumbed to all the terrible soreness from before—the type of discomfort that would convert to pleasure, reminding me of the first time I had sex.

I had been disinterested, and now I was not. Now I was single-minded. He did this to me. I closed my eyes. I saw it there: the mayhem. I wanted to be battered, twisted, bloodied like the thing in my head.

I jerked away, my heart thudding.

He smiled. "You okay?"

"Mm-hmm." My breathing was shallow.

He put a finger against my lip and came away with blood. He stared at it, rapt. "You bit yourself."

"Oh." I licked my lip. The chalky taste of metal met my tongue.

"God. You're never boring, are you?" He put his finger in his mouth and sucked it longer than he needed to for it to come out clean. I closed my eyes again and met rivers of blood in my brain. I felt like I might retch.

Remain steady. Remain in the present.

He was hovering just inches above me, close enough to tease me. "You like that?" he wanted to know. He put his mouth so close to mine, I could suck his breath into me, until I got no oxygen at all but was filled only with his expulsions. I played along, arching my back and flicking my tongue toward his mouth. He pulled away, teasing. Then he crushed his mouth to mine, allowing our tongues to intertwine, until I wrapped my arms around his shoulders and drew him to me, willing away the millimeters of distance that lingered between us. I tasted blood again, and when he raised his head, his lips were smeared with it.

I shut my eyes tight, gritting my teeth against the pictures in my head.

"Fuck me," I told him. "Hard." I needed him to make me see stars instead of blood and twisted limbs. To leave me wrecked liked I wanted. It was all I wanted.

He climbed on top of me, but I knew it wouldn't be enough. I put one palm against his chest and pushed him, hard, onto his back.

"Whoa," he said, grinning.

"Shut up," I told him.

"God, you're sexy."

"Shut up."

He was on his back, splayed out over the bed and looking at me in wonderment, like he'd never seen such a vision.

Neither had I. My own vision reared its ugly head at me, threatening to consume me from the inside out.

I clamped a hand over his mouth. I lowered my body onto his, allowing him to pulse against me. Then I pressed myself down. Hard. Hard enough to push everything out of my head.

He grunted. "Baby," he said, gasping as I moved. I tightened my hand over his mouth. I didn't want to hear it. I squeezed my eyes shut and rocked my hips on top of him until he couldn't talk—he could only gasp with pleasure—and I could finally remove my hand, because finally he was rendered helpless. His hands were around my hips, aiding my exertions, so each time I came down on him was harder and more powerful than the last.

"Fuck," he groaned once.

For a fleeting moment, I wished I could shut him up, really shut him up, see his hands rattling against the bars of the cell I made for him in my head, see him plead with me to let him out.

"Baby, please," he said.

"Please, what?" I asked, moving more slowly.

"Use me," he said. "Use me however you want."

"You mean that?" I lifted my body halfway, hovering above him until he answered. I was slick with sweat.

"Yes," he said.

His face flashed behind my closed eyes, pressed against the steel bars of a cage. I raked my nails over his skin, and in my head I left him bleeding. The visions were hideous and distorted, just as they were every time. I moved until all I saw was the flashing light of my own mounting release.

"Harder." I gasped, feeling my pleasure approach. But I was the one going harder, taking from him what I wanted, pulling the life out of him with each exertion of my own.

When I came, the visions stilled. The space behind my eyes was blank. The only thing I was aware of was my shuddering body. Every clench of pleasure pushed the ugliness away until I was empty.

I collapsed on top of him.

"Jesus," he said. "That was incredible. You were a woman possessed."

The room began to return to me. I pulled my body from his and rolled onto my side, resting a hand over my throbbing pelvis. "I've got to go clean up."

"Let me throw this away really fast." He pulled off the condom and tied it in a knot.

"I didn't know you came," I told him.

He laughed. "I didn't know you cared."

"I don't."

Then I looked at him, and his expression was so stunned that I had to laugh too.

"I'm kidding," I said, hoping he believed I wasn't broken. That I hadn't wanted to break him too. "Of course I care. Here, I'll throw that away for you."

I knew that even in our private universe, there were boundaries. There was a normal, and if I didn't play within the bounds of normal, he would leave. There were so many things I wanted from him, so many things I wanted him to do to me, to wipe out the intrusive thoughts. The things I wanted were abnormal—dangerous. I knew that much. These were the things I didn't dare say aloud.

I went to the bathroom and rested my head in my hands as I peed. When I wiped, there was a spot of blood on the toilet paper. It would hurt later. I was glad. I wiped myself clean with soap and stared at my face in the mirror. My eyes were bright under the tangle of my hair. My makeup had been rubbed off and my face was raw from his beard. Somewhere in another universe I was someone sweet and unencumbered and open to love, open to the things Ryan wanted to give me. But in this universe, I didn't want sweet.

A shadow in my periphery jolted me out of my head. I turned and realized I'd left the window cracked several inches, enough for someone to see way too much of my naked body. I yanked my towel off its hook and wrapped it around me, backing all the way up against the door opposite the window. My arms were covered in gooseflesh. Someone had been watching me, I was sure of it. They could still be out there. Watching. Waiting. I counted to three, then forced myself to step out from under the cover of the bathroom door in order to slide the window shut.

A knock sounded on the door, and I screamed.

"Maeve?"

"Oh god, I'm so sorry." I opened the door to Ryan, whose eyes were narrowed with concern. "I thought I saw something outside," I told him.

"I heard you whimpering . . ."

"I was whimpering?"

"Come here." Ryan drew me in to his chest, wrapping his arms around me until my chills subsided. "Are you okay? Do you want me to check outside?"

"No, no. It was probably just a raccoon or something." I tried hard to buy into my own explanation.

When we climbed back in bed, I was still prickling from fear. He pulled me toward him for a kiss. "Just a sec," I told him, dodging it. I wriggled away and pretended to look at my phone. "Busy day tomorrow," I said over my shoulder. The truth was, his tenderness made me uncomfortable. The times I was happiest with Ryan were when he was so deep inside me, I thought I'd split open from the physical agony.

When I rolled back over, Ryan was relighting his spliff, and I began to relax. This was the part I loved the best. When we hung out, smoking and watching something dumb and funny like *Bob's Burgers* or just chatting or playing silly made-up word games or fake-reading tarot. When my mind was still blank and my body was jelly. This was my favorite part—the not-fucking. The fucking itself, it was a means to an end.

He extended the joint toward me and I accepted. The best thing about Ryan was that I knew I'd never fall in love with him. But I liked him, and that was enough. And he didn't think I was a freak. Or he did and he enjoyed it.

"Yo," he said then, sounding uncharacteristically nervous. "I was serious before, Maeve. Why not just freelance? And, I don't know, rent this place out for a month or two online? You could stay with me for a while. Accomplish the same purpose as staying upstate, but you'd get to be here, taking meetings and job hunting and all that stuff. And also we wouldn't have to stop having sex."

I groaned and pinched him. "Move in with you?" I teased. "Don't you think it's a little fast?" But I felt a wave of relief. It would afford me the ability to get back on my feet. He was offering me the life preserver I needed, in an environment where I was comfortable.

"Just something to think about," he murmured into my hair. "You know. Get you a little extra income. Buy you some time. And, I don't know. Sure. See where things take us." It became clear that he was serious.

It wasn't a bad idea, I thought, as I began to drift off. If I ignored the last part, anyway. I didn't want to think about that, to change the nature of what we were. Staying with him wouldn't need to be for long. I could job hunt and freelance from cafés to stay out of his way during the week, then head upstate for the weekends to rebuild my relationship with Andrea at a comfortable pace while also preventing my relationship with Ryan from becoming too intense.

We fell asleep then, curled around each other, and I woke up periodically to kiss him on his shoulder, his back, wherever was available to my lips. In the night, nothing felt significant. The next day, I threw on my future dress, taking satisfaction in the routine, even though it was no longer necessary. A blue dress this time. Really just a light sack. I added a long gold necklace and some pumps and sprayed on perfume. Ryan groaned and rolled over, reaching for me. I leaned toward him, smiling into his sleepy face, then went in for a kiss.

"You look pretty," he said.

I left knowing he'd leave a Jolly Rancher on my nightstand when he went. Sometimes it was accompanied by old receipts or a few coins. I never knew for sure if the candy was for me or was just detritus from his pocket. I liked not knowing. I walked out knowing too that I'd see him again the following week, and we'd repeat the routine. I was like a dog that way, with men—always had been. I liked routine, structure. I rode the train into the city and waited in line at the pastry shop near the doctor's office for an iced green tea, extra lemon—my go-to hangover cure. Structure had always been scarce in my life; I had to take it where it came.

9

"C offee?"

I startled. It was the following morning, and Emily stood over me with two steaming mugs. The car Andrea had ordered dropped me at Rob and Andrea's place late the previous night, after a creeping journey delayed two hours by an accident on the highway. I hadn't been able to look at the charred shell of an SUV, but the mangled bits of it strewn across the road hadn't escaped me. I'd had to dry-swallow a Klonopin right there in the backseat. And even with the antianxiety drugs, I still slept fitfully the night before. I was up with the sun that morning, eager to escape the house and get outside, where I made my way to the hammock out back, novel in hand. The thinking was, if the treetops speckling the blue canvas of sky couldn't calm me, nothing could.

I'd read for a while, catching myself turning the pages without knowing how I'd gotten there. When it became clear I couldn't focus, I set the book next to me, my thumb marking the page. I closed my eyes, enjoying the feel of the crisp breeze offsetting the sun's relentless gaze.

I woke to the sound of Emily's voice. The sun was high above the trees and my exposed knees were turning a soft pink. I swung my legs over the side of the netting and blearily patted the empty canvas next to me. She sank down, lowering the seat of the hammock just a few inches above the lawn and splattering coffee across our laps in the process.

"Sorry. I knew that wasn't a good idea."

"So did I." We laughed, and I accepted the mug.

"Where are the others?" I leaned my head back against the

netting of the hammock, balancing my mug on my stomach as I stared at the trees. I had never been alone with Emily. I wanted her to like me, but I felt nervous and awkward, as though I were on a first date.

"Rob and Andrea took Henry to the farmers market. Figured they'd get him out of our hair for a while. Micah's still asleep."

"How does Micah feel about baby number two? Is he hoping it's another boy?"

Emily hesitated a beat too long, and I wondered if I'd overstepped. I searched her face for clues. Her features were half hidden by the shadows cast by the trees as we swung gently in and out of the sunlight. Finally she turned, offering me a tight smile. "We both want a girl," she said. "Which is great, because it's a girl. We were wandering around Red Hook the other day and stepped into this boutique I like . . . I can never remember its name."

"I know the spot."

"Yes, well, he couldn't stop pulling out these darling little bloomers and bonnets and stuff. He has an eye for the old-fashioned outfits. He was definitely all about the girl apparel."

"And how are you feeling about having another one?" I asked. "I bet Henry will be terrific with a little sister."

"It's fantastic," she said. "It's such a blessing to be able to bring children into the world. I'm lucky. I really do have it all." She bit her lip, loosening a bit of cracked skin with her teeth. "Having a girl will be the best thing that's ever happened to us."

"I think it's great that Micah parents just as much as you do." My words sounded wooden even to me.

"Why wouldn't he? Micah's a great dad. That's why I picked him. I could have picked anyone. But you have to choose right. A lot rides on it."

"He seems terrific," I acknowledged, lying to placate her. "I know you both work hard."

"Men aren't babysitters of their own children," Emily told me. "They shouldn't be *rewarded* for providing equal or more child care. Micah's contribution to Henry's upbringing shouldn't be notable. And if Micah isn't useful as a parent . . . well then . . ." She shrugged. "What's the point?"

"Well put." I wondered if Micah knew her thoughts on the matter. If he knew where he really stood.

"Anyway, rejection isn't right." She shook her head.

Her tongue emerged again, sliding across her reddened lower lip. She caught me staring.

"What?" she asked. She brought a hand to her lips. "Oh," she said when she pulled away her hand. She stared at the small smudge of blood on her fingertip. "How did *that* happen?"

"Are you okay?" I asked gently.

"Yes, fine." She wiped her mouth with the back of her hand. "Just chapped." She kicked hard at the ground, sending us gliding back through the air.

"What did you mean about 'rejection'?"

Emily looked at me strangely.

"You said, 'Anyway, rejection isn't right.'"

"Oh, yeah. Rejecting—rejecting a baby." I had a million questions I wanted to ask. "You asked how we were feeling about it. But you know, the mere act of not wanting a baby is wrong. It's almost akin to rejecting ourselves, because we have to reject a fundamental part of our womanhood in order to reject having children."

"I don't agree," I said carefully.

"Sorry, Maeve," she said, her voice tight. "We feel differently on this one. It's not as if no one ever struggles with pregnancy, you know. You just have to accept the challenge as part of the journey. That's the NewLife philosophy."

"Is that really what *you* think, though?" I turned to her. "Because, Emily . . . it isn't wrong. It's okay to *dislike* your kids sometimes. It's okay to dislike Micah. To be exhausted and angry. It's okay to feel whatever you want about the whole thing. It's not just okay; it's normal. You're this amazingly strong woman with an incredible career. You have a choice. This entire thing, it's a choice. Whether to have a partner. Whether to be a parent."

I thought I had her. I saw her eyes catch mine. Spark.

"You sound awfully patronizing, for someone who isn't a parent."

"What?" Then we swung back through the shadows. And when we emerged on the other side, her eyes were blank.

"You're the one who's got it wrong," she said. Then she placed her heel against the ground, jolting the hammock to a stop so suddenly I nearly toppled. "I know what you did to her. I know, and I think it's awful. After all her generosity. You're Andrea's *cousin*. If you didn't look practically identical, I'd never have believed it. Don't you want to help her fulfill her dream?"

She picked our up our mugs from the lawn and calmly headed back inside, leaving me speechless. The hem of her sundress lapped at her ankles as she walked, its folds a dozen tiny tongues. So that was it—the reason she'd been so visibly upset. Probably even the reason she'd joined me on the hammock. She saw my refusal to Andrea as a betrayal. Several long minutes after the screen door slammed shut behind her, her question lingered.

*　　*　　*

"I thought you three could enjoy some girl time this evening," Rob told us, as I walked back into the kitchen from the yard, trailing Emily by a few minutes, the wariness that now existed between us weighing on me. "Micah and I can handle Henry for a night. What do you think, bud?" Henry was looking at him curiously, having heard his name. "You want some more bro time?"

"The stand at the farmers market has the *best* quiche," Andrea said. She'd just emerged from the kitchen and bent to place the steaming dish atop a pot holder on the table. "I love that idea," she added. "We could go to that bar-restaurant in Cairo." Chunks of oily bacon oozed fat in tiny puddles across the surface of the quiche. "The one with live music and karaoke."

"That sounds fun," Emily said. "I can't drink, but I can definitely dance."

"Sounds great," I said neutrally. "I'm up for anything."

Rob shoveled a giant wedge of quiche onto his plate. "We've got this. Right, little dude? Your dad, too, if he ever wakes up from his beauty rest." Henry made a buzzing sound and slammed his palm on his tray, causing a Cheerios avalanche. Rob jumped to his feet and moved to pick the bits of cereal off the floor one by one.

"Looks like you've got it down," Emily said, shooting Rob a grateful smile. "They're all yours."

"Perfect," Andrea exclaimed. "It's settled! Let girls' night out commence at eightish."

"Just be safe," Rob prevailed, rubbing Andrea's head. "These locals can be vultures around beautiful women." He planted a kiss on Andrea's crown, and she gave him a return peck on the cheek.

Rob grabbed for the hot sauce and tipped the bottle upside down, puddling it over his quiche. He started talking about something—the weather, I thought. I was finding it difficult to tune in. He reached for the bread knife and began to saw at the loaf on the table. Front, back, front, back, like the steady ticking of a metronome. He glanced at Emily and laughed at something she said, taking his eyes from the loaf for a split second.

It happened so quickly.

The knife sliced neatly into the hand that was holding the loaf in place. The serrations cut through the fold of skin between his left thumb and forefinger. Reflexively, Rob yanked the knife back; it caught on his skin and dragged a ragged chunk away, exposing the thick muscle underneath. He dropped the knife, which clattered to the ground. He gripped his wrist as perspiration beaded his forehead, and he struggled to his feet. Andrea gasped and leaped from her chair.

It wasn't bleeding, until it was. And then a thick river of blood pulsed from it, trickling down his wrist as Andrea put a firm hand on his shoulder.

"Sit, Rob," she instructed, her voice tense. "I'll get a towel."

I watched the steady stream of red liquid pool in the center of Rob's quiche, making an audible *splat* as it mixed with the hot sauce and trickled down the sides of his eggs. Emily was already on the phone with the urgent care facility, which was good, because Rob's face had gone pale. He sank lower in his chair and the liquid kept pooling and trickling, covering every inch of his food until there was nothing left but red. *Splat. Splat. Splat.* An image of the doll, mutilated by Truman, rushed to mind, causing my hand to tremble. My fork slipped from my grasp with a clatter, to join Rob's knife on the floor.

Andrea rushed back into the room, towel in hand. A sweaty sheen had broken out on Rob's forehead. From his high chair, Henry began to cry.

"There's no wait at urgent care," Emily said. "We should get him there now. He'll probably need stitches."

"Okay," Andrea said. "Rob, you hear that? We're going to get you taken care of."

"I can drive," Emily told her. "You sit with Rob in the back and keep him comfortable. Maeve, can you stay with Henry for a while?"

Her words sounded like they were coming from the other

end of a tunnel. I stared at the blood, transfixed. The image of the doll's severed, shredded head refused to fade. Another image appeared, one I'd tried hard to keep buried.

"Maeve!"

I looked up, locking eyes with Emily's.

"I said, can you stay with Henry?" Emily sounded irritated. Andrea was already halfway across the room, her arm wrapped around Rob.

"Yes, of course," I said, flushing. "Go on. I'll clean up here, too."

Emily nodded and tossed her purse over one shoulder. Then she was out the door.

The blood was everywhere. I crouched to all fours to see the knife. It lay on its side, near Rob's chair. A raw, bloodied chunk of skin clung to its serrated edge. I eyed it, willing the image it had conjured back into the darkest and most remote recesses of my brain.

Henry shouted then, banging on his tray for attention. I looked up. He had stopped crying and was staring directly at me. When I met his eyes, he grinned wide and toothily. But it wasn't Henry who I saw through the haze of blood and hot sauce that covered the table. All I could see beyond the red was another child's stricken face.

10

They're a very nice couple," says the social worker, gripping my hand just a touch too firmly. "And I heard"—she leans down conspiratorially—"they're looking for a child to adopt. My, you're lucky to get such a fast placement."

We stand in front of a house, but it's all wrong. Front steps blue and shiny where they should be well worn by bare feet. A manicured yard, where weeds should warp reassuringly, forming their own protective netting around the house. This house is bald. Too new. Too perfect. It looks like it has no stories to tell. Its windows are blank like empty eyes. The social worker—Reuta—presses the doorbell with a finger. She holds it for a long beat. There is a pause. The light patter of anxious footsteps. My heart quickens; the door creaks open.

Behind it is a woman. Hair the color of straw, pulled into a bun at the nape of her neck. A smile stretched across her features. She reaches for me; I take a step back.

"She's shy," Reuta explains.

"That's okay," the woman says, smiling again, though it's dimmer now. "Whenever you're ready, sweetheart." I can tell from Reuta's look that I've messed up. I straighten my shoulders and move forward, wrapping my arms around this Mother's waist. When I check to see if I'm doing it right, her expression is sunny again.

"Well," she says. "What a sweet girl you are, Maeve."

"Hello, Mother," I say, releasing my arms. She shoots Reuta another glance, the kind Mother always had when Andrea was sick or hurt.

"You can call me Patty," she tells me gently.

"May we come in?" asks Reuta.

"Oh, jeez," Patty exclaims. "Of course. Come in, come in." We step over the threshold and into a great expanse of shiny foyer. There are thick rugs covering the floor of a room beyond the entrance. There are photographs in silver frames. The house behind her is still.

"You must be thirsty." Patty seems more comfortable, now that we're inside, as though she knows now what to do. "I'll make tea. And you can meet Tom." She leads us to another room, the kitchen. I feel myself calming slightly at the sight of familiar objects: knives, cutting boards, a sink, a table. But the table is not empty. At the table is a human form, larger than any of the Mothers. Dark and terrifying.

A man.

"Hello, there," he says, rising from the table and extending his hand like she did. My eyes dart to the kitchen knife on the counter. I know not to be afraid of men; I know they are powerless. I've known it all my life. But I can't help it. Seeing one in this house, walking among us unrestrained, terrifies me. His hand hovers in the air, and finally he drops it, when I don't take it.

He isn't supposed to be here. Not in this house. I stare, transfixed.

"I told you about Tom," Reuta says from behind me. Her voice has a sharp edge, like she is making this excuse not for my benefit at all. The man's eyes are kind, I notice.

"Tom is my husband, Maeve," Patty explains. "He lives here too."

I ignore her. "Where are all the Mothers?" I ask. I scan the house. It's so big, so empty. My heart quickens at all the space, and no one in it. No cousins, no Andrea, no Boy, no Mother. "Where are they?" I say again. I can hear my voice escalating, but I can't do anything to stop it. I yank my hand from Reuta's and walk into the next room, but there is no one.

"Mother?" I call. "Mother?"

"Oh, goodness," I hear Patty say. "Sweetheart, I—"

"Where are they?" I shriek. My heart is quickening, and my vision is going blurry. My pulse pounds in my ears, waves of rushing blood.

"Maeve! Calm down." Reuta grabs me, but I fight, kicking her several times until she lets me go.

"You said we were going home," I accuse, choking out sobs. The looks on their faces are too much for me to bear. It's clear there's been some sort of horrible misunderstanding. The three adults circle me, looking like they don't know what to do. Tears are streaming down my face now, as it becomes obvious. This is where I'm going to live. No Mothers, no cousins, no Andrea, no Boy. It is suddenly, painfully clear what I've done.

I've lost them all.

* * *

"She'll adjust quickly." Reuta's voice, firm and confident, reaches me with ease where I sit, a couple of hours later, at the top of the staircase to the second-floor bedrooms. I'm bleary from my nap but not so bleary that I don't know what they're talking about. I feel anxious over what I might have missed while I was asleep.

"Look," she says. "Her history is undoubtedly a psychologically damaging one. None of the children exhibited signs of physical abuse, and they seemed not to have any awareness of the . . . *violence* that was conducted in the locked-off wing. Maeve is on par with her peers—even ahead in certain ways—intellectually and academically. Her emotional development . . . That will likely need some work. Particularly her perception of men, and their role in her life. But with therapy, there is no reason she can't have a completely normal, healthy future."

"She didn't see any of it?" Patty is insistent, as though this answer could determine my fate.

"No. Her 'normal' was just different from ours. A good homeschooled education. Plenty of food and attention. A house without men. That's it."

"I don't know." Tom's voice. I hug my knees to my chest. "I'm not sure we were fully aware what we were getting ourselves into, and—"

"No." Patty silences him. "She's ours now. Our responsibility. Children are adaptable. We will be fine." Then, more plaintively: "She *needs* us, Tom. Maybe this is what we're meant to do."

"But my god." His voice is lower now, and I have to strain. "That place. It sounds much worse than the briefing they gave us in the initial call."

"I know," she says. "Don't you think that makes us even more necessary?" I peer over the staircase railing, craning my neck to see them in the rug room. Patty has an arm wrapped around Tom, comforting him. She is the strong one, just like Mother always said. There is no reason, I realize, to be afraid.

11

The week after my firing had been difficult. I felt uneasy, adrift, unsure what my next steps would be, let alone how to take them. The alopecia I'd battled since childhood began to flare up. I wasn't surprised; it had happened all through my life, during difficult periods. I mostly hid it by pulling my thin, extension-enhanced hair into a ponytail, but my extensions were old and it was becoming harder to hide the patches of bald that decorated the back of my scalp. I recognized the hair loss was speeding up, and maybe there would be no stopping it this time, but it wasn't as if I could afford any quick fixes.

A few hours after the incident at brunch, I removed the extensions, one by one. I combed what was left as best I could and popped into the kitchen for a quick midday snack. Emily was there, fiddling with her phone at the kitchen table, while Andrea worked at her computer.

"Oh, hey. How's Rob doing?" I asked. "Henry's napping now, by the way."

"Rob needed stiches, and he's resting now, but he's fine. He's on some pain meds," Andrea commented.

"Yikes," Emily said, trying hard to hide her shock as she eyed me teasing my hair self-consciously with one hand as I reached for an apple with the other. "What happened to you? Rough time babysitting Henry?"

I padded over to the coffeemaker and pulled out the pot, heedless of the drip cycle. Emily squinted, and I shifted my weight in the opposite direction, prickling.

"I unfastened my extensions," I admitted. "I'm . . . losing some hair. From the stress of losing my job, I guess. Extensions tend to make it worse." I felt my face begin to flush with embarrassment. "Are we staying in tonight, then?" I asked hopefully.

"Why would we do that?" Emily sounded incredulous.

"Oh," I said, surprised. "I assumed Rob wouldn't feel up to watching Henry, after what happened."

Emily shrugged. "Micah will have to step up. Listen, why don't I cut your hair for you?" She crossed the room to where I stood and examined the integrity of my strands. "Little-known fact: I used to do hair as a side hustle, back when I was in grad school. It'll be less obvious when it's short. We can sort of tease it up on this side." She worked her fingers in my scalp, the nails scratching bare skin.

"Let her, Maeve! Emily gives the best haircuts," Andrea said.

"That's sweet of you," I started, feeling a little embarrassed.

"I won't take no for an answer."

"Okay." I shrugged. "Sure."

Emily didn't have formal training as a hairdresser, she told me, but her mother had gone to beauty school. She'd taught Emily everything she knew, and Emily had made a killing in those early postcollege days. She'd even given Andrea a couple of haircuts in recent years, just for fun. "That's when I rocked asymmetrical bangs," Andrea reminisced, and Emily laughed.

I was sitting on the toilet seat in the upstairs bathroom near Emily and Micah's room, as she hovered above me with a pair of shears.

"If this keeps up, you might have to look into getting a wig," she commented. I felt the cold metal drag slowly across the back of my neck, watched Emily in the mirror as she leaned forward, examining my ends.

"They've got some really nice high-end ones now," she continued. Then she tilted my chin sideways, peering closely. Her hands steadied as she channeled all her focus onto me.

"Eyebrows and eyelashes still good, though. You should see a therapist."

"I did, until I couldn't afford it," I told her. "I'm about to lose my health insurance."

"It will pass," Emily said, after a pause. I didn't know if she meant the alopecia or my penniless state. Neither seemed very likely. "When did it start?"

"When I was a kid," I told her, leaving my answer purposefully vague. "Little. Six or seven. Not as bad as this, just a little bit here and there, until I went to college. Then it all grew back. I saw a doctor once after college, when I had a relapse, and he couldn't offer anything preventative. Every time there's a flare-up, I hope it doesn't go too far. And cross my fingers that it'll grow back." I spread my hands in a *What can you do?* sort of gesture.

Emily's eyes flickered to mine in the mirror, then away. I shifted in my chair as she continued to work. She was silent and focused; the only sound between us was the snipping of the shears. It was warm in the bathroom—too warm. The house had old, window-unit air conditioners, and this bathroom, on the second floor, didn't have a window.

"Hey. Sit still."

I'd jerked my body away from hers in an effort to open the bathroom door. It had come over me all at once, a wave of claustrophobia that threatened to suffocate me.

"Sorry. I was hot."

She moved on to the left side of my head. She was methodical, seemingly in her element, and I had to admit my hair looked lighter and fuller already, its volume concealing some of the thin spots. I wondered if I was glimpsing the Emily that existed before pregnancies and a husband.

"We're almost finished," she told me. For my part, I couldn't have been more relieved. I realized I was digging my fingernails into my palms under the towel. Another sign of stress—I'd accidentally gouged moon-shaped patterns in my hands that way as a kid. The lack of space in the room was getting to me.

"Well," Emily went on, "we'll all help you how we can, until you're back on your feet. I can always give you haircuts." She was brushing the stray hairs from my nose with a blush brush she'd found in the cabinet. "And I know Andrea would loan you whatever you need."

"I'm fine," I told her. "Thank you so much, but I've always been fine. Freelance doesn't pay horribly, it turns out. I have a couple of leads already." I'd gotten an email that morning through a freelance site I'd signed up for. The job would be tedious—a first-time writer with no sense of how to craft a story—but it paid $5,000. I'd also missed a call from Elena, and she'd left a voicemail saying she needed to speak with me urgently about a potential assignment. I was dreading calling her back—her failure to fight for me still stung.

"Just a second," Emily told me. I'd pulled the towel away from around my shoulders, thinking her done. "The back's uneven." She picked up the shears from where she'd laid them on the sink. "It'll only take another minute. You know, I was pretty stressed out before I met Micah, too. For a couple of years after college, I'd have to call in sick from work all the time because of diarrhea. I thought I had colitis. It turned out to be chronic stress."

"It's hard to imagine you being anxious."

"I'm not, anymore. I was before I really found myself. I grew up a lot after Andrea became my life coach and I found my family and my purpose. Back then I was a hot mess. So I took medication for a while to treat it. When I met Micah, it all went away, like that." She snapped her fingers, demonstrating how quickly her health had made a turnaround. "I put on, like, fifteen pounds and had never been happier."

"I suppose there's a silver lining to nerves," I mentioned dryly. "The weight management, not the lack of happiness."

"Totally," she agreed. "When Micah came around and suddenly I wasn't doing everything by myself, the anxiety evaporated. I had a partner. And we had a family. And a job that gave us both a sense of purpose. I went up a jean size, so what? Worth it for the mental gains."

"I'm glad he's been good for you."

"You can have it too," Emily told me. "And then you can have a real home of your own. A nice, forever place that you can fill up over time."

"I want that." *Just not your version of that.* More like a cute one bedroom apartment and a nice nest egg, and sure, maybe a partner, if the right one came along. But maybe not.

"Maybe you're looking for something that doesn't exist," Emily suggested, as if she'd read my mind. She shook her hair over one shoulder and looked at me. "Let's face it: there's nothing sadder than a woman in her late thirties or early forties who's all alone. God." She shuddered.

"It's just bad luck disguised as empowerment," she went on, patting my stiff shoulder. "Don't worry. That won't be you. There's still time to get your life together. New York is full of pretty women, but you're smart. Just don't waste all that intelligence on your job instead of building your own story. And I don't mean with someone like that bartender you've been seeing. I'm sure you have a hot connection and all, but meaningless hookups were a thing best left in our twenties. Perfect is the enemy of good, Maeve. I just know there's someone out there who'll be a devoted partner to you, even if you don't have fiery sex."

"What did Andrea tell you about the bartender?" I snapped, annoyed my cousin had been talking about my private life, and more annoyed still by Emily's transparent pity. "But impressive allusion to Voltaire, thanks."

"Nothing! I asked if you were dating anyone and she just said you were seeing a bartender but keeping it casual. I am of the opinion that you deserve more. I picked Micah because he's dedicated to me," she said. "Dedication is its own kind of passion. And it's way more useful in the long run."

I stared at her in the mirror. She patted the top of my head, oblivious. "All set," she said. "You look great."

"Thanks, Emily," I said stiffly. "You know, Ryan—the bartender—isn't the one holding back. And honestly? I don't think a man is the answer to all my problems. I don't want to be less happy just for the sake of not being alone."

"Is that what you think we're all doing?" Emily rinsed the scissors in the sink, then turned to me. They dangled there between her fingers, metal glinting with water.

I wasn't sure. Emily didn't seem to love Micah so much as tolerate his company. She was the powerful one; everything revolved around her. And it seemed like she was perfectly happy with that arrangement.

"Mama!" A faint wail broke in from the direction of Henry's bedroom. Emily jumped, startled, and lost hold of the scissors. They clattered to the floor, nearly grazing my bare foot.

"Why is he calling for me? I told Micah to keep an eye on him." Her mouth pulled at the corners. She retrieved the scissors and absently placed them on top of Micah's brown leather dopp kit. She flexed her palm; it was creased with deep, red grooves from where she'd handled the blades. She waited a moment before letting out an irritated sigh.

"I'd better go see what he needs."

"Thanks, Emily," I called, as she breezed out the door. "My hair looks a lot better."

I got no response other than the sound of a door opening and closing, and then Emily's stern tone mixing with the din of Henry's sobs.

12

We left the men to their own devices for dinner, since we planned to eat at the bar. The new haircut buoyed me, made me feel prettier and more confident. My hair was arranged in loose waves and Emily had woven my growing-out bangs into a braid that I'd pinned back against my crown. Andrea had let me borrow her clothes: an airy, silk sundress with V-neck in the front, spaghetti straps, a low back, and slits on both sides. Just the sort of thing I could wear barefoot and still feel glamorous in. I'd stained my lips a deep wine red and painted my toenails to match, and as they dried, I summoned the courage to return Elena's call. Andrea and Emily were downstairs in the kitchen, so I'd have privacy.

"Maeve!" Elena picked up on the second ring. Her voice was warm and friendly, as if she hadn't just stabbed me in the back and left me to rot. "Wonderful to hear from you! How are you? What's the latest? I miss you already."

"I'm just calling you back," I said, startled. Elena had apparently chosen to pretend nothing had gone down between us.

"Right, yes," she said. "I was wondering if you're open to freelance? I know it's soon, so I hope this isn't awkward. The truth is, Maeve, Mallory's about to be promoted. She's going to need backup on her edits, now that she's handling more management responsibility. You edit circles around most people in this industry, and I thought—"

"So I was right."

"Yes," Elena said, sounding chastened for the first time.

"I didn't expect the promotion to happen so soon myself, but Edward insisted all reorganizing of the imprint should happen at once, to minimize two separate structural shifts . . ." She trailed off. "It's not personal."

"Right," I said bitterly. "So you want me to take projects to back Mallory up. Basically, assist her."

"I wasn't thinking of it like that. We need help, and I assumed you might appreciate the work. I thought this would be a good thing, after Monday."

"I thought we were friends," I said quietly.

"We *are* friends!" Elena sounded surprised. "That's why I'm trying to give you work."

I drew in a deep breath. The fact was, I badly needed the money in order to keep covering rent for my own place. "How much does it pay?" I asked.

"We can give you a flat fee of fifteen hundred per project."

"You're lowballing me, Elena."

"The budget is tight. I would really like for you to have this job, Maeve. If you do well on this one, I'll have leverage to hire you for more."

"You already know I can edit," I snapped. "I shouldn't have to prove it to you. This can't be some kind of trial."

"I didn't mean it like that. Look, it's a way for us to continue working together."

"Can you go up to seventeen hundred?" I asked. At the very least, a negotiation would help me hang on to my self-esteem.

"I'm afraid not," Elena said. "Our budget can't handle that. What do you think? I'd rather have you than anyone else."

I sighed. "I want it," I agreed. It hurt, talking to Elena like this. At one point I'd thought of her as an older sister. I'd cared for her.

"Great! I'll send you a contract." Elena's voice was

sunny again. "I'm so glad this is working out for both of us, Maeve."

*   *   *

"You're pretty," Emily sad, scrutinizing me as if for the first time. We were perched on stools by the kitchen island. "You do look like Andrea, when you're all dolled up."

"We may as well have been twins as kids," I told her, choosing to ignore the uglier implications of the comment. I offered Andrea a careful smile. "So what's this place we're going to like? Have you guys been?"

"Nope," Andrea said. "I read about it online and have been wanting to go. Seems kind of like a trashy pub, if I'm honest. But, like, a fun one."

"I *love* a trashy pub," Emily said. "All the better if they have karaoke."

"Karaoke?" Andrea raised her eyebrows. "What are we, twenty-two and in search of thirst trap fodder for Instagram? Are your forty thousand followers not enough?" she teased.

I raised my eyebrows, expecting Emily to bite back, but she only smiled stiffly.

"You know I hardly ever post on my personal Instagram." She applied the finishing touches to her eye shadow, using a compact. "The followers are from NewLife publicity."

"It's cool." Andrea patted Emily on the shoulder. "We'd love you even if you *were* an attention hound. Wouldn't we, Maeve?" She looped her arm through mine. "Emily, you work too hard. All work and no play made Jack a dull boy."

"Right. I've been busy running a company and raising a kid while you play catch-up with your long-lost cousin," Emily shot back. "And I literally just suggested karaoke, which is the opposite of dull." I was kind of nice to see Emily's fiery side emerge.

"Me-oow." Andrea made a noise like a feral cat, then laughed. "It's not a competition. Relax."

Emily snapped her compact closed and placed it on the counter. "The car I ordered just pulled up," she told us. "I'll go hold it. Don't be long," she called over her shoulder, heading outside.

"Andrea," I whispered, grabbing her elbow as she moved to follow Emily. "Is Emily okay? She seems a little . . . I don't know. I can't help but think it's because of me being here."

"Oh, she's fine," Andrea said. "You are so sweet to worry. It's not you. Motherhood is hard, that's all. She might be a *little* jealous," she admitted, confirming my darker suspicions. "Three's a crowd, right? I'm sure it's pretty obvious to her that you and I are on a different level."

At that, Andrea slung her bag over her shoulder and skipped ahead of me into the foyer, then out the front door. I paused, staring after her. I couldn't imagine Emily—smart, sophisticated, model-gorgeous Emily—being jealous of me.

A horn sounded and I gathered my things hurriedly, locking the front door from the inside and pulling it shut behind me. Andrea turned back, looking up at me from the bottom of the porch stairs. She offered me her most dazzling smile, and I felt myself respond to its seduction like an addict to drugs.

"Come on, goofball." She laughed. "You look smokin'. Let's go show you off." I smiled and followed her to join Emily, who was already sitting in the car. I would follow Andrea anywhere, I realized. We all would.

*   *   *

A mere twenty-minute drive later, we reached the town of Cairo and stepped out of the car into a sweet, wood-paneled restaurant featuring a horseshoe-shaped bar and a steep set of stairs leading to a mezzanine decorated with strands of white lights. The effect was warm and cozy, and I was impressed. It was casual but beautiful—not a trashy pub at all. It was the perfect place to hang out and grab a quick drink or settle in for a full meal—a calling card for New York professionals desirous of a "home away from Brooklyn" feel. The live music had already started—some sort of indie rock band—and Emily was eyeing the lead singer. According to Andrea, Emily had had a serious thing for musicians before Micah came along.

"He is *cute*," I said, elbowing her, as we pushed our way to the bar. "Damn. All the things they say about corn-fed farm boys are true."

"You shouldn't get any ideas," Emily said. "Think long game."

"Thanks for the tip." Emily didn't seem to catch my sarcasm. "I meant for you, not me. Don't think I didn't see the way you were looking at him." We slipped our way around a crowd of college-age bros to the front of the bar.

"I've never been into younger men," Emily protested. "Half Micah's age with half the experience."

"You sure about that?" Andrea wiggled her eyebrows and broadened her mouth into a devilish grin that didn't quite reach her eyes.

"We'd never tell," I swore, crossing my heart. "Some passion never hurt anyone." Emily frowned.

"I'd never be with a man who didn't satisfy me," she said coldly. "Everything they say about men having needs that are different from women's is BS. I like to copulate as much as the next guy. Maybe more. And being pregnant makes me extra horny."

"'Copulate.' How sexy," Andrea teased. "Is that what you say when you're turned on? *Oh baby, my hormones are out of control. Wanna copulate?*"

Emily was visibly irritated—gnawing at her lip as she seemed wont to do when she was lost in thought—but Andrea didn't know about our conversation from earlier. Her harmless comments were hitting hard.

"Oh, for god's sake. You know what I meant. Mate. Bang. Reproduce. Fuck. Whatever."

"What's the weirdest thing a guy has ever sent you? Like on a text?" Andrea changed the subject, her eyes flashing.

"You mean like a dick pic?" Emily looked disgusted. "I've never been a fan of a noncontextualized penis."

"Oh, come on," Andrea said, cajoling. "You and Micah never had any sexy foreplay days? What about when you're traveling for work?"

"Well, with Micah it's different," Emily protested. "He's amazing at sex, but there isn't really any more mystery. Like, if he sent me something that didn't look like the lone tree amidst the shrubbery, I'd probably accuse him of using a filter."

"A grooming filter? Do they have those?" I scanned the packed bar, looking for an opening.

"They should, if they don't," Emily replied. "Portrait mode can only do so much."

Andrea laughed. "What about you, Maeve?"

I shrugged. "Ryan sent me a video once while I was at work."

"*What?*" gasped Emily, just as Andrea said, "A video of . . . Oh god, I'm afraid to ask. Not him and another *woman*."

"Or man?" Emily guessed.

"Just solo activities," I told them, laughing. "Which I like watching, for the record. But it was pretty much out of nowhere. I got this text and opened it in a meeting and it was like, *Bam!* Thank god I clicked off it before anyone saw. Or heard."

"Holy. Shit," Emily commented, looking both disgusted and enthralled. "I guess that's single life for you. How long was the video? I mean, it's like, if it's too long, you have to wonder if he has Ron Jeremy aspirations. If it's too short, he might look inadequate. Ego all the way down."

"Production of the video was apparently how he spent his entire afternoon," I informed them. "But the video itself was less than a minute long. He captured the grand finale. Men are so attached to their appendages. How often do you think your husbands masturbate?"

"Never," Emily replied. "Unless I'm traveling. He has *me*, after all." She paused, looking smug. "I honestly think he's so afraid of losing me that his erection would wither at the sight of another woman."

"I don't know, Emily," Andrea said. "Didn't you tell me that once he proposed a threesome with another man? There are certain . . . *needs* you can't fulfill." She flashed an evil grin, and I giggled uncertainly. Andrea had a sadistic streak when it came to teasing Emily, I was starting to realize.

"Micah worships the ground I walk on and craves me and only me."

"I know he does, sweetie." Andrea reached over and twirled a strand of Emily's hair between her fingers. "I was only teasing. Anyway, I honestly think Rob does it a few times a week. It doesn't seem to matter how often we're having sex."

"I could go weeks without thinking of sex," I interjected. "Possibly months. But if I'm sleeping with someone I'm into, I want it constantly."

"That's just your primal mating urge kicking in. I'm telling you. When we see someone we like, our bodies go all Neanderthal."

"Ugh, no shop talk tonight," Andrea groaned. "Everything isn't about having babies."

"I know it isn't." Emily's tone was sharp. "If it were, I'd have a lot more of them. So would you."

Andrea paled. "Right." The crowd shifted, and she pushed

her tote higher on her shoulder and muscled her way toward the front of bar. "Let's get a drink, already. Lord knows I need one. Em, have a spritzer before you switch to water. You need to loosen up, girl." We approached the bar, and Andrea flagged down a bartender with a chest-length beard and a PBR T-shirt. "Two gin and tonics with lime, and one white wine spritzer, please," she requested.

"Thanks," I said, pressing the drink against my forehead when she handed it to me. "Good *lord,* it is hot in here."

"You're telling me," came a voice from behind us. "Couldn't get any hotter."

I turned to find a drunk twentysomething swaying gently as he blatantly eyed us up and down. "Where are you ladies from? You come in from the city?"

"Brooklyn," Emily said primly. Then, motioning to me, she added, "At least the two of us. She used to live in Tribeca. Now she lives locally." She gestured to Andrea, who was already staring at the band with the expression of someone suffering from indigestion or boredom.

"Wow." The guy whistled, moving an inch closer to Andrea. It seemed he was the type who would take her reticence as a challenge. "Tribeca, huh? So you're pretty *and* rich. My lucky night, right Danny?" He turned, seeking his friend, then turned back to us when no one materialized. "He'll be right back," he mumbled.

Andrea sipped on her drink, clutching it with her left hand, ring facing out. "We're spoken for," she said, gesturing to Emily. "And she's too good for you," nodding her head at me. I winced. Despite my modest lifestyle back in Bushwick, it was easy to feel like a jerk in this place, which seemed filled with locals. We were clearly interlopers. I wondered how it looked from their perspectives.

"Ricky, my man!" A handsome, broad-shouldered guy pushed his way through the group and clapped a strong hand on Ricky's shoulder, subtly forcing him to take a step back. "I see you met my friends."

"Your—your friends?" Ricky's face had gone ashen.

"That's right," the guy said, sending a wink in our direction. "You wouldn't bother any friends of mine, would you?"

"No way," Ricky replied, shaking his head adamantly and listing sideways. "I didn't know you knew these girls, Ty. No offense, buddy." I frowned. He would be the type to call grown women "girls."

"No offense taken." Ty's voice was friendly but firm. "Now why don't you go around the back side of the bar and pick out a few karaoke tunes for later?"

We watched the man stumble off in the direction Ty had indicated.

"Spend a lot of time with that one?" I asked, quirking my lips.

"No way. Just a regular. Apologies—I should introduce myself. I'm Tyler," he said. "I'm the owner of this place. I'm so sorry he was bothering you like that. He knows I'll kick his butt if he tries anything with a customer."

"So you've been through this before," Andrea said shrewdly. "I'm Andrea, and this is my cousin Maeve and my friend Emily."

"Thanks for stopping by," Tyler told us. "I hope this horrible first impression won't inform your night." He looked at his wrist, which sported a smart watch. "It's nine already, so I'll give him about a half hour until his girlfriend gives him a lift home. But if he tries anything else in the meantime, I'll give him the boot."

"His girlfriend?" Emily looked shocked. "He hits on random girls a lot?"

"He's a drunk," Tyler said. "But a harmless one. Hillary's right over there." He waved at a woman perched at a bar stool, sipping a Corona.

"Ouch," I commented. "She saw the whole thing."

"Doesn't know how to handle her man," Emily said coolly. I winced.

"They've been together for a long time," Ty replied. Then, before I could ask him what that had to do with anything, he added, "Come on over here. There's a booth in the back that just opened up, and I'd like to order up a few appetizers on the house. I know I can't make up for Ricky's behavior, but I can at least make sure you have fun the rest of the night." He smiled, his eyes catching mine and making me blush.

"That's so sweet of you," Andrea said, with a pointed look in my direction. The look read, *We've found your future husband.*

"Yes, very thoughtful," I echoed, returning Andrea's pointed look with an eye roll. "Lead the way."

*   *   *

Two hours later, the band was packing up and Andrea and I were five comped drinks deep. I was getting sleepy, whereas Andrea was hopped up, inserting coins in the jukebox and starting spontaneous sing-alongs. I'd switched to wine after our gin and tonics. It turned out Tyler paid attention to his wine list, bringing in a lot of New York–based "locals" from the North Fork and even Brooklyn Winery. "Can't afford to disappoint the Brooklyn yuppies," he pointed out, giving me a nudge along with a playful grin.

Emily and I were hanging out in the booth, picking at the freebies Tyler had sent over on the house, while Andrea danced solo, seemingly oblivious to the circle of men in her orbit. I kept an eye on her. They looked predatory to me—Rob's description of them as vultures had been apt. It helped to know Tyler was right there—physically intimidating and stone sober—if we needed him. He'd already earned my trust with his easy manner and open disposition.

"I don't feel well," Emily was saying, placing her head on

her arms atop the table. "I want to go home." She seemed woozy.

"Maybe you just need some more food," I suggested. "You hardly touched the mushroom crostini. And it was really good. Shit." I eyed the menu more closely. "The dinner menu cuts off at eleven, and it's already ten fifty-five. Oh! But it says they have a late-night menu." I squinted at the blackboard posted over the bar. "Mac and beer cheese. Yum."

"Beer . . . cheese." Emily retched a little, straightening, her back rolling against her gag reflex. "God, I'm drunk."

"Emily!" I narrowed my eyes. "You *are*?"

"Maybe," she whispered, her eyes rolling around in her skull as she made a desperate attempt at seeking Andrea. "Make sure she doesn't know, okay, Maeve? It's just so hard being pregnant. I never wanted to be pregnant again anyway." She took a deep breath, looking pale. "She can't know," she repeated.

"Andrea would understand," I told her, although I wasn't sure she would.

"No." Emily shook her head hard from side to side. "I'm not this person anymore. This isn't who . . ." She trailed off, swallowing hard.

"Okay, okay," I told her, trying to stay calm. "Hold it together." I pushed a water—actual water this time, not the G&Ts she'd apparently been passing off as sparkling water all night—in her direction.

I never wanted to be pregnant again anyway. What the hell did that mean? I thought back to our conversation that morning, to her insistence that rejecting a baby was morally wrong. Was this some sort of screwed up, self-sabotaging behavior?

"Can you keep a secret?" Emily asked suddenly. She giggled then. "Nobody knows."

"Of course," I said. I felt dread beginning to build in the pit of my stomach. Emily pulled her phone from her purse and fiddled for a second. Then she flipped it around to show me a photo of a young woman in what looked like a mug shot. It was one of those pictures that immediately makes your heart sink. A face gaunt from addiction, eyelids half-mast, yellowed teeth, skin riddled with sores.

"Who is that?" I asked, disturbed. Emily's giggles grew louder. She put the phone away and laughed hysterically, until she began to hiccup.

"Drink more water," I instructed her. I was starting to feel alarmed. I needed to find Andrea and get Emily home.

Emily took a long sip of water. Then she looked me in the eyes, her own steady.

"You don't recognize me?" she asked.

My hands went cold. "What do you mean?"

"The girl in the picture. It was me," she said. "That's who I was before Andrea came along." She suddenly looked panicked again. "Oh, Maeve. What will I do?"

"You will keep drinking water," I told her, taking her hand. "You won't say anything to Andrea on the way home, if you can help it. Just pretend to sleep, or go to sleep. I'll find her and tell her you're not feeling well and it's time to go home. Okay?"

Emily nodded.

"You know, you aren't so bad," she mumbled, before she pulled her hand away and laid her head on her arms atop the table.

I pushed my way into the crowd, my heart thudding. It all made sense now. Why Emily worshipped Andrea. The reason she was so threatened by my presence. Andrea had helped her turn her life around.

It was difficult to move—the bar had become dense in the past hour. Bodies were pressed against sweaty bodies and I was having trouble squeezing through. I'd nearly reached Andrea when I felt a hand clamp down firmly on my butt. I whirled around, heart racing.

"What the hell?" I eyed a group of men in their thirties.

"Which one of you did that?" The men ignored me, continuing on with their conversation as if I wasn't there and nothing had happened. I felt a chill crawl up my spine. Their smiles looked distorted—freakish and leering—in the dim light of the bar. I turned my back to them and wiped my sweaty palms on my dress. I needed to help Emily. But first I needed to calm down, splash a little water on my face. I was nearly past the worst of the crowd when an arm snaked its way around my waist. I reacted before I had a chance to think, driving my elbow into the rib cage of whomever was grabbing me this time.

"Ow! Maeve, what the fuck?"

"Oh shit." I whirled around. "Oh, Andrea. I'm so sorry. I thought you were some guy. I was on my way to the bathroom, and—"

"And you thought you'd beat me up? Nice." She clutched her chest and winced, swaying. "I'm okay," she said, waving me away when I reached for her. "Nothing another drink can't fix."

"Andrea," I said. "We need to get going. Emily's over it."

"She's fine," Andrea said. "She's just bad at being pregnant." I winced. It was a harsh way of putting it, even if she was joking. "This is *so* fun." She gave her rib cage one last rub, then grabbed my hands in hers. "Isn't it so much fun?"

"It's fun," I lied, allowing her to twirl me with one hand. "But Emily's tired and feeling nauseated. It's almost eleven anyway. Let's call an Uber." I edged Andrea toward the bar and waved at Tyler to come over, hoping to get his attention for our check, and to thank him before taking off.

Andrea dropped my hand, pouting as he approached the counter. "Where's my party girl?" she asked me. "Don't you like bartenders anymore?"

Tyler gave me a bemused look. "Bartenders, huh? Darn. I was sort of hoping you were into restaurateurs." His smile was teasing, more than a little flirtatious.

I blushed and waved Andrea off. "She's just tipsy . . ." I trailed off. "Bartenders aren't like, a thing . . ." I let that sentence trail, too. I was digging myself into a hole, and from the look on Tyler's face, he was enjoying it.

"I'll go check on Emily while you settle up," Andrea said, disappearing back toward the booth.

"Did Ricky say anything else to you before he left?" Tyler wanted to know.

"No." I was relieved for the change of subject. "Apparently you wield some influence. Just not enough—the men here are kind of gross and wolfen."

"Yikes," he said. "I'm not sure I want to know . . . Are you okay?"

I nodded. "Nothing I can't handle."

"Good." He seemed relieved. "Frankly, I'd have orchestrated a different sort of meet cute, if it had been up to me. On a mini-golf course or something. But the world works in mysterious ways."

I laughed. "Meet cute, huh? Is that what this is?" I felt myself begin to relax, the tension draining from my shoulders. Was *I* flirting? He thumbed the cuff of my denim jacket, which I'd pulled on against the evening chill. I moved my hand away, grabbing a napkin from the stack on the counter. I hoped it came across as natural; his thumb had crept uncomfortably close to the scar that snaked down my left forearm. It wasn't exactly my best feature.

"Maybe yes, maybe no," he said, with a grin that made me weak. "You know, I read a book once where the protagonist met her lover when they were both being held hostage at gunpoint. And the entire rest of the book revolved around whether they could separate the trauma of that initial connection from their love."

"Whether there even *was* a love without the trauma," I said. "I know that book. God, what was it called . . . ?"

"Can't remember," he said. He ducked low behind the bar and grabbed a rag, then started wiping down the counter as the place began to clear out. "I read it back in college. I remember thinking it was a really interesting psychological dissection of love. For some people, it's an intersection of compatible neuroses. For the people in the book, it was a shared imprint of fear and isolation. I loved the premise but thought the execution could have been better."

"Wow." I evaluated him, impressed. "That's a really thoughtful analysis." My desire to retreat to the bathroom was fading, and fast.

"What can I say, I'm a regular Michiko Kakutani," he said, his lips quirking. "Not merely a barback-slash-restaurateur."

"I didn't mean . . ." I trailed off. *Michiko Kakutani.* Had Tyler name-dropped the legendary literary critic for the *New York Times*? Who was this guy?

"I know, I know. Only teasing," he said, oblivious to my surprise. "But yeah, I was an English major in school. I always had ambitions of being a writer, but that never really panned out."

"Maybe someday," I said. "And hey . . . if you ever need an editor . . ."

"Nah, it was definitely a good thing." He hesitated for a beat. "And I'm pretty sure if you were my editor, I'd be in trouble." He held my gaze. "How's that for psychological exploration? The woman whom I trust with my most intimate work, who dives into the trenches of my brain and is attractive, to boot . . ."

I laughed. "That's a little dramatic, but you're not wrong. Author–editor relationships can definitely get intense." I pulled back, looked around. "Shit," I said, realizing Andrea and Emily were no longer in the booth. "I hope Andrea's in the bathroom, because otherwise it looks like I've been ditched by my friends. I should settle our check also." I pulled my phone out of my pocket. Sure enough, I had three texts.

Rob picked us up
You two looked deep in convo ;)
Had to get Emily home, call an uber, k?

"Ugh," I groaned. "Looks like they left without me. I'm going to call an Uber."

"I can give you a lift home, if you don't mind sticking around while I close? Ubers aren't easy to get this late at night around here. And no worries about settling up. On the house."

I hesitated. "That's way too generous. I don't want to put you out. Let me at least try calling a car."

Tyler shrugged. "No worries. Just let me know. I'm going to ring these people up." He headed over to the register and I typed Andrea's address into my app. *Searching*, it read. I placed the phone on the counter while it did its thing, and helped myself to some water from the carafe at the edge of the bar. Five minutes later, the app was still searching. *God damn it, Andrea*, I thought. She was inebriated, sure, but she had to have known it wasn't going to be easy for me to get home.

"Verdict?" Tyler asked, when he returned to where I sat.

"I accept your offer," I told him. "Thank you. I really appreciate it."

"It's no trouble," he said. "Maybe this will keep you occupied while I close." He reached under the bar counter and pulled out a worn collection of short stories by an author whose name I recognized but whose work I'd never read. "This is one of my favorite books in the world," he told me. "You can borrow it if you're into it."

*   *   *

The bar cleared out completely an hour later. I'd received a text from Andrea that they were home safe, along with a reminder to take my time. Now it was just me and Tyler, who was wiping down the counters and counting tips when he wasn't refilling my wineglass. By now I was tipsy, far enough gone to struggle with the book in front of me—and more importantly, to understand that I needed to stop drinking. I placed a hand over my glass when he returned with the bottle. "Water, please," I told him. "Unless you're trying to take advantage of me. In which case: water, please."

I'd meant it as a joke. A bad joke. But he leaned in across the bar, and suddenly his lips were on mine and we were making out with an intensity I hadn't experienced since the early days with Ryan. He pulled back, leaving me stunned. "Here's more water," he said, bringing me a full carafe and a glass. "Give me two minutes."

I nodded, accepting the carafe gratefully. He disappeared into the kitchen, and when he returned a few minutes later, he'd lost his blazer and was wearing a black bomber over a T-shirt.

"Much more comfortable," he admitted. "I've never really been able to pull off the whole professional look. You ready to roll?"

In the car, Tyler turned on the radio and started singing along to something I recognized but couldn't place. He crooned the romantic lyrics, grabbing my palm in his. I giggled awkwardly.

"This is super familiar; what is it?" I asked, mostly to have something to say. The whole vibe of the ride was romantic, and it was making me nervous. I wasn't sure what he expected, and I also wasn't sure I was ready for much more.

"'Because the Night.' The 10,000 Maniacs version," he said. "Good, right? Kind of perfect for the moment, if I'm honest."

We pulled up to Andrea and Rob's place a few minutes later, Tyler still holding my hand. The mansion looked even more massive and hulking at this late hour. A curtain in an upper floor window—Emily's room?—fluttered then stilled.

Tyler killed the engine and leaned in, placing one palm

on the back of my neck as he drew my neck to his. We kissed again, sweetly, then with growing urgency, until he pulled back, breathless. "Damn," he said, raking a hand through his hair. "You are incredible."

I smiled. "I would invite you up, but . . ."

"Nah," he said, giving me a quick kiss on the cheek and reaching over to open my door for me. "You've had a lot to drink. Besides, some things get better with anticipation. Take care, beauty. I'll talk to you soon."

I stumbled ungracefully out of the car, a little surprised, but also overcome with relief. I prayed Andrea was long asleep so I could head straight to bed without the requisite recap. I waded through the grass, my feet dampening with dew. Tyler waited until I'd let myself in before he backed out of the long driveway and returned to wherever it was he came from.

I fell asleep fast but slept restlessly. A staticky noise was coming from the pipes, and nightmares plagued me, blending with reality as they sometimes do when you straddle that line between conscious and not. When I awoke around three, I flipped onto my stomach and flung my arm out to the side.

My hand collided with a solid object, as firm and warm and alive as a human. The thing let out a cry of pain. I turned, my head leaden, to find a doll propped limply on the pillow next to me, naked and furious. Sleep swallowed me whole before I could confront the meaning of it. When I woke up again later, the vision was replaced by a head, its skin tattered, the stump of its neck bloodied, its eyes lifeless—an image that had come to me unbidden in the past but hadn't in a long while. After that, I slept till morning, the half-lucid slumber of someone disturbed.

*   *   *

I found myself seated across from Andrea at the reclaimed wood kitchen table at eight a.m. the next morning, clutching a mug of coffee in both hands. Rob was making some concoction in his blender that he swore was a hangover cure. I was tense and jittery from lack of sleep.

"You look awful," Rob told me.

"Didn't sleep well," I said. "By the way, what's with the toilets in this house?" It came out blunt and aggressive—the way one talks when there's no room for a filter because one's brain is just so dramatically achy and shrunken. "Now the one off my bedroom doesn't work, and there's almost no water in the bowl."

"It's called hiring a plumber without checking their Yelp reviews. But I'm on it. Have a new guy coming out next week. Anyway, I can get it to flush. There's a trick to it." It was true that I'd seen Rob jiggling some things in the tank that morning and had eventually heard a flush coming from the hall bathroom nearest my room. I'd been too wrecked to worry about his proximity to my urine. "We wanted to talk to you before you left," he went on. Andrea nodded in the affirmative and I cradled my head in my palms. Good god, what could it be?

"We're . . . worried, Mae," Andrea said.

"Did I do something?" I asked, suddenly alarmed. "Did I see you when I got home?" Had I done something I couldn't remember? It wouldn't have been the first time, and the thought of it sent panic trailing down my spine. I remembered brushing my teeth, peeing in the broken toilet, fumbling with the flush mechanism to no avail, settling into bed with my makeup still on.

They exchanged a glance. One of genuine concern.

"No," Rob said gently. "You were fine. You didn't wake us." He poured the miracle smoothie into two cups and handed me one, reserving one for himself. "We really just worry about you . . . not having a job. Having to pay rent. Everything you're going through is a lot."

"I'm fine," I told them. "Really. Don't worry about it." I took a long sip of the drink.

"Mae, we'd really love for you to stay here," Andrea told me, searching my eyes with hers. My head ached. Their worry felt oppressive in my current state. "We've got this giant house"—she gestured around her—"and no one to enjoy it! It would be silly for you *not* to stay."

"I just . . ." I trailed off, trying to sort my thoughts into something coherent. I couldn't remember why, all of a sudden, I was opposed to their offer. What would be so bad about staying there? It would be calm, peaceful. Freelance work could be done anywhere.

Then I remembered. I couldn't stay there and owe them something. I couldn't have Andrea hoping I'd change my mind. And I needed to be in New York to find a new job.

"I've got a place to stay," I told Andrea and Rob. "I really appreciate your offer. But Ryan told me I could stay with him. And I need to be in the city to job hunt."

"Ryan?" Andrea looked blank.

"The guy I'm . . . My bartender friend? I told you about him. Remember?"

"Oh. The bartender?" She wrinkled her nose. "You're thinking of moving in together?"

I laughed. "No, no. We're friends more than anything. He said I can crash for a while, while I get things in order. It's better for me to be close to the city, for job hunting." Why did I feel as though I were trying to justify myself to a disapproving parent?

"Okay," Andrea said, looking disappointed. "We'll be here if you change your mind. We just want you to know you have a support system in us. No strings attached," she added, as if she could read my mind.

Rob nodded in agreement. "It's been great having you around," he said with a smile.

"And I've loved being here. It's been so nice to have somewhere to go to clear my mind while all this has been going on. You guys have been amazing. But I do think," I continued carefully, struggling for the right words, "that maybe we should ease back into the 'family' thing slowly, after what happened last week. I care about you, Andrea. And I am so happy you're back in my life. I want to get it right."

Andrea nodded, frowning. "That's probably wise," she said. "No need to rush things."

I returned to my room to collect my bag, ignoring their gazes on my back. Andrea elected to stay home and make breakfast for Emily, Micah, and Henry, while Rob took me back to the bus stop. The drive was less than ten minutes, but it felt like torture. My head was pounding—any remnants of my buzz having left my system—and I felt like throwing up.

"Are you okay?" Rob asked with concern. "You can stay another night, if you need to recover. Or just take a later bus today."

"I already bought the ticket," I explained. "I'm good."

"Well we could—"

"It's okay," I reassured him. "I'm good, I promise." When we pulled into the lot, Rob shifted into Park.

"You'll come back, won't you?" he asked. It was nice, I thought, to feel wanted.

"I will, but I don't know when," I said honestly. "I have some things to figure out back in the city. I'm so glad Andrea was willing to give it another shot."

"She feels the same way," he said. "You mean the world to her."

I thought of Andrea. The woman who so desperately wanted my fertility. Needed it. Did I mean the world to her? Or was it something inside me, a siren, a promise of DNA and cells and tissue that would eventually shape to form a mouth like hers, eyes like hers, a sloped jawline like hers? *You owe me,* she'd said in the heat of our argument the previous weekend. It was true that I'd taken something from her long ago. Could she really let it all go so easily?

13

ey," Ryan greeted me, as I walked into the bar ten minutes late. I smiled and hugged him, breathing in his familiar scent. *Normal*, his scent read. It had only been a week, but he felt like a relic from a past life, the one in which I had a job and a reality that was separate and distinct from the life of my cousin. I slid onto the bar stool next to him and he turned his legs toward mine, positioning them on either side of my knees. He rested one of his palms on my thigh, giving it a quick squeeze. The bartender placed a glass in front of me.

"Mine?" I asked. He nodded. "What am I having?"

His grin dimpled at the sides.

"Mmm . . . Old-Fashioned?" I guessed. The bar was divey but made some of the better cocktails in Brooklyn. It was a speakeasy of sorts, nearly invisible behind a set of heavy, floor-to-ceiling black doors that could have concealed a stable if we were anywhere else. Now the doors were open, allowing a cool evening breeze to filter through the windows.

"That's right." He smiled like I'd won a prize. The bartender poured the amber liquid into the glass he'd set out and mixed it with a long, metal stirrer.

It wasn't often that we met outside the confines of my bedroom, but my apartment had been snatched up immediately on Airbnb and my guests were due the following afternoon. Now that I was moving in, I would see him at different times— times that might ruin the magic of our nocturnal affair.

I tried not to worry about the possibility and tuned back in to our date. Ryan was telling me a story about goats. A time he had house-sat in Greece.

"They were in heat," he said. "They all wanted me. It was my pheromones." He reached for his glass, his hand extracting itself from my thigh, then finding its way to my hand after a long sip.

"Right. Because all things female want you."

"Well, I mean, kind of." He winked, then went on to describe how he had lost the goats. Misplaced them to another pasture. A kindly farmer found them. As he talked, I realized I did not much care what Ryan had to say. It wasn't that I didn't enjoy his company—I did. But like the goats, I was most interested in his pheromones.

We rode a moped home from the bar, one of the electric ones that appear as if by magic on the street, only to be abandoned later at will. A sort of metaphor for life in New York, I thought as we rode—or at least for apartment hunting and dating. I wrapped my arms around Ryan and held tight. "Keep your right foot raised," he said. "There's no pedal on that side."

"Be careful," someone shouted as we rode past. "Your feet could drag."

I imagined our feet dragging, skin scraping against pavement. I imagined what would happen if we collided with a car. Turned too fast. I imagined what it would take for Ryan to jolt the handlebars just so. I thought about the sort of power I was giving him just by being on the back of the bike. I closed my eyes and saw our bodies scraped raw, hot metal pressed against skin, blisters forming, helmets burning, flesh melting.

I opened my eyes. Shivered. I ran my right thumb over the jagged scar on my opposite forearm. Part of me wondered if it would offer relief: the violent satisfaction of my worst fears manifesting. An end to the relentless pain of anticipation.

"Here we are," he said, killing the engine. "You slide off first."

When he offered to help me with my helmet, I lifted my chin obediently, like a child, and he unfastened the buckle and slipped both our helmets inside the hood, where the beer had been stashed. We kissed as I unlocked my gate, our tongues moving in perfect accord. His belt buckle was undone before we reached my bedroom. He untied my dress with one tug on the sash—a wrap dress, a not unintentional sartorial decision. He went to the bathroom. I made myself naked and sprawled on the bed while he was gone.

"Beautiful," he told me when he returned, and I believed him, or rather I didn't care whether it was a lie.

"Turn over," he said, indicating that I should flip onto my stomach. I closed my eyes as he worked a finger down my spine, following it with his tongue. He stopped at the small of my back, using his mouth to trace the grooves just above my tailbone. I lifted my hips in the air, asking for more without having to actually ask. He traced the rest of me with his palms, toying with my vunerability as I squirmed underneath him.

When he finally pushed inside me it was more a relief than a promise. He moved over me, gripping my hips and rocking gently, then faster. I matched his rhythm, pressing back against him.

"I want to see you when I come," he said when he was close, motioning for me to turn over. He reentered me a second later, lifting my legs over his shoulders. Just before he came, his eyes rolled back and caught the glare of the bedside lamp, sending flickers of red and orange into his irises.

I jerked backward, away from his grasp, which was always tighter and more intense when he was outside himself. His features changed as his face contorted in an intense orgasm. His face took on a slackened, melted quality. His skin drooped from his cheekbones. I blinked. The fires in his eyes were gone. His features had righted themselves. Imagined. A waking nightmare. My breath caught and I stiffened. I separated myself from him and pushed to a seated position, pulling the bedsheet to my chest.

"Everything okay?" Ryan rolled to his side, propping himself up with one arm. "Hey. What's up?"

"Nothing." I took a deep, labored breath, trying to make sense of the moment. "Just a little intense, I think."

Ryan smiled, taking it for praise. "It had been a while."

He stood and walked naked to the bathroom, fetching a towel. Then he was wiping me down, absorbing the residue of our efforts. I liked this part. The routine of it brought me back to my head. When Ryan touched me this way, I felt like a valuable painting partway through restoration. I felt guilty for kissing Tyler. I felt like anything but a postcoital thirtysomething getting a careless rubdown with a fraying bath towel, courtesy of her non-monogamous lover.

"Would you like me to stay?" he asked then.

"Whatever you want," I told him. "I'm planning to get up around eight, though. So if you were hoping to sleep late, you might want to head back to your place." My plan for the following day was to tidy my apartment, pack a bag, and start hauling whatever I needed over to Ryan's.

"I'll opt to sleep in at my place, then. I can take a hint. Here." He pulled a key from his pocket. "It's my spare. We'll have plenty of sleepovers, starting tomorrow. Maybe this can be a symbolic last night of singledom, or something." He gave me a wink, and I tensed. *Last night of singledom.* The air in the room felt thick and stifling. We would have to talk about this later.

"Okay," I said. "I'll swing by with my things around ten or eleven."

He stood and pulled on his clothes, followed by his sneakers—a pair of red and black high tops I liked to tease him about, because to me they seemed childish. Then he crossed the room to the fridge and grabbed what was left of the beer.

"I'm looking forward to this," he said, kissing me on the forehead. And then he was gone.

14

It took me more than four hours the next morning to sort through my stuff and decide what I wanted to take to Ryan's while I rented out my apartment. Since I wasn't sure how long I'd be gone or what the logistics between tenants would be like, I packed enough for two months. Sundresses, two pairs of jeans, some T-shirts, a couple of sweaters for transition weather. I threw all my toiletries and makeup in a bag, then dropped in my meds. It was nearly noon when my phone buzzed: Andrea. My heart quickened.

How's it going down there? she wanted to know.

Great, I typed back. *About to head over to Ryan's.* She responded with a thumbs-up emoji. I switched back to my message log and clicked Ryan's name, shooting him a quick text.

On my way!

I waited for the ellipsis bubble to appear, and when it didn't immediately pop up, I switched back to Andrea.

How's stuff upstate? I asked.

Good, Andrea replied. Then, *Except there was a centipede in our bedroom last night and Rob was totally useless. It came slithering out of a pile of laundry (I know) and he was like, "oh these are fast motherfuckers" and I trapped it in about five seconds*

I sent back the cry-laughing emoji, and added, *Like what, he was just going to let it hang out?*

Yes!!!! typed Andrea. *He said, and I quote, "I heard centipedes are good tenants"*

LOL. Charge it rent. Maybe it can cover the rest of your renovations in exchange for shelter and your sanity. I waited, holding my breath.

Andrea hit the Ha-ha button and I took that as a sign to exit. I wasn't going to be desperate for her affection like Emily, if I could help it. But the warm thrill of our banter coursed through me as I flagged a car and hauled two suitcases and a duffle bag into the back. I checked my phone—no answer from Ryan. Probably still sleeping in after our late night.

I gave the driver directions to Ryan's place in the East Village. Things seemed okay with Andrea, and I was about to see Ryan, and I had an interview at a temp agency later that afternoon for a position at a publishing house, filling in for an editor who was out on maternity leave. Things were looking promising, if not exactly back to normal.

The car soared over the Williamsburg Bridge; traffic was light in the middle of the afternoon on a Tuesday. Below us, the water caught the sun, bouncing it back into my eyes. When I closed them, a phantom glare lingered behind my lids like two headlights. I imagined what it would be like to face a car head-on on this narrow bridge. To veer in the wrong direction, plummet into the water below. To be trapped in the sinking car, death's anchor. I shuddered and rolled down a window, unwilling to feel confined. I blinked hard several times, until the glare of the sun quit its relentless assault.

When we got to Ryan's block, the car slowed.

"You sure this is the right place?" The driver, an older gentleman with a sparse mustache, looked doubtful. The whole street was blocked off with yellow police tape. A strange odor filtered through the open window, the smell of a cookout, maybe. My euphoria began to dissipate.

"This is it," I told him. "Can you pull over and hang on a minute? I'll be right back." I left my suitcases in the car for insurance and speed-walked down Ryan's block, past the store that traded in mysticism, past the hole-in-the-wall Italian joint and the Laundromat that sold lotto tickets. I walked single-mindedly toward the crowd gathered midway down the block.

As I got closer, the trees cleared. And I saw it.

"No, no, no," I whispered. Black smoke residue blighted the exterior of a six-story brick building. Its windows were gone, its roof partially caved in. I walked faster, straining for the number on the building. I'd never been to Ryan's; he always came to me. I knew the neighborhood but didn't know what his building looked like, or which was his among this row of identical town houses. My breath stilled when I reached the site. Firefighters and cops were standing around, taking notes and talking into cell phones. The building address was just visible beneath the char.

787. Ryan's address. His building, burned top to bottom.

I scanned the crowd—no sign of him. I pulled out my phone and sent him another text: *Where are you?*

I didn't wait for an answer. I dialed his number. It went straight to voicemail.

A homeless woman rocked back and forth in her makeshift bed on the sidewalk, a dog in her lap. Its rib cage was visible. She laughed, loud and high, relentless, and when a policeman approached her and bent to speak, she spit in his face, then continued laughing, a high-pitched giggle that made me want to stuff cotton in my ears.

A few bystanders were talking in hushed whispers. When the door to the building opened, a woman gasped and covered her mouth with her palm. I followed her eyes to the entrance. An ambulance cot was emerging, covered in a sheet. As the EMTs made their way down the front stoop, one of them stumbled. He righted himself but lost his grip, and the sheet slipped up, revealing a set of black and red sneakers.

Ryan's sneakers.

I blinked, and they were covered again. I ran to the sidewalk and ducked under the police line, pushing my way to the ambulance. I had to see it for myself.

"Miss, you can't be here," said one of the EMTs, as they

loaded the body into the back. "You're crossing police lines. You need to get back."

"Who is that?" I asked, my voice sharp. "Who died in there?" I felt my heart accelerate, my hands growing damp and cold.

"We can't disclose any identities." The female EMT sounded exasperated. Her hair was stringy and there were pronounced bags under her eyes. "Please take a step back."

"I just need to know if my friend is okay. He—he isn't answering his phone, and he lives there . . ." I trailed off.

"You need to get back, or we'll have to escort you off the premises." The cop's voice held a warning. By then I was crying—thick, wet tears coating my cheeks and streaming toward my collarbone. I felt frozen, rooted to the spot. The female EMT said something to her partner and hopped out of the back of the ambulance. She touched my elbow and steered me away from the scene and back to the street, where the onlookers were beginning to dissipate, now that they'd seen what they came for.

"There were no survivors," she told me. "I'm so sorry."

"No," I said. "I just saw him last night. It was late when he left. That doesn't make sense."

"The fire happened early this morning," the EMT explained. Her eyes were kind. "Do you have someone who can take you home?"

"I don't have a home," I told her. "*This* was supposed to be my home."

The EMT's voice followed me back to the taxi, where my driver was waiting. Back to the car, where everything had been one way mere minutes before and was now altered. What was done could not be undone.

15

Ryan's spare set of keys in my tote may as well have been a brick, given how aware of them I was. Had those really been his shoes on the gurney? I called him four more times, but each time it went straight to voicemail.

"Ryan, it's Maeve. Call me when you get this, okay? I need to know you're all right." Each message a more frantic and pleading variation on the last. It occurred to me to ask the driver to go to the bar where Ryan worked, but I couldn't even do that. It didn't open until four, and it was before two.

"This okay?"

"What? Oh." The taxi was stopped in front of my apartment building. We'd gone all the way back into Brooklyn without me even noticing the bridge. I fumbled for my wallet.

"This one's on me," the driver said.

"Thanks." It was only when I climbed out, looked up at my unit, and saw the curtains flutter that I remembered: I couldn't go back inside. My renters were already there. I checked the lockbox I kept fastened to the gate outside, and sure enough, the spare keys had been retrieved. So I walked. I dimly realized at some point that I'd left my suitcases in the trunk of the cab.

I wandered on foot for what seemed like—and may have been—miles, calling Ryan's phone enough times to be sure that, yes, he was the man on the stretcher. No, it wasn't a sick joke or a parallel universe. The sun was bright, the pavement stank of piss, and every single New Yorker was bustling somewhere important—tripping over one another in their hurry to get wherever they were convinced they had to be.

I was the only one who had nowhere to be. My temp inter-view felt like a plan from another lifetime. That feeling I'd had since I was a kid—that my past was following me—had settled like a stone in my stomach. I thought about my adoptive par-ents: Patty, who now had severe Alzheimer's and lived in an assisted care facility. And Tom, who passed away when I was in college, from lung cancer. I thought of the people who'd loved me—Andrea, Patty, Tom, maybe even Ryan, in his way—and the people I loved, and their impermanence. I thought that this was why people made babies. Why Patty and Tom had taken me in to begin with. The cycle. The need for love, like some sort of emotional insurance policy. One I'd never quite man-aged to lock down. An outsider in the cycles of humanity.

Eventually it was dusk, and my feet hurt. I had nothing but the contents of my tote bag: my wallet, phone, computer, and a lip balm. My shoulder ached under the bag's weight. I felt so profoundly exhausted that I wondered how it was possi-ble for normal people to make decisions that catapulted them forward. Ryan had a family in L.A., but I'd never met any of them. I didn't have their numbers, or the numbers of any of Ryan's friends, and he hadn't been on social media.

Once again I had the feeling of being nonexistent, of the things and people around me being imaginary. I stood over the subway grates and let the foul air of an oncoming train blow up, swirling around my legs. I thought about the ways things started and stopped. Then stopped for good. I went to the bodega and bought a water, guzzling it down. I felt very, very thirsty. When I went to pay, the cashier had fires in his eyes. When he thanked me, smoke came from his mouth like a dragon.

Eventually I made my way back out on the street. I had my tote over my shoulder, my keys in my back pocket, Ryan's keys in my palm, my phone in my other palm. I found another subway grate and dropped Ryan's keys through it. I didn't like to be too close to death, and yet I had found myself there again. I sank down to the sidewalk and remembered Ryan's Jolly Ranchers. Finally, I began to cry.

In New York you can cry a surprising length of time before someone asks if you're okay. But it's not infinite. Eventually someone will care. It was an older person—man or woman, I couldn't say anymore—who walked me to the nearest urgent care facility, putting me carefully in a chair in the waiting room. A nurse eyed me skeptically from behind the registration desk at the clinic.

"Water's over there," she said, inclining her head. Her lips thinned, but she reserved for herself whatever she was thinking.

This must be the place for people like me, I thought.

*   *   *

When the door to the clinic creaked open, I jerked upright— I'd nodded off. A tall woman in a yellow sundress approached, her shoes clacking against the tiled floor. My eyes were having trouble focusing, but I'd have known her form anywhere. The ease with which she walked. The snarl of long, blond hair. My heart stood still.

"Mother?" I whispered. "How did you find me?"

"Maeve," she said.

"No. No," I whispered. I tried to rise from my chair, but I was weak from emotional exhaustion and fear, and my legs gave out. Mother's slender arms caught me, wrapped around me, held me tight as she sank into the chair next to mine.

I caught a whiff of vanilla on her neck. I breathed it in. The smell centered me.

"Maeve, sweetheart," the woman said. "It's okay. It's only me. You're okay."

"Andrea?" I pulled back from her embrace. Not Mother.

"Yes." She ran a hand through the back of my hair. "You're safe now, Mae. My poor, poor Mae. I'm so sorry this happened to you."

"But how did you know I was here?" My pulse was slowly returning to normal.

Andrea's eyes narrowed. She gave me a worried look. "You don't remember calling me?"

"What? No."

"You called me in a panic. You told me all about Ryan. There was a woman with you, helping you, and I asked her to bring you here."

"I don't remember," I said faintly.

"Here, let me see your phone." I handed it to Andrea. The battery was low from all the calls I'd placed to Ryan. Andrea clicked on my call log.

"See?" she said, indicating an outgoing call from a couple of hours ago. "That's when you called me."

I sighed, sinking back in the narrow, upholstered chair.

"I don't remember," I said. "I'm sorry."

"You were probably in shock," she told me, wrapping an arm around my shoulders. "Still are, if I had to guess. What happened is awful, Maeve. Nothing I can say is going to make it better. But you aren't alone, okay?"

"I've got nowhere to go," I said. "And Ryan is gone." The reality of it, acknowledged aloud, was crushing.

"You've got me," she said, drawing me closer, the armrests between our chairs our only separation. "I'm your family. You don't have to be alone ever again. I'm going to take you home with me. You can rest there and not worry about a thing."

"Oh, I don't—"

Andrea shushed me. "I won't take no for an answer. You need a support system right now. Anyone would."

I hesitated, then nodded. It would be okay for a while, I thought, not to have to worry.

It had occurred to Andrea to bring a blanket. I was intensely grateful, climbing into that car, for the people who were willing to take care of me. "Here," she said, handing me a warm travel mug. "It's soup, not coffee." She gave me a concerned look before starting the car.

"Thank you." I meant it. Suddenly I was ravenous—I realized I hadn't eaten since early that morning, and it was nearly seven o'clock. Andrea had driven three hours to retrieve me from the city.

I leaned my head back against the new-smelling leather of her SUV as she began to navigate traffic on the way back to the bridge. I took a long, slow pull from the mug. The broth was rich and salty, and I let out an involuntary hum of enjoyment. Andrea glanced over and smiled, looking pleased.

"How are you feeling?" she asked.

I lowered the mug to my lap. "You know, someone told me once that I was born under a bad sign," I said.

"Who would say something like that?"

I shrugged, looking at her, and she bit her lip. She knew who I meant. "Maybe it's the truth." I wrapped the red wool blanket more tightly around my legs. I hesitated, then pressed on. "Mother was the one who said it."

"Maeve, I really don't like to talk about those days." Andrea's voice was soft. Vulnerable. "Can we not?"

"Sure," I said. "It was just a memory."

"Well, I don't believe in signs," she told me. "You shouldn't either."

"You don't think it means something that we came back into each other's lives?"

"It means what we make of it." Andrea pulled onto the highway, merging smoothly. "We're all more in control of our destinies than you seem to think. *You're* in control. There are very few things we don't have any say over. This thing with Ryan, unfortunately, it's one of them."

"It doesn't feel like I have control," I replied. "Do you think it's my fault?"

Andrea looked shocked. "With Ryan? Of course not!" But

she couldn't know what I was referring to. I didn't mean the fire. I meant our shared past—the night that destroyed us. It was the sort of horror you put out of your mind, if you wanted to move on and build a life as a passable human.

"Sometimes things just happen," she said. "I'm really sorry about your friend. It was a horrible accident." She reached over and grabbed my hand, squeezing it tightly in her own.

*   *   *

When we entered the house, I stopped in my tracks. Babies were everywhere. In piles in the foyer, slung over the stairs, one even hanging from the banister by the crook of its arm, like a little monkey. Some were in motion—writhing and reaching toward the air for the hug of an invisible parent. Others were crying, their mewls piercing and angry.

I shuddered. Dolls; they were only dolls. My stomach sank at the sight of Emily, who was tending to them—rocking some, burping others. They were so lifelike, it frightened me.

"We're preparing to debut them wider," Andrea explained, her tone apologetic. "Emily's sorting through them and doing some quality assurance."

"How are you, Maeve?" asked Emily.

"Maeve needs rest," Andrea cut in, before I could respond. "Here, sweetie. Let me show you to your new room. The old one is being used for storage. It has a bunch of product boxes in it."

She didn't walk me up the front stairs toward the corridor where my old room had been; rather, she led me through the kitchen and up a smaller, spiral staircase. Its railing was coated in dust. I ran my finger along it as I walked, creating a slender trail. The landing was separated from the staircase by a door. Andrea pushed it open to reveal a long, dimly lit hallway.

"This is the east side of the house," she said. "Former

maid's quarters. Access to the kitchen and all that. It was empty before, but the furniture came in yesterday. I'll lend you a sleep mask; your room gets great light, but it might be too bright in the morning." She stopped in front of a wooden door with a cut glass knob. "Here it is," she said. "I hope you like it."

The bed—a four-poster queen—was much bigger than the last. I sank into it right away.

"Here, let me help you," Andrea said. She removed my shoes for me, placing them carefully next to the door. This small act of kindness nearly brought tears to my eyes.

"Andrea, I don't know how to thank you," I told her. "I know how busy you are right now. The last thing I want is to be a burden."

"You aren't, Maeve! Not even close. I love having you around. And besides, you're family. This is just what family does."

I nodded. "I won't impose on you for long. A couple of weeks to get my life together and—" I felt the sobs forming in the back of my throat, but it was too late to stop them. I had been *so close* to getting my life back on track. Now here I was, at thirty-three, broke, without prospects, and a guest in my cousin's home. How had she gotten it so right and I'd gotten it so wrong? But at least I had my life. Poor Ryan.

Andrea sat next to me on the bed and drew me close.

"I know it's not what you envisioned," she said. "But you can stay as long as you want. And I'll help you job hunt. We can update your résumé and make sure you're showcasing your skills. I'm good at that; I can help. When you're ready, I mean. For now, relax. I'll bring you some tea and a spare set of pajamas."

A breakup is like a death, someone told me once. You lose the person abruptly, entirely, just the same way. At the time I thought that sounded right, but in fact it wasn't. With a breakup, there existed a parallel dimension in which that rela-tionship continued to thrive if you wanted it to, preserved for eternity whenever you looked back on it. There were the gen-erous parts of a person that could feel happy at the thought of their partner moving on, finding new love, even indulging in occasional nostalgia over the past.

If Ryan and I had simply stopped fucking, he would have been fucking someone else eternally in a parallel universe—leaving someone else a Jolly Rancher in the morning, a Pe-ter Pan. Never aging, a constant, forever frozen at forty-two. Delusions like that weren't possible with death. Now Ryan was nowhere. He was gone forever. And when the people for whom he had been real stopped existing . . . well, there would be no one left to remember him. He may as well have never existed at all. When I thought about it that way, it was almost as if I'd made him up.

*   *   *

The following days were a blur. I slept the way newborns sleep: deeply, waking only for food, and then tumbling back to oblivion when sated. I dreamed of Olivia dolls surround-ing me in the bed, sucking and yawning. Another figment of my imagination, but one that was understandable. Ever since they'd begun popping up around the house, it seemed as if they were everywhere. Everyone wanted a piece of them, An-drea said at one point. *Everyone, who?* I'd wondered. But I didn't have time to wonder much, because sleep was always beckoning.

One morning, I woke at dawn, desperately needing to pee. I opened my door, noticing absently that it had no lock. I stumbled down the hallway, the soles of my feet gripping the wooden floorboards. Barely lifting in their shuffle. I wasn't surprised when a sliver of wood embedded itself in the tender part of my sole. I kept going. I felt disoriented, light-headed from not having eaten much.

The hallway was unfamiliar and grimy, as though no one had thought to clean way back here. My new room was in a completely different part of the house from the old one. This realization was even more disorienting. How had I found the bathroom? The rest of the house was still asleep.

I walked farther down the hall, raising a self-conscious hand to the back of my matted scalp. The hair was significantly thinner from stress. I stopped in front of one door. Tried the knob. It stuck. I made my way to another door. There was a slender bar of light, just barely visible where it made a seam with the floor. I pressed my palm to the knob, which felt warm, as though it had recently been touched. I let my eyes rove up and down the hallway—empty. I turned the knob, heedless of whether someone was inside.

For a brief moment, my breath caught in my throat. I wondered what I might find. Somewhere in my distant consciousness, in a more primitive place, I wished for a puppy. A moment of innocence lost that I could never reclaim.

The door swung open.

It wasn't a puppy that met my gaze. It wasn't even a toilet, a vanity, or the creature comfort of scented lotion.

It was a pile of wriggling, discarded babies. Dozens. A mound of them, as if the room were a mass grave. My eyes fixed on one, missing a leg. Its eyes blinked rapidly. Another, partially buried underneath it, had a split in its earlobe. It resembled a cloven hoof.

I heard a crackling noise from within the pile. The sound of static. I stepped into the room, my body seeking the source of the sound of its own accord. I had to find it. I had to make it stop.

There was a string attached to a bulb overhead. I gave it

a yank, and light flooded the room, illuminating the babies. Their expressions looked menacing in the light's harsh glare. The crackling noise came from the back of the room. I moved some of the dolls aside and waded through the rest, picking my way carefully over the piles until I reached the source of the noise.

It was coming from underneath three babies. I reached my hand into the pile of dolls, feeling around on the floor until my hand collided with a hard plastic object. I retrieved it, shuddering as my wrist connected with the dolls' lifelike casings. One doll moved, letting out a cry. I jumped back—startled—and lost my balance, landing among the rest. The dolls' arms poked into my body as if they were grabbing for me, trying to keep me there.

I scrambled to my feet, my heart thudding, and looked down at the object in my hand. It was a baby monitor. That was all. An older model. I was about to press Off when I heard a voice slice through the interference.

"You want a baby sister?" the voice crooned, then cut out. But I recognized it. It was Emily. I held the machine aloft, and the static lessened. "You do?" Emily's voice continued. It was sweet and high-pitched; she was talking to Henry. I could hear him murmuring in the background, though I couldn't make out his words.

"Well, Henry . . ." Emily's voice had turned cold and guttural—an abrupt shift from her baby talk. "I don't want a little girl at all. In fact, that's the last thing in the world Mommy wants." Goose bumps began to rise on my flesh.

"These are the dolls with defects." Andrea's voice came from behind me. I jumped. "Emily's found one or two in every box that arrives from the warehouse. It's maddening." She was cradling two of the imperfect babies in her arms. She tossed them onto the pile. "I see you found the baby monitor.

Emily was looking for that. She must have left it in here when she dropped off the dolls."

I handed my cousin the monitor. "It's such an old one," I said, struggling for something to say. "With all this technology, you'd think you'd have better monitors."

"It was Olivia's." Andrea shrugged. "Henry probably doesn't even need one at his age. Emily's just paranoid."

"God, I have to pee," I said, by way of explanation. *I was looking for the bathroom* reached my brain in a fragmented way a few seconds later. "I was looking for the bathroom," I repeated, aloud. "Did you know my bedroom door doesn't have a lock?"

Andrea looked at me with unmistakable pity. "We don't have locks on any of the doors," she informed me. "It's something we've been meaning to take care of. Do you want a lock on your bedroom? Would it make you feel safer, Mae?"

I nodded, shivering. Were there really no locks on the doors? None of them? I became aware of my thin tank top and the way it exposed my nipples. The odor emitting from my armpits. The thick layer of buildup on my teeth. I hadn't cared for myself in a while. I looked again at the discarded dolls.

"We didn't have anywhere to put them." Andrea followed my gaze. "We're keeping them for parts."

"A lot of them are boys," I noticed, looking around.

"Really?" She shrugged. "How can you tell, in that pile? Come on, let's get you to the bathroom."

I allowed myself to be led down the hall. I looked behind me, noticing the way our heels dragged moats in the dust coating the floor. We took a sharp turn to the left, then down a half-flight of stairs I didn't remember climbing, then another left, and then the corridor stretching in front of us was shinier, with fresh paint on its walls. It appeared I had been in the wrong wing entirely. Part of the house wasn't finished, I remembered then.

"Here you go," Andrea said, motioning me to a toilet in a room covered with daisies. It was familiar, somehow, triggering a memory I couldn't place. Someone had placed my toiletry and makeup bags next to the sink.

I closed the door, unzipped the toiletry case, and fumbled for my medicine; maybe if I took it, I'd feel more clearheaded. I came up empty. I tried my makeup bag next, but that was all mascara and blush and eyebrow gel. It was likely in the guest room somewhere, possibly on the nightstand at my bedside.

I breathed in the scent of freesia as I scrubbed my hands raw. Something in me was reacting to it, the same way I had reacted to the wallpaper. As if I was in a time warp. Some past bathroom in some past life I could no longer remember.

"Are you okay in there?" Andrea called. "Do you need help?" Again, as if I were a child.

I dried my hands and opened the door. "I need to go home," I told her. "I feel weird. I need to snap out of it and get back to my normal life."

Andrea tilted her head, bemused. "This *is* home."

16

French Louie is rolling around on the rug as he gnaws his rope toy, and I'm sitting next to him, playing tug-of-war. He's small, only four months, but Tom says he'll grow into a big dog. He was a gift from Tom and Patty for my ninth birthday. "But you need to walk and feed him," said Patty. "We old fogies don't have the energy for that."

It's true that Patty and Tom could easily be my grandparents—most people think they are. They're too old to chase after a puppy. And they've got their hands full with me. So I do take care of Louie. After a while, I discover I love brushing his fur and taking him on walks and even scooping his smelly poop. I enjoy having a thing to care for, something that's all mine. It makes me miss Boy a little bit less each day.

"French Louie, fetch!" I toss the rope toy to the other side of the room and French Louie runs after it. When he clears the carpet, he slides across the wood floors.

"No puppy toenails on my floors," calls Patty from the kitchen, but there's a laugh in her voice. Tom lowers his newspaper and gives me a wink, making me giggle. The sun is beginning to set and the smell of lasagna wafts into the living room from the kitchen. I lean back against the sofa and curl my toes into the shag rug while French Louie settles down with his rope toy, clutching it between his two giant paws—still too big for his body—as he chews.

We're watching football on a low volume. Tom seems not to care about it that much, only sometimes lowering his newspaper to say things like "Come on, D!" or "Penalty! Interference!" I'm still learning about football, but I like these quiet evenings before we all sit down to eat. Patty turns on some music in the kitchen and hums along.

"Almost ready," she calls.

Just then, the football game is interrupted by a large banner that reads "Breaking News." Then there's a flash to a roped-off house and my heart stops. I suck in a little breath and glance at Tom—his head is still buried in his paper. The roped-off house is *my* house. My *other* house. I focus my eyes on the screen. If I turn up the volume, Tom will shut off the TV. I know this. So I listen carefully and hope he doesn't notice.

"New developments have surfaced in the case concerning the Mother Collective, a Vermont-based commune colloquially referred to as the 'cult of motherhood.' As the excavation of the grounds has continued since the cult's raid last May, four bodies in varying states of decomposition have been recovered. All have been identified as male. Of the two victims originally found in critical condition, one has been released from the hospital. Five women who self-identify only as 'Mother' are standing trial, and two of their legal identities have been confirmed. One, a forty-three-year-old woman named—"

The TV goes black. My body is cold, freezing. A shudder rushes through me head to toe. It's been days since I've thought of that night, when everything fell apart. The night I last saw Andrea.

"Tom, are you kidding me?" Patty's cheeks are red, and wisps of hair have escaped from her ponytail. "Seriously? You're going to let this happen? Maeve. What did you see?"

"What?" Tom sets aside the paper, saving me from responding. His eyes meet mine. "What are you talking about? What did you see, Maeve?"

"The *news*," Patty says, venom in her voice. She waves a pot holder at him like a weapon. "We agreed."

"We were just watching football," Tom protests. "Weren't we?" He looks to me for validation.

"It switched," I admit in a small voice. I tense, waiting for their anger. I feel tears beginning to build behind my eyes. But Patty kneels next to me. She wraps her arm around me and pulls me close.

"It's okay, sweetie. You aren't in trouble," she says. "We just don't want you to have to go through all that again. What did you see on there?"

"What do they mean, bodies?" I ask, my voice trembling. Patty's wide eyes dart to Tom's. She takes a moment to answer.

"It's nothing for a child to hear about," she starts.

"Patty. The kid deserves to know—"

"She's too young."

Their bickering makes me nervous. Tom moves from the couch to kneel beside me. Patty is sitting with her legs crossed in front of me. We are all on the floor. The thought makes me giggle hysterically, but then I feel a trickle on my lip and reach up to touch my face and realize I'm crying.

"It's okay, sweetheart," Tom says, wrapping me in a hug. His whiskers tickle my neck. "You're with us now, and you're safe."

"But the bodies," I say again, more urgently. "What did they mean? Is Andrea safe? What about the Mothers?" Patty runs a hand through her hair. Her forehead has wrinkles on it and her mouth is turned down, like she's upset. "Are you mad?" I'm not supposed to ask questions about Before.

"No, of course not," Tom assures me. "And . . ." He hesitates. "Andrea and the Mothers are just fine, honey."

"Tom!"

"She's terrified—can't you see? She needs to know."

"Listen to me, darling," Patty says, taking my hands in hers. "There are some things that happened at your old house that you didn't know about. It's why you came to live here, with us. But remember what Dr. Miller says?"

"It's best to leave the past in the past," we say in unison.

Patty smiles. "That's absolutely right. The things that seemed . . . normal. . . . back then. Well. You have to put them out of your mind and start fresh. What you have here, with me and Tom, this is normal now. This is your normal, happy life. You get to start over. You're a lucky girl, Maeve. Not many kids get to start fresh."

"Does Andrea get to start fresh too?"

Patty and Tom exchange a glance. "Yes, darling. Andrea does too. But it's better for both of you, in your new lives, if you can let each other go. It's hard to start fresh when you're hanging on to people from your past, do you see?"

"And you'll make lots of friends at your new school," Tom adds. "Soon you'll hardly even remember the rest."

Tom is trying to make me smile, I can tell. I force the corners of my mouth up for him. He doesn't know, though, that the thought of forgetting Andrea makes my heart crack in a million spots.

"Are you okay, honey?" Patty wants to know. I nod, wiping my eyes with the back of my hand.

The one good thing about forgetting it all is that I don't have to tell Patty and Tom what I saw in the locked room that night. How could they love me if they knew what I did? If they knew I had one chance to help and I did nothing at all?

*   *   *

Later, we are wiping our mouths, our bellies full of Patty's delicious lasagna. French Louie barks twice and stands next to the door to the backyard, which is his way of telling us he needs to go potty.

"Smart boy," I say proudly. I taught him not to go in the house, and he's never once broken the rule. "Can I take him out?"

"Sure," Tom says, as he stands and begins to clear the table. "Just a few minutes, then we'll get ready for bed. You've got Dr. Miller in the morning." I like Dr. Miller. He talks me through the stuff that happened with the Mothers, while I play with toys at his office. I tell him most of my secrets. Some secrets, I'll never tell anyone.

I push back from the table and cross the Spanish tiles of the kitchen to the screen door, unlatching it and letting French Louie dash outside. I follow him, squinting into the waning light. It's nearly nine o'clock in late August, and the light is starting to fade earlier now. I'll be starting school— real school—in a few weeks, for the first time.

"Louie!" I grab a ball from the grass and hold it in the air to show him I'm going to throw it. He runs around my ankles in circles, excited. I throw the ball, but Louie has already set off in the opposite direction. I laugh. We all love Louie, but he's not the smartest. He's snuffling around and tugging at a stick that's way too big for him, while I go get the ball. I'm fishing it out of the grass bordering the wooden fence when Louie begins to bark madly. He jumps against the fence at the opposite end of the yard.

"What is it, Louie? Squirrel?" I peer through the slats but can't see anything. It's too dark. I'm about to turn away when I see it: a dark figure crossing the narrow beam of light cast by the streetlamps. The figure is slight, but unmistakably female. Her hair, waist-long, fans out behind her as she runs. Louie's going crazy now, hurling his entire body against the fence. The figure turns toward the source of the barking. Her eyes catch the light of the streetlamp.

There is no mistaking them. They flash green in the light. They are my own.

"Andrea?" I say once, my heart filled with hope and fear. I rush to the fence. But just as quickly as the figure appeared, it is gone, leaving me to wonder if I imagined it all. If I will always imagine her, wherever I go.

17

A week passed, maybe two. They were slow and foggy. Their passage was marked by routine: Rob delivered me a smoothie each morning. I read a book or fiddled on my computer. We ate evening meals. I'd become thin, my hip bones protruding like daggers from the cotton fabric of my sleep shorts. Andrea made dinner mandatory. In between meals, when I wasn't reading books, I more often than not napped. Follow-up emails from Elena had slowed to a trickle and then disappeared altogether. I couldn't work anyway. Fatigue had hit me hard. I'd begun dozing off soon after I cracked my laptop or the spine of a book.

One day Andrea caught me googling Ryan when she brought me my lunch.

"Oh, Maeve, don't torture yourself," she said.

"I just can't believe how much I learned from his obituary." My voice was thick, as if coming from below water. The sound of it sickened me. "I didn't know he could speak fluent Italian. Or that he played the piano by ear. I didn't even know he played the piano at all." My eyes welled with tears. "How could I have spent all that time with him and known so little?"

"Did he know everything about you?" Andrea asked, and I stopped short, sniffling.

"No," I said. "You know he didn't."

"Well." She shrugged. "There's your answer. It didn't mean you cared about him any less. People don't always reveal themselves up front. He probably would have told you those things eventually."

She was right. She was always right. Still, all the things I didn't know were crowding my brain, plaguing me, reminding me of what I'd lost that I'd never get back.

"I don't think all this googling is healthy," Andrea said, gently removing my laptop from my grasp. "Why don't I just hang on to it for a while. Uh-uh," she said, when I began to protest. "Just a few days."

Three days later, Andrea convinced me to give her therapy a try. "You never know. Taking care of something that depends on you might be beneficial. And if it isn't? No harm, no foul. Just try it out for a day or two."

"Thanks, but I—"

"I won't take no for an answer." Andrea's voice was firm. "Think of it as a favor to me. If the dolls can help the most reluctant case, I'll consider them a wild success."

My doll's name was Phoenix. I didn't find her helpful. She was temperamental, often crying when I was trying to sleep. It was disruptive to my hibernation. But, that, I supposed, was the idea. A way to get me to wake back up. I held Phoenix for an hour in the morning and an hour at night, while Andrea held Olivia. I didn't experience an ounce of maternal drive. I did it for Andrea.

My life upstate started to settle into a quiet cycle—wake up, eat, care for the doll, read, nap, eat dinner with Rob and Andrea—and, on weekends, Micah, Emily, and Henry. Emily was busy getting the NewLife conference organized. Emily, though more pregnant than ever, looked like she was losing weight. I wanted to ask her how she was, but I didn't have the strength to find the words.

I hardly remembered to bathe. I took my medicine when I needed help sleeping. If I couldn't enjoy the world, I would blot it out. I wore the same pajama shorts every day, all day. I wore a white shirt with a picture of Betty Friedan on the front until the armpits turned brown. I was tired, always. Sometimes the responsibilities of the doll got to me and I'd turn it off or hide it in the closet so I didn't have to look at it. Was there ever a time when a person wasn't tired? I no longer remembered. It seemed an intrinsic part of humanhood.

We were sitting at the dinner table one night when I realized the odor of my body may as well have been an assault weapon. The thought made me laugh. I took a bite of corned beef casserole and shoveled it into my mouth, glad for a thing like casserole, glad it was still being made by the Andreas and Emilys of the world. Emily watched me, her nose twitching like a rabbit's.

Micah's fork hit his plate with a clatter.

I looked up, pausing midbite.

"Couldn't you have . . . I don't know. I know you're in this *funk*, Maeve, but it's been more than two weeks. It's time to address your basic hygiene." He was fiddling in his pocket again. By now I knew Micah toyed with his pocketknife any time he was agitated.

"I'm sorry," I said, abashed. "I'm just so tired."

"Try having a new baby," said Emily. She was now six months along and seemed more exhausted than ever. Her comment stung, after what she'd shared with me at the bar. But maybe she didn't remember that night, I realized.

"I *have* one," I joked feebly, holding up Phoenix. Emily nodded and pursed her lips. For a second she seemed to have taken my words seriously, so I added, "I know, E. A real baby is harder. You can't exactly shove a real baby in a closet for an hour with a blanket wedged in its mouth so it doesn't cry while you nap." Emily recoiled, and Andrea looked horrified.

"God, the violence of that image," Emily said, aghast. She looked like she might be physically ill.

I laughed. I couldn't help it. "As though we haven't seen much worse. Right, Andrea?" Andrea froze. I took a great bite of casserole and chewed, feeling all the canned, oniony, salty things lump together inside my mouth. *Yum.*

Rob's eyebrows were raised. There was something in his expression . . . Pity? I didn't want it.

"What does she mean?" Micah asked. "What's she talking about?"

"Nothing," Andrea told him. Her voice was razor sharp. "She's exhausted."

"You guys always clam up about your childhood. You know that, right?" Micah pushed.

"Now's not the time, Micah," Andrea responded tersely. "Mae, let me draw you a bath after dinner. We have the most luxurious bath salts."

"Okay," I replied, and her face lit up, as if this would solve everything. "That's exactly what I need."

Emily rubbed her monstrous protrusion anxiously. She looked off, somehow. Then it hit me. She was wearing sweats and no makeup—I'd never seen her not perfectly turned out. She looked thinner in the face—practically gaunt despite her burgeoning womb—and wasn't teeming with her usual opinions and insights. She seemed quiet, distracted. The Emily I'd met at my birthday, on the other hand, had been radiant with her own womanhood. I wondered if it was work, then.

Henry reached for her from his high chair, but she ignored him. She palmed the bump viciously, as if in punishment. It wasn't even born yet, and her fetus was already feeling the wrath of its world. Her words through the baby monitor came back to me. She didn't want a girl. Was it because she wanted another boy?

And why was Andrea pretending a bath could wash away the stench of death that surrounded me? I had broken her only rule, but she was willing to look past it. It sounded nice, anyway. A long soak.

I stood, nearly stumbling. I felt weak but heavy, a bowling pin that had been toppled, with no way of righting itself. Rob stood, too, and extended an arm to catch me.

"I'm okay," I said, waving him away. "Just a little woozy. I've got this." I reached for my phone, registered the small number of missed calls and unanswered texts—from Tyler, mostly—and felt even more overwhelmed. I placed it back on the table and used my hand to support myself heavily on the chair behind me.

Andrea gave Rob a significant look.

"I insist," he told me, using both hands to support me up the hall stairs. Andrea followed behind, a bottle of wine in one hand.

They led me not to the small bathroom in the hall just outside my room but to the bathroom in Rob and Andrea's suite. It had been cleaned recently; the floor tiles quite literally sparkled, and lavender wafted from a candle burning on the edge of the spa-quality tub. Rob pulled a robe from the back of the door and handed it to me.

"Go slip that on while I run the water," Andrea instructed. "Rob will grab some towels."

Their bedroom may as well have been the picture of affluent normalcy. Their farmhouse bed was covered in an ivory linen duvet. Their patio doors were open to the night air, and the curtains fluttered in a gentle breeze. A walk-in closet revealed thousands of dollars' worth of athleisure in muted shades.

I shuffled into the closet and pulled the sliding door behind me, severing my path to the bedroom as well as the airflow from the patio. I pulled the chain bulb. The room wrapped me in its palm, oppressive. I shrugged off my T-shirt, then slipped my shorts to my ankles, and my underwear after them, wondering when I'd last changed them. I felt ripe, about to tip over into spoiling.

The robe was thick and plush around my shoulders. I belted it at the waist and made my way back into the bathroom. The tub was steaming and hazy, covered with a gentle layer of flowers—from the bath salts, I presumed. The lavender scent was even stronger now. Andrea was sitting on the edge of the tub, testing the temperature of the water with one hand. When I walked in, she gave me a compassionate smile.

"Burgundy?" Andrea asked, rising to her feet. She held a goblet of wine in an outstretched hand.

I nodded. I would have liked whatever she'd given me. Steam pooled around us in clouds, veiling our reflections in the mirror. Andrea didn't make any motions to leave. "Here, I'll help you in," she said.

Andrea retrieved the wine from my hand, placing it carefully on the edge of the sink, then pulled my robe off my shoulders and allowed it to slip to the floor before guiding me into the bath. I gasped when my body touched the water. The heat was searing. After a minute, my body adjusted, and it felt like exactly what I'd needed all along.

Andrea handed me back my wine and smiled, pleased with herself.

I took a long swallow and began to relax, relieved to be alone and away from the patter of dinnertime conversation. The room was becoming cloudier around me, shrouded in a dreamy mist. I heard the light sound of footsteps moving toward the door; the latch clicking. A while later, I stared at the sediment in my glass, vaguely realizing I must have finished off the bottle.

"Limestone." Andrea was suddenly behind me. I jumped, splashing water out of the tub and nearly dropping my glass.

"Easy," she said, moving to steady me. She caught my glass just in time, transferring it to the countertop. It was nearly empty—I'd managed to drain it. "The sediment is tartrates, bits of grape seeds, maybe some limestone from the soil. Harmless stuff."

"I didn't realize you were still here," I mumbled. I looked at the water, self-conscious in front of my cousin. I needn't have been; the bath was nearly opaque. Moody swirls of dried flowers made patterns in its surface, and the salt had clouded the water, obscuring my body.

"You need someone to keep an eye on you," she told me.

"I don't—"

"Not forever. Just for now," she said. "You've experienced trauma. Again. You can't be alone."

I felt myself accepting it, sliding deeper under the water's fragrant surface, my eyelids heavy. Maybe I could nap, just for a little while. Distantly, I heard the industrial, wood-paneled bathroom door slide open behind me. Then I heard Andrea's voice.

"Thanks, sweetheart. Maeve? It's only Rob with the towels," she said, but the heat of the water was getting to me. I was so tired. Too tired to respond, or even to open my eyes. I made efforts to nod. My head felt leaden.

"Of course," I heard Rob say, as if from a distance. "Do you need anything else?"

I didn't hear her reply.

18

I awoke in a cold sweat, disoriented, my heart pounding. I was apparently experiencing the mother of all hangovers. The night returned in snippets: dinner, the casserole that roiled in my stomach and on my breath, fighting to make its way from my body. I pushed it back down, holding my breath until the urge to vomit passed. Then I fumbled for my phone. 6:07 a.m. Fuck. The bath. Andrea. My head was pounding. I couldn't remember what had happened, how I got to my bed.

A night of too much drinking on too little food had likely led to a blackout. I reached for my Klonopin, eager to fall back into its hazy, medicated embrace, allowing it to suppress the rapid beating of my heart. I craved its calm. I fumbled in the morning's dim and my hand collided with the bottle, which shot off the nightstand and bounced around the floor. I jumped out of bed, heart racing. I hadn't heard its telltale rattling of pills.

"No. *No*," I muttered, thrusting open the blinds and blinking in the harsh glare of morning light that threw the disorder of my room into sharp relief. The bottle lay on the floor by my bed, and I practically leaped on it. My heart sank. *Empty*. I must have taken all my remaining pills the evening before. That explained the blackout. I had no money left. No access. A churning anxiety twisted my stomach. I sank onto the bed and pressed my hands to my forehead. Then I heard it.

A low rumbling—almost a growl—came from the hall-way, followed by a thud and a long grunt. Whatever it was, it was likely what had woken me up. I pulled my body from my bed with no shortage of effort; I ached everywhere. My hair was still wet from the bath, and I was wearing a fresh T-shirt and underpants. My entire *body* was shrunken. Even my underwear—not *mine,* but a pair Andrea had purchased for me—felt a size too big. I'd been stupid to drink wine after weeks of sporadic eating.

The noises in the hallway grew louder and more aggressive. Grunts. Frantic scrabbling. I stood in front of the door to the hall, willing myself to open it. Who was making noise at such an early hour? I placed a hand on the knob, then heard Andrea's voice, panicky.

"Emily! Emily, what are you doing?"

I flung open the door, no longer terrified by the possibility of what was on the other side.

I should have been.

I'd thought I'd find a caged beast, but what I found instead was Emily. She was wearing a long white nightgown that clung tightly to her pregnant form, and she carried a knife. She stabbed the knife repeatedly into the body of one of the NewLife dolls. The preemie models, I remembered Andrea saying. The baby was small enough for Emily to hold in her hand, small enough for me to fear she'd slice straight through it into the fragile skin of her palm. Andrea glanced at me and shook her head in warning, then moved forward, taking a step toward Emily. Emily wielded the knife high, seemingly unaware of our presence, and slashed it down on the doll, which was quickly becoming a heap of shredded rubber.

"Put it down, Emily," Andrea instructed in a measured tone.

"I don't. Want. This. Baby," Emily shouted, railing against the newborn in her arm.

"It's okay, Emily. You'll be okay." Andrea uttered soothing sounds like a mantra, but I knew my cousin. She was shaken by her own lack of control over what was unfolding.

Emily lowered the knife to hip level and focused on Andrea for the first time.

"I don't want it!" she shouted. "Do you hear me? I don't want another one." Andrea reached for her, but Emily slashed the knife through the air, allowing the baby to roll from her grasp to the floor.

"Rob! Micah! Where the hell are you?" Andrea yelled into the void of the house. Distantly, Henry began to cry.

"Emily, you're going to be okay," Andrea continued, moving carefully in Emily's direction. For a moment, Emily seemed to deflate. Then Andrea said, "You love this baby. You're just overwhelmed."

Andrea's reminder changed something in Emily, who froze. Then she bared her teeth. She turned the knife inward, blade facing her mounded front. She gripped the handle with both palms, dragged the blade up, readying for its descent.

She screamed, loud and guttural, and she sliced the blade through the air.

"No!" The shout came from Andrea or Emily.

The feeling of movement beneath my feet, belatedly, like a memory.

The muted sound of the blade against flesh.

I had her in my arms by the time Rob rounded the corner. The blood was everywhere. I'd been too late. She was shivering, tearful, in shock. Breathing low and shallow.

"What is this?" Rob's face betrayed his horror.

"Quick, Rob, call the ambulance," I ordered, suddenly aware of my nearly naked state and Emily's thin nightgown. "Then get us some robes. We need to keep her warm."

"I'll get them." Andrea eyed us warily. "Rob, you go make the call." Suddenly I felt alert, more alert than I had in weeks, as I encircled Emily's damaged body with my own. She felt frail, despite her girth. Her tears mingled with the damp of my sweat.

"Emily," I said, my voice clear—the sight of her had shocked me out of my fog. "What happened?" I was asking to keep her with me, not because I expected an answer. But she looked at me, her eyes bright and focused for a moment.

"I don't know," she said. "I love her, Maeve. I really do." She struggled for breath. *I love her.* The daughter she was carrying? Or my cousin? I didn't have time to wonder.

Then Emily jerked back, her spine stiff.

"I understand now," she whispered, her eyes unfocused. "You were never the problem, were you?"

"What?" I stared, confused.

"Poison. It's all poisonous." Her words were slurred. She was in the height of delirium, ranting and out of her mind with pain.

"Shh. You're okay, Emily. Just stay calm."

"You need to get out of this house," she told me, her voice clear for the first time. She grasped my forearm with surprising strength, her manicured nails biting into my skin. "It isn't safe for you here."

I heard Rob's feet on the stairs, Andrea's lighter patter behind him.

"Poison," she repeated, her words nearly incomprehensible now. Her head lolled downward, toward her broken body. "She poisoned me to you."

"To the baby? Who did? What do you mean? Emily?" But she was gone.

19

The following minutes passed in a blur. Emily was breathing, but unconscious, and then Rob was there with a blanket for her and a robe for me and sirens were blaring in the distance. Rob wrapped Emily tenderly in the blanket and lifted her in his arms, careful not to connect with the wound, which gushed blood from just above her abdomen. I pulled on the robe as the EMTs rushed up the stairs and took Emily from Rob. Andrea stood behind them, looking lost.

I watched as they loaded her on a stretcher with brutal efficiency. Then they were gone.

"Where's Micah?" I thought to ask. "Is he asleep? Someone needs to tell Micah. And Henry. Where is he?"

"I'll drive him to the hospital," Andrea said, all business. She began moving in the direction of Micah's room, invigorated with new purpose. "I'm sure they're both asleep. You two stay here with Henry while Micah and I are gone." Rob knelt to pick bits of rubber—now completely mutilated—off the floor.

"We should go to the hospital," I told him. "She'll be scared. We need to be there for her. We—"

"Andrea has it all under control," Rob said, his voice flat. "It's not for us to worry about."

"How can you be so callous? Don't you care?" My voice had risen in pitch. I was light-headed and disoriented.

Rob allowed himself to sink to the floor, still clawing a bit of rubber from a deep gap in the wooden floorboards. In the distance, I heard Micah's voice, loud and tense, and he and

Andrea clambered down the back stairs. A door slammed and they were gone.

"This is Micah's fault, you know," he said. "Andrea will certainly agree. Emily's done this before. He was supposed to look after her."

"What?" I took a step back. "What has she done before? She's stabbed herself?"

"Not that," Rob said. He raked a hand through his hair. "I'm just as horrified as you are, Maeve. Believe me. But we need to maintain status quo for Henry's sake. Micah and Andrea are on their way, and I'm sure Andrea's already called her therapist in the city, and he'll meet her there . . . I'll have to take Henry to his grandparents' later. *Emily's* parents," he clarified. "Micah hasn't talked to his parents in years."

"She has a therapist for this?" I was shocked by how blithely Rob ticked off the list. As if they'd been through it a hundred times.

"She went through this the last time, too. She has prepartum psychosis," Rob said grimly.

"And she got pregnant again? Knowing that, and when she didn't even want a second child?" I put my head in my hands and paced the hallway. "How could you have let this happen? Andrea was supposed to be her life coach. How could you both have *allowed* this?"

"Andrea hasn't been her life coach in years," Rob explained. "And Emily is a grown woman. Andrea and I can't allow or disallow anything. Emily wants the baby. She does. We've all wanted a girl for her since . . . well, for a long time. She just thinks she doesn't." His voice began to rise, to take on a more animated, angry quality. "She isn't in her right mind. She needs dedicated care. Maybe if Micah had been a better partner, that piece of shit . . ."

My mind snagged on something Rob had said.

"Why a girl?"

Rob looked at me strangely. "Isn't that every woman's dream? To have a little girl, a mini me? Girls rule the world. Who wouldn't want to have a hand in that?" Now his tone was serene.

"No," I said, shocked. "No, it isn't every woman's dream."

"That's right. You've made it clear. Your path is different."

I studied his face. Reached for the bloodied knife, discarded behind me. It was a butcher's knife. She'd gone for the sharpest, deadliest knife in the house. It was a miracle she hadn't done more damage.

"Rob, what happened last night?" I asked him, fortified by the knife in my hand, unbothered by Emily's blood smearing into my palm. Power wasn't something I wielded easily or well. I had learned early that very little about a woman could be weaponized.

Why do women manipulate men? Ryan had asked me once.

Do we? I'd replied, genuinely curious. Did we? *If we do,* I told him, *it must be because sometimes it's the only power we have.*

Now Rob eyed the knife in my hand and held my gaze. His was inscrutable.

"You came into the bathroom with towels," I told him. "I remember hearing your voice. Then I don't remember anything. I'm sore all over, and—"

"Whoa, whoa." Rob held up a hand. "You started passing out almost immediately after I came in," he said. "You were in a bad state. It took both of us to hold you upright. You practically fell once, which was scary. You were a mess. We wrapped you in a towel and I carried you to bed. Have you been taking too much Klonopin? You're jittery, Maeve. You're showing all the signs of some sort of withdrawal."

I nodded, disoriented. "I didn't realize I'd been taking too much," I protested weakly.

"We never would have given you wine, had we known things had gotten bad." Rob's forehead was creased with worry. "Andrea pulled some clothes on you, and we left."

"Okay." I nodded, taking a deep, steadying breath. "Okay, that makes sense. Sorry." It did make sense. Way more sense, in the light of day. "I'm sorry, I'm just . . ."

My words faded as Rob's phone began to ring. Andrea's name flashed across the screen. Rob held the phone to his ear.

"Uh-huh," he said. "Uh-huh. Okay. Oh, thank god."

When he hung up, I found myself scratching violently at my scar. I stilled my hand.

"Well?"

"She's going to be okay," he said, the relief palpable in his voice. "They both are. She didn't hit the baby or any vital organs. She'll be held overnight then go to the hospital in the city tomorrow. She'll be under observation by her psychiatrist there for a while."

"So much blood," I started. I was still feeling light-headed.

"She's going to be okay," Rob repeated. He stood, taking me in his arms. I smelled faint traces of whiskey on his breath. He pressed me to his chest, folding his arms around me. It felt good, comforting.

"You might want to lay off the wine for a while," he suggested gently, when he released me. "At least until you're feeling better."

"Yeah, you're right."

"Just give that to me," he said, gesturing to the knife and my palmful of severed baby parts. "I'll clean it up. Go get dressed. Maybe a trip to the farmers market is in order. What do you think?"

I nodded. I was willing to do anything, in that moment, to make everything seem okay again.

"Sure, I'll go," I told him. Rob's face broke into a grin, but I couldn't stop thinking about Emily's words.

It isn't safe for you here, she'd said. Prepartum psychosis. Her body had turned against her. Who was the "you" she'd been addressing? Her baby? Herself? I nearly laughed at my initial assumption that she'd meant her cryptic message for me. It was safer for me here than anywhere in the world. This house, I realized for the first time, was the only place I'd ever been where I didn't feel followed. I merely felt watched.

20

After breakfast, I shot off a quick email to Elena and heard back within minutes. She expressed gratitude that I'd finally gotten in touch, because they had more than they could handle. She didn't address any of my questions about her daughter or catching up. She didn't ask why I never completed the previous job. It seemed our friendship was a thing of the past. She told me she could pay premium for a quick turnaround. I accepted, and she sent over the novel—a benign historical romance, something midlist and forgettable. It would be an easy job—no major plot overhauls—and it paid double the usual rate. It would keep me occupied for now, and I was grateful for it.

The hours with the manuscript flew by, restoring a sense of normalcy I hadn't been sure I could reclaim. Purpose, even. It was funny how the smallest of tasks can level you, putting you back on a plane with the rest of humanity. I'd felt so dissociated; now, without my meds, I was starting to feel clearer-headed. Part of me felt guilty for *wanting* to return to regular life in the wake of Ryan's death. But the rest of me knew I had to.

I took a break only once, to get a glass of water, padding downstairs in my sweatpants and T-shirt. I could hear Rob in the sunroom, talking on his phone.

"Babe," he was saying, "we were lucky it went so well. But I don't like this new plan. There are too many variables." I'd been about to turn on the kitchen faucet, then I paused to eavesdrop, feeling only the tiniest pangs of conscience.

"Uh-huh." A note of panic in his voice. "You're right. I

spoke out of turn." An odd formality to the language—if he hadn't said *babe,* I'd never have known it was Andrea. Curious, I peered into the room from my vantage point in the kitchen. I could see the back of his head—a tuft of dark hair—rising just above a wing chair, facing south toward the opposite window and the trees beyond. His left hand curled around the arm of chair, gripping it tightly. His knuckles were red and raw. "I apologize . . . Of course . . . Of course." His tone had taken on an obsequious quality. "Yes, sweetheart, that sounds like the right course of action. I'll prepare."

Prepare what? I wondered, as I moved silently back to the kitchen sink and turned on the faucet full blast, announcing my presence. I filled my glass and pretended to be surprised when Rob entered the room.

"Hi there," I said, giving him a little wave. "I didn't realize you were back already."

"Yep," he said, seeming distracted. "I got back half an hour ago and was just catching up on some work. And connecting with Andrea. She hit the road a while ago and should be here in an hour or two."

"How is everything?" I asked. "How did it go with Henry?"

Rob shrugged. His face appeared wilted, the bags under his eyes pronounced. For the first time since I'd met him, he looked middle-aged. "It was tough," he admitted. "He was understandably confused about where his parents were, but I think his grandparents distracted him well enough with ice cream and an iPad. And Micah will be there to collect him soon." I felt a pang, remembering exactly how it felt to be yanked away from family and abruptly placed in someone else's care. At least Henry knew his grandparents.

"Emily is unfortunately going to be in the psych ward for a while," he explained. "She wound up being transferred immediately to the hospital in Manhattan. Andrea went over there to be with her and Micah." He opened the cupboard and reached for a bottle of scotch, pouring himself a few fingers' worth. "Emily's on suicide watch until she delivers."

"Oh my god. That's awful." I was shocked. Emily wasn't suicidal—or at least she hadn't seemed that way to me.

"Better than them thinking her intent was to kill the baby," Rob pointed out. He pulled out a chair at the kitchen table and motioned for me to join him. "That was the alternative. Micah and Andrea spent the whole morning trying to prove she was merely suicidal and not murderous. It's splitting hairs, really. She could still go to trial after the baby's born. But Andrea thinks it's unlikely, if she's compliant. Anyway. All that matters is the baby's safe."

"Rob, that's awful." I sank into the chair across from him, too sickened to bother disagreeing with his assessment.

He sounded tired. "The other thing is . . . well. You know Emily's essentially the face of NewLife. Andrea wants to respect her privacy, of course. She's announcing on the website that Emily's on bed rest for the duration of her pregnancy. It isn't so far from the truth." I nodded. That level of damage control seemed reasonable—even thoughtful, insofar as it protected Emily's privacy. "The only problem," Rob went on, "is that Emily was supposed to host the NewLife retreat here in September. It's too late to cancel, so Andrea's trying to get up to speed and handle it herself. It's a dozen people for a full week of hikes, meditation, coaching, motherhood workshops . . . that sort of thing. We'll have to prep the guest rooms. There's a lot of work to be done."

Well, that explained the cryptic phone call. "Maybe I should get out of your way before all this goes down," I suggested carefully. Truthfully, it was the first I was hearing of the retreat, and I wasn't sure I could handle being plunged into a group of NewLife enthusiasts for seven straight days, so soon after everything else. A two-month deadline would be a good motivator for me to figure my life out and get back to the city.

"Actually, we'd really appreciate a hand around here, when you're up for it," Rob said. "If you don't mind, of course. How are you holding up?"

I hesitated. "I can help for a little while," I said cautiously. I definitely didn't want to seem ungrateful, after all Andrea and Rob had done for me, and now with Emily gone, they were in a tight bind. "I'm feeling a little shaken, but for the most part okay. Thanks for asking." I curled one leg under the other and took a long sip of water. "It was really scary. Kind of a wake-up call. A brutal reminder that you never really know who's suffering."

Rob nodded. "It's hard to step out of ourselves sometimes and think about the bigger picture," he said. "What you went through is no small thing. I know you said your relationship with Ryan was casual, but it's clear you cared a lot about him."

"I did." I looked down and caught myself rubbing at my scar again. "I really did." I cleared my throat, thinking of the empty pill bottle on my nightstand and feeling shaky. Then I thought of Emily's desperation as she plunged the knife into her abdomen. That wouldn't be me. It couldn't. "I'm ready to start taking care of myself again."

Rob cleared his throat. "I'm really glad to hear that. Because Andrea has had one of her well-intended–slash–possibly misguided ideas, concerning dinner in a couple of days."

I looked at him blankly. "What's that?"

"Don't kill her, please. She meddled a bit. Your phone was lying out last week, and Andrea saw a call coming in from Tyler and picked up."

"*What?*" I clenched my glass hard, feeling my cheeks flame. "What would possess her to do that?"

"Yeah." Rob looked embarrassed. "You know Andrea means well." He fluttered his hand as if to say *What can you do?* "You were sort of out of it. I guess Andrea saw texts and missed calls from Tyler, and when she happened to see an incoming call, she felt bad for him. She picked up to, I don't know, explain. And put him out of his misery."

"She explained what happened with Ryan?" I was fully livid then. "It wasn't her place to tell him that. That's my business."

"She just told him you'd lost someone close to you and that you'd be in touch when you were feeling better."

"Ugh." I rested my forehead in my hands. "I guess there are worse things, but I wish she hadn't said anything at all."

"You know Andrea," Rob cajoled. "Her intentions are always pure. I really think she was trying to help, so Tyler didn't feel as though you were blowing him off."

"Well, who cares even if I was? What's her investment in that?"

"I don't know." Rob shook his head. "She gets these ideas in her head . . . She saw how much fun you two had at his restaurant that night, and she didn't want you to miss out on some amazing connection."

"Okay," I said slowly. It was true that I'd been ignoring my phone. I'd only half registered the texts and calls from Tyler when they'd rolled in. Partly because I'd been so out of it, and partly because being with Ryan again had made me feel more than a little guilty about my side flirtation.

"So what does all this have to do with dinner?"

"She invited him over for dinner on Saturday. I guess she took down his number and promised to give him updates on how you were doing. Then, after today, she just wanted to do something positive to lift everyone's mood."

"*What?*" Now I was mortified. "I'm not a child, Rob. I don't need this kind of assistance."

Rob raised both hands in the air. *Don't shoot the messenger.* "Take it up with your cousin," he said. "Frankly, Maeve, this might be more about her than you. I'll tell you one thing: she's hell-bent we restore normalcy to this house, after what happened today. She thinks this'll help you get back on your feet. Would it be the worst thing to humor her? She's had a tough time of it too, you know."

"Maybe you're right. It's been a long day. As you know. That's fine. I'll do whatever Andrea wants for dinner Saturday." One evening two days from now wouldn't kill me, would it? And part of me—though it felt like a guilty betrayal of Ryan's memory—was even excited at the possibility of seeing Tyler again. I pushed back from the table, filling my water at the sink one last time. I'd been largely in bed for three weeks, and the amount of activity I'd put in today had wiped out my reserves.

"I'm going to take a nap," I told Rob. "I'll catch up with you two later about Saturday." I walked out of the kitchen before he could reply, and ascended the stairs.

Once in my bedroom, I picked up my phone and scrolled through my texts until I found Tyler's name. Sure enough, there were several more texts that had gone unanswered. The first was a brief apology for not having gotten in touch sooner. Would I like to go out again? Sober, maybe? The second was a simple *Are you okay?* As I stood there scrolling, I felt my heart twinge. The third: *I'd love to talk. Call me when you get a chance.*

I hesitated, my thumb hovering over the keypad. Then I typed *I'm sorry I didn't get back to you sooner. I'm looking forward to seeing you on Saturday*, and hit Send.

I placed the phone back on my nightstand to charge, then stared at Phoenix for a long moment. The grief doll had been reclining against the pillows on my bed, and it suddenly seemed like an intruder. I picked it up and tossed it in the closet. After what had happened that morning, I was sure Andrea would understand.

I lay back on my bed and closed my eyes. The funny thing was, I realized, I sort of missed having the doll nearby. I was startled by the epiphany, but maybe I shouldn't have been. Andrea had created a company specifically tailored to the needs of women, to their grief and rebirth. Why had I thought myself immune to that? The doll had been a minor comfort all those weeks, just as Emily had promised it would be.

I tossed and turned for fifteen minutes before I returned to my closet, almost against my will. I removed Phoenix from the closet floor, where she was reclining atop my dirty laundry, and placed her instead on a small wooden chair near the bureau, where she could preside over my sleep.

21

Early Saturday evening, a few hours before Tyler was due to arrive, I took stock of my appearance in the downstairs bathroom. I'd rested all Thursday and Friday, and now I regretted not tackling my appearance sooner. I hadn't bothered to put effort into my upkeep for so long that I worried it was beyond me. Damage had been done. Unbuffed skin cells had formed weather-beaten layers on my face. My pigmentation was uneven, my pores inflamed. Rough patches of keratosis pilaris covered my thighs, where I hadn't bothered to shave or exfoliate. My hair was the thinnest it had ever been. Seeing Tyler again felt fraught. I shuffled to the kitchen, where Andrea was beginning meal prep.

My cousin looked up as I entered and clapped her hands. "I'm making some paella and a simple galette for dessert. We have tons of canned pears I've been meaning to put to use."

"What can I do to help?" I asked, resigned.

"Oh, just go and get yourself ready," Andrea said, looking pointedly at my pajama bottoms and sweatshirt. "Then maybe you can help set the table." I went back upstairs and turned on the shower in the guest bathroom. I stripped off my clothes, accidentally catching sight of myself in the mirror, and saw a false promise of what it meant to be a woman. I thought back to Andrea's request, trying to entertain the idea of changing my mind, but I couldn't. My cousin had forgiven me for ruining her life when we were children, and for refusing to mend it now, and still she offered me the only thing I'd ever wanted: a family, a home. It struck me that I was someone who would forever take from the world without giving.

I hated myself then more than I ever had, even on the worst days after the raid on the Mother Collective. I felt hollow inside and refused to be filled.

How had I let myself sink so low? I'd been submerged since Ryan died; everything had been thick and muted. But I didn't want to feel that way anymore. I filled the water glass by the sink. I gulped it down, realizing I'd only ever used that cup when swallowing pills. No more drugs, no more alcohol, no more numbing of emotions with hazy nights and underwater days. I hadn't seen Ryan for who he was until it was too late; I wasn't about to make that same mistake with Andrea. I would start doing more for my family.

I stepped into the scalding water, letting it stream over my shoulders and chest. It was so hot I could hardly stand it; I had to will myself to stay. I wanted it all gone—not just the events of the past month but also the baggage I'd carried with me all my life. I wanted it burned off me until all that was left was a new, shiny layer of personhood. I no longer wanted to fight. I wanted a rebirth.

*   *   *

I leaned back in my chair, cradling my water glass to my chest. Tyler was weaving elaborate patterns in the air with both hands to illustrate his story. I couldn't have said what the story was about, only that he'd been surprising me over and over with his quick-witted commentary on books, politics, and pop culture.

He'd worn a black T-shirt and black skinny jeans to the house, and his lean, muscled arms were on full display as he tapped the table and jabbed the air. Andrea and Rob were listening attentively.

"We were all so mad at him then, but to tell you the truth, it was a relief not to have to sleep in a filthy bus anymore, stealing sponge baths in gas station bathrooms. We were just privileged NYU kids at heart." Tyler caught me staring and winked. He'd been telling us about the band he'd been in in college, and how it had opened for Ben Folds once. Then the lead singer had knocked up his girlfriend and quit, leaving them all in the dust for a suit job at a wealth management firm. "There I go rambling again," he said. "Like any of this is interesting to anyone but me." He laughed at himself and took a long sip from his wineglass. Andrea leaned forward, her elbows resting on the table, chin propped on her clasped hands.

"No, no. Tell us more. You've lived such a bohemian life," she said, causing me to snort with suppressed laughter. "You know, Maeve works in publishing," she went on, cuing me. "There's probably some overlap there with the music industry, don't you think? The hustle, the way authors get pitched, the whole restructuring that happened with the digital boom." For a second I felt a flash of panic. I didn't want to get into my floundering career.

"Book publishing, right?" Tyler looked at me admiringly. "I remember you said you're an editor. There's tons of overlap. What house are you with?"

"Former," I corrected, spearing a bite of chicken. "I was formerly in publishing. I got fired recently."

"Oh, *fired* is such a harsh term," Rob interjected. "They were doing some restructuring," he told Tyler, by way of explanation. "And Maeve's been inundated with freelance work since then. You ask me, these jokers didn't want to pay for benefits and all that. They clearly still need her but are cutting back on costs."

I hadn't told Rob any of this, and it meant a lot that Andrea had.

"You don't want to be there anyway," Andrea said, with a dismissive wave of her hand. "You're better than whatever TikTok star is the next big thing. Fiction is *your* thing, Maeve. You've always had such a wild imagination."

I stiffened. *TikTok star?* I definitely hadn't told Andrea about Mallory's latest acquisition—the one that made her indispensable.

"How did you—"

"Relax, Maeve." Andrea fiddled on her phone for a second, then showed me her screen. *EW* had announced Quokka's deal with Mallory's newest author, who had more than 70 million followers on all his platforms combined. "It's all over the news," Andrea informed me. "But really. Better that you didn't get trapped into doing stuff you weren't passionate about. Money doesn't have to be the bottom line."

"Especially when it doesn't translate to a raise," I agreed, sighing. "You're right."

"Wow," Tyler said, peering at Andrea's phone before turning his full attention back to me. "So what types of books did you edit, then?"

"Fiction, mostly," I told him. "I'm still doing it, just as a freelancer." I felt my shoulders relaxing, my spine straightening. Talking about work, for whatever reason, had always made me feel calmer—more confident—than I typically was in social situations. I genuinely enjoyed work, for one. And for two, I felt a sense of ease at my job that I lacked in my personal life. They were inversely proportional.

"So what, you fix commas and stuff?" Tyler went on. I felt myself bristle in annoyance, then he gave me a wink. "I'm kidding! I know that's not all an editor does. I love reading. I read *Dear Scott / Dear Max* in my twenties. Max Perkins," he clarified, when I looked at him quizzically. "F. Scott Fitzgerald's editor."

"I know Fitzgerald's editor. I know who he was, I mean. I was just surprised—" I shook my head. "What I mean is . . . you're a Fitzgerald fan? I was obsessed in high school," I confided, leaning close. I'd known Tyler was well-read from our initial conversation at the bar, but I was excited to find we had even more in common than I had realized. We were seated on the same side of the table and it was only then that I noticed Rob and Andrea stealthily clearing away our dessert plates. I refocused on Tyler, trying not to blush.

"Big-time," he told me, angling his knees toward mine until we may as well have been patrons of a bar, seated at adjacent stools. "We had to read *Gatsby* for an English class in high school. I credit that melancholic midday party scene with turning me on to books."

"Okay," I said, delighted, "but can we agree that *Gatsby* is basically the worst of his books? *This Side of Paradise* was the best."

"I don't know if *Gatsby* was the worst." Tyler's tone was thoughtful. "I liked it better than *The Last Tycoon,* for sure. But I agree that *Paradise* was the best. With *The Beautiful and the Damned* in close second."

"Totally. Anything about debauched drinking and tortured love, basically."

He laughed. "Man. I wish I'd had you around to nerd out with on this stuff in high school. I couldn't talk to anyone about it."

"Did you grow up around here?" I asked, just as Andrea reentered the room. There was so much I hadn't bothered to ask him before, and suddenly I was full of questions.

"Sorry to interrupt! We're obscenely tired," she admitted. "It's been a really long day. Do you two mind if we head up to bed?"

"Oh—" Tyler said, rising from his seat. "I can get out of here. Thank you so much for the amazing meal."

Rob materialized behind Andrea. "No, no. You two hang out," he said. "Really. We're being so rude. It's only ten; you should absolutely stay." His tone was firm.

"I don't think so," Tyler said, examining the tablecloth. Why was he demurring?

"We insist," Andrea said firmly. "You're our guest, re-member? Good night, you two. See you in the morning, Mae. Rob and I are going antiquing in Hudson around noon and would love it if you came."

"Sure," I told her. "Of course." Tyler was still standing, awkwardly hovering between staying and leaving.

"You really can go," I told him, after they'd headed up-stairs. "Honestly. I won't be offended."

"I don't want to go," he said, seeming to choose his words carefully. "But—"

"But what? You have a girlfriend?" My tone was sharper than I'd intended. My mind flashed back to the weeks when he *hadn't* texted. Already defensive, already hunting for rea-sons to push him away.

"No!" He met my eyes, his own looking a little panicked. "It's not that at all. I'm . . . I'm afraid of getting carried away."

"Well, I appreciate that," I told him. "And you should go if you aren't comfortable. I'm having fun though, and I'm a grown woman. You can't get carried away on your own, I don't think. Unless there's something you're not telling me? Do you turn into a werewolf at midnight? Possess insatiable urges for blood?"

He bit his lip and shook his head slowly, smiling. "Nah," he said. "I'm good. Why don't we go sit somewhere more com-fortable?"

We moved into the living room, which was glass-enclosed and faced the woods of the backyard, an expanse now too dark to penetrate. We moved easily from sitting beside each other to curled into each other, my legs slung over his lap in a gesture of comfortable intimacy eons ahead of where we were. I couldn't remember putting them there; they just *were*.

"I'm going to call you Brennan from now on," Tyler said, tapping my nose. I pulled back to look at him.

"Why Brennan?" I asked, confused.

"Another hot, literary Maeve," he said. "She worked at *The New Yorker* back in the day. A friend lent me her biography. It was pretty solid."

"I've never heard of her." I lifted my phone and typed the other Maeve's name into the search bar. Her face was shrewd and beautiful. There were dozens of photos, but she wasn't smiling in any of them. I clicked on her Wikipedia entry. "Hey! It says here Maeve Brennan went crazy," I pointed out.

"She was unstable," Tyler allowed. "I blame it on the pa-triarchy."

"Sure you do."

"Usually that line works pretty well," he protested. I laughed and burrowed deeper into the crook of his arm.

"What brought you upstate?" I wondered aloud. "You're obviously engaged in books and film and music . . . Are you working on any side projects? Any writing? Not that the restaurant-bar combo isn't enough in its own right . . ." I trailed off, blushing. The last thing I wanted to do was make him feel like I thought what he was doing wasn't good enough. I'd met plenty of ambitious, smart men in New York. Tyler had conveyed more passion and genuine engagement with the world in the past two hours than most of them combined.

"I always worried that monetizing my passions would take away everything I love about them," Tyler confessed. "It sort of started to happen, that summer after college, when we were on the road with the band. We had a good thing going, you know? Then everyone got super intense about making it big. And the more successful we became, the more everyone wanted. It was this toxic cycle, and I knew at some point that nothing would ever be enough. We could have been on par with Aerosmith and it wouldn't have made us happy. I prom-ised myself, after that, that I wouldn't destroy the things I loved anymore. I'd just make money however I could. And use my downtime to enjoy what I love about life."

I nodded. His words had made my heart quicken; it was as if he was speaking directly to my own secret desires. I'd spent my life reaching for something bigger but wanting something easier. He'd somehow cracked the code. Everything I'd been doing—essentially validating my own ego with the glamor and prestige of it, all false motivators, in exchange for a life of constant scrambling—was thrown into harsh, naked relief. It was embarrassing. For the first time, I could imagine a different kind of life for myself. One with loved ones at the forefront, where ego took a backseat to the simple pleasure of reading a novel in the presence of a person you cared for. I wanted to see more of that life, to peel back the layers of it and discover what banal days looked like when you had people to call your own.

Andrea was the only person I'd ever really cared deeply about, it occurred to me then. The possibility that I could love a man—really love one, let one creep inside my heart—had never entered my mind. That kind of intimacy required truth. It would mean chipping below the veneer and airing the uglier stuff. It wasn't something I'd ever entertained.

"Do you ever get scared, looking out at that?" Tyler pointed out the floor-to-ceiling windows we faced, breaking my reverie.

"Not really," I said, shrugging off my ripple of unease. The fact was, it was nearly impossible not to be a little frightened in our big home in the middle of nowhere.

"It's so dark out there. Someone could be looking in now and we'd never even know," he said, pulling me close. "Many someones."

"You creep." I laughed, tickled his ribs. "Why would anyone do that?"

"Because they can. Because it's easy."

"You underestimate Andrea and Rob. I'm sure this place is rigged with a cutting-edge security system. The best of the best."

Tyler's eyes clouded, and he stared into the void of the backyard.

"Hey." I tugged at his T-shirt. "I'm right here. You seem a little . . . unsettled."

"I'm fine," he said, turning back to me, cupping my cheek in his hand. "What were we talking about before? Fitzgerald? Have we talked about the beguiling love of his life yet?" He traced my jawline with his index finger and thumb. "Because I think she's *fascinating*." He leaned in then and we were kissing roughly, my hand pressing against the back of his neck, willing him closer. He slipped his arm behind me, moving his palm to my lower back, his fingers creeping gently below the waistband of my jeans. He guided me down slowly, carefully, until I was lying on the sofa and his body hovered above mine. He moved from my mouth to my neck to my collarbone, teasing me with his tongue until I let out an involuntary gasp. Catching myself, I placed a palm against his chest.

"No?" he said.

"No." I laughed. "I feel like I'm in my parents' basement."

"Okay, okay." He pulled himself away, seeming almost relieved. "I guess there's no rush." He ran a hand through his hair and took a heavy breath. "I like you, you know?"

"I hope so," I said. "Isn't that the idea? I'm pretty sure it was Andrea's intention in orchestrating this whole thing."

"I just wasn't expecting it." He looked back outside. "Forget feeling like we're in your parents' basement." He laughed. "I feel like I'm cavorting in front of a chorus of deer."

"I hear deer are really good at keeping secrets." I curled back into him. He looped his arm around my shoulders and drew me against him. Our legs were propped on the coffee table, both sets intertwined. Maybe I could be close to someone. Maybe I could *date* someone, I thought. Maybe there was someone who wouldn't be afraid of my past, a person I could trust and respect. Maybe that was what all of this was about—the reason

Andrea and I got back in touch, the meaning of my lost job, the purpose I so badly wanted to believe existed behind these random sequences of events. All culminating in one thing: me learning how to let people into my life for real, not in the superficial way I'd collected Ryan and my coworkers.

"Andrea and Rob have taken such good care of me," I murmured, running a lazy palm over his chest.

"She's your cousin?"

"Yes." I was feeling relaxed, sleepy. "We were best friends as kids."

"As kids? And then what?" Tyler wanted to know.

"And then we lost each other," I said simply. "And found each other again."

Lying there with him, I thought about why I'd refused her. Why hadn't I wanted to give her something of myself that could make her as happy as she'd made me? My reasoning seemed nebulous, flimsy, and I wondered if it was yet another deeply ingrained response to intimacy. Maybe I was afraid to give of myself that way, to link myself to Andrea forever. Maybe I'd been horrified at the idea of bringing someone into the world who would perpetuate our bond. Of contributing to something meaningful and lasting.

I didn't want to be afraid anymore. I wanted deep ties. Commitments. I wanted to know I'd contributed to something bigger than I was. I resolved to talk it over with Andrea and Rob soon. To ask all the questions they surely had answers for. I'd even sit in on some of Andrea's NewLife retreat if she wanted. The only obstacle all along was me, I realized. There was no reason not to go all in. To finally, after all these years, give of myself.

Tyler and I fell asleep like that, intertwined on the couch. I awoke with a start around five a.m., my back screaming. When I straightened, he stretched sleepily, extending his arms over his head and revealing a sliver of his abdomen. Then he kissed me on the crown of my head. "I'm going to take off," he said, smiling down at me. "Can I see you again soon?"

I nodded. "How's tomorrow?" I asked. "And by that, I mean tonight?"

22

know we still need to go on a proper back-to-school shopping spree. Maybe we can go this weekend? I bought you this to tide you over for your first day." I can see Patty in the mirror as I brush my teeth in the bathroom that adjoins the room where I sleep. Her cheeks are flushed and she's smiling faintly. She lays a T-shirt and shorts on the bed, one above the other as if dressing a flat doll. She looks pleased with herself. It will be my first day ever at school, but I don't tell her that. I swirl water around my cheeks and spit into the sink, then blot my mouth with a towel and climb up on the bed next to her.

"It's pretty." The shirt is pale yellow with pink flowers. There are little sparkly pink circles sewn onto the petals; when I run my finger over them, they shift and change to purple.

"Sequins," Patty explains. She's watching me carefully. The shorts are long and narrow and yellow cotton like the shirt.

"It's the prettiest outfit I've ever seen," I explain. She looks startled at first, then smiles big and hugs me. I stiffen; I can't help it.

"Well, then." She pulls away and breaks the tags off the clothes.

"I've never had clothes with tags." I don't know where the Mothers got our clothes, but when something new showed up, it always had stains or loose threads or pilling. And all the clothes were in one place for sharing. We dug into the drawer and put on whatever fit best. Andrea always got first pick. Boy wore mostly tiny underwear and shirts that came down to his knees.

"Will there be boys at school?" It's the first time it's occurred to me. The hair on the back of my neck prickles.

"Yes." Patty's forehead squishes up into a pattern of wavy lines. "Tom and I were planning to talk with you about that tomorrow. There will be adult men there too—teachers—but we have asked for you to be assigned to a female teacher. The boys in your classroom will be your age. Is that okay?"

I nod. I think it will be. But I can't be sure. Patty and Tom explained there's nothing to be afraid of, with boys and grown-up men. But I know they're wrong. I think of the magic the Mothers used in times like these, and my pulse slows back to normal.

"If you feel uncomfortable at any time, even just a little, you can ask the teacher to help you call me. I'll tuck our number inside your lunch box, just in case you forget it."

"No way would I forget."

Patty laughs. It's the first thing she taught me, here at the new home. She made a game of it, giving me a square of chocolate for every time I remembered three, then four, then five, then seven, then all ten digits. I didn't try as hard as I could have, and when the game was over I was smeary with melted chocolate.

"Just in case," she repeats. "Now. Hop into bed. I'll bring French Louie in to sleep with you. Wake-up is seven o'clock sharp. You can always change your mind in the morning. We think this will be fun for you, but there's no rush, okay?"

I nod and climb into bed, pulling the covers up to my chest.

"I've got it under control," I tell Patty, and for some reason she laughs.

"Okay, sweetheart. I'll be right back."

On her way out, Patty pauses at my art table. She gathers the markers and places them inside their plastic cup. She organizes my drawings into an even stack, glancing at the top one, which is a drawing of the woods behind the Mothers' house. Patty tells me to draw my feelings, whenever I feel anything strongly, good or bad. When I drew the woods, I was feeling sick and crawly.

I feel sick and crawly now, but it's too late to draw.

When I wake up in the morning, French Louie bounds up to my pillow from the end of the bed and covers me in kisses. I close my eyes and lay my head back down, pretending to still be asleep, and he whines but retreats. By the time Patty comes in to officially get me out of bed, I have a plan.

"Be downstairs in twenty minutes," she says. "I'll have breakfast ready. How does baby-in-a-buggy sound to you? Tom's feeling inspired." She gives me a wink.

"Good!" I love the buttery, fried sliced bread with an egg in the center that Tom makes sometimes. It's the only thing Tom makes, as far as I can tell, but it's really good. He makes mine over easy so I can dip the small fried circle of cut-out bread in the yolk.

I hurry to pee, then I splash water on my face and brush my hair. After that I slip on my new outfit. It isn't right, but Patty didn't know. She's old and doesn't go out or meet anyone besides Tom. I saw the Mothers go out a hundred times, so I have a plan for making it right. I stand in front of the bathroom mirror and bunch up the fabric of the long sparkly shirt. I tie it in a big knot, but the shirt is meant to cover most of the tight cotton shorts, so even when I bunch it, there's still too much shirt covering my stomach.

I go to my craft table. I was hoping not to have to do it, but I can't go out like this. I pull the long shirt over my head and stand there, naked except for my shorts. Then I pick up my scissors and begin to cut. When I'm done, I slip the shirt back over my head. I run back into the bathroom and look at my reflection from every angle, turning this way and that.

It's perfect.

There's a mess of sparkles on the floor that I will clean up later, but I only have a few minutes before I have to eat breakfast. I run back to the craft table and sort through the plastic cup that contains all my markers. I find the red one and the blue one.

In the bathroom, I pull the cap off the red and run the tip of it over my mouth the way I've seen the Mothers do on the days they go out. I smack my lips. The taste is tangy and bitter, and I have to swallow hard in order not to gag. I turn on the faucet and run my mouth under the water, rinsing my tongue. When I straighten back up, there are smears of red on my chin. I grab my hand towel and scrub at it hard.

"Maeve! Time for breakfast." Patty's voice is faint, but it reaches me all the way in the bathroom.

"Just a minute!" I call back. I color my lips in again, re-sisting the urge to lick them this time. Then I uncap the blue marker and run it over my eyelids. When I'm done, it's per-fect. I look like them.

I run down the hallway to the stairs. The smell of but-tery fried bread drifts up and I take a deep breath, inhaling it all, reminding myself not to get used to it. If I get used to it, I'll forget how miraculous it is that it's there: this luxury, this good food and these clothes and the warm, soft bed I sleep in.

When I round the corner to the kitchen, Tom and Patty turn to me from their posts at the stove, where they are mix-ing, flipping, pressing. I lean against the door frame casually, letting their eyes rove over me. Is this what it feels like for Mother to be stared at? Patty's face is frozen, and Tom's eyes are wide, his neck flushed.

It feels like I've done something wrong, but it can't be. I did everything right.

I let out a high-pitched giggle. It echoes around the silence of the room, sounding strange even to me. "You like what you see?" It's a line I have heard Mother use a thousand times, late in the night. It's supposed to sound like play, but Tom and Patty don't say their line back: *Baby, you know I do.*

"What the fuck is she doing? That shirt doesn't cover half—"

Before Tom can finish bellowing, Patty swoops in and yanks my arm hard, dragging me out of the kitchen. I cry out, but she doesn't seem to care that she's hurting where her fingers twist the skin of my wrist.

"What have you done?" she hisses, when we're halfway up the stairs. I trip. She's moving too fast, and I fall against the carpeted staircase, skinning my knee. She hardly pauses for me to get to my feet, dragging me ahead so hard I stumble a second time before I catch my balance.

"What?" My eyes are filling by the time we get to my bedroom. "What did I do?" I feel tears rolling down my cheeks, and I wipe them with the back of my hand. It comes back blue.

Patty's eyes soften. She grabs a towel from the bathroom and holds it under the faucet.

"Here," she says when she's back. "Wipe off your face. We'll need to get cold cream, but blot it with water for now. What possessed you, Maeve?" She sits heavily on the mattress, then massages her forehead with both hands.

"I don't know what you mean," I choke out, pressing my face into the towel.

There's a pause.

"I know," Patty says after a minute, wrapping her arm around my shoulders and pulling me against her. "God. I know."

"I'm going to be late for school," I venture. Patty seems less mad now. Her eyes look sad when she turns to me.

"How about you start school tomorrow?" she suggests. "Today will just be you and me. I'll talk to Tom."

I nod. *Tomorrow.* Tomorrow, I'll know how to be.

23

"Are you seeing Tyler again today?" Andrea wanted to know. She was fiddling at her computer, ordering linens and other bedroom necessities for the retreat, which was only a day away.

"Is that okay?" I asked, feeling guilty. I'd spent almost every day for the past two months with Tyler, in lieu of pursuing freelance work or helping Andrea set up for the NewLife retreat. The house had populated around me with NewLife dolls in various stages of development. Delivery trucks had steadily streamed in with the spoils of Andrea and Rob's trips to antique shops around the Hudson Valley. Andrea had insisted on handling the planning of the week's menu as well as the procurement and prep of food, rather than bringing in a caterer for every meal. The first group of attendees was scheduled to arrive by chartered bus the following evening. I was starting to wonder what people were shelling out for the experience. It seemed high-end, but Andrea hadn't disclosed the financials, and when I'd checked the NewLife website, I'd noticed rates were available by inquiry only.

"More than okay," Andrea said. "I'm so glad to see you feeling more like yourself. I'll just be here prepping." She seemed cheerful about the undertaking, rather than daunted, whereas I felt guilty to have chosen that particular moment to indulge a crush.

Guilty—but preoccupied with what I'd begun to think of privately as a personal renaissance. I had a family. I was falling for a good person whose brain I was fascinated by, whose body I wanted, even though we hadn't explored fully the

depths of our sexual chemistry. I had some semblance of the
stability I'd lacked my whole life and tried so hard to find . . .
and all it had taken was opening my heart and trusting the
people around me, the simple acknowledgment that I didn't
have to go it alone. What had I been trying all those years to
prove?

I hadn't spoken to Andrea or even Tyler about it yet, but
I was reconsidering Andrea's proposition. What had seemed
like an egregious crossing of boundaries—a commodifica-
tion of my body, an act that could have lifelong emotional
consequences—now simply felt like a way I could give of myself to someone I loved. I wanted to be one hundred percent
sure before I told her. I was nearly there. Perhaps after the
retreat, when things around us had settled and there was time
for a private, serious conversation. I could almost picture it,
telling Andrea I could give her the thing she wanted most in
the world, an even exchange for what she'd given me these
months. My benevolence, my emotional growth, my ability to
behave generously toward the people I loved.

I found I liked the idea of my body being used for something generous and positive. For too long, its function had
been limited to pain and fear and longing. Now it could be
more, if I let it. In such a short time, Andrea had taught me
that connectivity was everything. How had she learned it, in
bouncing from foster family to foster family? How had she
been so much more enlightened than I, when I was the one
who had abandoned her and had by all accounts come out on
top, at least in childhood?

She had always been the better, stronger, smarter one.
The one the Mothers had loved best. Maybe *I* could finally
be better—stronger—than I was, for the sake of family. The
prospect frightened and thrilled me.

We didn't talk or think about the Mothers. It was as if
they'd never existed. As if our lives began the day that all

ended, separate courses destined to converge in the here and now. I had a home, a family, a partner prospect. As Emily had said, *What else is there?* The question had seemed offensive at the time, even ignorant. But now I wondered what exactly I'd been hoping to discover amid all that ceaseless striving.

"Is something about your coffee mug fascinating?" Andrea asked. I looked up and laughed, realizing I'd been staring at the lukewarm remnants of my coffee for several minutes.

"Just zoning out, I guess."

"Well you had a goofy smile on your face," Andrea informed me. "You look happy."

I pushed back from the table and crossed the room to where Andrea sat at the kitchen island, typing away at her laptop. "I *am* happy," I told her, wrapping my arms around her from behind. Andrea minimized whatever was on her screen before I could see it. Then she turned and gave me a peck on the cheek.

"I'm so glad," she said. "I knew you would be, if you learned to let yourself."

"Was it so obvious?" I straightened, looking down at her. Andrea's blond hair was pulled back in a low ponytail. She wore a white turtleneck and no makeup. She was radiant, angelic.

"You're one of the prickliest motherfuckers I know," she said, laughing. "Never have I had to work so hard for someone's trust. But you're worth it."

"Well, thanks for putting in the effort," I said. "I owe you one."

"You sure do. Now maybe you can help me. I am having a personal crisis. NewLife is driving me insane. This retreat is so much work! Like, should I switch careers? Should I be a manager or something instead of an entrepreneur?"

"Andrea," I said with a laugh, "what are you even talking about? A manager of what?"

She shrugged. "Just like . . . a successful person who manages . . . something."

I stood back, evaluating her. "Nah, I don't think you're the manager type."

Her jaw dropped.

I burst out laughing. "Girl, you are managing this entire retreat. That is exactly what you are doing right this very second."

"Brat," she said. Then she was giggling too. I wrapped my arms around my cousin again and leaned down to hug her, resting my head against her shoulder. These moments were it. There was nothing better—she had my whole heart. With maybe a small sliver left for a cute English major restaurateur.

*   *   *

Perhaps not shockingly, there wasn't much going on at night in our somewhat remote neck of the Catskills, which, I supposed, was why Andrea and Rob and I had spent so much time on their property—reading and talking in our own little bubble. It hadn't seemed stifling before, but now Tyler and I were struggling to find something to do.

"I can't believe there was a two-hour wait for the *diner*," he said, pounding his palm against the steering wheel in frustration.

"Hey." I put a hand on his thigh. "Relax. I don't care where we go."

"Maybe *you* don't, but I'm hungry, and it's irritating that we can't go anywhere within twenty miles of here because citiots flood every decent restaurant at the start of the weekend."

"It's just dinner," I said, taken aback. "And I'm one of those dumb city people."

"Not really. You don't live there anymore, at least."

"Ouch." I withdrew my hand. "I fully plan to, as soon as I can. What is with you tonight? I've never seen this side of you." *And I don't like it very much.*

"Nothing. I'm fine. Let's just try one more place. It's forty minutes away, but it's amazing." Tyler swore under his breath as we pulled out of the diner, and I tensed. His irritation had come out of nowhere, and it felt like a noose around my neck that tightened every time he made a sharp turn or drummed his fingers on the steering wheel. What started as a little bit of tension was looking more and more like a red flag.

"Look," I said to him, careful to keep my voice light. "Why don't we just grab a pizza and take it back to your place? When do I get to see your place?" I was teasing, sort of. We'd spent most of the past couple of months out at restaurants, hiking, or curled up together in my bed. We'd only been sleeping together for a few weeks—I hadn't been eager to jump into anything too fast—and when he'd nervously fumbled for a condom the first night, it had felt again like we were in high school, engaging in the nervous explorations of a couple more interested in getting it over with than in giving each other any real pleasure. In the morning, he'd been sheepish and I'd been anxious, wanting to reclaim our perfect, heightened haze and fearing one awkward moment would derail us altogether. I was anxious I hadn't been perfect, anxious he'd leave just as I was beginning to let him in.

"We're not going back to my place," he said stiffly.

"Like, ever?" I peered at him strangely. "Why not?"

He sighed, offering me a tight smile. "It isn't . . . as nice as what you're used to," he said finally. "It's basically a shack compared to Rob and Andrea's place."

"I don't care about that," I began, covering his hand where it rested atop the gearshift.

"*I* care," he said, removing his hand from mine and placing it back on the wheel. I was silent. He had professed not to take money seriously, to value a simple existence with the things he loved. But there it was. He cared just as much as any of us. We sat with the weight of his words. "I'm sorry," he said finally. "I'm not ready for you to see it yet. Can you be patient with me?"

I nodded, forcing a smile. It wasn't the first time it had occurred to me that Tyler was hiding something. But that was the voice from my past talking, the one that had sabotaged me all my life, preventing me from getting close to anyone until I'd formed a perfect glass house with myself as its sole occupant. I wasn't going to let anxiety stop me from seeing this thing through with Tyler. He was entitled to his privacy. And it had only been a couple months, I reasoned. It would be weird if he were spilling all his secrets at this stage.

We pulled into a narrow, partially filled lot. "Score," he said, letting out a breath. He pointed at the neon sign flickering "Open" in orange, fluorescent swirls near the entrance. "This is the best taco joint east of the Hudson," he announced, all his earlier tension seemingly vanished. He gave me an easy smile. It was odd how quickly he shifted from tense to relaxed. I could handle his mercurial tendencies if he could deal with my complete inexperience with emotional intimacy. And actually, I was more comfortable knowing he was flawed. The imposter syndrome was less intense during those moments; I didn't have to feel undeserving of what I was getting.

Twenty minutes later we were seated in a red vinyl booth, sharing chips and guac.

"So how old were you when you were adopted?" he asked, casually dunking a salted chip into the bowl of guacamole and emerging with an entire serving-sized scoop. I stiffened. Speaking of secrets...

"I don't remember telling you I was adopted," I said carefully. "Did Andrea say that?"

"Yeah," he said. "Sorry. I didn't mean to pry."

"No, it's okay," I said, drawing a deep breath. Tyler had

finally begun to chill out, and I didn't want to tip the scale. Besides, if I was going to get him to open up, I needed to be open with him. That meant giving him at least a basic over-view. But when were he and Andrea discussing these things? Had she called him, or had it come up organically sometime in the house, maybe when I was getting ready? If she accidentally let something slip, that was one thing. Going out of her way to tell him was something else entirely. It was a little odd, given that she preferred to avoid talking about those days.

"Andrea and I grew up together until she was eleven and I was eight," I explained. "Then we were put into the foster care system. I was adopted almost immediately."

Tyler looked confused. "Oh. I didn't realize you two lived together as kids."

Shit. Andrea must have mentioned my past without mentioning her own.

"Near each other," I hedged. "In the same neighborhood." This was the part that was hard. How could I be close to Tyler if I was lying to him? Why had Andrea broken the rules? Was she setting the terms of my relationship, sending the message that it was okay to talk about certain things and not others? "What else did she say?"

"Nothing really," he said. "She told me you were adopted; that's it." The waiter came and placed an enchilada in front of Tyler and shrimp tacos in front of me.

"Well, yeah, that's about it," I said. "Nothing to write home about. Could we get some extra salsa, please?" I asked the waiter, feeling Tyler's gaze burning into me.

"Look, Tyler," I said, trying to keep my voice even. "My childhood wasn't easy. I'll tell you about it sometime. Just not right now, okay?" It was the first time I felt I couldn't be fully open with Tyler. He knew some of the weirdest and darkest parts of me. I'd told him about the nightmares that plagued me almost nightly, my lack of any kind of real relationship in adulthood. He knew about Ryan, and my grief, and that I needed to move slowly. The only thing he didn't know about was my childhood.

He nodded, taking a giant bite of enchilada. "I understand," he said kindly. "We can talk about it whenever you're ready."

"Great," I said, feeling some of the tension in my shoulders subside. "Because I really want to have fun right now."

"Fun, I can do," he said. "Especially now that I'm not hangry."

"Hangry isn't real," I informed him. "Unless you're a toddler."

"Oh yeah?" he asked. "Is that so? Well then, I guess I'm a toddler. You know what else toddlers do?"

"Stop!" I squealed, laughing. But Tyler was already reaching back into the chip bowl, flinging a tiny blob of guacamole, slingshot style, at my head. I ducked just in time for the guac to sail past my head and hit the booth behind me.

"Real mature," I said to Tyler, but I was still smiling, and in it was a sense of relief. The tension had been broken.

Our high spirits continued in the car, all the way back to Andrea and Rob's. When we pulled into the driveway, he reached over and unbuckled my seat belt and pulled me toward him, kissing me hard until I was gasping for breath, then pulling back to tease me when I went in for more. I was hungry for him, leaning toward him, panicked by the sudden rush of full-body desire, aware only of my mouth on his and his hand slipping below the waistband of my jeans. Finally, he pulled back, his own breathing labored.

"I want you," he said. "But not here."

I nodded. He turned off the engine, and we ascended the dark stairwell, hand in hand. It was only nine thirty, but Andrea and Rob had made themselves scarce.

He kicked the door closed and pulled off my shirt, then led me to my bed. I lay on my back, his frame hovering above me. I shivered as his eyes roamed over my body, taking me in. I wiggled my hips, then drew my arms up to tickle his muscular forearms, trying to tempt him closer, to bridge the distance between us. His gaze was searing. I felt raw and vulnerable under its scrutiny.

"You're so beautiful," he told me. He pushed my arms above my head and let his lips wander from my neck to my chest. I was covered in goose bumps, my nipples erect. He paused on my right breast, flicking his tongue over its peak, and I moaned quietly. He moved to the left and stayed there until my entire body was writhing. Then he worked his way toward my stomach, still pinning my arms with one hand, and I felt my back arch toward him.

"I thought we'd try something a little different this time," he whispered. I looked for his eyes, but in the dim of the room I couldn't make out his expression. Was it a tremble of nervousness I'd heard? Or of excitement?

"What are we trying?" I asked. *Different* implied we'd done this before, countless times. *Different* didn't account for the fact that we'd only been having sex for a few weeks, that we were still discovering each other's bodies and comfort zones.

"It's a surprise," he said. "Do you trust me?" His voice quaked again, as if to say *Don't trust me.*

"I trust you," I told him. I *needed* to trust him. I needed to trust a man at some point in my life, and he was there in front of me, as good as any man. I needed him to prove me wrong about all the things I'd grown up knowing and fearing. More than that, I needed to *respect* a man, and respecting meant giving of myself in a reciprocal way. It went fully against my nature.

"I trust you," I said again, looking him in the eyes this time. Tyler rewarded me with a kiss.

"I like you, Maeve," he said. If I hadn't known better—in another situation—I'd have thought his voice sounded regretful, the words themselves inadequate.

"I like you too," I said, laughing awkwardly. One day, I hoped to love him, to prove all the broken parts inside me had been fixed. Tyler let me go, briefly, and rummaged in his backpack. At first I thought he was searching for a condom, but instead he brought out a long, narrow piece of black fabric. Then another, and another. He kept hold of one and set the other two on my bed. It astonished me that he'd planned this.

"It's a blindfold," he said, about the piece of fabric in his hand. "I'd like to cover your eyes and tie you up. Is that all right?" I hesitated. I'd used restraints and blindfolds before, with Ryan. That was when, if I was honest with myself, I didn't want to be treated gently by any man. I'd wanted punishment back then, so I could feel a measure of absolution.

I'd thought things with Tyler would be different.

But despite myself, I was aroused. My response to the sight of the blindfold was erotically Pavlovian. Intellectually I wanted respect, wanted to experience lovemaking at its gentlest and most cherished. I wanted what other, normal women had. On a more primal level, I *craved* punishment. Tyler waited expectantly.

I nodded.

I sat up and allowed him to tie the blindfold once, twice, to ensure there was no way I could see anything. He traced a finger down the side of my neck.

"Lie back," he said. I felt him draw my arms over my head and pull them uncomfortably taut while he made knots around my wrists and tightened the other ends to the bedposts. I shivered; my naked chest was exposed. I felt him unfasten my jeans, and I arched my hips to accommodate him.

He slid them down my thighs, pulling them past my ankles and abandoning them to the floor, where they landed with a light rustle. Finally, he removed my underwear. I was bare and trembling, my entire body vulnerable, and I could see nothing at all.

Then Tyler left the room, shutting the door behind him. Leaving me there alone, shaking. He was gone for a long time. Several minutes must have passed. My arousal transitioned to confusion and, finally, to apprehension. But, I reasoned, this was part of his game. When I reframed it that way, my heightened sexual awareness returned with a startling vengeance, until every nerve was firing, throbbing, begging for release. By the time the door opened again, I was breathless.

"You're back," I said. He placed a finger over my lips, and I moved to bite it, but he drew away. I felt the pressure of his body on the bed and rolled toward him as much as I could within the confines of the restraints. He flattened me onto my back with a calloused palm. He smelled like whiskey blended with vanilla, and I drank it in.

"Tyler." I uttered his name in a hoarse gasp. My pleasure was heightened by something new—fear—but the fear itself was beginning to crowd my consciousness. Soon it would block the pleasure out. Instead of answering, he placed his palm over my mouth. He lowered his body on mine, and began to touch me, gently at first, and then with more pressure.

I wanted his voice. I wanted to ask for it. He was silent, and I couldn't speak around his hand. I bit it lightly, hoping he would take the hint; instead, he simply accelerated his movements until I was panting against his palm. Then I felt him shift and enter me. I bit him harder then, sinking my teeth into his palm and causing him to jerk away with a grunt of

pain. Still he didn't speak. My heart was thrumming errat-
ically. It was impossible to distinguish panic from pleasure.

"Sorry," I whispered, tears crowding the edges of my eyes.
He didn't bother to respond. It was a sick, twisted game he
was playing, and I liked it.

He moved slowly at first, then quicker when the movements of my body betrayed my pleasure. Fear spiked again in
my brain, but the rational side of me knew it was my person,
the one I had agreed to trust. I allowed him to thrust wildly,
bringing me to an orgasm before he reached his own.

It was only when he came inside me, hot and pulsing, that
I realized two things: I had never come that intensely with
Ryan, not once; and Tyler hadn't been wearing a condom.

*   *   *

I awoke sore, curled against him. I turned over and met his
eyes. We hadn't talked about any of it the night before; he'd
simply exited the room to clean up and returned to untie me.
Then he'd cradled me against his chest and kissed the side
of my neck as if to establish a normal, postcoital comedown.
All night I'd slept fitfully, exhausted by my own confusion.
I'd consented to the blindfold. I'd known he wanted something kinky, something beyond the norm. I'd wanted it too.
And I'd indisputably been turned on, possibly more than
ever before. So why was it all bothering me to the extent that
I felt sick to my stomach, amped up, unable to sleep?

His eyes were wide and clear, as though he'd been awake
for hours.

"What was that last night?" I asked, resolving to be direct.

"I thought it was great sex," he replied. But the uncertainty
in his eyes betrayed him.

"No," I said. "No. Look at you. You've got guilt written all
over you."

"I thought you'd like it," he started. "Andrea said you liked it rough—"

"*What?*" I pulled back. "Andrea said that? Why were you and Andrea talking about my sex life? When is it that you two have so much time to talk behind my back?"

"It just . . . came up," he said lamely. I sat up in bed, securing the sheet over my chest with one arm. "How? When? When were you talking without me there? And why were you talking about this?"

"Maeve," he said, reaching for me. "We were just joking around. That night at my restaurant, I said how beautiful I thought you were, and she said something like *Well in bed she doesn't like to be sweet-talked,* and it went from there. I thought you'd like it, last night. You seemed to like it."

"That is so weird. Did Andrea also tell you not to use a condom too?" I snapped. "What was *that* about? Did it not occur to you that that's something we should have discussed? How do I know you aren't sleeping with other people? Have you been tested recently? Don't you care about your *own* health? What if *I* hadn't been tested?"

He looked down, ashamed. Then he began to climb out of bed.

"Where are you going?" I asked, shocked. "You aren't even going to bother talking this through?"

"I want to talk it through," he said. "But you're hysterical, and I think we should wait until we've both had some distance and a chance to calm down." He was being a coward, and he knew it. It was evident in his slumped shoulders and the way he averted his eyes.

"You're calling me hysterical. After *you* use my body however you want, scare the shit out of me, and neglect to use a condom. Are you seriously walking out on me right now?" I was fighting to control my rage; I couldn't remember the last time I'd been this furious. I'd slept with Ryan for a year—no pretense of dates, no pretense of love or romance—and he'd treated me better than Tyler had treated me after mere months as my supposed romantic interest.

"We can talk later," he said lamely, reaching for his jeans, which were lying in a bunch on the floor. He picked them up, and a small object rolled from one pocket and clattered across the floor, where it skidded and came to a rest against the leg of my bed frame. I looked over the edge and spotted it: a ring. Gold.

"What the actual fuck," I said to him. "Is that what I think it is?"

Tyler picked the ring off the floor. Met my eyes. He had the gall to look tragic, as though he were experiencing some sort of loss.

"You're *married*?" I shrieked, no longer caring about waking up Andrea and Rob. "Is that why we haven't been going to your house?"

"Maeve," he said, beginning to tear up. "I'm so sorry. Believe me. I never wanted it to be this way. I didn't think I'd start to care about you." He raked a nervous hand through his hair.

"Get out!" I shouted. He moved toward me, but I leaped out of bed, enraged. "Get the fuck out of here!" I yelled, shoving him toward the door until he turned and went.

I stood in my room like that—naked, my arms wrapped around myself—for a long time after I heard his footsteps reach the bottom of the stairs, then heard the front door open and close. I couldn't bring myself to get my robe until the thrum of his car engine filtered through my window, until his tires squealed down the driveway and away from the house. And then I did. I went through the motions of wrapping myself up, of sitting back on my bed, knees tucked to my chest, wondering how my trust had been so misguided.

Only then did I allow the full extent of my anger to wash over me. I gritted my teeth and imagined what I wanted to do to Tyler, the anguish I wanted him to feel. The ruthless sort of justice his betrayal warranted. I wanted him to feel as frightened and helpless as he'd made me feel. But Tyler wasn't worth despair or recriminations, I realized. Tyler had proven he wasn't worth anything at all.

24

I slept hard, until well past noon. Then I got up, threw on a sweatshirt and joggers, and looked for Andrea. The bus with the first wave of retreat attendees was arriving at seven p.m., and I wanted to be sure to catch her prior to a week of nonstop activity.

I found her sitting at her computer in the kitchen, perched atop a bar stool, as stunning as ever—her hair swept casually into a bun atop her head, her cheekbones a perfect blush pink, an oatmeal-colored sweater dress draped over her slender frame. When she saw me, she removed her reading glasses and placed them next to the computer.

"Are you okay?" she asked, a deep crease forming between her eyebrows.

"When did you talk to Tyler about my sexual preferences?" I asked her. My fingers, buried deep in the pockets of my hoodie, were shaking.

"What?" Andrea looked confused. She pushed back from the counter and slid off the stool. She grabbed my hand, and I allowed myself to be dragged into the living room and lowered to the sofa, where I burrowed into the corner cushion and blinked back tears. What had happened wasn't Andrea's fault, but I still wanted to know. She sat opposite me and curled her legs beneath her, her face betraying her concern.

"What's going on?" she asked. "Where's Tyler? I thought you guys were having a great time last night, so I figured I wouldn't wake you—"

I held up my hand to silence her. "He left around five

a.m.," I explained. Andrea pursed her lips as if to ask more questions, but I barreled along. "He was very rough with me," I told her. "He said you told him it's what I liked."

Andrea was silent for a minute, thinking. I waited her out.

"I think I said something that night at the restaurant, that first night," she admitted. She lowered her eyes. "Honestly, Mae, it was just a stupid joke. I was tipsy! I don't even know exactly how it came up." She shrugged helplessly. "God, did he—What did he do?" she asked, concerned. "Are you okay?"

"I'm fine," I told her. "He didn't do anything . . . physically . . . that I didn't condone." I paused. It was technically true, though the statement didn't paint an accurate picture. "He's a liar, Andrea. He's married. He didn't use protection, either, and obviously now I'm worried." I broke down, then, unable to hold it together any longer, said, "It wasn't violent; it was scary. And hearing him say you planted the idea—" I shuddered. "It felt like such a violation. This was a guy I trusted and cared about for two whole months."

"Wait a sec." Andrea had straightened. "He's *married*? And he didn't use a condom? First of all, let's take care of that. I have a Plan B I can give you. I got one ages ago at the pharmacy, when we found out I couldn't safely conceive, just to have around. In case. I never used it; you can take it. Stay here. Let me get it."

I nodded. At least that would be one minor relief in all of this. She stood up and covered me with a throw from the couch, as if to tuck me in firmly. Then she left the room in search of the contraceptive. A minute later, my phone buzzed in my back pocket. I pulled it out. Tyler's name illuminated my screen. I pocketed it again without bothering to look at the message. I didn't want anything to do with him, ever. Later, when I felt like looking at my phone again, I'd block him entirely.

Andrea returned with a small white pill and a glass of water. "It's a one-step," she told me. I accepted it gratefully, swallowing it quickly and downing the remainder of the water as she watched me.

"I'm sorry," she told me, her voice soft. "For what that fucker turned out to be, but also for telling him something so private. I never dreamed he'd . . . *use* that information, Mae."

"Yeah, well, it still wasn't yours to share," I said, my voice icy. "Nothing about my sexual preferences is yours to share. And if I'd thought you weren't trustworthy, I never would have told you that."

"You're absolutely right, and I'm so sorry." She shook her head. "It was a stupid thing to say. Please know I am furious with myself for breaking your trust." She grabbed my hands, and I searched her face. She looked genuinely disturbed—even sickened—by this turn of events. I didn't doubt she regretted it. But the fact that she'd thought it was okay to bring up, even tipsy, with a man I'd just started seeing . . . It didn't sit well.

"You need to respect my boundaries," I told her, as my phone buzzed again.

"God. Fucking *Tyler.*" I pulled my phone out of my pocket. Sure enough, there were seven messages from him.

"What's he saying?" asked Andrea, sounding worried. "Apologizing for being a married piece of shit, no doubt." She craned her neck, trying to see the screen.

"I'm not even interested in looking at his pitiful apologies," I admitted. "Now I'm going to have to get tested . . . And that's not the worst part," I said. I was embarrassed to hear myself choking up. "The worst part is, I'd decided—for whatever reason—that he was going to be someone I could try getting close to."

"Oh, sweetie," Andrea said, pulling me in for a hug. "Don't let this one asshole throw you off balance. He didn't deserve you."

"There were signs," I admitted, as my phone buzzed again. "He wouldn't even consider taking me back to his place."

"Maybe next time you move a little slower," she said, glancing at my phone, which was now vibrating loudly on the coffee table in front of us.

"Oh for god's sake. What could he possibly be saying?" I wiped my eyes and reached for the phone, unlocking the home screen with a quick swipe of my index finger.

I have to tell u smthing, the first text read, in a shorthand unusual for Tyler, who had claimed not to go in for that kind of thing.

Pls don't hate me

You already do, I know that

I was desperate, Maeve. Broke, a baby on the way

The restaurant's going under

I shuddered at this, a full-body tremor that didn't escape Andrea. What did him being broke have to do with the way he'd treated me? A baby on the way . . . Could he have been any more disgusting?

"What's he saying?" Andrea asked, an edge to her voice. "If he's asking you to forgive him . . . or making up some kind of sorry excuse to justify his lies . . . Well, Mae, you know you can't trust this loser anymore. Right?"

I ignored her. Tyler's texts were jumbled and incoherent.

I didn't know it would go that far

I did it for my family.

I'm so sorry, he'd written. *I'm a broke piece of shit. I thought if I could do one good thng, prove icould care for the baby, I'd be a better man.*

Definitely drunk. But why? Even for the worst wallowers, it was extreme. None of it made any sense, and his typing became more scattered as he went.

And again: *I didn't know theyd go that far.* More typos from the English major. The messages were the ramblings of some-one completely out of it.

"This doesn't even make sense," I said, frustrated. "He's

saying he did it for his family? What does that even mean?"
I started to type a reply, to ask him to explain himself, to explain away the piercing dread that had begun to work its way from my stomach to my chest. He was typing something too. The ellipses were moving again, indicating as much.

Andrea snatched the phone out of my hand.

"What are you doing?" I grabbed for it back, but she twisted away from me, deleting his existing texts and the new ones as they appeared on the screen.

"I think you need a break from this situation. I'm going to block him, okay?"

"Okay," I agreed. "I was going to anyway."

"I believe you," she said. "And I also believe it's hard. Do *not* unblock him or initiate contact. This guy doesn't deserve even the kindness of you reaming him out."

"Sure." I shrugged. "I'm just going to put it aside for a while. I'll read today and try to occupy myself. Maybe help you finish setting up the retreat and do yoga or something."

"That's great," she said. "Restore some normalcy. I am so sorry, Mae. This is all my fault. For inviting him over and encouraging it. You just . . . Well, none of us could have known."

"No," I said. "It wasn't your fault. He seemed like a nice guy. And I need to take some agency. You're not to blame for wanting me to be happy."

"On the bright side, at least you figured it out fast," she said. "What if you'd dated him for *years* before realizing he was married? What if you'd fallen in love with him?"

"I've never fallen in love," I told her. "I hardly expect to start now."

But that was the problem. I'd wanted to. I'd felt a spark of something different with Tyler. I'd felt more alive than I had with Ryan, or any other man. What worried me—on top of my suspicion that I wasn't capable of real love—was that I couldn't trust my instincts.

"Why don't you go get cleaned up," Andrea suggested. "I'm going to send Rob out to pick up some items I forgot for the retreat. I'll have him grab us lunch from the diner on the way back. What do you want? Avocado toast?"

"Sure," I told her. "That sounds nice."

"Maybe with a medium-boiled egg on top, the way you like," she suggested. I nodded, giving her as much of a smile as I could muster.

"Thanks, Mom," I joked lamely.

"I told you I'd take care of you," she said, returning my smile. "You'll see. By tomorrow this won't feel as immediate as it does now. Everyone will be here later tonight for the retreat and you'll be distracted. And by next week it'll be a distant memory."

"About that," I said hesitantly. "I was thinking I might go into the city while the retreat's going on, even if just for a couple of days. To take some meetings with former colleagues. See if I can rustle up some more jobs." Andrea paused halfway to the kitchen.

"Oh?" she said, furrowing her brow. "Well. Okay. I'm sure a day trip would be fine, but . . . I could really use your help around here."

"No, never mind," I said hastily. "I'll do it the following week. I can help however you need me." It was my guilt talking. I wanted some space. After what happened with Tyler, I knew it would be a long while before I could revisit the idea of giving Andrea a piece of my fertility. He had destroyed that for me. For a while, I needed my body to belong only to me.

*　　*　　*

I could really use your help. It was how I found myself distributing NewLife dolls as I greeted each guest at the door that evening. Give me your coat, take a doll, here's your gold-embossed name tag, please wear it for the first full day.

"Here you go," I said, pressing a doll with dark skin and rosy lips into the arms of a slender woman who'd made her way to the front of the line. "Welcome to NewLife!" The people in the group appeared to range from early twenties through late thirties; I pegged this one around twenty-eight or twenty-nine.

"She's beautiful," the woman whispered, misty-eyed, as though she were looking at a living, breathing baby.

"Andrea, I'm India," another—a redhead—gushed, reaching for my hand instead of accepting her doll. "It is *such* an honor."

"Oh, I'm not Andrea," I explained, removing my hand awkwardly as the group looked on with curiosity, clustered on the front porch like a bunch of hens around a prize chicken. "I'm her cousin, Maeve."

"I'm so sorry," the woman said, flustered.

"Happens all the time." I offered what I hoped was a reassuring smile. "Now let me—"

"You look just like her!" she said excitedly, cutting me off. She peered at me closely, scrutinizing. A lady wearing leather joggers and standing a few paces behind her nodded, looking awestruck. I could already tell Andrea was some sort of celebrity to these women. Strange. I'd thought I'd have to deal with their letdown over Emily's absence.

"I would have been able to tell," said someone with a thick topknot who had pushed her way into the foyer, craning her head toward the living room with curiosity. "I've met Andrea before." The others turned toward her, suddenly interested. Topknot preened, commanding new respect. "I went to a retreat last July," she explained. "And have been following the NewLife program ever since."

"So you thought it was worth it?" A petite blond woman asked.

"It changed my life. Would I be shelling out thirty thou again if it hadn't?" replied Topknot from the back, laughing.

I felt my eyes widen and fought to control my expression. *Thirty thousand dollars* for a seven-day retreat led by Andrea? By that math, I'd soaked in nearly a million dollars' worth of wisdom already.

"I'm Maeve," I repeated loudly. "Please form a line while I take your coats and check you in. Andrea will be down soon." I continued to check in a dozen guests, using the iPad Andrea had given me. I dutifully hung their coats in the hall closet and handed each one a NewLife newborn, tailored to their specific genetic makeups, using a program that digitally deconstructed and then blended images of the guests and their partners. The result was a doll that was meant to look exactly like their future offspring.

Some of the women, I noticed, were visibly pregnant already. Some did not appear to be. I wondered if any of them were single. There were three men in the mix, which had initially surprised me—after all, it was a retreat centered on motherhood.

"They're learning how to be better partners," Andrea had explained earlier, when we were going over the attendee list. "Part of motherhood is renegotiating your relationship with your spouse."

It occurred to me, then, that Andrea hadn't been a mother for long. How could she teach an entire course on motherhood? Had Emily given her tips or prepped presentations before her breakdown?

After showing the guests to their rooms—all of which were shared—I encouraged them to congregate in the living room once they got settled. Andrea would be joining us at eight

for welcome drinks. In the meantime, I lowered myself onto
the sofa and poured myself a glass of sauvignon blanc. I was
breaking my drinking moratorium for the retreat, and it was
looking like I was going to need it. A healthy fire was crackling in the old stone hearth on the wall opposite, providing
the room's only light, aside from two antique floor lamps, one
of which flickered stubbornly. It was a cozy, intimate atmo-
sphere. But the prospect of a dozen-odd guests descending
with their rubber progeny was making me want to grab the
wine bottle by the neck and guzzle it down in one swallow.

I'd been alone barely ten minutes when the first of the
guests came down, squirming dolls cradled in their arms, and
began to claim seats. They talked among themselves, occa-
sionally casting me curious looks but never drawing me into
conversation. I was glad. I wasn't sure what I had in common with these women, and my social anxiety was beginning to stir, making me shift uncomfortably in my seat. Just
then, Rob walked in with a tray of drinks. He was dressed in a
sharp button-down tucked into gray wool dress pants.

"Let me help you." I jumped up. Rob gave me a terse smile
and waved me away with his free hand. The women accepted
the water, champagne, and mocktails without bothering to
address Rob. Apparently he wasn't as big a celebrity as Andrea among this group.

"Rob," I said again, eager to have something to do. "Why
don't I fill a few more in the kitchen. Or I can grab the can-
apés."

"No need," Rob said, looking embarrassed. "You're our
guest too, Maeve. Please just sit and relax."

"But I told Andrea . . ." I trailed off as the three men I'd
noted earlier emerged from the vicinity of the kitchen, carrying trays loaded with finger sandwiches and tiny meatballs on
toothpicks.

"See?" Rob gave me a reassuring smile. "We've got this

under control. Actually, why don't I take this." He reached for my wineglass and traded it for a glass of chilled water. "You're supposed to be cutting back, remember? And besides, you're representing NewLife while our other guests are here."

I nodded and sank back in my armchair, watching the men circle the room and proffer their trays. None of the women seemed as surprised as I was. I wondered which women these men belonged to, and whether Rob had roped them into an evening of serving the women or whether they had offered. Not that I minded. Of course I liked being waited on. But there was something about how naturally they took to the job. As though they were assuming roles they'd performed a hundred times before, fully at ease with domestic tasks.

A few minutes of observation indicated there were two gay couples in the group. It occurred to me that despite the advanced technology it boasted, Andrea's organization wasn't all that progressive.

A second later, Andrea swept into the room in a long white gown and strappy heels. The dress—simple, high-necked silk with long sleeves and a cutout in the back—made her resemble a bride. She was beautiful. She appeared pure, virginal. As she made her way toward Rob, a hush fell. Twelve pairs of eyes followed her, riveted. Andrea accepted a glass of champagne and stood in front of the fire, turning to address the group. The flames illuminated her figure, making her look all the more striking.

"Welcome, mothers," Andrea said, raising her glass. "Thank you all for coming." Her use of that word made my blood run cold. Andrea met my eyes, then turned back to the group. "Mothers-to-be, of course." *Mothers*. It had been a trigger, but not a purposeful one, and not meant the way I'd interpreted it. I took a few long, slow breaths to calm the impact the simple phrase had had on me.

"A warm welcome to you all." She paused, and the guests

broke into a round of spontaneous cheers. "By now you've met my husband, Rob," Andrea continued, indicating Rob with her glass. "With the help of Alfredo, Matt, and Richard, he's here to serve you this weekend. If anything comes up that you need, please feel free to ask. And you've met our very special guest—someone closer to my heart than nearly anyone in the world."

Andrea met my eyes and lifted her glass toward me. "My dear cousin, Maeve, is with us this week. Her contributions to this retreat are uniquely important. We were recently reunited after a long time apart, and I can tell you . . ." She paused, seemingly gathering herself. "Our reunion was nothing short of fateful. The world works in mysterious ways, ladies. No more so than when it comes to motherhood."

At this, they cheered again. A woman with a name tag that read "Rosa" let out a whoop. They seemed tipsy, almost high, even though half the women were drinking mocktails. The energy in the room was running full tilt. Andrea's words had warmed me. In some ways, it felt like she was officially welcoming me into her family by acknowledging me publicly as her own.

"The upcoming seven days," Andrea went on, "will be full of challenges and opportunities for growth and reflection. We'll discuss why you've been called to motherhood. What it means to fulfill this sacred role. Why motherhood"—here, her voice rose in pitch—"is the single most important and valuable calling on this earth. And it'll all unfold in this historical house that I chose specifically because of its roots in Freemasonry, a tradition from which women were excluded. Well, here we are now, taking over," she said to cheers. "Fuck you, Freemasons! We won't be subdued. We are women, and we have the ultimate power. A power no man could ever have. The power of motherhood." At this, the cheers reached a cre-

scendo. I studied my cousin, absorbing it all. It took a while
for the guests to quiet. Andrea was *good* at playing to a crowd.

But that was to be expected. She was filling Emily's shoes,
after all. Representing the company, giving the guests what
they'd paid for. The women around me rocked their dolls
tenderly, caressing the dolls' backs when they let out fussy
mewls. One NewLife newborn, held by a woman named Sasha, began crying sharply, threatening to drown Andrea out.
Looking panicked, Sasha reached for her shirt, unbuttoning
the first few buttons of her blouse. She extracted a breast from
her bra and offered it to the newborn doll, encouraging it to
latch on. I recoiled, horrified.

When the doll found purchase, its cries turned to contented
gasps in between sucking. Sasha looked lost to the throes of
ecstasy, as though this experience alone were worth her ad-
mittance fee. A few of the others nodded at Sasha in approval.
I averted my eyes, embarrassed.

I wasn't at all opposed to women breastfeeding real babies
in public, but somehow this display with the doll felt tainted,
like I'd seen something I wasn't meant to see. Something
private and sacred but . . . warped. The sight of it brought
me back to my first day at the house, when I'd mistook my
own tearstains on Andrea's shirt for leaking breast milk. The
memory made me shudder. I shifted uncomfortably in my
seat and turned back to my cousin.

"Tonight, before the arrival of the second bus and the official commencement of our retreat, I encourage you to get to
know one another—and, of course, your 'babies.'" Andrea
had the grace to use air quotes, and a few in the audience
tittered. Sasha looked embarrassed. One or two others gazed
adoringly at their dolls, as if already experiencing the love
they were always promised they'd find.

"The mocktails are plentiful," Andrea wrapped up. "As is

the champagne—so, for those of you who aren't yet pregnant, let it flow. Here's to a wonderful group of true women. You have heard the calling and embraced it. Cheers, to you and to motherhood, the truest vocation, the ultimate source of your feminine power."

"To motherhood," said the women around me, lifting their glasses in euphoric synchrony. Rob and the other men seemed equally entranced by my cousin's speech, lifting their own glasses toward her triumphant silhouette. As the women began to whisper among themselves, I sat quietly and observed. Most of them commented on the lifelike quality of the dolls, wondering aloud if that's what their true offspring would look like. Some chattered animatedly about which lectures they wanted most to attend. Wisps of conversation flowed around me as easily as the drinks flowed into glasses.

"I heard there's a Bloody Mary here," one woman confided conspiratorially to her friend. At the sound of the phrase, I startled. Someone bad. A traitor. *Bloody Mary.*

"What did you say?" I asked, my hands beginning to tremble. My tone was harsher than I had intended.

"That's right." Andrea swooped in, overhearing us. "We're having a Bloody Mary bar with brunch tomorrow. Mimosas too—mango and pomegranate, for those among us who aren't expecting. And more mocktails. You're in for a treat." She turned to me, smiling. "Mae? Are you okay?"

I nodded, my fingers clasped so tightly around the stem of my water glass I feared the glass might break. How stupid I'd been. How skittish, in these women's company. Andrea crossed the room to chat up another guest, and when she glanced my way a minute later, I lifted my glass ever so slightly and mustered a smile. I tilted it in her direction, careful not to let my water spill. Her own grin in return was dazzling, pleased. Her warmth radiated through me, making me realize that like all the other women in this room, I'd do anything to be near her.

* * *

Three hours later, we had finished with cleanup and all the guests were in bed. Andrea had been giddy with the success of her opening ceremony. She had channeled Emily perfectly and had charmed a rapt audience. Poor Emily. I hoped she was okay. Andrea and Rob didn't seem to have much information. The hospital took patient confidentiality seriously, and Micah had so far been unreachable.

Late that night, I stood under the shower, allowing near-scalding beads of water to drum into the back of my neck like a dozen tiny fingers. The events with Tyler had left me confused, disoriented. Chores and retreat prep had been good distractions, but when I was alone in the shower, it all came rushing back. I took a deep breath, allowing the calming pressure of the hot water to make me feel more composed. I noticed a thick chunk of hair circling the drain and felt my pulse escalate. My hair had been getting thinner and thinner; if it didn't stop soon, I would definitely need a wig. Worrying about it would only make it worse. I tried to relax into the thick swirls of steam and allow my mind to wander.

I needed to get back to the city, to jump-start my life again—that much was clear. I couldn't stay forever in this life that wasn't my own. I'd go back to my apartment, do whatever it took to cover rent—waitress, whatever—anything to be independent again. Maybe it would be hard for a while, but the longer I relied on my cousin's generosity, the more I saw parts of myself beginning to slip away.

I turned the water off and stepped onto the thick, plush bath mat that covered the bulk of the bathroom floor. I toweled myself off, used the toilet, then washed my hands with a fragrant soap and slathered my body with scented oil. Everything Andrea invested in was high quality. Except, oddly, the plumbing. I wrapped the towel back around my torso and opened the door, allowing some of the steam to escape.

"Rob?" I called down the stairs, in case he and Andrea were still up. No answer. I heard murmurs, though, from somewhere on the ground floor—he and Andrea recapping the evening, most likely. I went back to the toilet, jiggling the handle once more.

I removed the lid to the tank and lifted the little suction stopper, allowing it to settle back into its suction groove. Nothing happened. I jiggled the handle again. The tank was silent. I looked under the bathroom sink for a plunger and, finding none, knelt on the bath mat and raised the seat to see if I could get a better look into the drain. Maybe there'd been blockage. The clogged toilet situation wasn't going to fly with all these other women in the house—all the spare bathrooms were in use.

I couldn't see anything unusual in the drain itself, other than that the water was low—I couldn't see much of *anything,* really—but as I started to lower the seat back down, I caught a glimpse of something green partially submerged in the bowl. It was a thin strip of paper, a scrap of some kind, the top piece green and the bottom white. Using a piece of toilet paper, I pulled at the part that rested against the side of the bowl above the urine level. It stuck. I pried it off with some effort and held it aloft—still dripping.

What had first looked like a tag or a ribbon appeared now to be a test strip of some sort, almost like those water-testing strips I'd seen at the drugstore. It contained various lines and markers I couldn't identify. Something related to the finicky plumbing or minerality levels, I assumed. I crumpled it in the wad of tissue and tossed it in the trash can. Then I reconsidered. Whatever it was, Rob would probably want to know it

bull moose
Music · Movies · Video Games · Books · and so much more

7/10/2022 12:44:55 PM @ Salem

New Items

austin,emily(everyone in this
room will someday be dead) $10.97T
  was $12.97
heltzel,anne(just like mother) $18.97T
  was $20.97

Total Purchases:	$29.94
CASH:	($50.00)
CHANGE:	$20.06

We buy your stuff! Ask about buybacks!

7/10/2022 12:44:55 PM @ Salem

New Items

austin emily (everyone in this
room will someday be dead) $10.97T
was $12.97

halfcat lance (just like mother) $18.97T
was $27.97

Total Purchases: $29.94
CASH: ($50.00)
CHANGE: $20.06

We buy your stuff! Ask about buybacks!

needed to be replaced. I slipped on my bathrobe and pulled the balled-up toilet paper from the trash can, resolving to ask Andrea.

I descended the stairs barefoot. When I reached the landing, the murmurs from below became clearer. It was not just Rob and Andrea, I realized, but also a third, masculine voice. I looked out the window and saw a police car parked in the driveway. Below me, Andrea's tone was hushed and insistent, Rob's mollifying.

I had the sudden, all-consuming sense that something was deeply wrong. Why would a policeman be here so late at night? I made my way down the last few stairs quietly, slipping around the corner and into the kitchen, just out of sight of where Rob, Andrea, and the policeman were seated in the living room.

"You can see why we're concerned," the officer was saying. "We heard from patrons at his bar that the victim was romantically involved with your cousin."

My heart quickened. *Victim?*

"They went out once or twice," Andrea said, her voice calm. "I'd hardly have called them romantically involved. It was very early stages; anyone will tell you that. In any case, she'll be devastated to hear."

"Devastated? I thought it was early stages," commented the police officer.

"She's suffered a recent job loss and is in a vulnerable place," Andrea explained. Her tone softened. "I'm protective of her, as you might imagine. She was enjoying getting to know Tyler. She'll of course be distraught. Who wouldn't be, to find out someone they knew has died?"

I bit my tongue and clapped a hand over my mouth to stifle a gasp. *Dead.* Tyler was dead. My entire body went cold, and I fought to keep myself from vomiting. Still, something told me I shouldn't enter the room. *What happened?*

"He was inebriated when he lost control of the car," the policeman said, seeming abashed. "But his brakes had frayed to the point of giving out. So you see, we have to cover all our bases. He was last seen at a restaurant with your cousin."

"And he left our home early this morning, according to my cousin," Andrea explained. "I can confirm that his car was gone when I woke up at eight." Her tone was respectful—calm, even—with a hint of sadness. "My cousin had no idea he had a wife. And a child on the way. What an awful business. I'm really not sure why you're here questioning us, though, when it's clear he went to his restaurant at some point today and proceeded to get very drunk before he plowed into that tree."

Rob interjected then. "I know he had financial issues," he said softly. "He mentioned them to me—was looking for work at our company. A side gig. I told him we didn't have anything right now . . ." He trailed off. "Anyway, I just mean that if the car was in a bad state, it's possible he couldn't afford repairs."

"Anything's possible," the officer said, clearing his throat. "Well then. I'll be leaving you folks alone. If you can think of anything that would help, please do give me a shout. And please have your cousin contact me when she's back from the city. We want to interview her about their relationship. Just a formality, of course."

I heard the shuffle of fabrics as they stood up and moved toward the front door.

I have to tell you something, Tyler had texted, mere hours before he drove to his death. *I didn't know they'd go that far.* I listened as my cousin and Rob exchanged final pleasantries with the officer. I waited until the door closed. Then I slid out of the shadows and into the living room, facing them as they returned.

"Maeve!" Andrea startled, then drew the blinds. The glow of red and blue lights pulsed behind them. "We thought you were upstairs sleeping."

"What happened to Tyler?"

"Maeve," Rob said, reaching for me. It was then that I saw clearly a dark purple outline on his palm. A bruise, in the shape of an oval. Rob noticed me looking and snapped his palm shut. The familiar, heady scent of whiskey trailed him as he withdrew his hand. It brought me back to the previous night. It wasn't a scent I'd ever associated with Tyler, but it had been present nevertheless as he'd fucked me, blindfolded. I remembered it on his breath when he leaned close, pressing his hand over my mouth until I could hardly breathe, until I bit down hard on his palm and—

My heart began to race. I fought to keep my expression neutral.

"I'm okay," I told them, struggling to keep my voice under control. "But I'm still pretty upset about Tyler and what he did. I *am* a little hysterical, I guess. I think I should spend a day in the city. Get a change of scenery."

"I don't think that would be such a good idea," Andrea warned.

"I'll be back to help with the retreat soon," I lied frantically. "I'm just going to go throw some things in a bag."

"You heard Andrea." Rob's voice was low. "We'd prefer it if you stayed."

"I—I overheard what happened to Tyler," I blurted out. "You told the police I was in the city, so I should be there, right?" I was talking faster, stumbling, my words tripping over each other in my haste to say something they'd buy.

"How do you think it would look to the police if they saw you leaving? We told them you were in the city to protect you. But don't you think it would be suspicious if they found out it was a lie?" Andrea's question was reasonable, but somehow it sounded threatening.

"Your boyfriends do seem to . . . *die,* don't they, Maeve?" Rob weighed in, in a speculative tone. "Death sort of follows you around, doesn't it? The police might start to do a little digging. Do some additional investigating into Ryan's death, maybe. And the other death."

My heart stopped. What did he know about the "other" death? My eyes flickered to Andrea, who was peering at something on the floor. The tissue, the strange strip of paper. It had fallen from my hand as Rob spoke.

"Oh!" Andrea gasped, and her eyes welled with tears. Then she clapped her hands and squealed, stooping low to pick up the strip of paper. "Isn't *this* perfect timing. I'm sorry, Maeve, I'm a little emotional. It's just . . ." She broke off. "Rob, take a look to make sure I'm not wrong. Oh, god, I hope I'm not wrong." She peered at the strip, then handed it to Rob, who examined it closely. "This is today's test? Of course it is!"

Rob looked up from the strip and let out a loud whoop. "You're not wrong, baby. She's pregnant!"

What the hell were they talking about? Andrea. He had to have meant Andrea.

She moved closer to me, placing a palm against my cheek, and I jerked back. "The test doesn't lie," she singsonged, waving the small strip in the air. "You're pregnant, Maeve."

I stared at it, my vision swimming in and out of focus.

I moved away and toward the back door. "I've got to catch the bus back to the city. I'll be back soon. I promise."

"We both know you're terrible at keeping promises," Andrea said, her eyes hard. "You certainly didn't keep your promise to me, did you? *Never alone, never apart, no matter what.*" Her words were bitter. "You're not going anywhere, Maeve. Not this time. Not when I'm finally about to get what I always wanted."

25

Every now and then, when I can't sleep, I climb from the bed Andrea and I share. I go down to the closet and bury myself behind the coats and listen for the thing in the locked room. I leave the closet door open, so it isn't scary the way it was when Mother shut me in there when I was bad.

I start with a gentle knock. Once, twice, lightly with my knuckles. If the thing doesn't answer right away, I knock a little harder. Then I hear a shift, a clanking of metal. And two knocks back. If I knock three times, it knocks three times. The thing in the locked room does whatever I do. It follows my lead.

Sometimes the thing makes muffled throat sounds. Moans or grunts. Sometimes I sing to it and it quiets. Singing the thing to sleep helps me fall back asleep, most days. The thing and I become friends this way with our monster lullabies.

One evening when I'm knocking and singing for the thing, I hear sounds like choking sobs. It's the noise I make when I'm very afraid or sad and don't want to wake the Mothers. I've never spoken to the thing directly, but now I do.

"Are you sad?" I ask. It pauses, then the noises get a little louder. "Shh," I tell it. "You'll wake the Mothers." It gets mad at this, makes a thud noise and its muffled roar. I shush it again, but it's become more frantic, like Boy in the throes of a tantrum. When Boy is like that, nothing will do, even though he knows he's not allowed to scream and fuss. Sometimes after those tantrums, Boy has bruises on his little arms and back where Mother strikes him.

"Please be quiet," I say now, but the thing's noises continue. If it goes on like this, all the Mothers will awake and be upset. Then they'll get upset with me, Boy, Andrea, and the littler girls. If one of us is bad, we all have consequences. It's the way it always goes—it teaches us responsibility to one another. If I'm not careful, none of us will sleep tonight.

"Do you want out?" I say suddenly, desperately. The thing stops its fussing. I am quiet for a long minute. The thing knocks on the wall, but I don't knock back. Maybe if I'm very still, it will think I'm gone, it'll forget I was here. But after another minute, it starts back up again even louder. *What have I done?*

I clutch my hair, tugging at it, and feel a few strands slip away in my sweaty palms. My heart thrums in my ears. There is no more time for reasoning. If it doesn't stop, there will be hell to pay. "Hell to pay" is what Mother says when there's big trouble. "Hell to pay" is what happened after one of the littler girls found Mother's phone one time and pressed the wrong button.

"Okay," I say. My body courses with fear. "Okay." Its moans lessen slightly, and I pull myself out from the closet, my heart pounding. I know if I don't open that door soon, the thing will start up again. Maybe louder than before. It'll wake the whole house and get everyone in trouble.

I know where the key is. Andrea showed me.

Mother with the baby inside her is snoring loudly when I creep inside the Mothers' room. The thing in the locked room is staying quiet. I told it I would be back soon. I have only a moment. I creep over to the bureau between the two big beds. I stand on my tiptoes and angle my chin, peering over its top edge, and lift my arm high, running my fingers over the smooth wood surface. I am feeling for a blue ceramic dish that keeps all the treasures we play with whenever Mother is out getting us food and clothes. I know from memory there's a hat pin, a pair of magnetic earrings shaped like snails, and a broken button that shines like a precious stone. Andrea saw the key there.

My hand connects with the dish and it rattles against the wood. I freeze, holding my breath. My nightdress wisps soundlessly against my ankles. Mother snores—one deep grunt—and rolls on her side. I reach my hand back into the dish and feel around until my fingers touch metal. I pinch the key between my thumb and forefinger and slowly back out of the room, holding my breath. I retreat into the hallway, then creep down the staircase and run on the tops of my toes. The locked room is just off the kitchen. The ridges of the warm metal key press painfully into my palm. Its teeth dig a groove in my skin. The house is quiet, still.

Maybe I shouldn't, I think. But I have to. I have to see it through. I want to be as brave as Andrea is. We look the same on the outside, but on the inside she's made of different, stronger stuffing. That's what Mother says.

I suck in a deep breath and step quietly toward the door. I press my ear against it. There is no sound. Maybe the thing is asleep, but now I have to know.

As soon as I put the key in the lock, the whining starts again. The thing moves around. From here, in front of the door, its noises are clearer. They are sad and searching, and suddenly I know I've made the right choice. *I don't have to let it out,* I tell myself. *I can just keep it company.*

I turn the key and the lock clicks. I ease the door open, pausing for an instant and glancing toward the ceiling, where the Mothers sleep. When the upstairs stays silent, I step all the way into the room and shut the door behind me.

There's a stench in there; the thing has pissed or shit. Its whining is louder, now that I've entered. More frantic. It scrabbles against the cement floor. As my eyes begin to adjust, I make out the frame of a cage in the room's center. Near the wall to my right is an old mattress, flat on the floor. There's a large, pacing thing in the cage. It's a bigger animal than I thought it would be. I squint, straining to make it out. It lets out a strangled-sounding noise. It bangs against the bars of the cage.

"Shh," I tell it. "I'm here to keep you company." I move closer, panicked now that it isn't keeping up its end of the bargain. It was supposed to stay quiet if I came, but now it is clamoring. If I can only get closer, maybe I can calm it down. I begin to hum, like Mother always did to the little girls when they were small and colicky. The blinds are drawn, and in the dark I can't quite tell what the animal looks like. I move to the window and carefully, slowly, begin to raise the shade. My back is to the cage.

When I turn, the moon shines bright in the room. My eyes land on the thing in the cage.

It is not an animal.

It is a man.

I'm too afraid to scream. The noise that comes out of me mirrors the noise coming out of him, around his gag: a strained, low groan. I'm rooted in place, unable to move my legs. My cousin is the brave one. She always has been.

I take a step backward, toward the door. My heart is in my throat. I turn, ready to run. All at once, the man lunges forward, pressing his face against the bars. His eyes are wild. He makes a sound behind his gag. Pounds his palms against the bars. His chest is naked and covered in long, bloody scratches. He is so thin I can make out all the ribs in his chest in the moonlight. His eyes are flashing. Wild, like the night animals we see from our window.

He makes the sound again. This time, I know what he's saying; a gag can't stifle the look in his eyes. *Please*. I could help him if I wanted. After all, we were friends. *Please*. I shake my head slowly from side to side. *No*.

I cross the room to the window, my mouth dry, my back drenched in sweat. I lower the blinds again. The man is thrashing around in the cage now, screaming around the gag as he rattles the bars with his hands, the tendons in his neck straining. I stand, breathing hollowly, until I feel the life returning to my legs.

Later—what feels like hours later but is really only minutes—I burrow into Andrea's shoulder. I am damp, both sweating and freezing. I have climbed into her bed, but I'm still trembling. I replaced the key and reached Andrea's room mere seconds before the Mothers were roused by the noise of the man in the cage.

"Shh," Andrea says, stroking my head gently when the sobs come. "There's nothing to be afraid of." She's hardly pulling my hair, but I feel a slight give where a chunk of strands comes away in her hand. My pillow will be littered with it tomorrow. "Don't worry, Mae. Mother will take care of it."

I shake my head against her shoulder, now wet from tears intermingled with sweat. We lie there, her murmuring sweetly while I sob. I can never tell Andrea what was down there. I can never reveal what I know, or we'll both be in danger.

A minute later, when the sound of a gunshot reverberates through the floorboards, I hardly flinch.

26

I awoke with a start, my mouth stuffed with something soft, chalky. Cotton, a wad of stiff fabric. I reared up, screaming behind the gag, but I could rise only a few inches at the pelvis. My wrists and ankles were bound to the bed with thick strips of something rough and taut. Not a perverse sex game this time—a nightmare. My instinct was to thrash wildly. I couldn't even do that; the restraints were too tight.

Through the clamor of my fear I became faintly aware of two things: I was in my bedroom, and I was bound. Whatever they had me in—a short-sleeved nightgown, it seemed, that stopped at my knees and left me shivering—was half drenched in sweat. The way my legs were spread to accommodate the restraints made me feel more vulnerable and exposed than I could remember feeling, ever. The light in the room was dim, but there were glimmers of sunlight behind the drawn drapes, and I could see the shadowy forms of five or six individuals peering down at me.

"She's awake," one of them shouted in the direction of the hallway. She tucked a NewLife doll close to her chest, crooning and swaying as if rocking it to sleep. There were heavy footsteps in the hallway, and a man burst into the room, flicking on the overhead light. Rob.

For a naive second I thought he would help me. Untie me and send me home, protect me from these women. I strained against my binds and growled into the gag, producing a muffled roar. I begged him with my eyes. But as he stared down at me, his betrayal—his violation—flooded back, and I knew it wasn't he who would set me free. It wasn't any of these people.

These Andrea worshippers. Because I knew then that my cousin had never been on my side.

I lay still, frozen by the expression in Rob's eyes, a curious blend of benevolence and pity. He turned from me, moving around the room with a confident ease, lighting candles that had begun to take shape in my periphery—more so now, with their flickering orange flames. When he was finished, he shut off the overhead light, illuminating the observers with a soft glow.

Two men entered the room.

One circulated with glasses of champagne and mocktails. Another positioned himself behind a seated woman, administering a back massage while she nursed her cooing doll.

Another arrived with stools, then returned again with stacks of blankets and began distributing them to the observers, who took them without bothering with thanks and arranged themselves comfortably around the bed in this room I'd thought of as my own, as a safe space. Rob exited, and for a while I was left alone with these people. They chatted quietly behind their champagne, allowed their eyes to rove over my body, making me wonder what they saw there.

My cousin would take what she wanted, no matter what the means.

I owed her, after all.

"Mothers." I heard the melodic tinkle of her voice as she entered the room, and I turned my neck, straining to see her. The others stood, murmuring their welcomes as she made her way to the foot of the bed. She, in full view of the body I'd once known as mine. I, in full view of my betrayer. Her eyes raked over me, lingering with near reverence at my midsection.

Mothers, she'd said. I knew what this was. I knew with a cold terror that filled my body from the inside out.

"Mothers, let us rejoice. Our Bloody Mary has returned

to her true purpose. Let us show her the joys of motherhood, which she has forsaken for so long, and welcome this wayward child into our fold." She glided to the top of the bed and ran her fingertips over mine where they were bound to the bed-post. She lowered her voice so only I could hear.

"I asked you nicely for your eggs, Maeve. This could have been so easy. If only you'd said yes. We could have remained a family. You could have even been a part of the child's life. But you were never good at understanding what it is to be a family, were you?" Her gaze went cold. "Maybe you just don't deserve one."

Then, at a louder pitch, she said, "Rob, sweetheart, will you bring the refreshments?" She didn't bother looking at Rob when she addressed him, but he scurried from the room, an obedient lackey. Andrea began to wash her hands in a basin that had at some point been placed on my nightstand. The room filled with the fragrant odor of lavender.

"What exactly is a Bloody Mary?" the woman named India whispered to a petite blonde sitting next to her, who shushed her with a condescending look. The two were seated closest to my bedside, and if I shifted my eyes as hard as they'd go to the left, I could catch their conversation.

The blonde hesitated before answering, keeping one eye on Andrea. "It's a term for a woman who aborts her child or—more generally—is hostile to the idea of motherhood," she explained quietly.

India gazed at me with a look of pity. "How sad for her," she commented. "She's so lucky to have Andrea intervene."

The blond woman glanced back at Andrea, then lowered her voice further, but not so low that I couldn't make out her words. "As little girls, we'd play a game Andrea made up, pretending to be a traitor to the cause. The ultimate scare."

"You were part of the community as a child?" India sounded reverential, even jealous.

"I was born into it," the blond woman said then. She met my eyes with her own, and her look was defiant. "All three of us were."

Everything slid into place. *Susie.* One of the smaller girls on the commune. Too little when everything fell apart for me to have recognized her as a grown woman. But it was clear in the slope of her nose and the dramatic arch of her full upper lip.

"That's right," Susie said, leaning forward in her stool so her face was mere inches from my own. "You're still the rotten one." Her voice was a hiss, and flecks of spittle connected with my face, where it was exposed above the gag.

Andrea moved back to the side of the bed, near enough that I could have touched her from where I lay, were I unbound. "That's enough, Susie," she said, laying a hand on Susie's shoulder. Then, to no one in particular, she said, "Remove the gag."

A man to her left, the one who had been circulating champagne, placed his tray on the bureau and lifted my head, struggling with the knot that secured my gag. When I was free, I let out a long scream, channeling all my rage into this noise that emitted from my throat, something animalistic and unencumbered. I screamed like that until my throat was sore and my vocal cords felt shredded from effort. The women winced, pressing their hands to the ears of their dolls in simultaneous gestures of maternal protectiveness. Andrea regarded me calmly, until I dissolved in choked sobs. Nothing I did would frighten or move her.

"We're in the middle of the woods, Maeve," she explained, as if to a child. "Who do you think will hear you?"

"Why are you doing this?" I choked out. Tears streamed down the sides of my face and wet my shoulders, mingling with my sweat.

"Well, because you made it so hard, of course." Andrea

reached out to stroke my cheek, but I gnashed my teeth at her fingers. "Oh, Maeve. Don't make me restore the gag." Andrea shook her head sadly. "Not when my greatest desire in all of this was for you to have a voice."

Maybe if I kept asking questions, I could gather enough information to figure some way out. "It was you all along with the fanatical agenda. Not Emily," I said, my throat raw.

"Well of course it was, silly. Emily is sweet and was a wonderful Mother. Or at least, that's what she became, after I fixed her mess of a life. But she could never run the show. Just look at what she did to herself," she added without emotion. "I am the one at the helm of the Mother Collective." She said it simply, without any of the grandiosity of the rest of her statements. "I've been at the helm since we were children. Studying, waiting for my time to rise. Gathering our sisters like Susie—and more and more sisters across the globe—so the Mother Collective could be even more powerful than before. We never really went away, you see. I know you gave up on our Mothers when you found a new family," she said with derision, "but I never did. That wasn't a surprise to anyone, though. I was always the chosen one. I'm Mother Superior, Maeve. How could I turn my back on my legacy?"

The women in the room sank to their knees, bowing at Andrea's feet.

"Please rise," she said. "Resume your positions. Care for your children."

At this they arose and sat once more on the stools that surrounded the bed. They cared for the dolls with renewed dedication.

"A sailor went to sea, sea, sea"

The lyrics to our old song floated over me, sending chills through my body. They continued singing the rhyme to their dolls until I couldn't stand to listen. I met Andrea's eyes and she smiled as if reading my mind.

"A sweet rhyme, isn't it?" she asked. "Does it bring back memories?"

"What do you want from me?" I asked, growing desperate. "Are you going to kill me?"

"*Kill you?* Of course not, Maeve. Not yet. You'll be here for a while, of course—just about nine months, I'd say. That's right." She laughed, self-satisfied. "We've been keeping you at peak fertility with those smoothies you love so much. Those have been ripe with hormone supplements. And poor you, thinking you were self-medicating so heavily. I felt a little bad about that, I admit. We added a few extra Klonopin to your wine here and there—it was just so easy. Once Ryan died . . . By then you would have believed anything, in your grief." Dread coursed through my body, but I was speechless. "You don't blame us, do you? You've always needed a firm hand, even in childhood. A willful child. So directionless." She shook her head ruefully.

"I haven't decided what to do with you in the long run." She paused. "But for now, you're merely going to perform your duty as a woman. You're not *really* a Bloody Mary. Not anymore." She made a clucking noise with her tongue. "I would never have let that fate befall you. God, no. I *love* you. That's why I'm doing this, Maeve, can't you see? I know what's best for you—I always have. You'll use the gifts you've been given, just as all the other women in this room gratefully use their gifts." At this, there were nods of assent. "We'll take good care of you, Mae. We'll make sure the child is born healthy and strong. We have doctors and midwives right in the Collective—you won't even have to go to a hospital to give birth. Rob," she called then. "You may return."

Rob entered the room almost immediately, carrying a tray on which rested a large, trembling mass. Next to it lay a fork and knife.

"Mmm," Andrea said, gazing at it hungrily. "Doesn't that look good?"

I drew back, horrified. "No," I whispered. "No. Andrea. What is this?"

"Call me Mother Superior," she said, her voice cold. "And I can do whatever I want to do." She bent low to the bed, until we could nearly kiss. "Don't worry, Maeve. You're safe for the time being. I would never do anything to hurt an unborn child. Do you hear me, Maeve? I am taking what I deserve to have. *What you owe me.*" Her hot breath filled my nostrils. And at this, Rob rested a hand on her back, as if to remind her of something. She straightened, composing herself.

"Andrea," I said desperately, my heart pounding as she turned toward the tray and accepted it from Rob. "Do these women know *you* don't have the gift?" There were gasps in the room, and Andrea froze long enough for me to know I was right. I hurried to finish, my words tumbling over themselves. "All these women think they're saving me from the awful fate of not bearing children. But they don't know Mother Superior is using me to *steal* a child and pass it off as her own."

"Get the gag," Andrea ordered Rob. "Gag her immediately."

Rob reached for the cotton strip that had guarded my mouth. As Rob descended with the gag, I saw some of the Mothers exchange looks of confusion. I talked fast, frantic. "How can you lead the Mother Collective if you don't have the power of womanhood? The *one single power* Mother Superior is supposed—"

And then the gag was in my mouth, thick and tight and more painful than before, biting into the flesh at the corners of my mouth. Without babies of her own, how could she continue to lead the cult? That's what this was about. I wasn't fulfilling my role as a woman, according to Andrea's vision; I was producing Andrea's very reason for being, the source of her power and wealth, in order that she might maintain her charade. And Rob, poor Rob. Surely he didn't know what would become of him. He was alive only because she needed his seed, so the baby would look like them. Like Olivia. Andrea had needed me all along, far more than I'd needed her.

I watched as Andrea cut into the bloody slab on the tray, as she explained to the women that finally I would stop squandering—*scoffing at*—my womanhood.

How long ago had this started? They had killed Ryan, that was clear to me now. Killed him soon after I mentioned I planned to live there and not here. They had killed Tyler when he became a liability—at that, a deep pain pierced my heart. Had I not shown Andrea his texts, she might never have known he was a threat. In a way, I was responsible for both their deaths.

Andrea sliced into the raw, gelatinous mass on the tray, cutting it into a dozen or more small pieces.

How far back did it go? My job? Had she ruined that for me, too?

What about my parents? Had she killed my father, who had stopped breathing in the night?

The bitch destroyed my life.

And for that, she would pay. One way or another, she would pay.

*   *   *

Andrea performed the Feeding three times per day for three days. During the ritual, my gag was removed only for the time it took to swallow ragged chunks of the placenta she'd frozen after Olivia's birth and thawed for me now, believing it would make us one. Believing it would somehow make the thing inside me more *hers* as it grew. More like her dead baby.

I tried to spit it out at first, but she stuffed it down my throat with her bare and bloodied hands, nearly choking me. After that, I swallowed the organ whole—and quickly—without chewing.

I learned to dissociate when Andrea approached with the platter, surgical gloves coating her hands. Without fanfare, she'd slice what remained of the placenta into ropy, browning chunks, the women from the retreat presiding in reverence. During these sessions, my gag—by now ripping into the corners of my mouth—would be removed so I could choke down the rotting meat of her womb. I was a mess of painful sores; if I could have smiled, it would have caused me excruciating pain.

Once, I heard a Mother whisper, "Poor thing. Such a lost soul. What else *is* there, other than having babies?" Another Mother clucked her tongue. "So true, Mother. Thank goodness Andrea saved her." Then, fearfully, her friend said, "She's one of the lucky ones, being guided to enlightenment." It made me wonder what happened to the other, unenlightened ones. What *they* thought happened to them.

The women, I supposed, still believed the child was to be mine. Some might have questioned Andrea's intentions. But others undoubtedly thought that when I saw it, I'd finally feel the love I was missing from my life and acknowledge the error of my ways. That Andrea was an evangelist. That in this way she'd save my soul. Andrea wouldn't let the women close to me after that first night; they only came around for the ritual, undoubtedly spending the rest of their time in seminars designed to program their brains.

Rob tended to my physical needs—giving me sponge baths, changing my clothes, feeding me his nutrient-rich shakes. Andrea didn't trust me with anyone else. Or rather, anyone else with me. And Rob, I couldn't break. He had always been either silent or agreeable; now he was impenetrable. Worse, he knew her secrets. There wasn't anything left to expose, not to him. One day he suggested they take me for a walk. I was losing feeling in my extremities by then, shitting and pissing into bedpans only, and I had begun to worry that they really intended to keep me bound like this until I gave birth. Surely, Andrea knew a baby couldn't thrive this way.

"It's too soon, darling," she said. "We need to wait until she's weakened a little. Just enough to be subdued. I know you're as excited as I am," she said, rewarding him with a kiss. "We'll have our Olivia back; don't worry."

"What if it's a boy?" I asked. My gag had been undone for breakfast, and it hadn't yet been replaced.

Andrea looked at me, her smile void of any soul. "Then we'll discard it and go again. We're in no rush. We have Mother eyes everywhere, Maeve. I only wish you hadn't been so . . . resistant. But then, you always were, weren't you? Troublesome. Favoring that worthless little Boy. Putting your whole life on the line for him—even our relationship.

"You know they asked me to take you under my wing when we were little? *That's* why we were 'best friends.'" Those words, and her mocking delivery, seared me more than anything. "They were hoping I'd be a good influence," she continued. "That I could train you to be more compliant. You were always so . . . strange. Coddling Boy as if he were one of our own. The Mothers knew that without my guidance you'd never be the right kind of woman, and they were correct."

Our relationship, I knew then, had meant nothing to Andrea. I was a simple transaction, a means to her own fulfillment. It wasn't clear how long she would have continued her sadistic game if the doorbell hadn't rung.

* * *

"Police! Open up!" The voice was loud enough to carry through my window, open to neutralize the odors of a sedentary body. At first I thought it was a dream, as I faded in and out of awareness. Even though I was alone in the room when they arrived, the police announced themselves three times at the front door, pounding on it before their words seeped into my consciousness.

And then I screamed harder than ever before into my gag and cast my body about within its chains like a madwoman, hurling my torso against the bed and arching it again in a desperate attempt to move the frame against the floor, to make any kind of noise at all.

The door to my room burst open, and Rob shut it gently behind him. Then he walked over to the window and slid it closed.

"It's no use," he told me. "Stop it, Maeve! They can't hear you all the way up here."

I thrashed anyway. Rob would never again tell me what to do, or how to be, or have any jurisdiction over my body, if I could help it. Finally he leaped on me, pinning me to the mattress with both hands. He lowered his face until it was inches from mine and hissed, "Shut up, you fucking whore. I need to get you out of here, now. They're searching the house."

My heart lifted, practically soared out of my chest. They were searching the house. Was it about Tyler? Or had they somehow found something tracing back to the Mother Collective? Rob untied my right arm and immediately I flailed, trying to hit him—a stupid thing, in hindsight, because I needed him to untie at least two hands in order to free myself all the way. The other men—the lackeys—came in then, and my heart sank again.

I hardly had feeling in the arm he'd untied; it was limp and dead from days of being lashed to the bedpost behind me, with only short intervals for roaming the bedroom. Sharp, searing pain traveled from shoulder to wrist, and a blueish bruise extended halfway up my forearm. One of the men twisted my arm behind me as the other assisted Rob in untying my other wrist. Then they bound the two together while the third man worked on my legs. It took all of two minutes.

When they were done, Rob was breathing heavily and

sweat dripped down his temples. I screamed again through my gag, an effort that came from my gut, forcing bile into the back of my throat. I tried to kick the men, but my legs had no life in them either. I could hardly move them at all.

The two lackeys grabbed me, securing my body tight between them so I had no option for wriggling to the ground and causing the kind of thump that might attract attention. They moved me out of the room and walked me rapidly through the hall. From there, I caught snippets of the conversation.

"Officers," Andrea was saying, in a placating tone, "you can see I'm hosting a retreat on motherhood. This isn't the time or place—"

"We have a warrant," said a male voice. "We are authorized to conduct a thorough search."

"This is bad for business," Andrea said pleadingly. "Surely you can understand that. You can come back in another couple of days, when the guests have cleared out, and tear the place apart. I don't care."

"With respect, ma'am, the timing isn't your decision."

I didn't catch more, because I was being shuttled rapidly down the hallway until we reached the hidden door that led to the passages in the wall, the ones where I'd lost my phone and fallen into a nest of spiders. The police would never find me there. The door was invisible if you didn't know how to find it. And even if I hadn't been gagged, it would have been impossible to hear me behind those walls.

They dumped me on the floor of the hidden corridor. Rob followed, closing the door behind him. Then he ripped off my gag, leaving me gasping and sucking in air mixed with blood from the sides of my mouth. I scooted as far away from him as I could get, pressing my shoulder blades painfully against the wall, my bound hands grazing the floor just behind my tailbone. The feeling was beginning to return to my legs, although I was certain that if I tried to stand, I'd stumble.

"It's soundproofed," he said. "They won't hear you in here, no matter how loud you scream."

"You fucking bastard," I said, inching away from him. "You raped me that night, when Tyler was here. Didn't you? *Didn't you?*" I yelled the last part, just in case we were both wrong and there was a way someone could hear me.

I could make out just enough of Rob's features in the dim of the passage to see he looked pleased with himself. "It worked out well, didn't it?" His tone was smug, even contemptuous. "We'd have let him live if he hadn't freaked out about the whole thing. Thought he was just being paid to seduce you. But to what end? So naive, that boy. So desperate to protect his loved ones. See, Maeve? Even *he* knew how important it is to build a family. If you hadn't been such a kinky slut in the first place, it wouldn't have worked. That part's on you."

"It's over, Rob. Don't you see? Now they know about the Mother Collective. Soon it will all be destroyed."

Rob laughed and shook his head. "All they know is that your fingerprints are all over Tyler's car," he explained. "And they didn't buy the lie about you being back in the city. They want a word. But we can't let them do that. Not in your condition."

Rob leaned forward so his musky breath overshadowed the damp and rot of the passage.

"Andrea already cleared out your room here and planted your phone in your apartment in the city. They'll do a cursory search of your things. And then they'll be gone. Eventually they'll trace your phone. And they won't ever find you, Maeve. Not even your cold, dead body after you deliver our child."

I pressed myself back and then propelled my leg in front of me until it connected with Rob's jaw, causing him to lurch backward. Something hard—his skull, I guessed—collided with the wall, and he slumped to the floor, groaning. I didn't waste a second. I stumbled to my feet and ran haphazardly down the corridor. I heard Rob rising behind me. I heard him laugh, off-kilter.

"Where do you think you're running to?" he asked, his voice slurred but mocking. "I'll catch you eventually."

I rounded a corner, my heart pounding. Rob must have hit his head hard; his speech was evidence enough of that. I had an advantage, but surely not for long. My legs were still aching and foreign, and I had no idea how long I could persist. I desperately searched my brain for anything I could remember. The passageways spanned the back length of the house, that much I knew. And there were three exits. But *where were they*? I could hardly see, let alone navigate, especially without my hands to guide me. The pungent smell of rot grew stronger as I made my way deeper into the exoskeleton of the house.

"I'm not even going to chase you, Maeve." Rob's voice was distant. "You hurt me, you know. That kick really hurt me. That's no way to treat a lover."

I connected with a solid mass. There shouldn't have been a dead end there. What was this? I pressed my body against the object. Without hands, I couldn't get a sense of it other than that it was covered in plastic. It appeared to be propped against the wall at a diagonal, like a slanted beam. I kicked around, identifying the amount of space beneath it—too tight for me to squeeze through.

I pushed into it, struggling to knock it over. But it was heavy and unwieldy; it hardly shifted an inch. I groaned in frustration. Behind me was Rob. The only way to escape was forward.

Then I heard something. The buzzing of a cell phone. Its attendant glow drew my eyes downward. The buzzing was coming from whatever was blocking my path. It was obscured by the heavy plastic that covered it. Even so, it highlighted a long, metal zipper. I reached for the tongue of the zipper with my teeth. As I pulled, the unmistakable smell of rot flooded my nasal passages, causing me to gag. I pressed on, clamping my teeth more securely around the zipper when they threatened to tremble. Once, twice, the zipper slipped out of my mouth, and in those paralyzing seconds I could hear Rob, dragging now, and coughing away the stench but pulling ever closer. The phone kept buzzing, its light revealing more as I went: the woolen material of dress pants. A blue button-down shirt.

I kept going. I had to be sure. I needed to know it was him. I moved my teeth, and the zipper, and in turn my face, up the figure. Toward its torso, its chest, its neck, its—

But Micah's body had no head. I found myself close enough to lick his putrid, decomposing stump. It was then that I screamed, until screams turned into chokes and gags.

Poor Micah. Micah, the reluctant father. Micah who loved death metal. Who was fond of his phone charger and other gadgets. Who cut the crusts off his own bread but left them on Henry's and didn't see the irony. Who fiddled with his pocketknife when he was nervous.

The phone stopped ringing. Went black.

His pocketknife.

I could hear Rob dragging himself closer. He seemed disoriented; his steps were irregular and plodding. Even so, without the use of my hands, I'd be helpless. Rob wouldn't kill me, not when I was pregnant. But I couldn't be held captive again and survive.

I turned my back to the body, fighting waves of nausea and tears and the encroaching feeling of claustrophobia that had begun to settle deep in my bones. I wiggled my fingers, trying desperately to restore feeling in them. They'd bound me tight enough to cut off circulation. I squatted, reaching along the body until I felt the lining in the wool of Micah's pants, then groped around in his left pocket, praying it was there. I felt the phone, and beside it a cold metal object, and for a fleeting second felt something like hope. Then the knob on the top clicked under my thumb and I realized it was only a pen. The knife was in the other pocket, then, if it was there at all. I couldn't reach the other pocket. Not without climbing on top of the dead man.

"Maeve, what are you doing?" Rob called, drawing out the syllables like they were a song or a game. "Come out, come out, wherever you are . . ."

He was mere feet away from me now. I climbed on top of the bag and laid my body against the corpse. Beyond it was solid wall, I knew now, from feeling with my feet. A dead end, after all. I'd made a wrong turn. The only way through was back, toward Rob. But the corpse had something I needed.

Micah's dead body was rigid enough from rigor mortis to withstand my weight even as I lay against him, my back to his stomach. I reached my hand into his right pocket, feeling around desperately until my fingers found purchase.

The knife.

I pulled it out, flicked it open, and placed it behind me, trapping it against the wall. I rubbed the binds on my wrists frantically against it. I felt one cord break. And then the hallway darkened, Rob's form obscuring any meager light.

"I found you," he whispered.

With a grunt, I yanked my wrists apart, loosening the cut cord until it was slack. I shook it off; my arms were free. I wielded the knife with my right hand and reached back for Micah's left pocket, for the phone. But I didn't press my hand to the button that would illuminate it. Rob was so close I could hear him breathing. I lowered the knife to my side, along with Micah's phone.

For a beat, we were silent.

"I can see you found Micah," he said. "Or rather, I can smell it." He coughed again, making a gagging sound. "I can't kill you," he lamented. "But oh, how I wish I could."

"Are you sure you don't want to kill Andrea? She's the one who did this to you, who turned you into this. You could confess to all of it. Tell the police downstairs. Get immunity."

"The police!" He laughed again. "No, Maeve. After all this time, you still don't understand. We are the enlightened ones," he said, casting spittle from his lips to mine. "This thing is bigger than you. Bigger than us, even. That pathetic commune you were born into?" He laughed again, then lost himself in a coughing fit that took precious seconds to subside—seconds in which the feeling returned to my arms and hands. "Mother Superior has made it a thousand times as big, a million times more profitable, infinitely more powerful. And that baby you carry inside you . . ." He took a step closer, and my hand twitched around the knife. "She'll be the next Mother Superior. Just as Andrea was groomed from birth, so shall she be."

I tried to take a step back. Rob was almost on top of me, and shudders of revulsion coursed through me.

"And if it's a boy?"

"Why do you keep asking this?" His voice was harsh. "If it's a boy, we'll discard it. We'll try again until we have a perfect replacement for Olivia."

"Just like you discarded Micah," I said, fighting to keep the emotion from my voice. *Just as they would have discarded Boy, in the end.*

"Yes." Rob sounded amused. "Yes, like that. He did too much digging. Asking about your and Andrea's childhood, sniffing around. Had mommy issues. On top of it, he was a bad partner to Emily. He didn't care well enough for their first child, so she felt the burden of it. His lack of devotion was clearly what led to her rejection of their second. So yes, we discarded him. It was an easy decision."

"And who's going to discard you, Rob?" With that, I shone the flashlight bright in his face, bright enough to make him blink, startled, and to illuminate all I needed. I didn't wait for him to respond.

"*I am*, you sick fuck."

Then I took the pocketknife and slashed it hard across his neck from Adam's apple to earlobe. Rob's blood spurted out at me, hot and wet. His body collapsed in front of me with a thud. He twitched and gurgled.

I kept the phone directed on his eyes, which stared—panicked—until they were lost and then gone. It didn't take long. Rob had never believed he'd be killed. As Andrea's husband, he thought he'd be safeguarded by her status. But I knew better. I knew that the second she found the positive pregnancy test, his clock had begun ticking. No matter if it was a girl or a boy. As soon as I brought a girl into the world, Rob's fate would have been sealed. It had been only a matter of time. And a matter of the hand that wielded the knife—hers or mine.

I hadn't been about to let her have the satisfaction of killing my rapist.

I fumbled in Rob's pocket for something—anything—of use. My fingers landed on a slender metal chain. I pulled it out, nearly fainting with relief at the sound of Rob's car keys. I gripped all three precious items—keys, phone, and knife. I clicked on the phone's home screen, desperately hoping for a lifeline, but it was locked.

I only knew the door we'd entered from, and I made my way back toward it, stepping carefully around the bodies. The narrowness of the corridors didn't scare me anymore, I realized; I'd dealt with far more frightening things by now. Nor did the spiders that crawled from the rafters and moved comfortably down the foundational beams, impervious to my presence. I moved down that hall for what felt like eternity, using the home screen of the phone to illuminate my path. And then I was there. I held an ear against the door, listening. As if I could have heard anything. It was eerily silent, but that didn't mean much.

I inched open the door a crack, allowing sound to seep back in. It was distant. The sounds of a struggle. I eased the door open and slid out. I could hear it more clearly now, and it was deafening, after the silence of the hidden passageways. There were screams—guttural and terrified—and thuds, and the voices of the Mothers coming from the lower level.

I crossed to the staircase near the room I'd taken when I first arrived. It was the only set of stairs that led directly to the foyer and out the door to the driveway, where Rob's car was parked.

"Please," I whispered. "Dear god, please."

I crept down the stairs barefoot, as soundlessly as possible. The grunts and cries grew louder with each step. When I reached the landing, the bloodbath in front of me made me rear back, accidentally knocking into the banister and falling onto the wooden stairs. All the Mothers' heads turned from their position across the room, where they had been mutilating the bodies of two policemen as Andrea looked on. Their fingers were slick with blood; they'd been tearing apart their victims with their bare hands.

Andrea saw me just a beat after they did, so transfixed was she with the scene before her. She was pristine in a white off-the-shoulder sweater and jeans as she observed, seemingly immune to the blood spurting through the air and coating the walls and furniture. Her eyes narrowed, and I leaped to my feet, darting to the right, toward the front door.

"Stop her," she shouted at the Mothers. I didn't look back. I couldn't. My heart was pounding, coursing energy through my still-weak legs in a desperate bid to keep them moving forward. But I heard their feet trampling the ground behind me—a whole horde of them—and it was as if I were living that night, twenty-five years ago, all over again. Running from a house I'd called home. Running from the only family I knew. The only thing missing was Boy in my arms.

I grabbed the doorknob and yanked it; it didn't budge. I fumbled desperately with the lock, yanking it again, and finally threw the door open with such force that it hit one of the women—whichever Mother had been closest to capturing me—with a thud.

I ran down the driveway until I reached the car. I pressed the Unlock button four times and then slid into the crisp leather driver's seat as they converged on me. I slammed the door on the fingers of another Mother. She screamed and yanked her hand back. It was hard to tell her blood from the blood in which she was already covered. I locked the car.

Now all I had to do was drive.

27

I t is my birthday, and I have run from the house with Boy in my arms. I am barefoot and my feet are scratched by a million brambles, but I don't slow until I reach the barn, and beside it, the old car.

The keys are in the ignition, like always. For a long time, it seemed to me that the Mothers just sat inside and the car magically went wherever they wanted it to go, as if it could read their thoughts or functioned as an extension of their desires. Then one day, Mother took me to the grocery. "I trust you," she said. "It's time."

I saw the way she turned the key, the way her foot pressed the pedal to make the car go. The car no longer seemed any more magical than the tractor or the machine we used to cut grass. But there was magic in taking the road all the way to the end, farther than I thought it could stretch, and following its bends past cornfields, a stream, even other cars like our own, until we reached the market.

The market was packed to the gills with food of all kinds— crunchy crackers I'd never seen before, cereals with marsh-mallows, cans of orange fizz Mother called "poison." And people. All the people, kids just like me, walking through the aisles like it was just a normal day. When a man crossed in front of me at the end of the aisle with pastas and grains, I nearly tripped into him.

"'Scuse me," he said, smiling. I stopped and stared until Mother gripped my arm hard and yanked me back over to the sauces. I'd seen men come into the house, but their eyes were always glazed, like when our cows got sick. *Men aren't like us,*

Mother had said. Seeing one walking around with the ease of belonging was a shock.

I will go to that market now. I will find that man and give Boy to him. He will know what to do. I fumble with the door on Mother's side, my heart pounding. It creaks open, screaming from rust, and the light inside flickers on. I hear shouts up the hill and glance back. Mothers' forms are rocketing toward me.

"Hush, hush," I say to Boy, as I slide in and nestle him on the passenger seat. I close the door and lock it, then fumble with Boy's belt. *Buckle your belt,* Mother said. *It isn't safe.* I want to keep Boy safe more than anything. That's why we have to go.

I pull the belt over Boy and slide it into the clasp with a hard *click,* looking up in the mirror at Mothers' forms, just a dozen yards away now, not far enough at all. Boy mewls, confused, then opens his mouth to wail. He reaches for me, wiggling right out over that belt.

There is a pounding on the window. I flinch. Mother is so close, right next to me. Mother claws at the door while Mother yells, "Unlock the door, Maeve."

Instead, I turn the key and the engine roars awake, startling Mother, who steps back. Mother's face is contorted in fury; I have never seen her so mad. I sit as tall as I can and look over the windshield until I can see the road stretching in front of me. I jam my foot onto the pedal and the car leaps forward, so fast I shove the brake and the car jolts again. My forehead collides with the wheel; I have forgotten my own belt. And Boy has tumbled to the floor, hurt and wailing.

The Mothers are surrounding the car now, banging on it, begging me to open up, and yelling. I scoop Boy up and put him on my lap, where I can hold him tight. I buckle the belt around us both. My foot hovers again over the pedal. Then I see Andrea. She presses a palm to the window by my face. Her face is streaked with tears.

"Mae," she says. "Don't go. Remember our promise."

I remember our promise. I think of it. I hesitate, reach for the lock on the door.

Then I remember the secret inside the locked room.

Andrea will be okay here. The Mothers will take care of her. Boy—I feel it deep down in my bones—will not be okay if he stays. I face forward and press my foot on the pedal, straining to see the road. We roar forward. I leave Andrea behind.

As the house recedes behind us, fading along with all their screaming voices, I am not prepared for how dark it is, or how bumpy the road. I keep one hand on Boy's belly and keep the other hand on the wheel, but it's hard to keep it straight and I can barely see over it. It's slick from my sweat and difficult to turn. The trees brush past me and we take a left at the end of the long road onto a paved road, the one I'm sure leads to the grocery.

But as we go, Boy wailing, I am no longer sure I turned the right way. I feel hot tears sliding down my cheeks and I blink rapidly to keep my eyes clear. "Just a little further," I tell Boy. "Don't you worry."

I focus on the yellow line on the road and try to keep the car right on top of it, so we don't leave the road. Some cars come toward me head-on before they blare their horns and swerve around. Why don't they follow their own yellow line? My tears turn to choking sobs. The yellow line curves. I don't see what is beyond it. But I keep the car centered on it. I am doing so well, and surely the store must be close.

I follow the line so carefully around the corner, and when the truck comes and blares its horn, I can't understand why it is breaking the rules, why it hasn't found its own line to follow, why it is heading straight toward us instead of around us like all the rest.

When it hits us, Boy is jolted from my lap and there is an emptiness beneath the seat belt where he was before. The car tumbles, rockets, the wheel no longer any good, and anyway I'm not reaching for the wheel anymore; I'm desperately grasping the air to reclaim Boy, his wails reaching me around the noises of horns and breaking glass.

The car hits its side and skids that way down the road for a long time. When it stills, I am hanging on my side from my seat belt and Boy is nowhere to be seen. The big window on the front of the car is completely smashed. I unbuckle the belt, letting my body crash to the other end of the car—the side pressed against the road. The door above me creaks open and hands reach for me and frantic voices scream, "Is she okay?" I hear, "My god, she's only a little kid." And I'm wrenched from the car.

A man crouches over me, yelling, and before long there are red and blue lights pulsing around me. Then more men. I am surrounded by men. Big men, scary ones, and I scream and cry for Boy. I crane my neck, straining to find him. I have to find him.

It's when one of them lifts me on top of a thin bed on wheels that I see it: not Boy, but a small animal lying in the road, twisted and broken. Not Boy. It doesn't look like Boy at all. It doesn't look like anything but a mass of bloodied flesh— maybe a raccoon or a baby deer. But people are surrounding it, a woman is shrieking, and the big men are kneeling, and then I catch a glimpse of the worst thing. I have a vision I don't want to have, and after that everything goes black.

When I wake up, I am inside a big white van and someone is pressing a mask on top of my face and wrapping something around my left arm, which for the first time I see is gushing blood and hanging limply from my side. Somewhere in all of it, I fall asleep, letting my body sink into the curious sounds of panic surrounding me.

I never see Boy after that, except in the visions I would do anything to end.

28

My cousin looked at me looking at her, daring me to turn on the engine and drive away. I held her gaze as the car rocked more precariously, as cracks from the larger rocks formed on the windshield. *I know you,* her eyes said. *You'd never do it again. Not when it's only you to save. Deep down, you're just a scared little child.*

But what she didn't know was that all those years of being on my own had taught me something: I was also a survivor.

So I turned the key. I put the car into Drive. Watched her expression change from smug to confused to astonished.

I pressed my foot on the pedal and accelerated as hard and fast as I could—very hard, very fast; it was their top-of-the-line Range Rover, after all—aiming straight for my cousin. I saw her react, move out of the way. I felt the crunching of obstructions—a body, or bodies—beneath my wheels. I had no idea if one was hers. I prayed it was.

I drove like that, not knowing how to drive, really, tears clouding my vision, for what must have been ten minutes before I heard it: the buzzing of Micah's phone. He was getting another call.

I reached frantically for the device, which had slid somewhere between the driver's seat and the center console. On the fourth ring I hit Accept.

"Hello, this is Linda from NYC Health," came a voice, blessedly clear and composed. "May I speak with Micah Winters? I'm calling about his wife, Emily."

"Micah is dead," I told her. "Please, I need help."

29

I awoke gasping for air, shrieking, certain I was trapped in those same walls where Micah's and Rob's bodies had been discarded. But instead of a dark, musty corridor cloaked in the smell of death, I was confronted by the bland sterility of a hospital room. I kicked hard, eager to be free of the sheets twining my legs. I fought to catch my breath as I registered the details: gleaming white speckled tiles, the sun just starting to set behind uniform white blinds, a blue metal door that reminded me of my public high school, a man in a dark suit seated next to me.

"You've been through an ordeal." He offered me a cup of water, but I shook my head. I wasn't about to trust this guy, like I'd trusted Andrea and all the others.

"Where am I? Who are you?" My tongue felt thick, like a slab of meat that didn't belong to me. The words came out garbled.

"Troy Atkinsen. FBI." He offered me the cup again, and this time I accepted—not because I'd changed my mind about him but because my sudden thirst was overwhelming, a physical need rather than a desire. I gulped down the water, watching him out of the corner of my eye. My body ached. My muscles felt stiff and leaden. When I was done drinking, he pulled a plastic pitcher off the nightstand and refilled my cup.

"You're at Bellevue," he explained. "Do you remember what happened?"

I nodded, draining the paper cup a second time and sinking back against my pillows. Troy took the cup and tossed it into the trash can with the finesse of a former athlete.

"Basketball?" I asked.

"Yeah. Georgetown."

"It was the follow-through. And your height."

He smiled. "Observant."

"Not observant enough." Pain was beginning to wash over me. I hadn't remembered this whole-body stiffness when running. The pain in my wrist hadn't bothered me when I clutched the steering wheel. "You're here because you didn't get her," I said as I realized.

"We made a dozen arrests—"

"What are you doing?" I bolted upright again, pain shooting from my wrists to my elbows as I pushed myself to a seated position. "Why aren't you out looking for her?"

"We did, for days," the investigator explained. I stared. "Still are."

"What do you mean, '*days*'?"

"You've been out for three days. The police gave you a sedative when they found you, and they brought you straight here. You've been sleeping since. It's the shock."

"Brought me here . . . to Bellevue."

"Not my call," he told me. "But you were in bad shape when you were picked up. We're getting you out, though. Transferring you to Mount Sinai. They have a good long-term program. We'll be able to keep an eye on you there."

"What do you mean?" I studied his face, panicked. "Am I under investigation? You can't check me in anywhere against my will. I can go home. I live in the city. My apartment is in Brooklyn. I could go home today." But I couldn't, I realized. I had renters. I hardly had any money. I needed the modest surplus from the renters in order to survive even a few more months.

"You're not under investigation." Agent Atkinsen leaned forward and rested his clasped hands on the bed's guardrail. "But you're a key witness, and we need to keep you safe. And you've been through trauma," he repeated. "It wouldn't be the worst thing." His eyes flickered to the opposite wall, where a TV I hadn't noticed before was showing the local news. Even without the sound, I could tell what was being broadcast. The scenes flickering across the screen—of a taped-off crime scene—were identical to my nightmares.

Throngs of people milled outside the house. It was pandemonium.

Agent Atkinsen reached for the remote and clicked the volume. The sounds of chaotic fury filled the room and "Breaking" flashed across the screen.

"As the search for bodies continues," said the newscaster, "more questions arise over the Mother Collective: How the cult slipped under the government's radar while generating billions of dollars in profit behind the NewLife label and its revolutionary Vigeneros technology, patented just five years ago. Where the money went, now that 'Mother Superior' is missing. How the worship of false idols hid behind an international life coaching franchise. Stay tuned for answers to these and other revelatory questions, after the break."

After the break, they did flash a picture—Andrea's. Mother Superior, at large. "If you see this woman, alert authorities immediately," instructed the reporter solemnly. Andrea's delicate jawline and green eyes were so familiar, I could have been looking at myself. *Just like twins.* The reporter held the mic out to a man in his mid- to late twenties, burly and red-faced, who was standing toward the front of the crowd.

"What would you do if you spotted her?" the reporter asked.

"I'd rip her to shreds," the man replied without hesitation. "I'd make sure that murdering bitch never saw the light of—"

The producers cut to a commercial, an ad featuring children peeling the cellophane off a prepackaged lunch.

"People are riled up," Troy said, matter-of-factly. "And you look like her. Even if you don't want psychological care, the psych ward is high security. It's a safe space for you to ride this out. Wait until the worst of it dies down. Let us keep an eye on you. And maybe you'll cooperate. Give us something that'll help us catch her." He paused. "Your care will be paid for by the state, if you do."

There it was. I leaned back in the hospital bed, feeling a fresh wave of nausea. The room tilted. My head was pounding. I was sick. Too sick to continue the conversation. *Pregnant*. I was pregnant, not sick. I gagged, choking on my own bile. I lifted a corner of the thin coverlet to my face, breathing deeply. The thick smell of antiseptic wasn't helping.

"I'll get someone," he said. "I'll come back for you in the morning." As he strode from the room in his predictable black suit—I hadn't thought they wore those in real life—I coughed, hacking, until I did throw up, all over my sheets, and a nurse rushed in, calling for support, and then they were surrounding me and fiddling with my IV and dabbing my face and chin with a cold washcloth.

A nurse approached me with a needle. "Just a little something to make you feel better."

"What is it?" There were the stirrings of fresh panic.

"Shh," the nurse whispered, motioning to her aide, who gripped my forearm, pinning it flat to the bed. "All this upset isn't good for the baby."

"Who are you?" I hissed. She bent over me with the syringe and I kicked hard, watching her face contort with surprise as I connected my knee with her shoulder.

"Backup!" shouted the aide, pressing a button on the side of my bed. The nurse moved to a corner of the room and was rubbing her shoulder, her face twisted in pain.

Three people rushed in—two men and a woman. I heard myself shrieking and wailing as if through a tunnel while the men held me down and the woman prepared a new needle and jabbed it into my arm before I had time to think of another strategy, another way to fight. I couldn't fight and win, I realized, as my vision began to blur. The world wasn't set up that way, not for me.

The rest of the night was fitful. I awoke multiple times in a drugged haze, certain at one point that Andrea was standing in the corner of the room, watching me. Later, I thought a robe hanging from a hook on the door was Rob hanging from a hook on the door, his head sliced at the neck.

At five o'clock I awoke again, shuddering but clearheaded. She had only given me a sedative. I wondered how long it would be before I stopped being terrified of every woman I encountered.

The first hints of dawn were breaking through the flimsy plastic blinds that covered the only window in the room. I slid from the hospital bed and tested my balance before reaching back for the IV drip. I shuffled toward the door, pulling the IV station after me.

Agent Atkinsen wasn't wrong, I realized. I was too fragile for the outside world. Even if I weren't, I had nowhere to go. A hospital would be good, safe. I would simply check out as soon as I was ready and head straight to an ob-gyn. I would work with the FBI as long as they were willing to protect me. It was my only choice. Anything else would be suicide.

Something told me Andrea wouldn't hurt me—not as long as I had what she wanted. But after I terminated the pregnancy? I wasn't ready to think about the after. Maybe I wouldn't have to. Maybe they'd catch her before my time ran out.

The room felt tiny and airless. I heaved open the heavy metal door and moved into the hallway, eager for air, space, something other than those four walls, which may as well have been a prison cell. The ward wasn't much bigger, I realized. From where I stood, I could see two sets of doors on either end of the hall. Between them was a reception area—empty save for one orderly, who nodded as I inched by—and six or seven rooms. I shuffled toward one set of doors. Block letters, facing the opposite direction, created signage over the triple-pane glass. I squinted at their outlines.

"Maximum security wing," I read aloud. Of course. It hadn't occurred to me to wonder why I didn't have a roommate, but now I understood. I didn't bother testing the door. Instead I turned and shuffled back toward the opposite end of the corridor.

"Stretching my legs," I muttered at the orderly as I approached.

"Make it quick," he said, but he smiled kindly. He knew.

I made the trek four times, relishing the feeling of circulation returning to my legs, before I heard it: a low keening coming from one of the other rooms. Something about it sounded familiar. I shot the orderly a look; he was typing into his phone. I moved toward the source of the noise and pushed the door open as quietly as I could. I peered in.

Fuck.

Emily was on one of two cots, staring vacantly into space. The other cot sat empty. I looked from the room to the machine I was tethered to. There was no way I could drag it into the room without the orderly hearing.

I drew a breath and yanked the IV from my arm, letting the tube fall to the floor. I clutched my forearm and slid noiselessly into the room, shutting the door gently behind me. My arm stung, and a drop of blood seeped from the needle's insertion point. I wiped it on the corner of my gown.

Emily's wrists were shackled to the sides of her bed. I gasped audibly, and as I did, the door swung open behind me.

"Hey!" The orderly's voice was sharp. "How did you get in here? You can't be in here. Did you pull out your drip?"

"I just wanted to see her," I pleaded. "I . . . We . . . I'm a friend."

He eyed me warily. But he didn't make any move to usher me out. There'd been a glimmer of sympathy in his eyes earlier. He knew our story. Maybe he felt bad for us. And there was something more, something else. I watched his eyes travel over me, then dart to Emily. They widened, taking in her pregnant form. The glimmer wasn't just sympathy, I realized. It was morbid fascination.

"You can stand outside the door," I said softly, taking the gamble. "To make sure I don't do anything funny. I just want to talk. I haven't seen her since . . . well. Since we were last together." I'd never been much for charming men, and I certainly wasn't about to then, as I stood there covered in bruises in a flimsy hospital gown. But this man didn't want charm; he was hungry for something else. I met his eyes and focused on projecting all the pain and hurt I'd felt from Andrea's betrayal, allowing it to bubble to the surface. He winced.

"You have five minutes," he muttered, looking away. "Don't work her up. She's easily exhausted."

I nodded. Emily's arms were draped listlessly against her restraints, her enormous stomach presiding above the rest of her form, which looked thinner and more wasted than when I'd last seen her.

"She's facing serious legal charges." The orderly was as eager to share as I'd assumed he'd be. "I can't say much, but the state doesn't look kindly on women who possess violent tendencies toward their unborn children, let alone women associated with . . . illegal behaviors. Still . . ." He straightened and composed his face, which had slipped into a look of disgust. "Everyone needs friends. Even sadistic cult members. Maybe especially them. I'll step outside for a couple of minutes, but I'm leaving the door open. Try to bring her some peace."

He wasn't all bad, then.

"Emily," I said loudly. "Emily, can you hear me?" Her eyes flickered to where I stood, focusing and slipping back out of focus as if she were under water. Finally they cleared. Her expression changed from confusion to recognition.

"Maeve?" she asked, slurring slightly. It was clear she was on tranquilizers of some kind; she was having a hard time enunciating. "Your hair is gone. Did you bring Henry?"

"No," I said, sorry. "But he's being looked after." I hoped it was true.

Her eyes were wet, her lips chapped. She had a red rash along her collarbone, where her hospital gown didn't cover her. Her forearms were covered in hives.

"I'm so sad," she told me. "So, so sad." Her head lolled to the side, and I wondered again about what they'd put her on. Her sorry state shocked me. I had five minutes to get answers. To see how much Emily had known about Andrea and Rob's plan for me. Whether she knew where Andrea was now. But she was so pathetic, so broken, that I wasn't sure she could tell me anything at all. It was hard to believe this was the same woman I'd seen gracing the front page of so many publications. That woman had been magnetic. This one was a husk.

"I'm sorry, Maeve," she told me then.

"For what?" I asked carefully, wanting to encourage her without sending her over the edge.

"You were right," she mumbled, tears leaking from her eyes and streaming down the sides of her face. "She said it was you who was the problem, but it was her all along." I moved closer, pulled a tissue from the box next to her, and dabbed at her cheeks.

"You mean Andrea?" My voice was low, cautious.

Emily nodded. Her expression contorted in fear. "Where is she?" she asked urgently.

"You don't know where Andrea is?" I asked.

"No. No," she said again, her voice rising to fever pitch. So she had heard something about the bust, but not from Andrea herself. She looked too terrified for it to be anything but the truth. Emily wasn't going to be of any use to me now.

"The police have her," I lied, wanting to soothe her. "She's gone now. She can't hurt you. Everyone from the Collective was arrested."

Emily shook her head vehemently. "You don't understand," she said, whispering. "They're everywhere."

"What are you talking about? Andrea controlled everything. And they got all twelve women who came for the retreat. They're in jail now."

"She's not gone for good, Maeve. Even if the police have her, even if they got every single person from the retreat, the Collective is like a net gun. There are tendrils everywhere." Her chapped lips pursed, causing the skin around her mouth to break and bleed where she'd clearly been gnawing at it again, even more so than before. But she sounded more lucid now than she had a moment ago.

"The Collective is over," I told her firmly. "The FBI took it down. Everyone is in jail."

Emily laughed. Her eyes were clearing. A chill worked its way down my spine.

"It's everywhere," she said simply. "It has thousands of members. It's the biggest and most egalitarian organization that exists in the world right now. It doesn't discriminate by race, socioeconomic divide, religion, age. Its devotees won't let it crumble."

It did discriminate, though, I realized. It celebrated womanhood only as it pertained to a working uterus. It excluded trans and nonbinary people, men, people who couldn't have kids or didn't want to. It was the antithesis of inclusive, the opposite of feminist.

Emily's face darkened. I watched her come back to herself, her eyes widening in fear as she returned to her present circumstances.

"What is it?" I asked, dreading the answer.

"Why do you think I had to have another baby?" she whispered.

Then I realized. "Henry wasn't enough."

"No. Oh no, Henry wouldn't do. I needed a little girl. But that was the problem. I didn't want another baby. You understand, don't you?" She looked up at me, her eyes desperate. "I'm sorry for what we did to you," she went on, and I went cold. "Did it work? Did the plan work?" She gazed at my midsection, evaluating. "I should have given her mine," she told me. "I didn't want it. You understand, don't you, Maeve?"

I shook my head slowly from side to side. "No," I whispered. "I'm sorry, Emily. I don't."

At this she let out a sob. She bucked against her restraints and began to howl, her eyes rolling back in her skull.

"They're everywhere!" she screamed. "Everywhere, don't you see? They're always watching." I stared at her, panicked. The orderly burst back in, shooting me a furious look.

"You were supposed to keep her calm," he said. "I could get fired for this. Go back to your room." Then he turned to Emily. "Okay, Emily, none of that, you hear me? It isn't good for your condition." Emily continued to thrash.

"The baby," she moaned in between snarls and shrieks. "I don't want it. Get it out of me." Whatever had been left of her mind when I saw her last was no longer there; that much was clear. Andrea's world had broken her.

"Didn't you hear me?" the orderly snapped, glaring in my direction. "Get back to your room before you get me fired!" I backed slowly out of the room as he pressed the red button by Emily's bed, summoning help. But Emily was beyond help now, I realized, as I pulled my IV drip back to the room with me, my heart pounding against my ribs. Emily had been reduced to an anxious, manic vessel whose sole purpose was to give birth. It was the exact thing she'd tried, along with the others, to do to me.

The next day, I resolved, I would go to the other hospital. I would work with the FBI. I would give them whatever they needed. Because here, on my own, I could trust no one.

'd arranged to meet up with Mallory for coffee prior to my doctor's appointment, but now I was regretting it. I'd awoken to the sharp staccato of my heartbeat at seven a.m., two hours before my meeting with my former colleague. I forced myself to lie there, determined to seize any respite from reality. But the reality was I wanted to race straight to the clinic, leap onto the examining table, spread my legs wide in stirrups, and expel the thing inside me, which had begun to feel as though it were taking over my body.

It had been nearly four months since I'd escaped Andrea's clutches, and she was still at large. The clock had been ticking from the moment I'd entered Mount Sinai under FBI supervision, and I'd checked myself out yesterday out of necessity, heading back to the tiny, familiar apartment that had been empty for nearly two weeks by then. The first thing I did was take a long, hot shower. The second was set up a doctor's appointment. And the third was to email Mallory to see if she was available the next day to discuss freelance work and "catch up." My reprieve was over.

When it became clear I wasn't going to fall back asleep, I rolled out of bed and began to get ready. I splashed water on my face, catching a glimpse of my reflection in the small, cracked mirror that hung over my sink. I hardly recognized myself lately. My cheeks were gaunt, my midsection and feet swollen. I looked old, far older than my thirty-three years. The encounter with Emily had left me shaken. It was all I could think about at Mount Sinai—that and Andrea, of course. Agent Atkinsen made sure she was always on my mind, with his daily visits and relentless questions about everything from Andrea's favorite foods to her mannerisms to our childhoods.

Now, as I brushed my teeth and ran a brush through my hair, it struck me how much it was costing me to undo what the Collective had done to *me*. I knew I ought to be grateful to be alive. To be on the receiving end of Mallory's freelance scraps, which might keep me afloat, if I was lucky. I ought, even, to be more afraid. But I was none of those things. I was angry. By then, the police had linked Tyler's death to Andrea. No one had connected the dots back to Ryan and the apartment fire that killed him, but I knew, and it was enough.

When I arrived at Le Pain Quotidien an hour and a half later, Mallory appeared decidedly uncomfortable.

"Hi!" I said, forcing a sunny smile and wrapping my arms around her. I was aware of the shadows under my eyes, my bald head partially concealed by a jaunty hat, my pale complexion. I could feel Mallory's healthy, athletic frame through the shift dress that separated my fingers from her body. I was Mallory once. And now here I was. How quickly I'd lost myself.

"Congratulations on your promotion," I told her. "It's such great news for you."

"Thanks! And I owe you a congratulations also. I can't believe it! Expecting." She eyed my bump. I'd tried to hide it, but it had moved past conspicuous into an obvious protrusion, a tumor I hadn't yet expelled. "How incredible! Who's the lucky guy?"

"No guy," I said.

"Oh. Oh!" She exclaimed. "I didn't realize! Sorry." She scrambled to walk back her heteronormative assumption, and I didn't bother to clarify. "Well, I'm so happy for you. What a modern family."

It *was* a modern family. All too modern. I rewarded her comment with a tight smile. Let her think whatever she wanted.

"I tried to get ahold of Elena," I mentioned. "Turn in some of those freelance assignments she had me doing, stuff she said you were too busy to take on. But I got her bounce-back."

"Oh," Mallory said again. She looked downward. "You know, Elena's been gone for a while. She was having a really good year, between you and me." Mallory's voice turned conspiratorial. "Her wife came into a bunch of money. Some dead relative, I guess. So Elena retired early. Wouldn't *that* be nice? She's been posting photos of that smug wife of hers and their kids in Prague and, like, Senj. Which, frankly? Where even *is* Senj?"

"Croatia," I answered faintly.

"Well she's pretty much living the dream now." At this, Mallory's expression soured. So the promotion hadn't done much for her salary level. Poor Mallory. Single, struggling. We were so alike, except for the shit show I'd been born into and barely escaped, and barely escaped again. Suddenly I found myself missing Patty and Tom with a ferocity I didn't expect. I was truly alone this time.

I leaned back, focusing on what Mallory had revealed. Elena's story sounded familiar. Eerily so. Her wife got a significant cash flow at some point between when I was fired and now. Then she disappeared. It was too coincidental.

"Could you check on these freelance titles Elena gave me before she left? Maybe keep the invoices moving?" I asked Mallory. "I'd love to get them accepted and paid. And of course, if you have any other leads, I'd really appreciate you keeping me in mind."

"Sure," she said. "Just email me. I'll ask Edward too."

I laughed, and she looked at me oddly.

"Sorry," I said. "It's just funny."

"What is?"

"Oh, I was thinking of Edward. How few men there are in publishing, yet how they all manage to be at the top. I wonder what would happen if men sort of . . . ceased to exist." I threw the fingers of my right hand in the air and made a *poof* sound. Mallory laughed awkwardly and eyed me, clearly trying to determine how serious I was.

"That's a little intense, don't you think?"

I tried to course-correct. "I only mean if they became irrelevant. In publishing," I stammered. "You know. If more women rose to the top."

Mallory shrugged. "I think things would be mostly the same," she said. "Except it would be women and not men making bad judgment calls. And I happen to like the guys we work with. Then again, if it gets me a higher salary, I'm all in." She laughed ruefully. "If I'm going to have a baby in the next year or two, I'll need to pay for a nanny."

This time I was the shocked one.

"Oh! I didn't tell you? I'm engaged." Mallory waved her left hand between us, and a cluster of diamonds glittered proudly against her olive skin. How had I not noticed?

"Well, congratulations," I told her. "That's exciting news. I had no idea you were seeing someone."

"We've only been together for a year and a half," she explained, shrugging. "I don't know. I usually keep my personal life quiet. You of all people should understand that."

"What do you mean?"

"Oh, Maeve, come on," she said. "Don't take this the wrong way, but everyone knew you were impenetrable." She peered at me as I fought to keep my astonishment under control. "What? Don't tell me this is coming as a surprise. You never let anyone in. I always figured you thought you were better than the rest of us."

I cleared my throat and took a long sip of coffee.

"Well," I said, trying to make light of it. "I guess no time like the present to start opening up."

"Sure."

I stared at my coffee, flushing. Mallory—a woman whom I'd openly disregarded—had seen right through me. Everything she'd said was right. The Mothers' old phrase leaped into my head: *If you're born to be hanged, you'll never be drowned.* I hadn't let the Mother Collective destroy me. The person I could be was still undetermined. So what now? How did I fix things?

"I'm so sorry," I said, meeting her eyes. "You are absolutely right. You've been nothing but kind to me, and I've been jealous. You're younger than I am, more successful, and have your life together. I was projecting my insecurity onto you."

"It's okay," she said, shaking her head as if to clear it. "But a piece of advice, Maeve? Earning people's trust goes a long way."

I nodded. She was right. It was going to be the most impossible road, but I would get there one way or another. Something Andrea had said once had seared itself into my brain: *You can choose happiness.* Maybe for some people happiness was a choice. I didn't think it was as easy as all that—luck played a large part in things, after all. But why had I always believed, on some level, that *misery* was my destiny? What a silly, self-centered thought.

"I'm curious to know which season my projects with Elena were in," I said, steering the conversation back to freelancing. "The ones you couldn't take on. I would think they'd be fall of next year? Or are they spring?"

Mallory fidgeted uncomfortably. "I can't give out confidential information," she said.

"No, no." A dismissive wave of my hand. "I'm just curious to know when they're coming out, so I can grab a copy."

"Which ones were you working on?" Mallory softened.

I rattled them off. I'd been working on *Three Strikes Till Midnight* and *The Last of Her Kind*. I was slated to receive $3,000 altogether for the two projects—a paltry sum, but one I needed nevertheless. When I told Mallory, her brow furrowed quizzically.

"Sorry, what did you say the titles were? *Three Strikes . . .*? Elena said these were projects of mine? I've never heard of that."

"I can show you my correspondence with Elena," I offered.

"No. Those aren't our books. You must be getting your assignments mixed up."

"Here," I said, pulling up an email and showing Mallory my screen.

"That's really weird," she said, staring hard at the email. "Why would Elena send out a freelance assignment on a personal account? And I thought her personal email was her maiden name, not her last name . . ."

"Oh," I said. "I'm not sure. Maybe they were early projects that got canceled? In any case," I went on, quickly, not wanting the weirdness of the situation to put her off, "I'd love to take on more freelance moving forward. I would be so grateful." My words sounded pandering, but I was sincere. My well-being was in large part in the hands of my acquaintances, acquaintances whom I hadn't treated all that well or made much effort to get close to.

I spent the next twenty minutes endearing myself to Mallory. Asking more about her fiancé, her personal life, her new role at the company. Mentioning my enthusiasm for just about all the content no one else wanted to handle, my willingness to accept rush jobs on a shoestring budget. Money would be a problem sooner than I wanted to admit.

During lulls in the conversation, I found my mind wandering to Andrea and Rob. *Those bastards,* I thought as Mallory spoke, picturing Rob's decaying body and Andrea's twisted sneer. *Those lying, Mother-worshipping sacks of shit.*

*   *   *

Later that day, I lay back on the examining table at the clinic and tried hard not to think about what it meant to finally be outside hospital walls—vulnerable. My legs were splayed apart, my butt scooted to the end of the examination table, my feet propped in stirrups. I'd elected to go to a random Planned Parenthood in Inwood rather than my old gynecologist, just in case. Everything had been a "just in case," after my final conversation with Emily. I wondered if I'd ever be able to live without a degree of paranoia again. Until they found Andrea, I knew I'd never settle into a permanent job; I'd never see the same doctor twice; I'd hop from sublet to sublet.

"Take a breath," said the OB, who'd introduced herself as Dr. Kapadia. "You're tense."

You'd be tense in this position, too, if you'd been raped by your cousin's husband and bound to a bed for days, I thought but did not dare say. *If you'd been lied to for months and fed hormones in smoothies and given a placebo pill you thought was Plan B and made to eat a raw placenta.*

"I'm interested in pursuing an abortion," I'd told her. "As soon as possible."

"You're far along," she'd said, eyeing the thing my body had grown.

"Not so far," I'd said. "Maybe toward the start of my second trimester. I think I just show more than most women do at this stage." By my estimation, I was sixteen to eighteen weeks along. And it wasn't all that uncommon for some women to show more than others. It was further along than I would have liked, for what I was about to do. Far enough for me to be aware of the thing inside me, for it to take on traits that were too human, too real. It was less a sickness now and more a living entity, depending on me for survival. I didn't like that. I didn't want it to feel human at all. It wouldn't change what I was about to do. It would only change how I felt about it.

I took a deep breath, unfisting my hands. I tried hard not to clench up against the doctor's instrument probing my vaginal canal. She moved the transvaginal ultrasound wand inside me. My body fought hard against it, even as I told myself to relax. Sweat pooled at the base of my tailbone, in the hollow of my lower back. It was taking so long. Why was it taking so damn long?

And then it was gone. Dr. Kapadia pulled the wand out abruptly, and my body shut its access points. She pushed back her stool and gave me a long look.

"Everything looks healthy in there. But you're not at eighteen weeks." Her voice was matter-of-fact.

"I am," I insisted. "Give or take." That was when Tyler and Rob had blindfolded and raped me.

I shut my brain against the memory.

"No." She shook her head.

"What do you mean, 'No'?" I asked. Could I be wrong? Could I have gotten pregnant by Tyler, despite that we'd used condoms every time? I did the math. Still plenty of time.

"I'll have to run some tests, but I'd guess you're roughly twenty-seven weeks along," she informed me. "Actually showing a little less than average for this stage."

"No. That's impossible." I sat upright on the table, crossing my legs at the knee. They were covered by a fine layer of goose bumps, the dark protrusion of hairs emerging from pores. Tyler and I hadn't even slept together at that point, which by my quick calculations fell shortly after Ryan's death. She had to be off by a few weeks one way or the other.

Dr. Kapadia gave me a long look. "Stay calm," she said. "Let's look again. I want to get a better sense of the baby's age and sex. Lie back." I acquiesced, nodding when she asked if she could reinsert. She spread a blue gel over the base of the condom-clad wand and inserted it back into my vagina. I shuddered from the surprising cold of it and turned my head away as she began to move the wand over the thing in my body.

I didn't want to see it. How different this all could have been, with Ryan, who might still be here, alive, if I had only wanted a future with him. If I hadn't been so *alone* when Andrea made connection. So in need of someone to love me. But it wouldn't have mattered, I realized. Andrea would have gotten to me one way or another, once she made me her target. No one around me was safe. No one would be, until she was gone.

"Doctor," I said absently, as she peered at the screen. "I ran out of a prescription recently, and I need it to do my work." I faltered, knowing it sounded strange. "Anyway, I was wondering if you could refill it for me."

"Which medicine?"

"Adderall."

"I wish I could help you, but—"

"I have ADD," I said defensively.

"It's not that," the doctor reassured me. "No judgment here. It's just that you shouldn't be on Adderall when you're pregnant. It increases the risk of premature delivery." There was a long silence.

"Oh." The doctor's explanation made clear how I had seemingly lost my bottle. *Andrea.* I rested my hands at my sides and refused to look at the screen. I wanted no attachment to the baby.

"Well!" came the doctor's voice then. She was very pleased with herself, whatever the news. "Do you want to know the sex of the baby?"

"I'm not sure," I told her. Then, because, despite myself, part of me desperately wanted it to be a boy, I said, "Okay."

"It's a girl . . ." she began, and I felt my heart sinking. It would be harder, with a girl. I tried to forgive myself for the thought. It wasn't my fault how fucked up I was. "And another girl," she finished.

"What?" I was sure I'd misheard.

"Identical twins," she told me. "Two baby girls, twenty-five weeks along. We should talk about your options."

Two little girls who'd look exactly alike. Would they have green eyes and blond hair? It was so ironic I nearly laughed. I laid my head back against the crinkly white paper covering the exam chair and tried hard not to pass out.

*   *   *

The options, it seemed, were limited, since abortion wasn't a possibility in New York for late-term pregnancies. I would put the babies up for adoption.

"If we secure a family quickly," the doctor mentioned, "they may be willing to cover a portion of your medical expenses up to the birth." She referred me to an adoption agency. I called right then, in the waiting room of the doctor's office, to set up an appointment. Then I went home and thought back to where I was twenty-five weeks ago.

Of course the blindfold incident hadn't done it. I had been an idiot to think a pregnancy test could have tracked a day-old conception. It had happened before then; they just hadn't known it yet.

I made note of as many significant dates as I could remember. When I looked at the reservations on my Airbnb calendar, my heart stood still.

Twenty-five weeks prior, Ryan was definitely already dead.

"No, no. That isn't right," I whispered to myself, double- and triple-checking the dates on the messages against the weeks I'd marked off on the calendar.

But it was. Twenty-five weeks ago I was living in the house, in my Grief Fog, which was how I'd begun to think of those disorienting weeks. My heart jackhammered as I searched my memory, came up empty, convinced myself the doctor was wrong.

I curled up on my side atop my mattress and peeled off my sweater, trying not to panic. The old radiators made my small apartment hot in the dead of winter—too hot. I felt a sharp pain in my pelvis and shifted, trying to get comfortable. I wondered how much the things inside me were like Andrea and me. I wondered if one would be born a psychopath. Would living with a good family help my little psychopath, like it had me? Or would she be doomed to repeat the cycle?

I pulled myself to my feet, losing my tank top and the sweats I'd been living in on the way to the bathroom. A bath would relax me; baths always had. Once in the bath, I'd be able to think more clearly. I'd sort through this new information and figure out a course of action.

I filled the tub, leaving the door open so the room wouldn't get too hot. When the water hit the two-thirds mark, I lowered my heavy body in, nearly gasping from the decadent pleasure of it. I was glad my body still fit, but then, as it turned out, I was actually smaller at this stage than was average, at least for women pregnant with twins. The twins were nestled up against each other right that second, plotting. Whispering secrets. Devising a way to rip me in two.

I blinked. The heat was making me woozy. I wasn't sure where that last thought had come from. I eased my head back against the porcelain rim and allowed my eyes to close. I only wished I had a glass of wine.

Then I felt it: his hands on my shoulders. His lips against my neck.

I gasped, jolting upright, causing the water to slosh over the side of the tub. My heart was pounding, and I scanned the room for any sign of him.

But Rob was dead.

I drew my knees up and wrapped my arms around them,

shuddering despite the heat. My rounded belly broke the surface of the water, an island on which my naked breasts were moored. It came back to me, all at once. The long, eerie bath. Rob's hands on my shoulders, kneading them. The blackout. The strange, musky odor the following day—a foreign sheen of sweat. The depleted Klonopin bottle. The way I ached everywhere. The way nothing made sense the next day.

Rob had done more than rape me while I was blindfolded.

Rob had raped me *two* times. It was so obvious, I couldn't believe I hadn't listened to my gut before.

I screamed until I heard a banging on my apartment door. When I managed to pull myself up to answer, there was more water on the floor than in the tub. I saw myself in the mirror, a madwoman, remaining hair hanging in damp, wild wisps around my gaunt face and hollow eyes.

I answered the door naked. Why not? My body was no longer mine to protect. It had been taken by Rob, by Andrea, by the leeches growing inside it. Privacy no longer meant anything to me.

I am okay, I told them. *I stumbled on a piece of glass. I am okay.*

Just another crazy lady, they probably thought. Hormones.

I shut the door and dragged myself back to bed. As I passed the kitchen, I saw the glint of a knife. I remembered Emily, the knife poised over her stomach. I thought about doing what she hadn't quite pulled off.

In the end, it all came back to me and to what little control I could still wield. And I wanted the things inside me gone.

But I wanted to stay alive.

I hated myself for my selfishness.

Andrea's eyes were on me, even then; I felt it.

Just like twins. Just like Mother.

We were so much alike, she and I. It was hard to tell, sometimes, where one of us ended and the other began.

31

V ery bold, refusing a scheduled C-section," the nurse said, as he wheeled me, panting and keening, toward the labor and delivery ward. "Twins usually arrive early. Better for you, though; no worries there. Don't worry, mama, they'll be perfectly healthy." His voice was cheerful and impersonal, the sort of voice you might expect to hear from a cashier at the 7-Eleven, collecting $3.30 for a Slurpee.

I nodded, gritting my teeth through the pain, wanting to disembowel this youthful, smug person. For weeks, I'd wanted them out. I'd been assured they'd vacate my body long before term. But here we were, *at* term, weeks of pacing and squats and castor oil and pineapple core having amounted to little more than dashed hopes and indigestion. It was as if they were hell-bent on torturing me, latching themselves to my body until they gutted me from the inside out.

I could have had a C-section. But I couldn't stand the idea of one more scar. Of my body being ripped open and sewn back together like a rag doll they'd infested. After it was all over, I wanted my body to bear no trace of what my cousin had done to me. I wanted to start over, smooth and undefiled. I wanted to look at my body and buy into the lie that it had always been mine and mine alone.

"Up, up, up," the nurse said, hoisting me onto my hospital bed. The paper beneath me dampened and crinkled, already slick with cold sweat. "The doctor will be with you shortly." I nodded, heaving and bearing down against the initial throes of labor.

Before he could exit, there were three knocks. A striking

thirtysomething woman with close-cropped natural hair rushed in.

"I came as soon as I could," Celeste told me, the pitch of her voice revealing her excitement. "I was in the middle of a brief when I got your text, and I rushed right over. Oh god, Maeve, how are you feeling?"

I nodded, gritting my teeth. Sweat trickled down my face and I allowed her to mop it with a tissue as she clasped my hand in her own. "You're going to be wonderful, Maeve," she assured me. "You're going to bring our babies into this world with so much courage."

I met her eyes. "Yours," I forced out. My teeth were gritted, pressed so tight I thought I'd grind them out, pulverize them to dust in my cheeks. My body felt alien. The pain was powerful and dissociative, intensifying to a degree I couldn't comprehend. It felt like something happening to someone else, empathy pain for someone much stronger than I. "They're your babies."

"How's Mom doing?" A doctor I'd never seen entered the room, looking at her chart. Both Celeste and I opened our mouths, then Celeste let out an embarrassed-sounding giggle.

"I'm the adoptive mom," she explained.

"I'm Dr. Rudolph." The doctor was brusque, unreceptive to Celeste's fawning. "And you must be Maeve." She moved to occupy the space at my bedside, gently nudging Celeste away. "Maeve, your regular doctor had a family emergency and couldn't be here. I'll be overseeing the delivery of your babies. I'm glad to see my attending"—she nodded at the man I'd assumed was a nurse—"has been taking good care of you."

"They're hers," I spat. Disowning the things inside me felt singularly imperative. Dr. Rudolph glanced at Celeste.

"We'll need you to step right outside," she told her. Celeste appeared as if someone had slapped her.

"I was told—"

"I don't care what you were told," Dr. Rudolph said, leveling her with a look. "This is my patient, and I'll need the room cleared during delivery." Celeste's mouth gaped like a fish's, and her cheeks colored, but finally she nodded. She exited the room quickly, allowing the door to slam shut behind her.

Dr. Rudolph turned to me while her attending physician wheeled in a tray of medical apparatuses. She leaned over me, resting her palms on the metal bed frame. "Your babies need their birth mother to welcome them into this world," she said, her voice somber. "And you need to have a chance to change your mind about the adoption, if you wish."

"I'm not changing my mind." I had to say it. I needed everything to go a certain way.

A wave of pain chased the words, and I let out a long, guttural moan.

"Fair enough," Dr. Rudolph said. "But for now, you're still their mother. They need you. Now, your chart says you want a vaginal delivery. We'll do all we can to make that happen. Right now, both babies are head down and your cervix is free of obstruction. So it shouldn't be a problem. I'm going to administer an epidural for the pain," she explained, filling a syringe. "You'll feel much better when I'm done."

*　*　*

When the first one came out, the one who would be called Julia, my vagina felt as though it were being ripped apart with a thousand flaming swords. The epidural hadn't done what it was supposed to do—or maybe it had all been a lie. Maybe epidurals were meant to make women think they could get through this agony; otherwise, we'd all bow out long before the great push. The pain of Julia entering this world nearly killed me, and when it was Esther's turn, my body shut down. Inside, I could feel Esther clawing at me, fighting her way out with miniature talons, determined to rip me straight through if she could. She was shifting, a wild thing, no longer a part of me but something that had invaded me for the sole purpose of administering death.

"She's hemorrhaging." It was the attending's voice, alight with panic.

It happened, though, right? It happened that women bled like this.

"Relax, Maeve." Dr. Rudolph now. "Maeve, we're going to need you to help us get the other baby out."

"I can't feel anything," I whimpered. "I can't feel my body."

"She's shutting down," the attending said, full of wonder. "She's closed up completely. But at the same time, she's bleeding out. I've never seen anything like this."

"Stanch the bleeding, quick. Her blood pressure is plummeting. Page Dr. Ursu, now."

From somewhere, I heard a siren. A low wail to match my own. I leaned back on the bed. For the first time, I saw the metallic sheen of the ceiling; it was something like a mirror. I watched as doctors and orderlies flooded the room, swarming around me, as they worked at my vagina with red-soaked hands, as they moved efficiently and quickly, a team of worker bees, each with a particular role.

The pain had stopped. In its place was a sense of peace.

They dropped a sheet, blocking my view of my lower half.

I tried to lift my head, but immediately the world around me swirled. I lay back, watched them again in the ceiling as they abandoned my vagina and bore down on my large, inflated womb. I nearly laughed. They didn't know I could see their betrayal. I tried to whisper for them to stop.

The swarm invaded my body with knives. They sliced me apart. The red of my guts shone clear in the ceiling, as clear as if I were bending over my own body, administering the cuts.

"Stay calm," one said.

"What is she saying?"

"She's losing a lot of blood."

Get it out of me.

The creature writhed inside me. I saw my body split in two, saw their hands reaching for the thing.

"It shifted positions. God damn it." The voice of Dr. Rudolph. "Stay with me, honey." It was unclear whether she meant me or it.

"Get it out of me," I said. I began to feel the rage mounting in a maelstrom of energy. Everything I had left was building at the base of my throat. I resolved not to let it kill me.

"Get it out of me!" It was a scream, or something like it. It was loud enough to get their attention, for all their faces to turn toward the sheet that concealed my head.

"How is she even talking right now? Sedate her further."

It was then that I noticed the shadowy form, a face pressed up against the room's sole window, a small rectangle of glass gracing the door. It was hard to tell if the woman was real or a specter, but she brought with her a strong sense of foreboding—the feeling of being followed.

The ceiling's shifting reflections drew my attention back to the birth, and I saw them take it from me. It resisted at first; I could feel in every cell its desire to stay with me until it had wrought me dead. But they pulled and pulled, the bed red, their gloves stained with my fluids.

I stared at the ceiling, transfixed. I watched as they lifted the child above my ruined form. I stared deep inside the gaping, torn whole of me, even as the world began to shift just slightly, as the woman in the window flickered in and out of vision, until the ceiling faded and I was aware only of the hollow sensation within my desecrated womb.

* * *

When I awoke, my body was racked with pain and the babies were gone. I fumbled with the button to the right of my hospital bed, pressing it several times until a nurse burst in.

"What is it?" she asked. She glanced at my heart monitor and seemed relieved. I tried to sit up, but she rushed to my bedside and put a hand on my shoulder, pressing me back down. "You've been through a lot," she told me. "But you're okay now. You're a fighter."

My mouth was dry, cottony. "It hurts," I told her.

"Shh. Don't worry. You're due for some more meds."

She walked over to a medicinal drip that was attached to the IV at my wrist.

"Wait," I told her, my voice hoarse. I needed to say it while I was lucid. "My babies. Did she take them?" I meant the figure I'd seen in my delirium.

"Your babies are in the NICU," the nurse said. "No one can take them anywhere for a few days, but they're doing fine. You'll need to sign the paperwork to release them to their adoptive mother before they can be discharged. She's been staring at them for hours, you know. I've never seen someone want something so bad. You're doing a good thing."

I swallowed. Celeste would be devastated. But I remembered what Agent Atkinsen had told me in recent conversations, and I knew for certain what I had to do.

"Tell her I've changed my mind," I said, wincing a little. "Tell her I'm not giving them to her."

32

pushed the double stroller over a bumpy cobblestone street in Brooklyn Heights. A cop car idled nearby, its engine sending puffs of exhaust into the otherwise pristine street. I glanced down from time to time to make sure the infants weren't being jostled. Their little hands rested peacefully at their sides as they slept, their pink cheeks partially obscured by raindrops speckling the stroller's transparent rain cover.

We were headed to a park I didn't often visit, an overgrown hideaway that used to function as respite for hospital patients but had long since been abandoned. It was elevated, offering a soaring view of the highway from its north side. Now tree branches burst with spring buds and tulips were in full bloom along the walkway. Despite the flowers, the park had been abandoned to the rain.

A bench in the far west corner of the park had been wiped off by the last visitor, leaving a somewhat dry patch behind. Two trees flanked it, their limbs stretching toward the ground, nearly grazing the bench with heavy, crooked fingers. I pushed the stroller to the bench. Good. The rain was light under the trees, despite coming down in sheets beyond. Once settled, I could hardly see through the mist it produced.

I took a long breath. It was just us now.

I turned the stroller to face me. I felt nothing when I looked down on them, aside from a current of protectiveness. No swell of tenderness, none of the love I was promised I'd never known and would eventually find. They may as well have come from someone else's body.

Celeste had contacted me repeatedly since I left the hospital. I felt awful for her, but I'd ignored her calls. I needed to trust my instincts.

"Hello, sweet girl," I cooed. "Hello, baby Esther." In response, a quiet mewl. The sound a cat makes when it's asking for more. More food, more strokes. In this case, more attention. "Hello, Julia. I am so lucky. So lucky to have you girls." I smiled down into the stroller, performing. Watching as they shifted and yawned and turned in their seats, stretching out the kinks of their nap and beginning to fuss wonderfully. Watching, even as I felt watched.

Good, I encouraged them silently. *Fuss louder.*

Out of the corner of my eye, I noticed the flash of a dark trench coat. I couldn't help it; I jumped, suddenly skittish. The babies began to wail. They were sensitive to my emotional cues, and they read me eerily well—two tiny, perfect reactor systems attuned to my every emotional tell. I jolt, you jolt.

"Shh." I calmed them, keeping one eye on the park entrance, which I had to squint to see. The figure in the bulky raincoat advanced closer. Perhaps just another pedestrian, enjoying the brisk spring air.

Perhaps.

A shudder racked my body. My heart climbed in my throat. This person walked with an odd gait—a distinctive limp-and-drag. They limped and dragged toward me. I gripped the handle of the baby carriage, willing myself not to stand and flee. There was no one else in sight. But I was perfectly safe now. I knew that. I had been reassured of it countless times.

The person was closer now. Close enough to speak, if they only unwrapped the light scarf covering their nose and mouth.

"Hello, there," I called. On cue, the babies began to wail.

The figure raised its head. Met my eyes. Green, a startling emerald green, made brighter with some intense emotion. Love? Fear? Anger? Desire? There were common elements to each, I'd learned. Sometimes, if you didn't know what you were looking for, they were nearly identical.

I refocused on the two squirming things in the stroller, my heart pounding. I knew to expect it, but I was no less afraid.

"It's okay, sweethearts," I said. I brushed a tender palm over their cheeks; only my trembling fingers, hidden under the cast of the umbrella casing, betrayed me. I allowed my smile to widen as I looked at them. "You're okay. Mother will protect you."

The figure was standing mere inches away now, observing me silently.

My senses were acute from years of being watched.

I lifted my eyes from the babies, leveling her with my gaze.

"Mother," I said coldly. "Welcome home."

The woman reached for the stroller, fumbling with Esther's buckles. I rose to my feet, looking left and right. There was no one in sight. Then I shoved her back, hard, away from the girls. She moved toward Julia, but I blocked the stroller with my body. This wasn't right. This wasn't what I'd expected at all. I was meant to have protection.

"Give them to me," Andrea snarled, her eyes venomous.

"No," I told her, my own voice cold. "They're not yours to take."

"You knew I'd never let you have them." She tilted her head back and laughed, loud and brittle. "You couldn't possibly have thought you'd run away and live this little fairy tale life with your two newborns." She stopped, her mouth twisting in a cruel smile. "Or did you forget what happened the last time you ran away? Do you need me to remind you of what happened to that child?"

"No," I said, my voice firm. Inside, I was quaking. "I could never forget that." It was natural to say, because it was true. It was the reason I had not done the easy thing in the hospital, when I'd wanted to. I had not given the girls away then because everything—my whole life since the day I fled the Collective at age eight—came down to this moment. I needed this moment to work.

Andrea shoved me out of the way and reached for the stroller, fighting to wrench it from my grip.

"What are you going to do with them?" I shouted. I needed to push her further, I realized. I needed her to say it aloud. "You think you can kidnap my babies?"

"That's exactly what I think," she snarled. "You idiot. Of course I'm taking them from you. You were never powerful enough to get in my way."

"You're wrong," I said quietly.

There was a quick rustling sound from behind me.

I closed my eyes, bracing for the end.

It came swiftly. The FBI agents were on her before she could so much as scratch my face. Sounds of her shrieking filled the park. She kicked and flailed, but she was no match for them. When they dragged her away, she turned back, craning her neck to look at me.

This time, I kept my eyes open.

EPILOGUE

Baby, did you see the news?" Otis is home early, announcing himself from the front door in his usual way: loudly, and as if we were already in the middle of a conversation.

"Nope," I call back. "Come in here if you want to talk!"

He enters the bedroom, where I'm folding laundry. He pulls me into his arms and nuzzles my neck. "Really? You aren't just saying that? Because I think we should talk about it."

I shift back and scan his face. "Hon, I just got home. Today was insane at work. I may as well be living in a bubble."

I secured a creative development job at a literary start-up several months after I gave birth, naming a wage I had thought astronomical. I'd been shocked when they readily agreed to my terms. I wasn't used to valuing myself at a high level. I've been there ever since. Part of me feels guilty, like I've stolen someone else's life; another part feels fearful, as if just around the corner is a grenade. It's been fading gradually, but I still have a long way to go.

"What's going on?" I set down the towel I was folding, a yellow one with blue stripes. Otis notices and smiles a little. He takes my hand, pulling me onto the bed next to him. "Why are you always making me talk?" I complain. But I'm not mad, just a little wary. My husband knows my history. He's a partner—a best friend, despite a rocky road getting there. He's someone I respect and feel challenged by . . . and to a degree, need. Not for what he can provide me with but for the tremendous love he's taught me to accept and return. He holds me accountable when it comes to facing my fears. And this, unfortunately, seems like an accountability moment.

"It's a good thing," he says. "Sort of. I feel weird saying that."

"Just tell me. You're freaking me out."

Otis wraps one arm around my waist and uses the other to fiddle with his phone. Finally, he brings up an article in *The New York Times*. It takes me a second to understand what I'm seeing. Then my eyes focus, and I realize it's a photo of Andrea's face.

A photo of Andrea's face.

My eyes have long since scanned the headline by the time I'm able to process it.

"Mother Superior Found Dead."

My vision blurs. I blink rapidly, forcing my eyes to focus on the article's lengthy copy. I'm vaguely aware of Otis stroking my shoulder and murmuring comfortingly. The sounds of his words fade as paragraphs leap from the screen and jostle their way into my consciousness.

Billionaire cult leader Andrea Rothko, known to her followers as Mother Superior, was found dead in her jail cell this afternoon. Police have ruled it a suicide. Rothko's death comes as a shock just days before she was due to testify before a grand jury on new findings on the Mother Collective, a cult reported to have powerful members on every continent.

Questions remain regarding who controls this female-operated cult, how money is transferred, and how deep the history of violence extends in a cult that is known for its fanatical perspective on motherhood. Confirmed instances include the grisly murders of seven men on a Vermont compound in 2001, as well as the murders of four men in an upstate New York compound in 2015, two of whom were men in uniform and one of whom was Rothko's husband. Fraud investigations and lawsuits continue concerning NewLife, a business and lifestyle brand cofounded by Rothko, as well as the groundbreaking Vigeneros technology that drove its profits. Will the "cult of motherhood" disband, or was Mother Superior just one arm of the organization's powerful infrastructure? With the loss of Mother Superior, we may never have the answers we seek.

I stare at Andrea's face, her eyes sparkling and seeming very much alive in the photo. I feel nothing but emptiness at the news of Andrea's death. She's been out of my life since I helped Agent Atkinsen and the FBI lure and capture her, ensuring the safety of the children to whom I gave birth—a safety that would have remained uncertain if I'd handed them over to Celeste in the hospital. But for the past seven years, I have continued to feel followed. Finally, with her death, I am free.

"Are you okay?" Otis's eyes are wide and concerned. He's waiting for a reaction.

"Yeah, I really am," I tell him. "I promise."

"I just don't want you to do that thing—"

"O! Chill. I'm not. I promise. I'm not repressing anything. Or at least I don't think I am. We can definitely talk more later, but right now I have to go. I'm late."

Realization dawns on him. "Oh, right," he says. "Are you sure I can't come?"

"Unfortunately not," I tell him. "No boys allowed." I roll my eyes, then give him a kiss. "We'll talk more later, okay?"

He pulls my hips toward him and kisses me again. "More of that later, too, please."

"You got it." I wink, then grab my bag and a light jacket and let myself out the door.

* * *

"I choose . . . that one!" A small voice reaches my ears from just inside the playground.

"Silly—those are for boys. Gross! I choose this one. I'm a strong, powerful woman, so I get the crown."

I smile. Their voices are as familiar to me as my own. They aren't far off, really, in their cadences and intonations, the way they pause at odd moments in a sentence and pitch up at the end of a thought. I've got two presents tucked into my tote, belated gifts for Esther and Julia on their seventh birthdays.

Celeste, their adoptive mother, initially felt betrayed by my role in the FBI sting. But it had been necessary to keep her in the dark; we needed everyone to believe I'd chosen to keep the girls. Celeste was right to be angry that I agreed to use the girls as bait—it was a risk, and she'd never have allowed it to happen if she'd known. But the second she held the babies in her arms after Andrea was behind bars, all was forgiven.

Through the railings of the fence I see the girls playing in the sand pit. I skipped the party the week before. I'm not much for crowds these days, not since Andrea's arrest made me a recognizable figure in the mommy circles, despite the dark wigs I use to conceal my naked scalp.

My meetings with the girls are always private affairs, and Celeste and I have developed a careful friendship, spurred on by landmarks in the girls' lives. To them, I am Aunt Maeve, and Otis is Uncle O. But I don't bring him by very often. "Just us girls," Celeste likes to say, banishing Otis from our special brunches at Alice's Tea Cup and our Saturday Broadway matinees: *Matilda, Lion King,* whatever the girls could want. Normally, I love these outings. Normally, I practically run from the office to the park, to their town house on Park Avenue, or

to the Plaza for Tea with Eloise. Today, though, I hesitate to
enter the playground. Because today is more than a birthday
celebration. I have something very important to tell the girls.

"Aunt Maeve! What did you bring us?" Julia asks, leap-
ing up from where she crouches in the sand, not bothering to
brush granules off her tights before running over to me and
enveloping me in a hug.

"Well, wouldn't you like to know?" I tease, tugging one
of her braids. Esther looks over her shoulder and smiles, giving me a small wave. She's fashioning an extravagant sand
castle—an empire, really, from the look of it—and can't be
bothered to come say hello.

Despite myself, I have a favorite, and it is the one who re-
minds me of me. Julia is sweet and guileless, the first to vacate my womb. Esther is also sweet, but cunning, and already
aware of her manipulations—for candy, for an extra story at
night. I try not to think about how she nearly killed me. I try
not to remember the placenta I ate. I try hard to believe my
wariness toward her is unrelated to any of it, especially to that
miserable day when she was yanked from my body. I walk
over to the sand pit, holding Julia's hand.

"Hi, cutie," I say to Esther, who reluctantly abandons her
post in the sand. "Happy birthday."

"My birthday was last week," she informs me.

"I know," I tell her. "But haven't you heard of a birthday
week? You get to celebrate all week long." Esther looks skep-
tical. "But if you don't want to, I can just take these presents
back to the store . . ." I gesture toward the brightly wrapped
packages poking over the rim of my bag.

"*No!*" Julia shrieks. "We want them! Esther, tell her."

Esther looks at her sister and smiles. "Thanks, Aunt
Maeve," she says, her green eyes serious. "We want them."

"Great," I tell them. "Let's go over to the picnic table to
open them. Where's your mom?"

"Over there." Esther gestures absently to the opposite end of the park. I squint, then recognize Celeste with another woman. They're talking animatedly, and although Celeste's back is to me, I recognize the telltale tension she carries in her shoulders. The other woman's mouth is pursed. She's wearing an odd flannel coat, a man's hunting jacket, too heavy for the season. Her face is absent of makeup and her hair is striped with gray—an unusual choice among this moneyed crowd.

"Who's that?"

"That's Mother," Esther says, digging through my bag.

"No, the other woman," I clarify, stiffening. Esther is already squealing over the deluxe Lego set I got her, a pirate ship, complete with mermaids and a palm tree–laden island. Julia opens hers next: an RV with a camping tent and speedboat.

"We both got boats!" Julia squeals. I watch as Celeste crosses the expanse of the park to join us, giving me a wave.

"Oh Maeve, you didn't have to," she tells me. She smiles, but her eyes look hollow, and the skin around her fingers is cracked and raw. "You know the girls have plenty of toys."

"You know I was happy to," I tell her, giving her a warm smile. "Are you okay, Celeste? You didn't answer my last few texts. I was starting to worry."

"I'm fine," she says. "Just a little stressed out about work." Celeste's job as in-house legal counsel for a start-up often keeps her up all night, and in the years I've known her, she's aged dramatically. She's still tough as nails, but as a single, working mom—one of the reasons I chose her—the youthful radiance she had when we first met has long since vanished.

"You know I can help out more with the kids."

She smiles at me reassuringly. "Don't worry, Maeve. They've got the best nanny money can buy. Let's preserve your cool aunt image while we can."

Julia and Esther are already assembling their sets, Esther

humming under her breath faintly. I strain to listen, but Celeste is talking over their din.

"—have a production next month, *Robin Hood*," she's saying. "At the school." The girls attend a private, all-girls kindergarten on the Upper East Side. Celeste settles next to me on the bench and absently watches the girls play. "Maeve, weren't you saying you had news for us? Something exciting?"

But I've picked up on the faint rhythm of Esther's song, as she pieces together the pirate ship.

"A sailor went to sea, sea, sea," she mumbles quietly. My heart sinks to my stomach, and my hands turn cold. I lean toward her, straining harder to capture her words.

"Esther, what are you singing?"

"To see what she could see see see," my biological daughter continues. Julia looks up then, noticing my attention on her sister.

"But all that she could see see see," Julia joins in, ever needy, smiling up at me, seeking my approval.

"Was the bottom of the deep blue sea sea sea."

They sing together, while I fight the wave of nausea threatening to invade my throat.

"Where . . . where did you two learn that?" I ask. I rub my eyebrows, which feel suddenly itchy.

"Mother," answers Esther.

Julia nods. "Mother taught us."

I look at Celeste.

Celeste looks at me. Her mouth crooks into a smile. Her eyes narrow into slits.

"Your news, Maeve?" She lowers her gaze to my abdomen, where I've unconsciously rested a protective palm. "Is it a girl or a boy? A girl would be such a blessing. I just knew you'd come around to motherhood one day. It really is the only path, don't you think?"

ACKNOWLEDGMENTS

I began working on this book in earnest in 2018, shortly after I turned thirty-four. "In earnest" because I thought about it for an entire year before I got to work. Thirty-three, I guess, was the year I stopped assuming my uneasy ambivalence toward motherhood would figure itself out. I drafted those initial pages during a week spent upstate with my late dog on a solo writing retreat that mainly consisted of me "finding my voice" and taking advantage of my B&B's extensive streaming options. In the end, I produced only twenty pages, and I'd be hard-pressed to find a single paragraph that made it into the book you hold now. I have many supportive people in my life to thank for that, and I say that with genuine gratitude.

I knew Elisabeth Weed was the right agent for me when she said, "I love the concept, but I don't love the execution." I knew she would push me, and I needed to be pushed. She read draft after draft, brainstorming for hours, mercilessly trimming the fat. So much fat! An additional book's worth of fat, probably. Elisabeth is patient, smart, creative, and very, very funny. Best of all, she doesn't shy from honesty. Elisabeth, thank you—your dedication to this manuscript has meant more than you know.

Kelly Lonesome has been an incredible champion of this book from the beginning, and her offer to work together was the best gift I could possibly have received. (It arrived the day before my thirty-seventh birthday.) Having Kelly in my corner—and being welcomed so warmly into the Nightfire "coven"—has been a dream. Thank you, Kelly, for your insight, gentle guidance, and endless patience. Thank you for allowing me the freedom to take risks. Thank you also to Kristin Temple, whose astute notes helped guide the narrative, to Fritz Foy, for supporting my career and sternly yet wisely advising me not to shake hands with anyone when we met in early March 2020.

Thank you to the marketing, publicity, design, managing editorial, and production teams at Nightfire. It takes so many people to publish a novel well. I am very proud and grateful to be a Nightfire author.

Much gratitude to Michelle Weiner and Jenny Meyer; to Hallie Schaeffer and DJ Kim.

To Caroline Donofrio, whose friendship and support are unparalleled and who brings humor and wisdom to everything she does.

To all the friends and fellow writers who read early drafts and offered invaluable feedback: Jill Santopolo, Eliot Schrefer, Marie Rutkoski, Marianna Baer, Anna Godbersen, Jessie Gaynor, Corinna Barsan, and Emily Daluga.

To my Abrams family, in particular, Andrew Smith.

To Susan Van Metre, Tamar Brazis, Traci Todd, and Jessica Brigman for your genuine enthusiasm, encouragement, and friendship and for setting the bar high.

To Alyssa Sheinmel, Danielle Rollins, Jocelyn Davies, and Jackie Resnick. I am lucky to have found the most wonderful friendships in adulthood.

To my family. Inevitably you will hate this book, but I consider myself lucky to know you'll continue to love me anyway.

Thank you to my cousins, who are sisters to me.

Finally, to Andy Marino, the most dedicated writer, partner, and dog dad. You amaze me every day. I am so (underlined twice) glad we met again in the author-sphere.